... routinely app...

... on numerous awards, inc...

... Reader's Choice Award. A seven-time non...

... the prestigous RITA® award from Romance Writers of America, one of her books was made into a CBS-TV movie called *The Soul Collecter*. Maureen recently moved from California to the mountains of Utah and is trying to get used to snow.

USA TODAY bestselling author **Kat Cantrell** read her first Mills & Boon novel in third grade and has been scribbling in notebooks since she learned to spell. She's a former Mills & Boon So You Think You Can Write winner and former RWA Golden Heart finalist. ...at, her husband and their two boys live in north Texas.

A Surprise Family

Against
the Odds

ANN MAJOR

MAUREEN CHILD

KAT CANTRELL

MIX

Paper from
responsible sources

FSC

FSC C007484

This book is produced from independently certified FSC™ paper
to ensure responsible forest management.

For more information visit www.harpercollins.co.uk/green

Printed and bound in Spain
by CPI, Barcelona.

MILLS & BOON

First Published in Great Britain 2020
By Mills & Boon, an imprint of HarperCollins*Publishers*
1 London Bridge Street, London, SE1 9GF

A SURPRISE FAMILY: AGAINST THE ODDS © 2020
Harlequin Books S.A.

Terms of Engagement © 2012 Ann Major
A Baby for the Boss © 2016 Maureen Child
From Enemies to Expecting © 2017 Kat Cantrell

ISBN: 978-0-263-28170-5

TERMS OF
ENGAGEMENT

ANN MAJOR

To Ted, with all my love.

And as always I must thank my editor, Stacy Boyd, and Shana Smith, along with the entire Harlequin Desire team for their talented expertise. I thank as well my agent, Karen Solem.

One

No good deed goes unpunished.

When would she ever learn? Kira wondered.

With her luck, never.

So, here she sat, in the office of oil billionaire Quinn Sullivan, too nervous to concentrate on her magazine as she waited to see if he would make time for a woman he probably thought of as just another adversary to be crushed in his quest for revenge.

Dreadful, arrogant man.

If he did grant her an audience, would she have any chance of changing his mind about destroying her family's company, Murray Oil, and forcing her sister Jaycee into marriage?

A man vengeful enough to hold a grudge against her father for twenty years couldn't possibly have a heart that could be swayed.

Kira Murray clenched and unclenched her hands. Then

she sat on them, twisting in her chair. When the man across from her began to stare, she told herself to quit squirming. Lowering her eyes to her magazine, she pretended to read a very boring article on supertankers.

High heels clicked rapidly on marble, causing Kira to look up in panic.

"Miss Murray, I'm so sorry. I was wrong. Mr. Sullivan *is* still here." There was surprise in his secretary's classy, soothing purr.

"In fact, he'll see you now."

"He will?" Kira squeaked. *"Now?"*

The secretary's answering smile was a brilliant white.

Kira's own mouth felt as dry as sandpaper. She actually began to shake. To hide this dreadful reaction, she jumped to her feet so fast she sent the glossy magazine to the floor, causing the man across from her to glare in annoyance.

Obviously, she'd been hoping Quinn would refuse to see her. A ridiculous wish when she'd come here for the express purpose of finally meeting him properly and having her say.

Sure, she'd run into him once, informally. It had been right after he'd announced he wanted to marry one of the Murray daughters to make his takeover of Murray Oil less hostile. Her father had suggested Jaycee, and Kira couldn't help but think he'd done so because Jaycee was his favorite and most biddable daughter. As always, Jaycee had dutifully agreed with their father's wishes, so Quinn had come to the ranch for a celebratory dinner to seal the bargain.

He'd been late. A man as rich and arrogant as he was probably thought himself entitled to run on his own schedule.

Wounded by her mother's less-than-kind assessment of her outfit when she'd first arrived—"Jeans and a torn shirt? How could you think that appropriate for meeting a man so important to this family's welfare?"—Kira had stormed out of the house. She hadn't had time to change after the crisis at her best friend's restaurant, where Kira was temporarily waiting tables while looking for a museum curator position. Since her mother always turned a deaf ear to Kira's excuses, rather than explain, Kira had decided to walk her dad's hunting spaniels while she nursed her injured feelings.

The brilliant, red sun that had been sinking fast had been in her eyes as the spaniels leaped onto the gravel driveway, dragging her in their wake. Blinded, she'd neither seen nor heard Quinn's low-slung, silver Aston Martin screaming around the curve. Slamming on his brakes, he'd veered clear of her with several feet to spare. She'd tripped over the dogs and fallen into a mud puddle.

Yipping wildly, the dogs had raced back to the house, leaving her to face Quinn on her own with cold, dirty water dripping from her chin.

Quinn had gotten out of his fancy car and stomped over in his fancy Italian loafers just as she got to her feet. For a long moment, he'd inspected every inch of her. Then, mindless of her smudged face, chattering teeth and muddy clothes, he'd pulled her against his tall, hard body, making her much too aware of his clean, male smell and hard, muscular body.

"Tell me you're okay."

He was tall and broad-shouldered, so tall he'd towered over her. His angry blue eyes had burned her; his viselike fingers had cut into her elbow. Despite his overcharged emotions, she'd liked being in his arms—liked it too much.

"Damn it, I didn't hit you, did I? Well, say something, why don't you?"

"How can I—with you yelling at me?"

"Are you okay, then?" he asked, his grip loosening, his

voice softening into a husky sound so unexpectedly beautiful she'd shivered. This time, she saw concern in his hard expression.

Had it happened then?

Oh, be honest, Kira, at least with yourself. That was the moment you formed an inappropriate crush on your sister's future fiancé, a man whose main goal in life is to destroy your family.

He'd been wearing faded jeans, a white shirt, his sleeves rolled up to his elbows. On her, jeans looked rumpled, but on him, jeans had made him ruggedly, devastatingly handsome. Over one arm, he carried a cashmere jacket.

She noted his jet-black hair and carved cheekbones with approval. Any woman would have. His skin had been darkly bronzed, and the dangerous aura of sensuality surrounding him had her sizzling.

Shaken by her fall and by the fact that *the enemy* was such an attractive, powerful man who continued to hold her close and stare down at her with blazing eyes, her breath had come in fits and starts.

"I said—*are you okay?*"

"I was fine—until you grabbed me." Her hesitant voice was tremulous…and sounded strangely shy. "You're hurting me, really hurting me!" She'd lied so he would let her go, and yet part of her hadn't wanted to be released.

His eyes narrowed suspiciously. "Sorry," he'd said, his tone harsh again.

"Who the hell are you anyway?" he'd demanded.

"Nobody important," she'd muttered.

His dark brows winged upward. "Wait…I've seen your pictures… You're the older sister. The waitress."

"Only temporarily…until I get a new job as a curator."

"Right. You were fired."

"So, you've heard Father's version. The truth is, my professional opinion wasn't as important to the museum director as I might have liked, but I was let go due to budget constraints."

"Your sister speaks highly of you."

"Sometimes I think she's the only one in this family who does."

Nodding as if he understood, he draped his jacket around her shoulders. "I've wanted to meet you." When she glanced up at him, he said, "You're shivering. The least I can do is offer you my jacket and a ride back to the house."

Her heart pounded much too fast, and she was mortified that she was covered with mud and that she found her family's enemy exciting and the prospect of wearing his jacket a thrill. Not trusting herself to spend another second with such a dangerous man, especially in the close quarters of his glamorous car, she'd shaken her head. "I'm too muddy."

"Do you think I give a damn about that? I could have killed you."

"You didn't. So let's just forget about it."

"Not possible! Now, put my jacket on before you catch your death."

Pulling his jacket around her shoulders, she turned on her heel and left him. Nothing had happened, she'd told herself as she stalked rapidly through the woods toward the house.

Nothing except the enemy she'd feared had held her and made her feel dangerously alive in a way no other man ever had.

When she'd reached the house, she'd been surprised to find him outside waiting for her as he held on to her yapping dogs. Feeling tingly and shyly thrilled as he handed her their tangled leashes, she'd used her muddy clothes again as an excuse to go home and avoid dinner, when her father would formally announce Quinn was to marry her sister.

Yes, he was set on revenge against those she loved most, but that hadn't been the reason she couldn't sit across the table from him. No, it was her crush. How could she have endured such a dinner when just to look at him made her skin heat?

For weeks after that chance meeting, her inappropriate attachment to Quinn had continued to claim her, causing her much guilt-ridden pain. She'd thought of him constantly. And more than once, before she'd returned his jacket to Jaycee, she'd worn it around her apartment, draped over her shoulders, just because his scent lingered on the soft fabric.

Now, retrieving the magazine she'd dropped, she set it carefully on the side table. Then she sucked in a deep breath. Not that it steadied her nerves.

No. Instead, her heart raced when Quinn Sullivan's secretary turned away, saying, "Follow me."

Kira swallowed. She'd put this interview off to the last possible moment—to the end of the business day—because she'd been trying to formulate a plan to confront a man as powerful and dictatorial and, yes, as dangerously sexy, as Quinn Sullivan.

But she hadn't come up with a plan. Did she ever have a plan? She'd be at a disadvantage since Sullivan planned everything down to the last detail, including taking his revenge plot up a notch by marrying Jaycee.

Kira had to sprint to keep up with the sleek, blonde secretary, whose ridiculous, four-inch, ice-pick, gold heels clicked on the polished gray marble. Did *he* make the poor girl wear such gaudy, crippling footwear?

Quinn's waiting room with its butter-soft leather couches and polished wainscoting had reeked of old money. In truth, he was nothing but a brash, bad-tempered upstart. His long hallway, decorated with paintings of vivid minimalistic splashes of color, led to what would probably prove to be an obscenely opulent office. Still, despite her wish to dislike everything about him, she admired the art and wished she could stop and study several of the pictures. They were elegant, tasteful and interesting. Had he selected them himself?

Probably not. He was an arrogant show-off.

After their one encounter, she'd researched him. It seemed he believed her father had profited excessively when he'd bought Quinn's father out of their mutually owned company. In addition, he blamed her father for his father's suicide—if suicide it had been.

Quinn, who'd known hardship after his father's death, was determined to make up for his early privations, by living rich and large. Craving glamour and the spotlight, he never attended a party without a beauty even more dazzling than his secretary on his arm.

He was a respected art collector. In various interviews he'd made it clear nobody would ever look down on him again. Not in business; not in his personal life. He was king of his kingdom.

From the internet, she'd gleaned that Quinn's bedroom had a revolving door. Apparently, a few nights' pleasuring the same woman were more than enough for him. Just when a woman might believe she meant something to him, he'd drop her and date another gorgeous blonde, who was invariably more beautiful than the one he'd jilted. There had been one woman, also blonde, who'd jilted him a year or so ago, a Cristina somebody. Not that she hadn't been quickly forgotten by the press when he'd resumed chasing more beauties as carelessly as before.

From what Kira had seen, his life was about winning,

not about caring deeply. For that purpose only, he'd surrounded himself with the mansions, the cars, the yachts, the art collections and the fair-haired beauties. She had no illusions about what his marriage to Jaycee would be like. He had no intention of being a faithful husband to Kira's beautiful, blonde sister.

Rich, handsome womanizer that he was, Kira might have pitied him for being cursed with such a dark heart— if only her precious Jaycee wasn't central in his revenge scheme.

Kira was not gifted at planning or at being confrontational, which were two big reasons why she wasn't getting ahead in her career. And Quinn was the last person on earth she wanted to confront. But the need to take care of Jaycee, as she had done since her sister's birth, was paramount.

Naturally, Kira's first step had been to beg her father to change his mind about using her sister to smooth over a business deal, but her father had been adamant about the benefits of the marriage.

Kira didn't understand the financials of Quinn's hostile takeover of Murray Oil, but her father seemed to think Quinn would make a brilliant CEO. Her parents had said that if Jaycee didn't walk down the aisle with Quinn as agreed, Quinn's terms would become far more onerous. Not to mention that the employees would resent him as an outsider. Even though Quinn's father had been a co-owner, Quinn was viewed as a man with a personal vendetta against the Murrays and Murray Oil. Ever since his father's death, rumors about his hostility toward all things Murray had been widely circulated by the press. Only if he married Jaycee would the employees believe that peace between the two families had at last been achieved and that the company would be safe in his hands.

Hence, Kira was here, to face Quinn Sullivan.

She was determined to stop him from marrying Jaycee, but how? Pausing in panic even as his secretary rushed ahead, she reminded herself that she couldn't turn back, plan or not.

Quickening her pace, Kira caught up to the efficient young woman, who was probably moving so quickly because she was as scared of the unfeeling brute as Kira was.

When his secretary pushed open Quinn's door, the deep, rich tones of the man's surprisingly beautiful voice moved through Kira like music. Her knees lost strength, and she stopped in midstep.

Oh, no, it was happening again.

She'd known from meeting him the first time that he was charismatic, but she'd counted on her newly amassed knowledge of his despicable character to protect her. His edgy baritone slid across her nerve endings, causing warm tingles in her secret, feminine places, and she knew she was as vulnerable to him as before.

Fighting not to notice that her nipples ached and that her pulse had sped up, she took a deep breath before daring a glance at the black-headed rogue. Looking very much at ease, he sat sprawled at his desk, the back of his linebacker shoulders to her as he leaned against his chair, a telephone jammed to his ear.

She couldn't, wouldn't, be attracted to this man.

On his desk she noted a silver-framed photograph of his father. With their intense blue eyes, black hair and strongly chiseled, tanned features, father and son closely resembled each other. Both, she knew, had been college athletes. Did Quinn keep the photo so close out of love or to energize him in his quest for revenge?

"I told you to buy, Habib," he ordered brusquely in that

too-beautiful voice. "What's there to talk about? Do it."
He ended the call.

At least he was every bit as rude as she remembered.
Deep baritone or not, it should be easy to hate him.

His secretary coughed to let him know they were at the
door.

Quinn whirled around in his massive, black leather
chair, scowling, but went still the instant he saw Kira.

He lifted that hard, carved chin, which surprisingly
enough had the most darling dimple, and, just like that,
dismissed his secretary.

His piercing, laser-blue gaze slammed into Kira full
force and heated her through—just like before.

Black hair. Bronze skin. Fierce, brilliant eyes... With a
single glance the man bewitched her.

When his mouth lifted at the edges, her world shifted as
it had that first evening—and he hadn't even touched her.

He was as outrageously handsome as ever. Every bit as
dark, tall, lean and hard, as cynical and untamed—even
in his orderly office with his efficient secretary standing
guard.

Still, for an instant, Kira thought she saw turbulent grief
and longing mix with unexpected pleasure at the sight of
her.

He remembered her.

But in a flash the light went out of his eyes, and his
handsome features tightened into those of the tough, heart-
less man he wanted people to see.

In spite of his attempt at distance, a chord of recognition
had been struck. It was as if they'd seen into each other's
souls, had sensed each other's secret yearnings.

She wanted her family, who deemed her difficult and
frustrating, to love and accept her for herself, as they did
her sister.

He had longings that revenge and outward success had failed to satisfy. What were they? What was lacking in his disciplined, showy, materialistic life?

Was he as drawn to her as she was to him?

Impossible.

So how could he be the only man who'd ever made her feel less alone in the universe?

Hating him even more because he'd exposed needs she preferred to conceal, she tensed. He had no right to open her heart and arouse such longings.

Frowning, he cocked his dark head and studied her. "I owe you an apology for the last time we met," he drawled in that slow, mocking baritone that turned her insides to mush. "I was nervous about the takeover and the engagement and about making a good impression on you and your family. I was too harsh with you. A few inches more…and I could have killed you. I was afraid, and that made me angry."

"You owe me nothing," she said coolly.

"I don't blame you in the least for avoiding me all these weeks. I probably scared the hell out of you."

"I haven't been avoiding you. Not really," she murmured, but a telltale flush heated her neck as she thought of the family dinners she'd opted out of because she'd known he'd be there.

If only she could run now, escape him. But Jaycee needed her, so instead, she hedged. "I've been busy."

"Waitressing?"

"Yes! I'm helping out Betty, my best friend, while I interview for museum jobs. Opening a restaurant on the San Antonio River Walk was a lifetime dream of hers. She got busier faster than she expected, and she offered me a job. Since I waited tables one summer between college semesters, I've got some experience."

He smiled. "I like it that you're helping your friend

realize her dream even though your career is stalled. That's nice."

"We grew up together. Betty was our housekeeper's daughter. When we got older my mother kept hoping I'd outgrow the friendship while Daddy helped Betty get a scholarship."

"I like that you're generous and loyal." He hesitated. "Your pictures don't do you justice. Nor did my memory of you."

His blue eyes gleamed with so much appreciation her cheeks heated. "Maybe because the last time I saw you I was slathered in mud."

He smiled. "Still, being a waitress seems like a strange job for a museum curator, even if it's temporary. You did major in art history at Princeton and completed that internship at the Metropolitan Museum of Art. I believe you graduated with honors."

She had no idea how she'd done so well, but when her grades had thrilled her father, she'd worked even harder.

"Has Daddy, who by the way, has a bad habit of talking too much, told you my life history?"

For a long moment, Quinn didn't confirm her accusation or deny it.

"Well, is that where you learned these details?"

"If he talked about you, it was because I was curious and asked him."

Not good. She frowned as she imagined her parents complaining about her disappointments since Princeton during all those family dinners she'd avoided.

"Did my father tell you that I've had a hard time with a couple of museum directors because they micromanaged me?"

"Not exactly."

"I'll bet. He takes the boss's side because he's every bit

as high-handed and dictatorial. Unfortunately, one night after finishing the setup of a new show, when I was dead tired, the director started second-guessing my judgment about stuff he'd already signed off on. I made the mistake of telling him what I really thought. When there were budget cuts, you can probably guess who he let go."

"I'm sorry about that."

"I'm good at what I do. I'll find another job, but until I do, I don't see why I shouldn't help Betty. Unfortunately, my father disagrees. We frequently disagree."

"It's your life, not his."

Her thoughts exactly. Having him concur was really sort of annoying, since Quinn was supposed to be the enemy.

In the conversational lull, she noticed that his spectacular physique was elegantly clad in a dark gray suit cut to emphasize every hard sinew of his powerful body. Suddenly, she wished she'd dressed up. Then she caught herself. Why should she care about looking her best for a man she should hate, when her appearance was something she rarely thought about?

All she'd done today was scoop her long, dark hair into a ponytail that cascaded down her back. Still, when his eyes hungrily skimmed her figure, she was glad that she'd worn the loosely flowing white shirt and long red scarf over her tight jeans because the swirls of cloth hid her body.

His burning gaze, which had ignited way too many feminine hormones, rose to her face again. When he smiled as he continued to stare, she bit her bottom lip to keep from returning his smile.

Rising, he towered over her, making her feel small and feminine and lovely in ways she'd never felt lovely before. He moved toward her, seized her hand in his much larger one and shook it gently.

"I'm very glad you decided to give me a second chance."

Why did his blunt fingers have to feel so warm and hard, his touch and gaze so deliciously intimate? She snatched her hand away, causing his eyes to flash with that pain he didn't want her to see.

"That's not what this is."

"But you *were* avoiding me, weren't you?"

"I *was*," she admitted and then instantly regretted being so truthful.

"That was a mistake—for both of us."

When he asked her if she wanted coffee or a soda or anything at all to drink, she said no and looked out the windows at the sun sinking low against the San Antonio skyline. She couldn't risk looking at him any more than necessary because her attraction seemed to be building. He would probably sense it and use it against her somehow.

With some difficulty she reminded herself that she disliked him. So, why did she still feel hot and clammy and slightly breathless, as if there were a lack of oxygen in the room?

It's called chemistry. Sexual attraction. It's irrational.

Her awareness only sharpened when he pulled out a chair for her and returned to his own. Sitting down and crossing one long leg over the other, he leaned back again. The pose should have seemed relaxed, but as he concentrated on her she could see he wasn't relaxed—he was intently assessing her.

The elegant office became eerily silent as he stared. Behind the closed doors, she felt trapped. Leaning forward, her posture grew as rigid as his was seemingly careless.

His hard, blue eyes held her motionless.

"So, to what do I owe the pleasure of your visit this afternoon…or should I say this evening?" he asked in that pleasant tone that made her tremble with excitement.

She imagined them on his megayacht, sailing silently across the vast, blue Gulf of Mexico. Her auburn hair would blow in the wind as he pulled her close and suggested they go below.

"You're my last appointment, so I can give you as much time as you want," he said, thankfully interrupting her seduction fantasy.

Her guilty heart sped up. Why had she come at such a late hour when he might not have another appointment afterward?

The sky was rapidly darkening, casting a shadow across his carved face, making him look stark and feral, adding to the danger she felt upon finding herself alone with him.

Even though her fear made her want to flee, she was far too determined to do what she had to do to give in to it.

She blurted out, "I don't want you to marry Jaycee." Oh, dear, she'd meant to lead up to this in some clever way.

He brought his blunt fingertips together in a position of prayer. When he leaned across his desk toward her, she sank lower in her own chair. "Don't you? How very strange."

"It's not strange. You can't marry her. You don't love her. You and she are too different to care for each other as a man and wife should."

His eyes darkened in a way that made him seem more alive than any man she'd ever known. "I wasn't referring to Jacinda. I was talking about you…and me and how strange that I should feel…so much—" He stopped. "When for all practical purposes we just met."

His eyes bored into hers with that piercing intensity that left her breathless. Once again she felt connected to him by some dark, forbidden, primal force.

"I never anticipated this wrinkle when I suggested a marriage with a Murray daughter," he murmured.

When his eyes slid over her body again in that devouring way, her heart raced. Her tall, slim figure wasn't appealing to most men. She'd come to believe there was nothing special about her. Could he possibly be as attracted to her as she was to him?

"You don't love her," she repeated even more shakily.

"Love? No. I don't love her. How could I? I barely know her."

"You see!"

"Your father chose her, and she agreed."

"Because she's always done everything he tells her to."

"You, however, would not have agreed so easily?" He paused. "Love does not matter to me in the least. But now I find myself curious about his choice of brides. And…even more curious about you. I want to get to know you better." His tone remained disturbingly intimate.

She remembered his revolving bedroom door and the parade of voluptuous blondes who'd passed through it. Was he so base he'd think it nothing to seduce his future wife's sister and then discard her, too?

"You've made no secret of how you feel about my father," she whispered with growing wariness. "Why marry his daughter?"

"Business. There are all these rumors in the press that I want to destroy Murray Oil, a company that once belonged to my beloved father."

"It makes perfect sense."

"No, it doesn't. I would never pay an immense amount of money for a valuable property in order to destroy it."

"But you think my father blackened your father's name and then profited after buying your father out. That's why you're so determined to destroy everything he's built, everything he loves…including Jaycee."

His lips thinned. Suddenly, his eyes were arctic. "My father built Murray Oil, not yours. Only back then it was called Sullivan and Murray Oil. Your father seized the opportunity, when my dad was down, to buy him out at five cents on the dollar."

"My father made the company what it is today."

"Well, now I'm going to take it over and improve upon it. Marriage to a Murray daughter will reassure the numerous employees that family, not a vengeful marauder, will be at the helm of the business."

"That would be a lie. You are a marauder, and you're not family."

"Not yet," he amended. "But a few Saturdays hence, if I marry Jaycee, we will be…family."

"Never. Not over my dead body!" She expelled the words in an outraged gasp.

"The thought of anything so awful happening to your delectable body is hateful to me." When he hesitated, his avid, searching expression made her warm again.

"Okay," he said. "Let's say I take you at your word. You're here to save your sister from me. And you'd die before you'd let me marry her. Is that right?"

"Essentially."

"What else would you do to stop me? Surely there is some lesser, more appealing sacrifice you'd be willing to make to inspire me to change my mind."

"I…don't know what you mean."

"Well, what if I were to agree to your proposal and forgo marriage to your lovely sister, a woman you say is so unsuited to my temperament I could never love her—I want to know what I will get in return."

"Do you always have to get something in return? You wouldn't actually be making a sacrifice."

His smile was a triumphant flash of white against his deeply tanned skin. "Always. Most decidedly. My hypothetical marriage to your sister is a business deal, after all. As a businessman, I would require compensation for letting the deal fall through."

Awful man.

His blue eyes stung her, causing the pulse in her throat to hammer frantically.

"Maybe…er…the satisfaction of doing a good deed for once in your life?" she said.

He laughed. "That's a refreshing idea if ever I heard one, and from a very charming woman—but, like most humans, I'm driven by the desire to avoid pain and pursue pleasure."

"And to think—I imagined you to be primarily driven by greed. Well, I don't have any money."

"I don't want your money."

"What do you want, then?"

"I think you know," he said silkily, leaning closer. "*You. You* interest me…quite a lot. I believe we could give each other immense pleasure…under the right circumstances."

The unavoidable heat in his eyes caused an unwanted shock wave of fiery prickles to spread through her body. She'd seriously underestimated the risk of confronting this man.

"In fact, I think we both knew what we wanted the moment we looked at each other today," he said.

He wanted her.

And even though he was promised to Jaycee, he didn't have a qualm about acknowledging his impossible, unsavory need for the skinnier, plainer, older sister. Maybe the thought of bedding his future wife's sister improved upon his original idea of revenge. Or maybe he was simply a man who never denied himself a female who might amuse him, however briefly. If any of those assumptions were true, he was too horrible for words.

"I'm hungry," he continued. "Why don't we discuss your proposition over dinner," he said.

"No. I couldn't possibly. You've said more than enough to convince me of the kind of man you are."

"Who are you kidding? You were prejudiced against me before you showed up here. If I'd played the saint, you would have still thought me the devil…and yet you would have also still…been secretly attracted. And you are attracted to me. Admit it."

Stunned at his boldness, she hissed out a breath. "I'm not."

Then why was she staring at his darling dimple as if she was hypnotized by it?

He laughed. "Do you have a boyfriend?" he asked. "Or dinner plans you need to change?"

"No," she admitted before she thought.

"Good." He smiled at her as if he was genuinely pleased. "Then it's settled."

"What?"

"You and I have a dinner date."

"No!"

"What are you afraid of?" he asked in that deep, velvet tone that let her know he had much more than dinner in mind. And some part of her, God help her, wanted to rush toward him like a moth toward flame, despite her sister, despite the knowledge that he wanted to destroy her family.

Kira was shaking her head vehemently when he said, "You came here today to talk to me, to convince me to do as you ask. I'm making myself available to you."

"But?"

He gave her a slow, insolent grin. "If you want to save your sister from the Big Bad Wolf, well—here's your chance."

Two

When they turned the corner and she saw the gaily lit restaurant, Kira wished with all her heart she'd never agreed to this dinner with Quinn.

Not that he hadn't behaved like a perfect gentleman as they'd walked over together.

When she'd said she wanted to go somewhere within walking distance of his office, she'd foolishly thought she'd be safer with him on foot.

"You're not afraid to get in my car, to be alone with me, are you?" he'd teased.

"It just seems simpler...to go somewhere close," she'd hedged. "Besides, you're a busy man."

"Not too busy for what really matters."

Then he'd suggested they walk along the river. The lovely reflections in the still, brown water where ducks swam and the companionable silences they'd shared as they'd made their way along the flagstones edged by lush vegetation, restaurants and bars had been altogether too enjoyable.

She'd never made a study of predators, but she had a cat, Rudy. When on the hunt, he was purposeful, diligent and very patient. He enjoyed playing with his prey before the kill, just to make the game last longer. She couldn't help but think Quinn was doing something similar with her.

No sooner did Quinn push open the door so she could enter one of the most popular Mexican restaurants in all of San Antonio than warmth, vibrant laughter and the heavy beat of Latin music hit her.

A man, who was hurrying outside after a woman, said, "Oh, excuse us, please, miss."

Quinn reached out and put his strong arm protectively around Kira's waist, shielding her with his powerful body. Pulling her close, he tugged her to one side to let the other couple pass.

When Quinn's body brushed against hers intimately, as if they were a couple, heat washed over her as it had the afternoon when she'd been muddy and he'd pulled her into his arms. She inhaled his clean, male scent. As before, he drew her like a sexual magnet.

When she let out an excited little gasp, he smiled and pulled her even closer. "You feel much too good," he whispered.

She should run, but the March evening was cooler than she'd dressed for, causing her to instinctively cling to his hot, big-boned body and stay nestled against his welcoming warmth.

She felt the red scarf she wore around her neck tighten as if to warn her away. She yanked at it and gulped in a breath before she shoved herself free of him.

He laughed. "You're not the only one who's been stunned by our connection, you know. I like holding you as much as you like being in my arms. In fact, that's all I want to do…hold you. Does that make me evil? Or all too human because I've found a woman I have no will to resist?"

"You are too much! Why did I let you talk me into this dinner?"

"Because it was the logical thing to do, and I insisted. Because I'm very good at getting what I want. Maybe because *you* wanted to. But now I'd be quite happy to skip dinner. We could order takeout and go to my loft apartment, which isn't far, by the way. You're a curator. I'm a collector. I have several pieces that might interest you."

"I'll bet! Not a good idea."

Again he laughed.

She didn't feel any safer once they were inside the crowded, brilliantly lit establishment. The restaurant with its friendly waitstaff, strolling mariachis, delicious aromas and ceiling festooned with tiny lights and colorful banners was too festive, too conducive to lowering one's guard. It would be too easy to succumb to temptation, something she couldn't afford to do.

I'll have a taco, a glass of water. We'll talk about Jaycee, and I'll leave. What could possibly go wrong if I nip this attraction in the bud?

When told there was a thirty-minute wait, Quinn didn't seem to mind. To the contrary, he seemed pleased. "We'll wait in the bar," he said, smiling.

Then he ushered them into a large room with a high-beamed ceiling dominated by a towering carved oak bar, inspired by the baroque elegance of the hotels in nineteenth-century San Antonio.

When a young redheaded waiter bragged on the various imported tequilas available, Quinn ordered them two margaritas made of a particularly costly tequila he said he had a weakness for.

"I'd rather have sparkling water," she said, sitting up straighter, thinking she needed all her wits about her.

"As you wish," Quinn said gallantly, ordering the water as well, but she noted that he didn't cancel the second margarita.

When their drinks arrived, he lifted his margarita to his lips and licked at the salt that edged the rim. And just watching the movement of his tongue across the grit of those glimmering crystals flooded her with ridiculous heat as she imagined him licking her skin.

"I think our first dinner together calls for a toast, don't you?" he said.

Her hand moved toward her glass of sparkling water.

"The tequila really is worth a taste."

She looked into his eyes and hesitated. Almost without her knowing it, her hand moved slowly away from the icy glass of water to her chilled margarita glass.

"You won't be sorry," he promised in that silken baritone.

Toying with the slender green stem of her glass, she lifted it and then tentatively clinked it against his.

"To us," he said. "To new beginnings." He smiled benevolently, but his blue eyes were excessively brilliant.

Her first swallow of the margarita was salty, sweet and very strong. She knew she shouldn't drink any more. Then, almost at once, a pleasant warmth buzzed through her, softening her attitude toward him and weakening her willpower. Somewhere the mariachis began to play "La Paloma," a favorite love song of hers. Was it a sign?

"I'm glad you at least took a sip," he said, his gaze lingering on her lips a second too long. "It would be a pity to miss tasting something so delicious."

"You're right. It's really quite good."

"The best—all the more reason not to miss it. One can't retrace one's journey in this life. We must make the most of every moment…because once lost, those moments are gone forever."

"Indeed." Eyeing him, she sipped again. "Funny, I hadn't thought of you as a philosopher."

"You might be surprised by who I really am, if you took the trouble to get to know me."

"I doubt it."

Every muscle in his handsome face tensed. When his eyes darkened, she wondered if she'd wounded him.

No. Impossible.

Her nerves jingled, urging her to consider just one more sip of the truly delicious margarita. What could it hurt? That second sip led to a third, then another and another, each sliding down her throat more easily than the last. She hardly noticed when Quinn moved from his side of the booth to hers, and yet how could she not notice? He didn't touch her, yet it was thrilling to be so near him, to know that only their clothes separated her thigh from his, to wonder what he would do next.

His gaze never strayed from her. Focusing on her exclusively, he told her stories about his youth, about the time before his father had died. His father had played ball with him, he said, had taken him hunting and fishing, had helped him with his homework. He stayed off the grim subjects of his parents' divorce and his father's death.

"When school was out for any reason, he always took me to his office. He was determined to instill a work ethic in me."

"He sounds like the perfect father," she said wistfully. "I never seemed to be able to please mine. If he read to me, I fidgeted too much, and he would lose his place and his temper. If he took me fishing, I grew bored or hot and squirmed too much, kicking over the minnow bucket or snapping his line. Once I stood up too fast and turned the boat over."

"Maybe I won't take you fishing."

"He always wanted a son, and I didn't please Mother any better. She thought Jaycee, who loved to dress up and go to parties, was perfect. She still does. Neither of them like what I'm doing with my life."

"Well, they're not in control, are they? No one is, really. And just when we think we are, we usually get struck by a lightning bolt that shows us we're not," Quinn said in a silken tone that made her breath quicken. "Like tonight."

"What do you mean?"

"Us."

Her gaze fixed on his dimple. "Are you coming on to me?"

He laid his hand on top of hers. "Would that be so terrible?"

By the time they'd been seated at their dinner table and had ordered their meal, she'd lost all her fear of him. She was actually enjoying herself.

Usually, she dated guys who couldn't afford to take her out to eat very often, she cooked for them in her apartment. Even though this meal was not a date, it was nice to dine in a pleasant restaurant and be served for a change.

When Quinn said how sorry he was that they hadn't met before that afternoon when he'd nearly run her down, she answered truthfully, "I thought you were marrying my sister solely to hurt all of us. I couldn't condone that."

He frowned. "And you love your sister so much, you came to my office today to try to find a way to stop me from marrying her."

"I was a fool to admit that to you."

"I think you're sweet, and I admire your honesty. You were right to come. You did me one helluva favor. I've been on the wrong course. But I don't want to talk about Jacinda. I want to talk about you."

"But will you think about…not marrying her?"

When he nodded and said, "Definitely," in a very convincing manner, she relaxed and took still another sip of her margarita with no more thoughts of how dangerous it might be for her to continue relaxing around him.

When he reached across the table and wrapped her hand in his warm, blunt fingers, the shock of his touch sent a wave of heat through her whole body. For a second, she entwined her fingers with his and clung as if he were a vital lifeline. Then, when she realized what she was doing, she wrenched her hand free.

"Why are you so afraid of me, Kira?"

"You might still marry Jaycee and ruin her life," she lied.

"Impossible, now that I've met you."

Kira's breath quickened. Dimple or not, he was still the enemy. She had to remember that.

"Do you really think I'm so callous I could marry your sister when I want you so much?"

"But what are you going to do about Jaycee?"

"I told you. She became irrelevant the minute I saw you standing inside my office this afternoon."

"She's beautiful…and *blonde*."

"Yes, but your beauty affects me more. Don't you know that?"

She shook her head. "The truth isn't in you. You only date blondes."

"Then it must be time for a change."

"I'm going to confess a secret wish. All my life I wished I was blonde…so I'd look more like the rest of my family, especially my mother and my sister. I thought maybe then I'd feel like I belonged."

"You *are* beautiful."

"A man like you would say anything…"

"I've never lied to any woman. Don't you know how incredibly lovely you are? With your shining dark eyes that show your sweet, pure soul every time you look at me and defend your sister? I feel your love for her rushing through you like liquid electricity. You're graceful. You move like a ballerina. I love the way you feel so intensely and blush when you think I might touch you."

"Like a child."

"No. Like a responsive, passionate woman. I like that… too much. And your hair…it's long and soft and shines like chestnut satin. Yet there's fire in it. I want to run my hands through it."

"But we hardly know one another. And I've hated you…"

"None of the Murrays have been favorites of mine either…but I'm beginning to see the error of my ways. And I don't think you hate me as much as you pretend."

Kira stared at him, searching his hard face for some sign that he was lying to her, seducing her as he'd seduced all those other women, saying these things because he had some dark agenda. All she saw was warmth and honesty and intense emotion. Nobody had ever looked at her with such hunger or made her feel so beautiful.

All her life she'd wanted someone to make her feel this special. It was ironic that Quinn Sullivan should be the one.

"I thought you were so bad, no…pure evil," she repeated.

His eyebrows arched. "Ouch."

If he'd been twisted in his original motives, maybe it

had been because of the grief he'd felt at losing someone he loved.

"How could I have been so wrong about you?" Even as she said it, some part of her wondered if she weren't being naive. He had dated, and jilted, all those beautiful women. He had intended to take revenge on her father and use her sister in his plan. Maybe when she'd walked into his office she'd become part of his diabolical plan, too.

"I was misguided," he said.

"I need more time to think about all this. Like I said…a mere hour or two ago I heartily disliked you. Or at least I thought I did."

"Because you didn't know me. Hell, maybe I didn't know me either…because everything is different now, since I met you."

She felt the same way. But she knew she should slow it down, reassess.

"I'm not good at picking boyfriends," she whispered.

"Their loss."

His hand closed over hers and he pressed her fingers, causing a melting sensation in her tummy. "My gain."

Her tacos came, looking and smelling delicious, but she hardly touched them. Her every sense was attuned to Quinn's carved features and his beautiful voice.

When a musician came to their table, Quinn hired him to sing several songs, including "La Paloma." While the man serenaded her, Quinn idly stroked her wrist and the length of her fingers, causing fire to shoot down her spine.

She met his eyes and felt that she had known him always, that he was already her lover, her soul mate. She was crazy to feel such things and think such thoughts about a man she barely knew, but when dinner was over, they skipped dessert.

An hour later, she sat across from him in his downtown

loft, sipping coffee while he drank brandy. In vain, she tried to act unimpressed by his art collection and sparkling views of the city. Not easy, since both were impressive.

His entrance was filled with an installation of crimson light by one of her favorite artists. The foyer was a dazzling ruby void that opened into a living room with high, white ceilings. All the rooms of his apartment held an eclectic mix of sculpture, porcelains and paintings.

Although she hadn't yet complimented his stylish home, she couldn't help but compare her small, littered apartment to his spacious one. Who was she to label him an arrogant upstart? He was a success in the international oil business and a man of impeccable taste, while she was still floundering in her career and struggling to find herself.

"I wanted to be alone with you like this the minute I saw you today," he said.

She shifted uneasily on his cream-leather sofa. Yet more evidence that he was a planner. "Well, I didn't."

"I think you did. You just couldn't let yourself believe you did."

"No," she whispered, setting down her cup. With difficulty she tried to focus on her mission. "So, what about Jaycee? You're sure that's over?"

"Finished. From the first moment I saw you."

"Without mud all over my face."

He laughed. "Actually, you got to me that day, too. Every time I dined with Jacinda and your family, I kept hoping I'd meet you again."

Even as she remembered all those dinner invitations her parents had extended and she'd declined, she couldn't believe he was telling the truth.

"I had my team research you," he said.

"Why?"

"I asked myself the same question. I think you intrigued

me…like I said, even with mud on your face. First thing tomorrow, I will break it off with Jacinda formally. Which means you've won. Does that make you happy? You have what you came for."

He was all charm, especially his warm, white smile. Like a child with a new playmate, she was happy just being with him, but she couldn't admit that to him.

He must have sensed her feelings, though, because he got up and moved silently toward her. "I feel like I've lived my whole life since my father's death alone—until you. And that's how I wanted to live—until you."

She knew it was sudden and reckless, but she felt the same way. If she wasn't careful, she would forget all that should divide them.

As if in a dream, she took his hand when he offered it and kissed his fingers with feverish devotion.

"You've made me realize how lonely I've been," he said.

"That's a very good line."

"It's the truth."

"But you are so successful, while I…"

"Look what you're doing in the interim—helping a friend to realize her dream."

"My father says I'm wasting my potential."

"You will find yourself…if you are patient." He cupped her chin and stared into her eyes. Again she felt that uncanny recognition. He was a kindred soul who knew what it was to feel lost.

"Dear God," he muttered. "Don't listen to me. I don't know a damn thing about patience. Like now… I should let you go…but I can't."

He pulled her to him and crushed her close. It wasn't long before holding her wasn't enough. He had to have her lips, her throat, her breasts. She felt the same way. Shedding her shirt, scarf and bra, she burst into flame as he kissed her. Even though she barely knew him, she could not wait another moment to belong to him.

"I'm not feeling so patient right now myself," she admitted huskily.

Do not give yourself to this man, said an inner voice. *Remember all those blondes. Remember his urge for revenge.*

Even as her emotions spiraled out of control, she knew she was no femme fatale, while he was a devastatingly attractive man. Had he said all these same wonderful things to all those other women he'd bedded? Had he done and felt all the same things, too, a thousand times before? Were nights like this routine for him, while he was the first to make her feel so thrillingly alive?

But then his mouth claimed hers again, and again, with a fierce, wild hunger that made her forget her doubts and shake and cling to him. His kisses completed her as she'd never been completed before. He was a wounded soul, and she understood his wounds. How could she feel so much when they hadn't even made love?

Lifting her into his arms, he carried her into his vast bedroom, which was bathed in silver moonlight. Over her shoulder she saw his big, black bed in the middle of an ocean of white marble and Persian carpets.

He was a driven, successful billionaire, and she was a waitress. Feeling out of her depth, her nerves returned. Not knowing what else to do, she pressed a fingertip to his lips. Gently, shyly, she traced his dimple.

Feeling her tension, he set her down. She pushed against his chest and then took a step away from him. Watching her, he said, "You can finish undressing in the bathroom if you'd prefer privacy. Or we can stop. I'll drive you to your car. Your choice."

She should have said, "I don't belong here with you,"

and accepted his gallant offer. Instead, without a word, she scampered toward the door he'd indicated. Alone in his beige marble bathroom with golden fixtures and a lovely, compelling etching by another one of her favorite artists, she barely recognized her own flushed face, tousled hair and sparkling eyes.

The radiant girl in his tall mirror *was* as beautiful as an enchanted princess. She looked expectant, excited. Maybe she did belong here with him. Maybe he was the beginning of her new life, the first correct step toward the bright future that had so long eluded her.

When she tiptoed back into the bedroom, wearing nothing but his white robe, he was in bed. She couldn't help admiring the width of his bronzed shoulders as he leaned back against several plumped pillows. She had never dated anyone half so handsome; she'd never felt anything as powerful as the glorious heady heat that suffused her entire being as his blue eyes studied her hungrily. Still, she was nervy, shaking.

"I'm no good at sex," she said. "You're probably very good… Of course you are. You're good at everything."

"Come here," he whispered.

"But…"

"Just come to me. You could not possibly delight me more. Surely you know that."

Did he really feel as much as she did?

Removing his bathrobe, she flew to him before she lost her nerve, fell into his bed and into his arms, consumed by forces beyond her control. Nothing mattered but sliding against his long body, being held close in his strong arms. Beneath the covers, his heat was delicious and welcoming as she nestled against him.

He gave her a moment to settle before he rolled on top of her. Bracing himself with his elbows against the mattress, so as not to crush her, he kissed her lips, her cheeks, her brows and then her eyelids with urgent yet featherlike strokes. Slowly, gently, each kiss was driving her mad.

"Take me," she whispered, in the grip of a fever such as she'd never experienced before. "I want you inside me. Now."

"I know," he said, laughing. "I'm as ravenous as you are. But have patience, darlin'."

"You have a funny way of showing your hunger."

"If I do what you ask, it would be over in a heartbeat. This moment, our first time together, is too special to me."

Was she special?

"We must savor it, draw it out, make it last," he said.

"Maybe I want it to be over swiftly," she begged. "Maybe this obsessive need is unbearable."

"Exquisite expectation?"

"I can't stand it."

"And I want to heighten it. Which means we're at cross-purposes."

He didn't take her. With infinite care and maddening patience he adored her with his clever mouth and skilled hands. His fevered lips skimmed across her soft skin, raising goose bumps in secret places. As she lay beneath him, he licked each nipple until it grew hard, licked her navel until he had all her nerve endings on fire for him. Then he kissed her belly and dived even lower to explore those hidden, honey-sweet lips between her legs. When she felt his tongue dart inside, she gasped and drew back.

"Relax," he whispered.

With slow, hot kisses, he made her gush. All too soon her embarrassment was gone, and she was melting, shivering, whimpering—all but begging him to give her release.

Until tonight she had been an exile in the world of love. With all other men, not that there had been that many, she had been going through the motions, playing a part, searching always for something meaningful and never finding it.

Until now, tonight, with him.

He couldn't matter this much! She couldn't let this be more than fierce, wild sex. He, the man, couldn't matter. But her building emotions told her that he did matter—in ways she'd never imagined possible before.

He took her breast in his mouth and suckled again. Then his hand entered her heated wetness, making her gasp helplessly and plead. When he stroked her, his fingers sliding against that secret flesh, she arched against his expert touch, while her breath came in hard, tortured pants.

Just when she didn't think she could bear it any longer, he dragged her beneath him and slid inside her. He was huge, massive, wonderful. Crying out, she clung to him and pushed her pelvis against his, aching for him to fill her even more deeply. *"Yes! Yes!"*

When he sank deeper, ever deeper, she moaned. For a long moment he held her and caressed her. Then he began to plunge in and out, slowly at first. Her rising pleasure carried her and shook her in sharp, hot waves, causing her to climax and scream his name.

He went crazy when she dug her nails in his shoulder. Then she came again, and again, sobbing. She had no idea how many climaxes she had before she felt his hard loins bunch as he exploded.

Afterward, sweat dripped off his brow. His whole body was flushed, burning up, and so was hers.

"Darlin' Kira," he whispered in that husky baritone that could still make her shiver even when she was spent. "Darlin' Kira."

For a long time, she lay in his arms, not speaking, feeling too weak to move any part of her body. Then he leaned over and nibbled at her bottom lip.

The second time he made love to her, he did so with a reverent gentleness that made her weep and hold on to him for a long time afterward. He'd used a condom the second time, causing her to realize belatedly that he hadn't the first time.

How could they have been so careless? She had simply been swept away. Maybe he had, too. Well, it was useless to worry about that now. Besides, she was too happy, too relaxed to care about anything except being in his arms. There was no going back.

For a long time they lay together, facing each other while they talked. He told her about his father's financial crisis and how her father had turned on him and made things worse. He spoke of his mother's extravagance and betrayal and his profound hurt that his world had fallen apart so quickly and brutally. She listened as he explained how grief, poverty and helplessness had twisted him and made him hard.

"Love made me too vulnerable, as it did my father. It was a destructive force. My father loved my mother, and it ruined him. She was greedy and extravagant," he said. "Love destroys the men in our family."

"If you don't want to love, why did you date all those women I read about?"

"I wasn't looking for love, and neither were they."

"You were just using them, then?"

"They were using me, too."

"That's so cynical."

"That's how my life has been. I loved my father so much, and I hurt so much when he died, I gave up on love. He loved my mother, and she broke his heart with her unrelenting demands. When he lost the business, she lost interest in him and began searching for a richer man."

"And did she find him?"

"Several."

"Do you ever see her?"

"No. I was an accident she regretted, I believe. She couldn't relate to children, and after I was grown, I had no interest in her. Love, no matter what kind, always costs too much. I do write her a monthly check, however."

"So, my father was only part of your father's problem."

"But a big part. Losing ownership in Sullivan and Murray Oil made my father feel like he was less than nothing. My mother left him because of that loss. She stripped him of what little wealth and self-esteem he had left. Alone, without his company or his wife, he grew depressed. He wouldn't eat. He couldn't sleep. I'd hear the stairs creak as he paced at night.

"Then early one morning I heard a shot. When I called his name, he didn't answer. I found him in the shop attached to our garage. In a pool of blood on the floor, dead. I still don't know if it was an accident or…what I feared it was. He was gone. At first I was frightened. Then I became angry. I wanted to blame someone, to get even, to make his death right. I lived for revenge. But now that I've almost achieved my goal of taking back Murray Oil, it's as if my fever's burned out."

"Oh, I wouldn't say that," she teased, touching his damp brow.

"I mean my fever for revenge, which was what kept me going."

"So," she asked, "what will you live for now?"

"I don't know. I guess a lot of people just wake up in the morning and go to work, then come home at night and drink while they flip channels with their remote."

"Not you."

"Who's to say? Maybe such people are lucky. At least they're not driven by hate, as I was."

"I can't even begin to imagine what that must have felt like for you." She'd always been driven by the need for love.

When he stared into her eyes with fierce longing, she pulled him close and ran her hands through his hair. "You are young yet. You'll find something to give your life meaning," she said.

"Well, it won't be love, because I've experienced love's dark side for too many years. I want you to know that. You are special, but I can't ever love you, no matter how good we are together. I'm no longer capable of that emotion."

"So you keep telling me," she said, pretending his words didn't hurt.

"I just want to be honest."

"Do we always know our own truths?"

"Darlin'," he whispered. "Forgive me if I sounded too harsh. It's just that…I don't want to hurt you by raising your expectations about something I'm incapable of. Other women have become unhappy because of the way I am."

"You're my family's enemy. Why would I ever want to love you?"

Wrapping her legs around him, she held him for hours, trying to comfort the boy who'd lost so much as well as the angry man who'd gained a fortune because he'd been consumed by a fierce, if misplaced, hatred.

"My father had nothing to do with your father's death," she whispered. "He didn't."

"You have your view, and I have mine," he said. "The important thing is that I don't hold you responsible for your father's sins any longer."

"Don't you?"

"No."

After that, he was silent. Soon afterward he let her go and rolled onto his side.

She lay awake for hours. Where would they go from here? He had hated her family for years. Had he really let go of all those harsh feelings? Had she deluded herself into thinking he wasn't her enemy?

What price would she pay for sleeping with a man who probably only saw her as an instrument for revenge?

Three

When Kira woke up naked in bed with Quinn, she felt unsettled and very self-conscious. Propping herself on an elbow, she watched him warily in the dim rosy half light of dawn. All her doubts returned a hundredfold.

How could she have let things go this far? How could she have risked pregnancy?

What if... No, she couldn't be that unlucky.

Besides, it did no good to regret what had happened, she reminded herself again. If she hadn't slept with him she would never have known such ecstasy was possible.

Now, at least, she knew. Even if it wasn't love, it had been so great she felt an immense tenderness well up in her in spite of her renewed doubts.

He was absurdly handsome with his thick, unruly black hair falling across his brow, with his sharp cheekbones and sculpted mouth. She'd been touched when he'd shown her his vulnerability last night. Just looking at him now was enough to make her stomach flutter with fresh desire.

She was about to stroke his hair, when, without warning, his obscenely long lashes snapped open, and he met her gaze with that directness that still startled her. Maybe because there were so many imperfections she wanted to keep hidden. In the next instant, his expression softened, disarming her.

"Good morning, darlin'." His rough, to-die-for, sexy baritone caressed her.

A jolt sizzled through her even before he reached out a bronzed hand to pull her face to his so he could kiss her lightly on the lips. Never had she wanted anyone as much as she wanted him.

"I haven't brushed my teeth," she warned.

"Neither the hell have I. I don't expect you to be perfect. I simply want you. I can't do without you. You should know that after last night."

She was amazed because she felt exactly the same. Still, with those doubts still lingering, she felt she had to protect herself by protesting.

"Last night was probably a mistake," she murmured.

"Maybe. Or maybe it's a complication, a challenge. Or a good thing. In any case, it's too late to worry about it. I want you more now than ever."

"But for how long?"

"Is anything certain?"

He kissed her hard. Before she could protest again, he rolled on top of her and was inside her, claiming her fiercely, his body piercing her to the bed, his massive erection filling her. When he rode her violently, she bucked like a wild thing, too, her doubts dissolving like mist as primal desire swept her past reason.

"I'm sorry," he said afterward. "I wanted you too much."

He had, however, at the last second, remembered to use a condom. This time, he didn't hold her tenderly or make small talk or confide sweet nothings as he had last night. In fact, he seemed hellishly annoyed at himself.

Was he already tired of her? Would there be a new blonde in his bed tonight? At the thought, a sob caught in her throat.

"You can have the master bathroom. I'll make coffee," he said tersely.

Just like that, he wanted her gone. Since she'd researched him and had known his habits, she shouldn't feel shocked or hurt. Hadn't he warned her he was incapable of feeling close to anyone? She should be grateful for the sublime sexual experience and let the rest go.

Well, she had her pride. She wasn't about to cling to him or show that she cared. But she did care. Oh, how she cared. Her family's worst enemy had quickly gained a curious hold on her heart.

Without a word, she rose and walked naked across the vast expanse of thick, white carpet, every female cell vividly aware that, bored with her though he might be, he didn't tear his eyes from her until she reached the bathroom and shut the door. Once inside she turned the lock and leaned heavily against the wall in a state of collapse.

She took a deep breath and stared at her pale, guilt-stricken reflection, so different from the glowing wanton of last night.

She'd known the kind of guy he was, in spite of his seductive words. How could she have opened herself to such a hard man? Her father's implacable enemy?

What had she done?

By the time she'd showered, brushed her hair and dressed, he was in the kitchen, looking no worse for wear.

Indeed, he seemed energized by what they had shared. Freshly showered, he wore a white shirt and crisply pressed dark slacks. He'd shaved, and his glossy black hair was combed. He looked so civilized, she felt the crazy urge to run her hands through his hair, just to muss it up and leave her mark.

The television was on, and he was watching the latest stock market report while he held his cell phone against his ear. Behind him, a freshly made pot of aromatic coffee sat on the gleaming white counter.

She was about to step inside when he flicked the remote, killing the sound of the television. She heard his voice, as sharp and hard as it had been with the caller yesterday in his office.

"Habib, business is business," he snapped. "I know I have to convince the shareholders and the public I'm some shining white knight. That's why I agreed to marry a Murray daughter and why her parents, especially her father, who wants an easy transition of power, suggested Jacinda and persuaded her to accept me. However, if the older Murray sister agrees to marry me instead, why should it matter to you or to anyone else…other than to Jacinda, who will no doubt be delighted to have her life back?"

Habib, whoever he was, must have argued, because Quinn's next response was much angrier. "Yes, I know the family history and why you consider Jacinda the preferable choice, but since nobody else knows, apparently not even Kira, it's of no consequence. So, if I've decided to marry the older sister instead of the younger, and this decision will make the shareholders and employees just as happy, why the hell should you care?"

The man must have countered again, because Quinn's low tone was even more cutting. "No, I haven't asked her yet. It's too soon. But when I do, I'll remind her that I told her yesterday I'd demand a price for freeing her sister. She'll have to pay it, that's all. She'll have no choice but to do what's best for her family and her sister. Hell, she'll do anything for their approval."

One sister or the other—and he didn't care which one. That he could speak of marrying her instead of Jaycee as a cold business deal before he'd even bothered to propose made Kira's tender heart swell with hurt and outrage. That he would use her desire for her family's love and acceptance to his own advantage was too horrible to endure.

Obviously, she was that insignificant to him. But hadn't she known that? So why did it hurt so much?

He'd said she was special. Nobody had ever made her feel so cherished before.

Thinking herself a needy, romantic fool, she shut her eyes. Unready to face him or confess what she'd overheard and how much it bothered her, Kira backed out of the kitchen and returned to the bedroom. In her present state she was incapable of acting rationally and simply demanding an explanation.

He was a planner. Her seduction must have been a calculated move. No longer could she believe he'd been swept off his feet by her as she had by him. She was skinny and plain. He'd known she desired him, and he was using that to manipulate her.

Last night, when he'd promised he'd break it off with her sister, she'd never guessed the devious manner in which he'd planned to honor that promise.

She was still struggling to process everything she'd learned, when Quinn himself strode into the bedroom looking much too arrogant, masterful and self-satisfied for her liking.

"Good, you're dressed," he said in that beautiful voice. "You look gorgeous."

Refusing to meet the warmth of his admiring gaze for fear she might believe his compliment and thereby lose her determination to escape him, she nodded.

"I made coffee."

"Smells good," she whispered, staring out the window.

"Do you have time for breakfast?"

"No!"

"Something wrong?"

If he was dishonest, why should she bother to be straight with him? "I'm fine," she said, but in a softer tone.

"Right. That must be why you seem so cool."

"Indeed?"

"And they say men are the ones who withdraw the morning after."

She bit her lip to keep herself from screaming at him.

"Still, I understand," he said.

"Last night is going to take some getting used to," she said.

"For me, as well."

To that she said nothing.

"Well, the coffee's in the kitchen," he said, turning away.

Preferring to part from him without an argument, she followed him into the kitchen where he poured her a steaming cup and handed it to her.

"Do you take cream? Sugar?"

She shook her head. "We don't know the most basic things about each other, do we?"

"After last night, I'd have to disagree with you, darlin'."

She blushed in confusion. "Don't call me that."

He eyed her thoughtfully. "You really do seem upset."

She sipped from her cup, again choosing silence instead of arguing the point. Was he good at everything? Rich and strong, the coffee was to die for.

"For the record, I take mine black, very black," he said.

"Without sugar. So, we have that in common. And we have what we shared last night."

"Don't…"

"I'd say we're off to a great start."

Until I realized what you were up to, I would have agreed. She longed to claw him. Instead, she clenched her nails into her palms and chewed her lower lip mutinously.

The rosy glow from last night, when he'd made her feel so special, had faded. She felt awkward and unsure…and hurt, which was ridiculous because she'd gone into this knowing who and what he was.

Obviously, last night had been business as usual for him. Why not marry the Murray sister who'd practically thrown herself at him? Did he believe she was so smitten and desperate for affection she'd be more easily controlled?

Why had she let herself be swept away by his looks, his confidences and his suave, expert lovemaking?

Because, your stupid crush on him turned your brain to mush.

And turned her raging hormones to fire. Never had she felt so physically and spiritually in tune with anyone. She'd actually thought, at one point, that they could be soul mates.

Soul mates! It was all an illusion. You were a fool, girl, and not for the first time.

"Look, I'd really better go," she said, her tone so sharp his dark head jerked toward her.

"Right. Then I'll drive you, since you left your car downtown."

"I can call a cab."

"No! I'll drive you."

Silently, she nodded.

He led the way to stairs that went down to the elevator and garage. In silence, they sped along the freeway in his silver Aston Martin until he slowed to take the off-ramp that led to where she'd parked downtown. After that, she *had* to speak to him in order to direct him to her small, dusty Toyota with several dings in its beige body. She let out a little moan when he pulled up behind her car and she saw the parking ticket flapping under her windshield wipers.

He got out and raced around the hood to open her door, but before he could, she'd flung it open.

"You sure there isn't something wrong?" he asked.

She snatched the ticket, but before she could get in her car, he slid his arms around her waist from behind.

He felt so solid and strong and warm, she barely suppressed a sigh. She yearned to stay in his arms even though she knew she needed to get away from him as quickly as possible to regroup.

He turned her to face him and his fingertips traced the length of her cheek in a tender, burning caress, and for a long second he stared into her troubled eyes with a mixture of concern and barely suppressed impatience. He seemed to care.

Liar.

"It's not easy letting you go," he said.

"People are watching us," she said mildly, even as she seethed with outrage.

"So what? Last night was very special to me, Kira. I'm sorry if you're upset about it. I hope it's just that it all happened too fast. I wasn't too rough, was I?"

The concern in his voice shook her. "No." She looked away, too tempted to meet his gaze.

"It's never been like that for me. I…I couldn't control myself, especially this morning. I wanted you again… badly. This is all happening too fast for me, too. I prefer being able to plan."

That's not what he'd said on the phone. Quinn seemed to have damn sure had a plan. Marry a Murray daughter. And he was sticking to it.

"Yes, it is happening…too fast." She bit her lip. "But… I'm okay." She wanted to brush off his words, to pretend she didn't care that he'd apologized and seemed genuinely worried about her physical and emotional state. He seemed all too likable. She almost believed him.

"Do you have a business card?" he asked gently.

She shook her head. "Nope. At least, not on me."

He flipped a card out of his pocket. "Well, here is mine. You can call me anytime. I want to see you again…as soon as possible. There's something very important I want to discuss with you."

The intensity of his gaze made her heart speed up. "You are not going back on your word about marrying Jaycee, are you?"

"How can you even ask? I'll call it off as soon as I leave you. Unfortunately, after that, I have to be away on business for several days, first to New York, then London. Murray Oil is in the middle of negotiating a big deal with the European Union. My meeting tonight in New York ends at eight, so call me after that. On my cell."

Did he intend to propose over the phone? Her throat felt thick as she forced herself to nod. Whipping out a pen and a pad, she wrote down her cell phone number. "Will you text me as soon as you break up with my sister?"

"Can I take that to mean you care about me…a little?" he asked.

"Sure," she whispered, exhaling a pent-up breath. How did he lie so easily? "Take it any way you like."

She had to get away from him, to be alone to think. Everything he said, everything he did, made her want him—even though she knew, after what she'd heard this morning, that she'd never been anything but a pawn in the game he was playing to exact revenge against her father.

She wasn't special to him. And if she didn't stand up for herself now, she never would be.

She would not let her father sell Jaycee *or* her to this man!

Four

"You're her father. I still can't believe you don't have a clue where Kira could be. Hell, she's been gone for nearly three weeks."

Shaking his head, Earl stalked across Quinn's corner office at Murray Oil to look out the window. "I told you, she's probably off somewhere painting. She does that."

Quinn hated himself for having practically ordered the infuriating Murray to his office again today. But he was that desperate to know Kira was safe. Her safety aside, he had a wedding planned and a bride to locate.

"You're sure she's not in any trouble?"

"Are *you* sure she didn't realize you were about to demand that she marry you?"

Other than wanting Kira to take Jaycee's place, he wasn't sure about a damn thing! Well, except that maybe he'd pushed Kira too fast and too far. Hell, she could have overheard him talking to Habib. She'd damn sure gotten quiet and sulky before they parted ways.

"I don't think—"

"I'd bet money she got wise to you and decided to let you stew in your own juices. She may seem sweet and malleable, but she's always had a mind of her own. She's impossible to control. It's why she lost her job. It's why I suggested you choose Jaycee in the first place. Jaycee is biddable."

Quinn felt heat climb his neck. He didn't want Jaycee. He'd never wanted Jaycee. He wanted Kira…sweet, passionate Kira who went wild every time he touched her. Her passion thrilled him as nothing else had in years.

The trouble was, after he'd made love to her that morning, he'd felt completely besotted and then out of sorts as a result. He hadn't wanted to dwell on what feeling such an all-consuming attraction so quickly might mean. Now he knew that if anything had happened to her, he'd never forgive himself.

"I couldn't ask her to marry me after our dinner. It was too soon. Hell, maybe she did figure it all out and run off before I could explain."

"Well, I checked our hunting lodges at the ranch where she goes to paint wildlife, and I've left messages with my caretaker at the island where she paints birds. Nobody's seen her. Sooner or later she'll turn up. She always does. You'll just have to be patient."

"Not my forte."

"Quinn, she's okay. When she's in between museum jobs, she runs around like this. She's always been a free spirit."

"Right." Quinn almost growled. He disliked that the other man could see he was vulnerable and crazed by Kira's disappearance. The need to find her, to find out why she'd vanished, had been building inside him. He couldn't go on if he didn't solve this mystery—and not just because the wedding date loomed.

His one night with Kira had been the closest thing to perfection he'd known since before his dad had died. Never had he experienced with any other woman anything like what he'd shared with Kira. Hell, he hadn't known such closeness was possible. He'd lost himself completely in her, talked to her as he'd never talked to another person.

Even though she'd seemed distant the next morning, he'd thought she'd felt the same wealth of emotion he had and was running scared. But no—something else had made her vanish without a word, even before he'd told her she'd have to marry him if Jaycee didn't. Thinking back, all he could imagine was that she'd felt vulnerable and afraid after their shared night—or that she *had* overheard him talking to Habib.

Then the day after he'd dropped her at her car, Quinn had texted her, as he'd promised, to let her know he'd actually broken it off with Jacinda. She'd never called him back. Nor had she answered her phone since then. She'd never returned to her tiny apartment or her place of employment.

Kira had called her friend Betty to check in, and promised she'd call weekly to keep in touch, but she hadn't given an explanation for her departure or an estimation for when she'd return.

Quinn had to rethink his situation. He'd stopped romancing Jacinda, but he hadn't canceled the wedding because he planned to marry Kira instead. Come Saturday, a thousand people expected him to marry a Murray daughter.

Apparently, his future father-in-law's mind was running along the same worrisome track.

"Quinn, you've got to be reasonable. We've got to call off the wedding," Earl said.

"I'm going to marry Kira."

"You're talking nonsense. Kira's gone. Without a bride, you're going to piss off the very people we want to reassure. Stockholders, clients and employees of Murray Oil. Not to mention—this whole thing is stressing the hell out of Vera, and in her condition that isn't good."

Several months earlier, when Quinn had stalked into Earl's office with enough shares to demand control of Murray Oil, Earl, his eyes blurry and his shoulders slumped, had sat behind his desk already looking defeated.

The older man had wearily confided that his wife was seriously ill. Not only had Earl not cared that Quinn would soon be in charge of Murray Oil, he'd said the takeover was the answer to a prayer. It was time he retired. With Murray Oil in good hands, he could devote himself to his beloved wife, who was sick and maybe dying.

"She's everything to me," he'd whispered. "The way your father was to you and the way your mother was to him before she left him."

"Why tell me—your enemy?" Quinn had asked.

"I don't think of you as my enemy. I never was one to see the world in black or white, the way Kade, your dad, did—the way you've chosen to see it since his death. Whether you believe me or not, I loved your father, and I was sorry about our misunderstanding. You're just like him, you know, so now that I've got my own challenge to face, there's nobody I'd rather turn the company over to than you.

"Vera doesn't want me talking about her illness to friends and family. She can't stand the thought of people, even her daughters, thinking of her as weak and sick. I'm glad I finally have someone I can tell."

Quinn had been stunned. For years, he had hated Earl, had wanted revenge, had looked forward to bringing the man to his knees. But ever since that conversation his feelings had begun to change. The connection he'd found with Kira had hastened that process.

He'd begun to rethink his choices, reconsider his past. Not all his memories of Earl were negative. He could remember some wonderful times hunting and fishing with the blunt-spoken Earl and his dad. As a kid, he'd loved the stories Earl had told around the campfire.

Maybe the bastard had been partially responsible for his father's death. But maybe an equal share of the blame lay with his own father.

Not that Quinn trusted his new attitude. He'd gone too far toward his goal of vengeance not to seize Murray Oil. And he still believed taking a Murray bride would make the acquisition run more smoothly.

"I will get married on Saturday," Quinn said. "All we have to do is convince Kira to come back and marry me."

"Right. But how? We don't even know where she is."

"We don't have to know. All we have to do is motivate her to return," Quinn said softly.

Seabirds raced along the beach, pecking at seaweed. Her jeans rolled to her knees, Kira stood in the shallow surf of Murray Island and wiggled her toes in the cool, damp sand as the wind whipped her hair against her cheeks. Blowing sand stung her bare arms and calves.

Kira needed to make her weekly phone call to Betty after her morning walk—a phone call she dreaded. Each week, it put her back in touch with reality, which was what she wanted to escape from.

Still, she'd known she couldn't stay on the island forever. She'd just thought that solitude would have cleared her head of Quinn by now. But it hadn't. She missed him.

Three weeks of being here alone had changed nothing. None of her confusion or despair about her emotional entanglement with Quinn had lifted.

Maybe if she hadn't been calling Betty to check in, she would be calmer. Betty had told her about Quinn's relentless visits to the restaurant. Thinking about Quinn looking for her had stirred up her emotions and had blocked her artistically. All she could paint was his handsome face.

Well, at least she was painting. When she'd been frustrated while working at the museum, she hadn't even been able to hold a paintbrush.

Since it was past time to call Betty again, she headed for the family beach house. When she climbed the wooden stairs and entered, the wind caught the screen door and banged it behind her.

She turned on her cell phone and climbed to the second floor where the signal and the views of the high surf were better.

Betty answered on the first ring. "You still okay all alone out there?"

"I'm fine. How's Rudy?"

She'd packed her cat and his toys and had taken him to Betty's, much to his dismay.

"Rudy's taken over as usual. Sleeps in my bed. He's right here. He can hear your voice on speakerphone. He's very excited, twitchin' his tail and all." She paused, then, "I worry about you out there alone, Kira."

"Jim's around. He checks on me."

Jim was the island's caretaker. She'd taken him into her confidence and asked him not to tell anyone, not even her father, where she was.

"Well, there's something I need to tell you, something I've been dreadin' tellin' you," Betty began.

"What?"

"That fella of yours, Quinn…"

"He's not my fella."

"Well, he sure acts like he's your guy when he drops by. He's been drillin' the staff, makin' sure you weren't datin' anyone. Said he didn't want to lay claim to a woman who belonged to another."

Lay claim? Kira caught her breath. Just thinking about Quinn in the restaurant looking for her made her breasts swell and her heart throb.

Darn it—would she never forget him?

"Well, today he comes over just as I'm unlocking the door and launches into a tirade about how he's gonna have to break his promise to you and marry your sister, Jaycee! This Saturday!

"I thought it right funny at first, him sayin' that, when he comes by lookin' haunted, askin' after you all the time, so I said up front I didn't buy it. Called him a liar, I did.

"He said maybe he preferred you, but you'd forced his hand. He had to marry a Murray daughter for business reasons, so he would. Everything is set. He told me to read the newspapers, if I didn't believe him. And I did. They're really getting married. It's all over the internet, too."

"What?"

"Tomorrow! Saturday! I know he told you he broke off his wedding plans, but if he did, they're on again. He's every bit as bad as you said. You were right to go away. If I was you, I'd never come back."

So, since he'd never cared which Murray sister he married, he was going to marry Jaycee after all.

Well, she'd stop him. She'd go back—at once—and she'd stop him cold.

Five

A sign in front of the church displayed a calendar that said Murray-Sullivan Wedding: 7:30 p.m.

It was five-thirty as Kira swung into the mostly empty parking lot.

Good. No guests had arrived. She'd made it in time.

The sun was low; the shadows long; the light a rosy gold. Not that she took the time to notice the clarity of the light or the rich green of the grass or the tiny spring leaves budding on the trees. Her heart was pounding. She was perspiring as she hit the brakes and jumped out of her Toyota.

The drive from the coast hadn't taken much more than three hours, but the trip had tired her. Feeling betrayed and yet desperate to find her sister and stop this travesty before it was too late, Kira ran toward the back of the church where the dressing rooms were. Inside, dashing from room to room, she threw open doors, calling her sister's name. Then, suddenly, in the last room, she found Jaycee, wearing a blue cotton dress with a strand of pearls at her throat. With her blond hair cascading down her back, Jaycee sat quietly in front of a long, gilt mirror, applying lipstick. She looked as if she'd been carefully posed by a photographer.

"Jaycee!" Kira cried breathlessly. "At last… Why aren't you wearing…a wedding dress?"

Then she saw the most beautiful silk gown seeded with tiny pearls lying across a sofa and a pair of white satin shoes on the floor.

"Oh, but that's why you're here…to dress… Of course. Where's Mother? Why isn't Mother here to help you?"

"She's not feeling well. I think she's resting. Mother and Quinn told me to wait here."

Odd. Usually when it came to organizing any social affair, their mother had endless reserves of energy that lasted her until the very end of the event.

"Where are your bridesmaids?"

Turning like an actress compelled by her cue, Jaycee pressed her lips together and then put her lipstick inside her blue purse. "I was so worried you wouldn't come," she said. "I was truly afraid you wouldn't show. We all were. Quinn most especially. But me, too. He'll be so happy you're here. I don't know what he would have done if you hadn't gotten here in time. You don't know how important you are to him."

Right. That's why he's marrying you without a qualm.

As always, Jaycee worried about everyone she loved. Kira very much doubted that Quinn would be happy with her once she finished talking to Jaycee.

Guilt flooded Kira. How would she ever find the words to explain to her trusting sister why she couldn't marry Quinn? Jaycee, who'd always been loved by everybody, probably couldn't imagine there was a soul in the world who wouldn't love her if she tried hard enough to win him. After all, Daddy had given his blessing.

"You can't marry Quinn today," Kira stated flatly.

"I know that. He told me all about you two. When Daddy asked me to marry Quinn, I tried to tell myself it was the right thing to do. For the family and all. But...when I found out he wanted to marry you...it was such a relief."

"Why did you show up here today if you knew all this?"

"Quinn will...explain everything." Jaycee's eyes widened as the door opened. Kira whirled to tell their visitor that this was a private conversation, but her words died in a convulsive little growl. Quinn, dressed in a tux that set off his broad shoulders and stunning dark looks to heart-stopping perfection, strode masterfully into the room.

Feeling cornered, Kira sank closer to Jaycee. When he saw her, he stopped, his eyes flashing with hurt and anger before he caught her mood and stiffened.

"I was hoping you'd make it in time for the wedding," he said, his deep baritone cutting her to the quick.

"Damn you!" Her throat tightened as she arose. "Liar! How could you do this?"

"I'm thrilled to see you, too, darlin'," he murmured, his gaze devouring her. "You do look lovely."

Kira, who'd driven straight from the island without making a single stop, was wearing a pair of worn, tight jeans and a T-shirt that hugged her curves. She hadn't bothered with makeup or a comb for her tangled hair. She could do nothing but take in a mortified breath at his comment while she stared at his dark face, the face she'd painted so many times even when images of him had blurred through her tears.

"What is the meaning of this?" she screamed.

"There's no need for hysterics, darlin'," he said calmly.

"Don't *darlin'* me! You have no right to call me that!"

she shrieked. "I haven't even begun to show you hysterics! I'm going to tear you limb from limb. Pound you into this tile floor... Skin you alive—"

"Kira, Quinn's been so worried about you. Frantic that you wouldn't show up in time," Jaycee began. "Talk about wedding jitters. He's had a full-blown case..."

"I'll just bet he has!"

"I see we misunderstand each other, Kira. I was afraid of this. Jacinda," he said in a silky tone that maddened Kira further because it made her feel jealous of her innocent sister, "could you give us a minute? I need to talk to Kira alone."

With a quick, nervous glance in Kira's direction, Jaycee said, "Kira, are you sure you'll be okay? You don't look so good."

Kira nodded mutely, wanting to spare Jaycee any necessary embarrassment. So Jaycee slipped out of the room and closed the door quietly.

Her hand raised, Kira bounded toward him like a charging lioness ready to claw her prey, but he caught her wrist and used it to lever her closer.

"Let me go!" she cried.

"Not while you're in such a violent mood, darlin'. You'd only scratch me or do something worse that you'd regret."

"I don't think so."

"This storm will pass, as all storms do. You'll see. Because it's due to a misunderstanding."

"A misunderstanding? I don't think so! You promised you'd break up with my sister, and I, being a fool, believed you. Then you slept with me. How could you go back on a promise like that after what we—"

"I wouldn't. I didn't." His voice was calm, dangerously soft. "I've kept my promise."

"Liar. If I hadn't shown up, you would have married my sister."

"The hell I would have! It was a bluff. How else could I get you to come back to San Antonio? I was going mad not knowing where you were or if you were all right. If you hadn't shown up, I would have looked like a fool, but I wouldn't have married your sister."

"But the newspapers all say you're going to marry her. Here. Today."

"I know what they say because my people wrote the press releases. That was all part of the bluff—to get you here. We'll have to write a correction now, won't we? The only Murray sister I plan to marry today is you, darlin'. If it'll help to convince you, I'll repeat myself on bended knee."

When he began to kneel, she shrieked at him, "Don't you dare…or I'll kick you. This is not a proposal. This is a farce."

"I'm asking you to marry me, darlin'."

He didn't love her. He never would. His was a damaged soul. He'd told her that in plain, hurtful terms right after he'd made love to her.

The details of the conversation she'd overheard came back to her.

"Let me get this straight," she said. "You always intended to marry a Murray daughter."

"And your father suggested Jaycee because he thought she would agree more easily."

"Then I came to your office and asked you not to marry her, and after dinner and sex, you decided one sister was as good as the other. So, why not marry the *easy* sister? Is that about it?"

"Easy?" He snorted. "I wish to hell you were easy, but no, you disappeared for weeks."

"Back to the basics. Marrying one of the Murray daughters is about business and nothing more to you?"

"In the beginning…maybe that was true…"

"I repeat—I heard you talking to Habib, whoever the hell he is, the morning after we made love. And your conversation made it seem that your relationship with me, with any Murray daughter, was still about business. Your voice was cold, matter-of-fact and all too believable."

"Habib works for me. Why would I tell him how I felt when I'd only known you a day and was still reeling, trying to figure it out for myself?"

"Oh, so now you're Mr. Sensitive. Well, I don't believe you, and I won't marry you. I've always dreamed of marrying for love. I know that is an emotion you despise and are incapable of feeling. Maybe that's why you can be so high-handed about forcing me to take my sister's place and marry you. I think you…are despicable…and cold. This whole situation is too cynical for words."

"It's true that our marriage will make Murray Oil employees see this change of leadership in a less hostile way, as for the rest—"

"So, for you, it's business. I will not be bought and sold like so many shares of stock. I am a human being. An educated, Western woman with a woman's dreams and feelings."

"I know that. It's what makes you so enchanting."

"Bull. You've chosen to ride roughshod over me and my family. You don't care what any of us want or feel."

"I do care what you feel. I care too damn much. It's driven me mad these last few weeks, worrying about you. I wished you'd never walked into my office, never made me feel… Hell! You've made me crazy, woman."

Before she had any idea of what he was about to do, he

took a long step toward her. Seizing her, he crushed her against his tall, hard body.

His hands gripping her close, his mouth slanted across hers with enough force to leave her breathless and have her moaning…and then, dear God, as his masterful kiss went on and on and on, she wanted nothing except more of him. Melting, she opened her mouth and her heart. How could she need him so much? She'd missed him terribly—every day they'd been apart.

Needle-sharp thrills raced down her spine. His tongue plunged inside her lips, and soon she was so drunk on his taste and passion, her nails dug into his back. She wanted to be somewhere else, somewhere more private.

She'd missed him. She'd wanted this. She hadn't been able to admit it. His clean, male scent intoxicated her. The length of his all-too-familiar body pressing against hers felt necessary. Every second, asleep and awake, she had thought of him, craved him—craved this. Being held by him only made the need more bittersweet. How could she want such a cold man so desperately?

"We can't feel this, do this," she whispered in a tortured breath even as she clung to him.

"Says who?"

"We're in a church."

His arms tightened their hold. "Marry me, and we can do all we want to each other—tonight…and forever," he said huskily. "It will become a sacred marital right."

How could he say that when he didn't care which Murray sister walked down the aisle as long as it saved him a few million dollars?

The thought hissed through her like cold water splashed onto a fire.

Her parents' love had carried them through many difficulties. Her dad was a workaholic. Her mother was a perfectionist, a status-seeking socialite. But they had always been madly in love.

Kira had grown up believing in the sanctity of marriage. How could she even consider a marriage that would be nothing more than a business deal to her husband?

A potential husband who had lapped up women the way she might attack a box of chocolates. Maybe he temporarily lusted after her, but he didn't love her and never could, as he'd told her. No doubt some other woman would soon catch his fancy.

Even wanting him as she did, she wasn't ready to settle for a marriage based on poor judgment, a momentary sexual connection, shallow lust, revenge and business.

She sucked in a breath and pushed against his massive chest. His grip eased slightly, maybe because the handsome rat thought he'd bent her to his will with his heated words and kisses.

"Listen to me," she said softly. "Are *you* listening?"

"Yes, darlin'."

"I won't marry you. Or any man who could dream up such a cold, cynical scheme."

"How can you call this cold when we're both burning up with desire?" He traced a fingertip along her cheek that made her jump and shiver before she jerked her head away.

"Cheap tricks like that won't induce me to change my mind. There's nothing you can say or do that will convince me. No masterful seduction technique that you honed in other women's bedrooms will do the job, either."

"I wish I had the time to woo you properly and make you believe how special you are."

Special. Now, *there* was a word that hit a nerve. She'd always wanted to feel beloved to those she cared about. How did he know that? It infuriated her that he could guess her sensibilities and so easily use them to manipulate her.

"What you want is revenge and money. If you had all of eternity, it wouldn't be long enough. I won't have you or your loveless deal. That's final."

"We'll see."

His silky baritone was so blatantly confident it sent an icy chill shivering down her spine.

Six

"You told him—the enemy—that Mother might be dying, and you didn't tell me or Jaycee! And you did this behind my back—weeks and weeks ago!"

Kira fisted and unfisted her hands as she sat beside her father in the preacher's library. Rage and hurt shot through her.

"How could you be so disloyal? I've never felt so completely betrayed. Sometimes I feel like a stray you picked up on the side of the road. You didn't really want me—only you have to keep me because it's the right thing to do."

"Nonsense! You're our daughter."

He blanched at her harsh condemnation, and she hung her head in guilt. "I'm sorry," she muttered.

She wanted to weep and scream, but she wouldn't be able to think if she lost all control.

"You know your mother and how she always wants to protect you. I thought only of her when I confided in him."

"First, you sell Jaycee to him because, as always, she's your first choice."

"Kira…"

"Now, it's me."

"Don't blame me. He wants *you!*"

"As if that makes you blameless. Why didn't either of my parents think about protecting their daughters from Quinn?"

"It's complicated. Even if your mother weren't sick, we need someone younger at the top, someone with a clearer vision of the future. Quinn's not what you think. Not what the press thinks. I knew him as a boy. This can be a win-win situation for you both."

"He grew into a vengeful man who hates us."

"You're wrong. He doesn't hate you. You'll never make me believe that. You should have seen how he acted when you disappeared. I think he'll make you a good husband."

"You don't care about that. You don't care about me. You only care about Murray Oil's bottom line, about retiring and being with Mother."

"How can you say that? I care about you, and I care about this family as much as you do. Yes, I need to take care of your mother now, but like I said—I know Quinn. I've watched him. He's good, smart, solid. And he's a brilliant businessman who will be the best possible CEO for Murray Oil during these tumultuous economic times. He's done great things already. If I had time, I'd fill you in on how he helped organize a deal with the EU while you were gone. He's still in the middle of it at the moment."

"For years he's worked to destroy you."

"Hell, maybe he believed that's what he was doing, maybe others bought it, too, but I never did. I don't think *he* knew what was driving him. This company is his heritage, too. And I saw how he was when you were gone.

The man was beside himself. He was afraid you were in trouble. I don't know what happened between the two of you before you ran away, but I know caring when I see it. Quinn cares for you. He's just like his father. You should have seen how Kade loved his wife, Esther. Then you'd know the love Quinn is capable of."

"You think Quinn will come to love me? Are you crazy? Quinn doesn't believe he can love again. The man has lived his life fueled by hate. Hatred for all of us. How many times do I have to repeat it?"

"Maybe so, but the only reason his hatred was so strong was that the love that drove it was just as strong. You're equally passionate. You just haven't found your calling yet." Her father took her hands in his as he continued, "You should have seen him the day he came to tell me he had me by the balls and was set to take over Murray Oil. He could have broken me that day. Instead, he choked when I told him about Vera because he's more decent than he knows. He's ten times the man that his father ever was, that's for sure. Maybe you two didn't meet under ideal circumstances, but he'll make you a good husband."

"You believe that only because you want to believe it. You're as cold and calculating as he is."

"I want what's best for all of us."

"This is a deal to you—just like it is to him. Neither of you care which daughter marries Quinn today, as long as the deal is completed for Murray Oil."

"I suggested Jaycee primarily to avoid a scene like the one we're having, but Quinn wants you. He won't even consider Jaycee now, even though he was willing to marry her before you meddled."

"Oh, so this fiasco is my fault."

"Someday you'll thank me."

"I'm not marrying him. I won't be sacrificed."

"Before you make your decision, your mother wants to talk to you." He pressed a couple of buttons on his phone, and the door behind him opened as if by magic. Her mother's perfectly coiffed blonde head caught the light of the overhead lamp. She was gripping her cell phone with clawlike hands.

She looked so tiny. Why hadn't Kira noticed how thin and colorless her once-vital mother had become? How frail and tired she looked?

"Dear God," Kira whispered as she got up and folded her precious mother into her arms. She felt her mother's ribs and spine as she pressed her body closer. Her mother was fading away right before her eyes.

"Please," her mother whispered. "I'm not asking you to do this for me, but for your father. I need all my strength to fight this illness. He can't be worried about Murray Oil. Or you. Or Jaycee. I've always been the strong one, you know. I can't fight this if I have to worry about him. And I can't leave him alone. He'd be lost without me."

"I—I…"

"I'm sure your father's told you there's a very important international deal with the EU on the table right now. It can make or break our company."

"*His* company."

"Your father and I and the employees of Murray Oil need your help, Kira. Your marriage to Quinn would endorse his leadership both here and abroad. Have I ever asked you for anything before?"

Of course she had. She'd been an ambitious and very demanding mother. Kira had always hoped that when she married and had children, she'd finally be part of a family where she felt as if she belonged, where she was accepted, flaws and all. How ironic that when her parents finally needed her to play a role they saw as vital to their survival,

their need trampled on her heartfelt dream to be at the core
of her own happy family.

Would she ever matter to her husband the way her
mother mattered to her father? Not if the man who was
forcing her to marry him valued her only as a business
prize. Once Quinn had Murray Oil under his control, how
long would she be of any importance to him?

Still, what choice did she have? For the first time ever,
her family really needed her. And she'd always wanted that
above all things.

"I don't want to marry you! But yes!" she spat at Quinn
after he had ushered her into one of the private dressing
rooms. She'd spun around to face him in the deadly quiet.
"*Yes!* I will marry you, since you insist on having your
answer today."

"Since I insist we marry today!"

Never had she seemed lovelier than with her dark, heavily lashed eyes glittering with anger and her slender hands
fisted defiantly on her hips. He was so glad to have found
her. So glad she was all right. So glad she'd agreed without
wasting any more precious time. Once she was his, they'd
get past this.

"Then I'll probably hate you forever for forcing me to
make such a terrible bargain."

Her words stabbed him with pain, but he steeled himself not to show it. She looked mad enough to spit fire and
stood at least ten feet from him so he couldn't touch her.

Looking down, staring anywhere but at her, he fought
to hide the hurt and relief he felt at her answer, as well as
the regret he felt for having bullied her.

Bottom line—she would be his. Today. The thought
of any man touching her as Quinn had touched her their

one night together seemed a sacrilege worthy of vengeful murder.

"Good. I'm glad that's finally settled and we can move
on," he said in a cool tone that masked his own seething
passions. "I've hired people to help you get ready. Beau-
ticians. Designers. I selected a wedding gown that I hope
you'll like, and I have a fitter here in case I misjudged your
size."

"You did all that?" Her narrow brows arched with icy
contempt. "You were that sure I'd say yes? You thought I
was some doll you could dress up in white satin…"

"Silk, actually, and no, I don't think you're some doll—"
He stopped. He wasn't about to admit how desperate he'd
felt during the dark days of her absence, or how out of control, even though his silence only seemed to make her angrier.

"Look, just because you bullied me into saying yes
doesn't mean I like the way you manipulated my family
into taking your side. And, since this is strictly a business
deal to all of you, I want you to know it's nothing but a
business deal to me, too. So, I'm here by agreeing to a marriage in name only. The only reasons I'm marrying you are
to help my father and mother and Murray Oil and to save
Jaycee from you."

His lips thinned. "There's too much heat in you. You
won't be satisfied with that kind of marriage…any more
than I will."

"Well, I won't marry you unless you agree to it."

He would have agreed to sell his soul to the devil to have
her. "Fine," he said. "Suit yourself, but when you change
your mind, I won't hold you to your promise."

"I won't change my mind."

He didn't argue the point or try to seduce her. He'd

make the necessary concessions to get her to the altar. He'd pushed her way too far already.

He was willing to wait, to give her the time she needed. He didn't expect it would be long before he'd have her in his bed once more. And perhaps it was for the best that they take a break from the unexpected passion they'd found.

Maybe he wanted her to believe his motive for marrying her was business related, but it was far from the truth. Need—pure, raw, unadulterated need—was what drove him. If they didn't make love for a while, perhaps he could get control over all his emotions.

After they'd made love the last time, he'd felt too much, had felt too bound to her. Her power over him scared the hell out of him. She'd left him just as carelessly as his own mother had left his father, hadn't she?

He needed her like the air he breathed. Kira had simply become essential.

But he wasn't about to tell her that. No way could he trust this overwhelming need for any woman. Hadn't his father's love for Quinn's own mother played the largest part in his father's downfall? And then his own love for his father had crushed him when his father died.

Grief was too big a price to pay for love. He never wanted to be weak and needy like that again.

Seven

"You look…absolutely amazing," her mother said, sounding almost as pleased as she usually did when she complimented Jaycee. "Don't frown! You know you do!"

In a trancelike daze, Kira stared at the vision in the gilt mirror. How had Quinn's beauty experts made her look like herself and yet so much better? They'd tugged and pulled, clipped and sprayed unmercifully, and now here she was, a sexy, glowing beauty in a diaphanous silk gown that clung much too revealingly. The dress flattered her slim figure perfectly. How had he known her exact size and what would most become her?

All those blondes, she told herself. He understood glamour and women, not her. The dress wasn't about her. He wanted her to be like them.

Still, until this moment, she'd never realized how thoroughly into the Cinderella fantasy she'd been. Not that she would ever admit that, on some deep level, he'd pleased her.

"How can I walk down the aisle in a dress you can see straight through?"

"You're stunning. The man has flawless taste."

"Another reason to hate him," Kira mumbled, brushing aside her mother's hard-won approval and pleasure for fear of having it soften her attitude toward Quinn.

"Haven't I always told you, you should have been playing up your assets all along," her mother said.

"Straight guys aren't supposed to know how to do stuff like this."

"Count yourself lucky your man has such a rare talent. You'll have to start letting him dress you. Maybe he knows how to bring out your best self in other areas, as well. If he does, you'll amaze yourself."

The way he had during their one night together. A shiver traced through her. "May I remind you that this is not a real marriage?"

"If you'd quit saying that in such a sulky, stubborn tone, maybe it would become one, and very soon. He's very handsome. I'll bet there isn't a single woman in this church who wouldn't trade places with you."

"He doesn't love me."

"Well, why don't you start talking to him in a sweet voice? More like the one that you always use with that impossible cat of yours?"

"Maybe because he's not my loyal, beloved pet. Maybe because being bullied into a relationship with him does not make me feel sweet and tender."

"Well, if you ask me, the men you've chosen freely weren't much to brag about. Quinn is so well educated and well respected."

A few minutes later, when the wedding march started, Kira glided down the aisle in white satin slippers holding on to her father's arm. When she heard awed gasps from the guests, she lifted her eyes from the carpet, but in the sea of faces it was Quinn's proud smile alone that made her heart leap and brought a quick, happy blush to her cheeks.

Then her tummy flipped as their souls connected in that uncanny way that made her feel stripped bare. Fortunately, her father angled himself between them, and she got a brief reprieve from Quinn's mesmerizing spell.

Not that it was long before her father had handed her over to her bridegroom where she became her awkward, uncertain self again. As she stood beside Quinn at the altar, she fidgeted while they exchanged rings and vows. With a smile, he clasped her hand in his. Threading her fingers through his, he held them still. Somehow, his warm touch reassured her, and she was able to pledge herself to him forever in a strong, clear voice.

This isn't a real marriage, she reminded herself, even as that bitter truth tore at her heart.

But the tall man beside her, the music, the church and the incredibly beautiful dress, combined with the memory of her own radiance in the mirror, made her doubt what she knew to be true. Was she a simple-minded romantic after all, or just a normal girl who wanted to marry a man she loved?

After the preacher told Quinn he could kiss his bride, Quinn's arms encased her slim body with infinite gentleness. His eyes went dark in that final moment before he lowered his beautifully sculpted mouth to hers. Despite her intention not to react to his lips, to feel nothing when he kissed her, her blood pulsed. Gripping his arms, she leaned into him.

"We'd better make this count because if you have your way, it will probably be a while before I convince you to let me kiss you again," he teased huskily.

She threw her arms around his warm, bronzed neck, her

fingers stroking his thick hair, and drew his head down. Fool that she was, it felt glorious to be in his arms as he claimed her before a thousand witnesses.

Such a ceremonial kiss shouldn't mean anything, she told herself. He was just going through the motions. As was she.

"Darlin'," he murmured. "Sweet darlin' Kira. You are incredibly beautiful, incredibly dear. I want you so much. No bridegroom has ever felt prouder of his bride."

The compliment brought her startled eyes up to his, and his tender expression fulfilled her long-felt secret desire to be special to someone. For one shining instant, she believed the dream. If a man as sophisticated as he was could really be proud of her and want her...

He didn't, of course... Oh, but if only he could...

Then his mouth was on hers. His tongue inside the moist recesses of her lips had her blood heating and her breath shuddering in her lungs. Her limbs went as limp as a rag doll's. When she felt his heart hammering against her shoulder blade, she let him pull her even closer.

The last thing she wanted was to feel this swift rush of warm pleasure, but she couldn't stop herself. How could a single, staged kiss affect her so powerfully?

He was the first to pull away. His smile was slow and sweet. "Don't forget—the last thing I want is for our marriage to be business-only," he whispered against her ravaged lips. "You can change your mind anytime, darlin'. Anytime. Nothing would please me more than to take you to my bed again."

"Well, I won't change my mind! Not ever!" she snapped much too vehemently.

He laughed and hugged her close. "You will. I should warn you that nothing appeals to me more than a challenge."

After a lengthy photography session—she was surprised that he wanted photos of a wedding that couldn't possibly mean anything to him—they were driven by limousine to the reception, held at his opulent club in an older section of San Antonio.

Once again he'd planned everything—decorations in the lavish ballroom, the menu, the band—with enough attention to detail that her critical mother was thoroughly impressed and radiantly aglow with pride. Vera sailed through the glittering throng like a bejeweled queen among awed subjects as she admired the banks of flowers, frozen sculptures and the sumptuous food and arrangements. Kira was secretly pleased Quinn had at least married her under circumstances that gave her mother, who loved to impress, so much pleasure.

With a few exceptions, the majority of the guests were employees and clients of Murray Oil. The few personal friends and family attending included Quinn's uncle Jerry, who'd been his best man, and her friend Betty. The guest list also included a few important people from the Texas art world, mostly museum directors, including Gary Whitehall, the former boss who'd let her go…for daring to have an opinion of her own.

Since the wedding was a business affair, Kira was surprised that Quinn had allowed his employees to bring their children, but he had. And no one was enjoying themselves more than the kids. They danced wildly and chased each other around the edges of the dance floor, and when a father spoke harshly to the little flower girl for doing cartwheels in her long velvet gown, Quinn soothed the child.

Watching the way the little girl brightened under his tender ministrations, Kira's heart softened.

"He's very good with children," Betty whispered into her ear. "He'll make a wonderful father."

"This is not a real marriage."

"You could have fooled me. I get all mushy inside every time he looks at you. He's *so* good-looking."

"He's taken over my life."

"Well, I'd be glad to take him off your hands. I think he's hunky. And so polite. Did I tell you how nice he was to Rudy after he found out the reason the beast wouldn't stop meowing was because he missed you? He sat down with that cat and commiserated. Made me give the beast some tuna."

"I'll bet he got you to feed him, too."

"Well, every time Quinn came to the restaurant he did sit down with me and whoever was waiting tables, like he was one of us. He bragged on my pies."

"Which got him free pies I bet."

"His favorite is the same as yours."

"Your gooey lemon meringue?"

"I thought he was sweet to remember to invite me to the wedding. He called this evening after you showed up."

Betty hushed when Quinn appeared at his bride's side and stayed, playing the attentive groom long after his duties in the receiving line ended. Even when several beauties—one a flashy blonde he'd once dated named Cristina, whom he'd apparently hired as a junior executive—came up and flirted boldly, he'd threaded his fingers through Kira's and tucked her closer.

For more than an hour, ignoring all others, he danced only with Kira. He was such a strong partner, she found herself enjoying the reception immensely as he whirled her around the room. She could see the admiring glances following them. He smiled down at her often, no doubt to give the appearance that she delighted him. The women who'd flirted with him watched him with intense interest, especially Cristina, whose lovely mouth began to pout.

"I've never been much of a dancer," Kira confessed during a slow number.

"You could've fooled me. Just goes to show that all you need is a little self-confidence."

Had his attentiveness given her that, at least briefly? When Gary Whitehall's gaze met hers over Quinn's broad shoulder, he smiled tightly. As Quinn's wife, she'd taken a huge step up in the art world. Was Gary wishing he'd let someone else go other than her when the budget had been tight? Why had Quinn included him on the guest list?

After a fast number, when Kira admitted she was thirsty, Quinn left her to get champagne. Seeing his chance, Gary rushed up to her.

"You look lovely," he said, smiling in the way he used to smile at major artists and important donors. How rare had been the smiles and compliments he'd bestowed on his lowly curator for her hard work. "I'm very happy for you," he said.

She nodded, embarrassed to be so pleased that her marriage had won his respect.

"If I can do anything for you, anything at all, just call me. I am rewriting your letter of recommendation. Not that you'll need to work now."

"I intend to work again. I loved my job."

"Your husband has been most generous to the museum. We value his friendship and expertise almost as much as we will value yours—as his wife," he gushed. "I have a feeling we may have a position for a curator opening up soon. If so, I'll give you a call."

She thought about what Gary had said about a position possibly being available and was surprised she was so pleased. Maybe…she would consider working for him again…if he made her the right offer. She would, however, demand to have more power.

Stunned, she stared at him. Then Quinn returned with her champagne. The two men shook hands and exchanged pleasantries. When Quinn made it clear he preferred his bride's conversation to art talk, Gary quickly eased himself back into the crowd. But every time after that conversation, when their eyes met, Gary smiled at her.

For a man who supposedly hated her family, Quinn was excessively attentive to her mother and father and Jaycee. He talked to them, ordered them wine and appetizers, acted as if he actually wished to please them. He was especially solicitous of her mother, who positively glowed.

Kira watched him during dinner, and his warm smiles and polite comments rang with sincerity. If she hadn't known better, she wouldn't have believed he was simply acting a part in order to reassure oil company clients and executives that Murray Oil was in good hands.

Never had a bridegroom appeared more enthusiastic, even when his uncle Jerry congratulated him on his marriage.

"Kira, he's had his nose to the grindstone so long, we were beginning to think that's all he'd ever do," Jerry said. "We'd given up on you, son. Now I see you just hadn't met the right girl. Sooner or later, if we're lucky, love comes our way. The trick is to know it and appreciate it. When you fall in love, wanting to spend the rest of your life with the same woman doesn't seem that hard to imagine."

Quinn stared at her as if he agreed. The two men shook hands again and laughed. But since Quinn's heart wasn't really in their marriage, she wondered how soon he'd give up trying to pretend to people like his uncle. After that, when she felt herself too charmed by one of Quinn's thoughtful smiles or gestures, she reminded herself that she'd be a fool if she fell for his act. Their marriage was a business deal. She didn't matter to him. She never would.

All too soon the dinner and dancing came to an end, and she and Quinn had changed into street clothes and were dashing out to his limo while cheering guests showered them with birdseed. When someone threw seeds straight at her eyes, and a tear streamed down her cheek, Quinn took out his monogrammed handkerchief and dabbed her face while everybody cheered.

She expected to be driven to his loft. Instead, the limo whisked them to his sleek private jet, which had been prepared for flight and was waiting outside a hangar at the San Antonio International Airport.

"Where are we going?" she asked as he helped her out into the blinding glare of dozens of flashes.

"Honeymoon," he whispered, his mouth so close to her ear she felt the heat of his breath. Her heart raced until she reminded herself he was only staging a romantic shot for the press.

Putting his arm around her, he faced the reporters, who asked him questions about his pending international oil deal as well as his marriage.

With abundant charm and smiles, he answered a few and then, grabbing her by the elbow, propelled her into his jet.

"Surely a honeymoon isn't necessary," she said when they were safely on board.

He smiled down at her. "A man only marries once."

"Like that reporter asked—how can you afford the time when you're working on that important EU deal?"

"You have to make time...for what's important."

"So, why did you notify the press about our honeymoon? Was it only so the EU people would know you married into the Murray family?"

"Why don't you relax? Step one, quit asking so many questions. Step two, just enjoy."

"You're thorough. I'll have to give you that. Even so,

how can I leave town when I haven't even packed for a trip," she said. "Besides, I have a cat—Rudy. I promised Betty I'd relieve her... He's been crying for me."

"I know. Rudy's all taken care of. Jacinda's going to look after him at your apartment. So, he'll be on his own turf. I bought him a case of tuna."

"You shopped for Rudy?"

"Okay—so I sent my assistant. And your mother helped me shop and pack for you."

"I'll bet she loved that."

"She did—although I did make certain key choices."

"Such as?"

"The lingerie and bikinis."

"Lingerie? I'm not much for lingerie! Or bikinis!"

"Good. Then you'll be exquisite in nothing. You slept in my arms like that all night, remember."

Hot color flooded her face. "Don't!"

"With your legs wrapped silkily around me," he added. "You were so warm and sweet, I can't believe you really intend to sleep alone tonight."

The images he aroused in her, coupled with his warm gaze and sexy grin, made her blood hum.

"I meant I feel bad about going away again so soon without telling Betty."

"Already done. Betty's fine with the idea."

"You *are* thorough."

When her temples began to throb, Kira squeezed her eyes shut. "Did everyone, absolutely everyone, know I was getting married to you today before I did?"

"Not me, darlin'. I was scared sick you wouldn't turn up or that you'd order me straight to hell after I proposed."

Had he really felt that way? Did he care a little?

No! She couldn't let herself ask such questions.

Or care at all what the answers might be.

Eight

An hour later, after a flight to the coast and a brief but exciting helicopter ride over Galveston Island, they dropped out of the night sky onto the sleek, upper deck of the white floating palace he kept moored at the Galveston marina. She took his arm when the rotors stopped and sucked in a breath as he helped her onto his yacht. Gusts of thick, humid air that smelled of the sea whipped her clothes and hair.

Promising to give her a tour of the megayacht the next day, the captain led them down a flight of steep, white stairs and through a wood-lined corridor to Quinn's master stateroom. Clearly the captain hadn't been told that they would not be sharing a room. Crewmen followed at a brisk pace to deliver their bags.

Once alone with Quinn in his palatial, brass-studded cabin, her brows knitted in concern as she stared at the mountain of bags.

"Don't worry. If you really insist on sleeping alone, I'll move mine."

Shooting a nervous glance toward his big bed, she felt her body heat.

Above the headboard hung a magnificent painting of a nude blonde by an artist she admired. The subject was lying on her tummy across a tumble of satin sheets, her slender back arched to reveal ample breasts. Long-lashed, come-hither eyes compelled the viewer not to look away. Surely such a wanton creature would never send her husband away on their wedding night.

"Last chance to change your mind," he said.

Feeling strangely shy, Kira crossed her arms over her own breasts and shook her head. "So, where will you sleep?"

"Next door." There was a mesmerizing intensity in his eyes. "Would you like to see my room?"

She twisted her hands. "I'll be just fine right here. So, if that's settled, I guess we'll see each other in the morning."

"Right." He hesitated. "If you need anything, all you have to do is punch this button on your bedside table and one of the staff will answer. If you want me, I'll leave my door unlocked. Or, if you prefer me to come to you, you could ring through on that phone over there."

"Thanks."

He turned, opened the door, shoved his bags into the passageway and stepped outside. When the door slammed behind him, and she was alone with his come-hither blonde, a heavy emotion that felt too much like disappointment gripped her.

To distract herself, she studied the painting for another moment, noting that the artist had used linseed oil most effectively to capture the effect of satin.

Feeling a vague disquiet as she considered the nude,

she decided the best thing to do was shower and get ready for bed. As she rummaged in her suitcase, she found all sorts of beautiful clothes that she never would have picked out. Still, as she touched the soft fabrics and imagined her mother shopping for such things without her there to discourage such absurd purchases, she couldn't help smiling. Her mother had always wanted to dress Kira in beautiful things, but being a tomboy, Kira had preferred jeans and T-shirts.

What was the point of fancy clothes for someone who lived as she had, spending time in art vaults, or painting, or waiting tables? But now, she supposed, for however long she was married to a billionaire with his own jet and mega-yacht, she would run in different circles and have fundraisers and parties to attend. Maybe she did need to upgrade her wardrobe.

Usually, she slept in an overlarge, faded T-shirt. In her suitcase all she found for pajamas were thin satin gowns and sheer robes, the kind that would cling so seductively she almost regretted she wouldn't be wearing them for Quinn.

Instead of the satin gown, which reminded her too much of the blonde above the bed, she chose black lace. Had he touched the gown, imagining her in it, when he'd picked it out? As the gossamer garment slipped through her fingers she shivered.

Go to bed. Don't dwell on what might have been. He's ruined enough of your day and night as it is.

But how not to think of him as she stripped and stepped into her shower? What was he doing next door? Was his tall, bronzed body naked, too? Her heart hammered much too fast.

Lathering her body underneath a flow of warm water, she imagined him doing the same in his own shower. Leaning against the wet tile wall, she grew hotter and hotter as the water streamed over her. She stood beneath the spray until her fingers grew too numb to hold the slippery bar of soap. When it fell, she snapped out of her spell.

Drying off and then slipping into the black gown, she slid into his big bed with a magazine. Unable to do more than flip pages and stare unseeingly at the pictures because she couldn't stop thinking about Quinn, she eventually drifted to sleep. But once asleep, she didn't dream of him.

Instead, she dreamed she was a small child in her pink bedroom with its wall-to-wall white carpet. All her books were lined up just perfectly, the way her mother liked them to be, in her small white bookcase beneath the window.

Somewhere in the house she heard laughter and hushed endearments, the sort of affection she'd never been able to get enough of. Then her door opened and her parents rushed inside her bedroom. Only they didn't take her into their arms as they usually did. Her mother was cooing over a bundle she held against her heart, and her father was staring down at what her mother held as if it were the most precious thing in the world.

She wanted them to look at her like that.

"Kira, we've brought your new baby sister, Jaycee, for a visit."

A baby sister? "Where did she come from?"

"The hospital."

"Is that where you got me?"

Her mother paled. Her father looked as uneasy as her mother, but he nodded.

What was going on?

"Do you love me, too?" Kira whispered.

"Yes, of course," her father said. "You're our big girl now, so your job will be to help us take care of Jaycee.

She's *our* special baby. We're all going to work hard to take very good care of Jaycee."

Suddenly, the bundle in her mother's arms began to shriek frantically.

"What can I do?" Kira had said, terrified as she ran toward them. "How can I help? Tell me what to do!"

But they'd turned away from her. "Why don't you just play," her father suggested absently.

Feeling lonely and left out as she eyed her dolls and books, she slowly backed away from them and walked out of her room, down the tall stairs to the front door, all the while hoping their concerned voices would call her back as they usually did. She wasn't supposed to be downstairs at night.

But this time, they didn't call her. Instead, her parents carried the new baby into a bedroom down the hall and stayed with her.

They had a new baby. They didn't need her anymore.

Kira opened the big front door. They didn't notice when she stepped outside. Why should they? They had Jaycee, who was special. They didn't care about Kira anymore. Maybe they'd never really cared.

Suddenly, everything grew black and cold, and a fierce wind began to blow, sweeping away everything familiar. The house vanished, and she was all alone in a strange, dark wood with nobody to hear her cries. Terrified, she ran deeper into the woods.

If her family didn't love her anymore, if nobody loved her, she didn't know what she would do.

Hysterical, she began sobbing their names. "Mother! Daddy! Somebody! Please…love me. I want to be special, too…"

Quinn opened her door and hurled himself into her stateroom.

"Kira!" He switched on a light. She blinked against the blinding glare of gold with heavy-lidded eyes.

"Are you okay?" he demanded. "Wake up!"

"Quinn?" Focusing on his broad shoulders, she blinked away the last remnants of that terrifying forest. He was huge and shirtless and so starkly handsome in the half shadows she hissed in a breath.

Her husband. What a fool she'd been to send him away when that was the last thing she really wanted.

When he sat down on the bed, she flung herself against his massive bare chest and clung. He felt so hard and strong and hot.

Snugging her close against his muscular body, he rocked her gently and spoke in soothing tones. "There…there…"

Wrapped in his warmth, she almost felt safe…and loved.

"I was a little girl again. Only I ran away and got lost. In a forest."

He petted her hair as his voice soothed her. "You were only dreaming."

She stared up at his shadowed face. In the aftermath of her dream, she was too open to her need of him. Her grip on him tightened. She felt his breath hitch and his heart thud faster. If only *he* loved her…maybe the importance of her childhood fears would recede.

"Darlin', it was just a dream. You're okay."

Slowly, because he held her, the horror of feeling lost and alone diminished and reality returned.

She was on his megayacht. In Galveston. He'd forced her to marry him and come on a honeymoon. She was in his bed where she'd been sleeping alone. This was supposed to be their wedding night, but she'd sent him away.

Yet somehow *she* was the one who felt lonely and rejected.

She liked being cradled in his strong arms, against his

virile body. Too much. She grew conscious of the danger of letting him linger in her bedroom.

"You want me to go?" he whispered roughly.

No. She wanted to cling to him…to be adored by him…. Another impossible dream.

When she hesitated, he said, "If you don't send me packing, I will take this as an invitation."

"It's no invitation," she finally murmured, but sulkily. Her heart wasn't in her statement.

"How come you don't sound sure?" He ran a rough palm across her cheek. Did she only imagine the intimate plea in his voice? Was he as lonely as she was?

Even as she felt herself softening under his affectionate touch and gentle tone, she forced herself to remember all the reasons she'd be a fool to trust him. Squeezing her eyes shut, she took a deep breath. "Thanks for coming, but go! Please—just go."

She felt his body tighten as he stared into her eyes. Time ticked for an endless moment before he released her.

Without a word he got up and left.

Alone again, she felt she might burst with sheer longing. When she didn't sleep until dawn, she blamed him for not going farther than the room next to hers. He was too close. Knowing that all she had to do was go to him increased her frustration. Because he'd made it clear he would not send her away.

Twisting and turning, she fought to settle into slumber, but could not. First, she was too hot for the covers. Then she was so cold she'd burrowed under them.

It was nearly dawn when she finally did sleep. Then, after less than an hour, loud voices in the passageway startled her into grouchy wakefulness. As she buried her head in her pillow, her first thought was of Quinn. He'd probably slept like a baby.

When the sun climbed high and his crewmen began shouting to one another on deck, she strained to hear Quinn's voice among theirs shouts, but didn't.

Sitting up, alone, she pulled the covers to her throat. Surely he couldn't still be sleeping. Where was he?

A dark thought hit her. Last night he'd left her so easily, when what she'd craved was for him to stay. Had she already served her purpose by marrying him? Was he finished with her?

Feeling the need for a strong cup of coffee, Kira slipped into a pair of tight, white shorts and a skimpy, beige knit top. Outside, the sky was blue, the sun brilliant. Normally, when she wasn't bleary from lack of sleep, Kira loved water, boats and beaches. Had Quinn been in love with her, a honeymoon on his luxurious yacht would have been exceedingly romantic. Instead, she felt strange and alone and much too needily self-conscious.

Was his crew spying on her? Did they know Quinn hadn't slept with her? Did they pity her?

Anxious to find Quinn, Kira grabbed a white sweater and left the stateroom. When he didn't answer her knock, she cracked open his door. A glance at the perfectly made spread and his unopened luggage told her he'd spent the night elsewhere. Pivoting, she stepped back into the corridor so fast she nearly slammed headlong into a crewman.

"May I help you, Mrs. Sullivan?"

"Just taking a private tour," she lied. On the off chance he'd think she knew where she was going, she strode purposefully past him down the wood-lined passageway.

Outside, the gulf stretched in endless sapphire sparkle toward a shimmering horizon. Not that she paid much attention to the dazzling view. Intent on finding Quinn, she was too busy opening every door on the sumptuously appointed decks. Too proud to ask the numerous crew members she passed for help, she averted her eyes when she chanced to meet one of them for fear they'd quiz her.

The yacht seemed even bigger on close inspection. So far she'd found six luxury staterooms, a cinema, multiple decks, a helipad and a grand salon.

Just when she was about to give up her search for Quinn, she opened a door on the uppermost deck and found him slumped over a desk in a cluttered office. Noting the numerous documents scattered on chairs, desks, tables and even the floor, she crossed the room to his side. Unfinished cups of coffee sat atop the jumbled stacks. Obviously, he'd worked through the night on a caffeine high.

At the sight of his exhausted face, her heart constricted. Even as she smoothed her hand lightly through his rumpled hair, she chastised herself for feeling sympathy for him. Hadn't he bullied her into their forced, loveless marriage?

Now that she knew where he was, she should go, order herself coffee and breakfast, read her magazine in some pristine chaise lounge, sunbathe—in short, ignore him. Thinking she would do just that, she stepped away from him. Then, driven by warring emotions she refused to analyze, she quickly scampered back to his side.

Foolishly, she felt tempted to neaten his office, but since she didn't know what went where, she sank into the chair opposite his. Bringing her knees against her chest, she hugged them tightly and was pleased when he slept another hour under her benevolent guardianship. Then, without warning, his beautiful eyes snapped open and seared her.

"What the hell are you doing here?" he demanded.

She nearly jumped out of her chair. "He awakens—like a grumpy old bear," she teased.

Managing a lopsided grin, he ran a hand through his

spiked, rumpled hair. "You were a bit grumpy...the morning after...you slept with me in San Antonio, as I recall."

"Don't remind me of that disastrous night, please."

"It's one of my fondest memories," he said softly.

"I said don't!"

"I love it when you blush like that. It makes you look so...cute. You should have awakened me the minute you came in."

"How could I be so heartlessly cruel when you came to my rescue in the middle of the night? If you couldn't sleep, it was my fault."

When his beautiful white teeth flashed in a teasing grin, she couldn't help smiling back at him.

"I could bring you some coffee. Frankly, I could use a cup myself," she said.

He sat up straighter and stretched. "Sorry this place is such a mess, but as I'm not through here, I don't want anybody straightening it up yet."

She nodded. "I sort of thought that might be the case."

"What about breakfast...on deck, then? I have a crew ready to wait on us hand and foot. They're well trained in all things—food service...emergencies at sea..."

"They didn't come when I screamed last night," she said softly. "You did."

"Only because you didn't call for their help on the proper phone."

"So, it's my fault, is it?" Where had the lilt in her light tone come from?

Remembering how safe she'd felt in his arms last night, a fierce tenderness toward him welled up in her heart. He must have sensed what she felt, because his eyes flared darkly before he looked away.

Again, she wished this were a real honeymoon, wished that he loved her rather than only lusted for her, wished that she was allowed to love him back. If only she hadn't demanded separate bedrooms, then she would be lying in his arms looking forward to making love with him again this morning.

At the thought, her neck grew warm. She'd been wishing for the wrong stuff her whole life. It was time she grew up and figured out what her life was to be about. The sooner she got started on that serious journey, one that could never include him, the better.

Nine

Breakfast on deck with his long-limbed bride in her sexy short shorts was proving to be an unbearable torture. She squirmed when his gaze strayed to her lips or her breasts or when it ran down those long, lovely legs.

If only he could forget how she'd clung to him last night or how her big eyes had adored him when he'd first woken up this morning.

"I wish you wouldn't stare so," she said as she licked chocolate off a fingertip. "It makes me feel self-conscious about eating this and making such a mess."

"Sorry," he muttered.

He tried to look away, but found he could not. What else was there to look at besides endless sapphire dazzle? Why shouldn't he enjoy watching her greedily devour her fresh-baked croissants and *pain du chocolat*? The way she licked chocolate off her fingers made him remember her mouth and tongue on him that night in his loft. *Torture.*

Even though he was sitting in the shade and the gulf breeze was cool, his skin heated. His bride was too sexy for words.

If he were to survive the morning without grabbing her like a besotted teenager and making a fool of himself, he needed to quickly get back to his office and the EU deal.

But he knew he wouldn't be able to concentrate on the deal while his forbidden bride was aboard. No. He'd go to the gym and follow his workout with a long, cold shower. Only then would he attempt another try at the office.

Dear God, why was it that ever since she'd said no sex, bedding her was all he could think about?

With the fortitude that was so much a part of his character, he steeled himself to endure her beauty and her provocative sensuality, at least until breakfast was over and they parted ways.

"So, are we heading somewhere in particular?" she asked playfully.

"Do you like to snorkel?"

"I do, but I've only snorkeled in lakes and shallow coves in the Caribbean."

"Once we get into really deep water, the gulf will be clear. I thought we'd snorkel off one of my oil rigs. It's always struck me as ironic the way marine life flourishes around a rig. You're in for a treat."

Her brief smile charmed him. "I read somewhere that rigs act like artificial reefs." She stopped eating her orange. "But you don't need to interrupt your precious work to entertain me."

"I'll set my own work schedule, if you don't mind."

"You're the boss, my lord and master. Sorry I keep forgetting that all-important fact." Again her playful tone teased him.

"Right." He smiled grimly. What could he say?

They lapsed into an uncomfortable silence. Focusing on his eggs and bacon, he fought to ignore her. Not that he didn't want to talk to her, because he did. Very much. But small talk with his bride was not proving to be an easy matter.

"I'd best get busy," he said when he'd finished his eggs and she her orange.

"Okay. Don't worry about me. Like I said, I can entertain myself. I love the water. As you know, I spent the past few weeks on Murray Island. I don't know where we are, but we probably aren't that far from it."

Scanning the horizon, he frowned. He didn't like remembering how much her stay at her family's isolated island had worried him.

How had he become so attached—or whatever the hell he was—to her so fast? They'd only had one night together!

Biting out a terse goodbye that made her pretty smile falter, he stood abruptly. Pivoting, he headed to his gym and that icy shower while she set off to her stateroom.

The gym and shower didn't do any good. No sooner did he return to his office on the upper deck than who should he find sunbathing right outside his door practically naked but his delectable bride.

She lay on a vivid splash of red terry cloth atop one of his chaise lounges, wearing the white thong bikini he'd picked out for her while under the influence of a lurid male fantasy.

He'd imagined her in it. Hell, yes, he had. But not like this—not with her body forbidden to him by her decree and his unwillingness to become any more attached to her. He would never have bought those three tiny triangles if he'd had any idea what torture watching her would give him.

Clenching his fists, he told himself to snap the blinds shut and forget her. Instead, mesmerized, he crossed his office with the long strides of a large, predatory cat and stood at a porthole, staring at her hungrily, ravenous for whatever scraps of tenderness the sexy witch might bestow. He willed her to look at him.

She flipped a magazine page carelessly and continued to read with the most maddening intensity. Not once did she so much as glance his way.

Damn her.

She was on her tummy in the exact position of the girl in the painting over his bed. He watched her long, dark hair glint with fiery highlights and blow about her slim, bare shoulders. He watched her long, graceful fingers flip more pages and occasionally smooth back flying strands of her hair. Every movement of her slim wrist had her dainty silver bracelet flashing.

Was she really as cool and collected as she appeared?

How could she be, when she'd given herself to him so quickly and completely that first night? Her eyes had shone with desire, and she'd trembled and quivered at his touch. She hadn't faked her response. He'd bet his life on it. He would never have forced her to marry him if he'd thought her cold and indifferent.

And last night he'd definitely felt her holding on to him as if she didn't want to let go.

So, she must be clinging to her position of abstinence out of principle. Wasn't she turning those pages much too fast? Was she even reading that magazine? Or was she as distracted as he was? Did she sense him watching her and take perverse delight in her power over him?

Damn the fates that had sent her to him!

Always, before Kira, he'd gone for voluptuous blondes with modern morals, curvy women who knew how to dress, women who thought their main purpose was to please a man. Women with whom he'd felt safe because they'd wanted his money and position more than they'd valued his heart.

This slim, coltishly long-limbed girl hadn't yet learned what she was about or even how to please herself, much less how to seduce a man. But her innocence in these matters appealed to him.

Why?

Again, he told himself to forget her, but when he went to his desk, he just sat there for a full half hour unable to concentrate. Her image had burned itself into his brain. She had his loins hard and aching. The woman lured him from his work like the Sirens had lured Ulysses after Troy.

He began to worry that she hadn't put on enough sunblock. Weren't there places on that long, slim body she couldn't reach?

Hardly knowing what he was about, he slammed out of his office and found himself outside, towering grimly over her. Not that she so much as bothered to glance away from her damn magazine, even though she must have heard his heavy footsteps, even though he cast a shadow over the pages.

He felt like a fool.

"You're going to burn," he growled with some annoyance.

"Do you think so? I've got lotion on, and my hat. But maybe you're right. I need to turn over for a while." She lowered her sunglasses to the tip of her nose and peered up at him saucily with bright, dark eyes.

Was she flirting with him? Damn her to hell and back if she was.

"Since you're out here, would you mind being a dear and rubbing some lotion on my back for me?"

He sank to his haunches, his excitement so profound at the thought of touching her that he didn't worry about her request for lotion on her back being illogical. Hadn't she forbidden his touch? And didn't she just say she intended to turn over onto her back?

He didn't care.

The lotion was warm from the sun, and her silky skin was even warmer as he rubbed the cream into it.

A moan of pure pleasure escaped her lips as his large palm made circular motions in the center of her back, and his heart raced at her response. He felt a visceral connection to her deep in his groin.

"You have strong hands. The lotion smells so deliciously sweet. Feels good, too," she whispered silkily, stretching like a cat as he stroked her.

"Thanks," he growled.

She rolled over and lay on her towel. Throwing him a dismissive glance, she lifted her magazine to shut him out.

"You can go now," she whispered.

Feeling stubborn and moody, he didn't budge. Only when he saw his oil rig looming off the starboard side did he arise and ask his crew to assemble their diving gear: fins, wet suits, marker floats and masks.

So much for working on the EU deal…

Later, when he and she stood on the teak diving platform at the stern of the yacht in their wet suits, she noticed nobody had thrown out an anchor.

"What if your yacht drifts while we're in the water?"

"She won't," he replied. "*Pegasus* is equipped with a sophisticated navigational system called dynamic positioning. On a day this calm she'll stay exactly where we position her. Believe me, it's much better than an anchor, which would allow her to swing back and forth."

"You plan so much that you think of everything. Does your planning and your fortune allow you to have everything you want?"

"Not quite everything," he murmured as he stared hungrily at her trim body.

Didn't she know she had changed everything?

For years, he'd been driven to avenge himself against her father, but no sooner had he been poised to seize his prize than he'd learned of Vera's illness. From that moment, his victory had begun to feel hollow.

Just when he'd wondered what new challenge could ever drive him as passionately as revenge once did, Kira had walked into his office to fight for her sister. He'd known he had to have her.

Trouble was, he was beginning to want more than he'd ever allowed himself to dream of wanting before. He wanted a life with her, a future, everything he'd told himself he could never risk having.

Kira stood on the platform watching Quinn in the water as he adjusted his mask.

"Come on in," he yelled.

She was removing her silver jewelry because he'd told her the flash of it might attract sharks.

"You know how I told you I've mainly confined my snorkeling to lakes or shallow lagoons," she began. "Well, the gulf's beginning to seem too big and too deep."

"I'll be right beside you, and Skip and Chuck are in the tender."

"I've seen all the *Jaws* movies."

"Not a good time to think about them."

She squinted, searching the vast expanse of the gulf for fins.

"Are you coming in or not?" he demanded.

Despite her doubts, she sucked in a deep breath and jumped in.

As she swam out to him, the water felt refreshingly cool.

After she got her mask on she and Quinn were soon surrounded by red snapper and amberjack. She was enjoying their cool, blue world so much that when he pointed out a giant grouper gliding by, she stared in awe instead of fear. Quinn's sure presence beside her in the water instilled in her a confidence she wouldn't have believed possible.

Snorkeling soon had her feeling weightless. It was as if she were flying in an alien world that dissolved into endless deep blue nothingness. As he'd promised, Quinn stayed beside her for nearly an hour. Enjoying herself, she forgot the vast blue darkness beneath them and what it concealed.

Just when she was starting to relax, a tiger shark zoomed out of the depths straight at Quinn. In her panic, she did exactly what she shouldn't have done. Kicking and thrashing wildly, she gulped in too much water. Choking, she yanked off her mask. As the fin vanished, Quinn ordered her to swim to the yacht.

In seconds, the fin was back, circling Quinn before diving again. Then the shark returned, dashing right at Quinn, who rammed it in the nose and made a motion with his arm for her to quit watching and start swimming. Staying behind her so he could keep his body between hers and the shark, he headed for the yacht, as well.

A tense knot of crewmen on the platform were shouting to them when she finally reached the yacht.

"Quinn," she yelled even as strong arms yanked her on board. "Quinn!" She barely heard his men shouting to him as she stood on the teak platform panting for breath. Then the dorsal fin slashed viciously right beside Quinn, and her fear mushroomed.

"Get him out! Somebody do something! Quinn! *Darling!*" she screamed.

Quinn swam in smooth, rapid strokes toward the stern. When he made it to the ladder, his crewmen sprang forward and hauled him roughly aboard, slamming him onto the teak platform.

Quinn tore off his mask. When he stood up, he turned to Kira, who took the desperate glint in his eyes as an invitation to hurl herself into his arms.

"You're as white as bleached bone," he said, gripping her tightly. "You're sure you're okay?"

The blaze of concern in his eyes and his tone mirrored her own wild fears for him.

"If you're okay, I'm okay," she whispered shakily, snuggling closer. She was so happy he was alive and unhurt.

"You're overreacting. It would take more than one little shark—"

"Don't joke! He could have torn off your arm!"

"He was probably just curious."

"Curious! I saw the movies, remember?"

He stared down at her in a way that made her skin heat. "In a funny way I feel indebted to the shark. Because of him, you called me darling."

"Did not!"

"Did, too," he drawled in that low tone that mesmerized her.

When she wrenched free of him, he laughed. "Okay. It must have been wishful thinking on a doomed man's part. Guess it was Chuck who let out the *d*-word."

She bit her lip to keep from smiling.

After they dressed, they met on the upper deck where they'd had breakfast earlier. Quinn wore jeans and a blue Hawaiian shirt that made his eyes seem as brilliant as the dazzling sky.

He ordered pineapple and mangoes and coffee. She was still so glad he was alive and had all his body parts she couldn't take her eyes off him.

"I have an idea," she said. "I mean…if we're looking for a less exciting adventure."

"What?"

"I could show you Murray Island."

"Where is it?"

"South of Galveston. Since I don't know where we are, I can't tell you how to get there. But it's on all the charts."

He picked up a phone and talked to his captain. When he hung up, he said, "Apparently, we're about forty nautical miles from your island. The captain says we could run into some weather, but if you want to go there, we will."

"What's a raindrop or two compared to being lunch for Jaws?"

"I love your vivid imagination."

In little over an hour, *Pegasus* was positioned off the shore of Murray Island, and Kira and Quinn were climbing down into the tender together. After Quinn revved the outboard, they sped toward the breaking surf, making for the pass between the barrier islands and the tiny harbor on the island's leeward side.

The bouncy ride beneath thickening gray storm clouds was wet and choppy. Heedless of the iffy weather, she stared ahead, laughing as the spray hit them. Quinn's eyes never strayed from his course—except when they veered to her face, which secretly thrilled her. She knew she shouldn't crave his attention so much, but ever since the shark incident, her emotions refused to behave sensibly.

He's alive. I have this moment with him. It's our honeymoon. Why not enjoy it? Why not share this island sanctuary I love with him?

Ten

Quinn watched his beachcombing bride much too avidly for his liking. He hated feeling so powerfully attracted to her. It was incomprehensible. She was Earl's daughter, a woman he barely knew, a wife who wouldn't even share his bed.

She'd slept with him once and then she'd left him, causing a pain too similar to what he'd felt after his father's death. The tenderness he continued to feel for her put him on dangerous ground, but still she possessed him in a way no other woman ever had.

It was the shark. Before they'd snorkeled, he'd been able to tell himself that he was under a temporary spell, that he could vanquish his burning need for her simply by staying out of her bed.

But he'd been afraid for her when she'd been swimming for the boat, more afraid than he'd ever been in his life.

Then he'd seen her bone-white face and the wild terror in her eyes when she'd imagined him in danger.

Once he'd been safely on board, her slim face had become luminous with joy. She'd hurled herself into his arms so violently she'd all but knocked them both back into the water again.

Nobody had ever looked at him like that.

Surely his father had loved him more, but she was here, and so beautiful, and so alive, and his—if only he could win her.

The prevailing southeasterly wind, cooler now because of the dark gray clouds, licked the crests of the waves into a foaming fury and sent her dark chestnut hair streaming back from her face as she scampered at the surf's edge. Every few steps, she knelt, not caring if a wave splashed her toes. Crouching, she examined the beach debris: tangles of seaweed, driftwood and shells.

Her long slim feet were bare, her toenails unpolished. Flip-flops dangled from her left hand.

For twenty years, his determination to succeed and get revenge had made time seem too valuable for him to waste on a beach with a woman. Most nights he'd worked, and most mornings, he'd left for his office before dawn. Driven by his dark goals, he'd often worked through entire weekends and holidays. His main sources of relaxation had been the gym or a willing woman and a glass of scotch before he hit his bed or desk again. He'd been more machine than human.

But that was before Kira.

Memories, long suppressed, stirred. As a child, he'd looked forward to the hour when his father's key would turn in the lock and he'd holler Quinn's name.

Quinn would race into his father's arms. After hugging him close, his father would lift him so high in the air

Quinn could touch the ceiling. So high, he'd felt as if he was flying. Then his dad would set him down and ruffle his hair and ask him about his day.

Never had his father been too tired to pass a football around the yard or take him to the park to chase geese. His father had helped with Quinn's homework, helped him build models, played endless games with him. His mother, on the other hand, had always been too busy to play. Then his father had died, and Quinn had known grief and loneliness.

For the first time, while indulging in this simple walk on the beach with Kira, Quinn felt a glimmer of the warmth that had lit his life before his father's death.

His father would want him to stop grieving, he realized. He'd want him to choose life, to choose the future.

Kira didn't realize she was beautiful, or that her lack of pretention and artifice made her even more attractive. Her every movement was graceful and natural. On the beach, she seemed a lovely wild thing running free.

This island was her refuge. For however long they were together, he would have to accept her world if he wanted her to accept his. No doubt, she would need to come here again from time to time.

He frowned, not liking the thought of her leaving him to stay out here all alone. Anyone could beach a small boat or tie up at her dock. Jim, the island's caretaker, had the faraway look of a man who'd checked out of life a long time ago. Quinn wasn't about to trust a dropout like him as her protector. No, he would have to get his security team to figure out how to make her safe here without intruding on her privacy. She was a free spirit, and Quinn wanted her to be happy, the way she was now, but safe, as well.

The sky was rapidly darkening from gray to black. Not that Kira seemed concerned about the gathering storm as she leaned down and picked up a shell. When she twisted, their gazes met. At her enchanting smile, his heart brimmed with way too much emotion. Then she ran over to show him her newfound treasure. When she held it up, her eyes shone, and the tiny window that had opened into his soul widened even further.

"Look, it's a lightning whelk," she cried.

"It's huge," he said, turning the cone-shaped shell over in his hand to properly admire it.

"At least a foot long. I've never seen one so big. And it's in perfect condition. Did you know it's the state shell of Texas?"

Shaking his head, he shot a glance at the darkening sky before he handed it back to her. "Do you collect shells?"

"Not really, but I'd like to give you this one. So you can remember Murray Island."

And *her,* he thought. "As if I could ever forget," he said. "I'll cherish it."

"I'm sure." She attempted a laugh and failed. "A new gem for your art collection."

"It's already my favorite thing."

Stronger now, the wind whipped her hair, and the sand bit into his legs.

"We should take cover," he said. "Storm's coming in. Fast. I think we'd better make a run for the house!"

"I'll race you!" Giggling as she danced on her toes, she sprinted toward the house, and because he liked watching her cute butt when she ran, he held back and let her win.

Darting from room to room as the wind howled and the frame structure shuddered, she gave him a quick tour of the house. A shady front porch looked out onto the raging gulf. Two bedrooms, a bath and a kitchen were connected by screened breezeways to each other and to the porch.

The southern bedroom had a wall of windows. "This is my favorite room," she said. "There's always a breeze, so I usually sleep here."

When she cracked a window, the room cooled instantly as storm gusts swept through it.

Deliberately, he stared outside at the rain instead of at her narrow bed. Since it was much too easy to imagine her long, lithe body on that mattress beneath him, he concentrated on the fat raindrops splatting on sand.

"With all the doors and windows open, the prevailing breezes cool the house on the hottest summer days," she said.

"If you open everything up, doesn't that make you vulnerable to a break-in?"

"No one usually comes here except me and Jim."

All anybody had to do was slit a screen to get inside. She would be defenseless. If Quinn had known how vulnerable she was while she'd been gone, he would have been even crazier with worry.

"Would you like some tea?" she said. "While we wait out the weather?"

"Sure."

When he nodded, she disappeared into the kitchen, leaving him to explore the room. A violent gust hit the house as the storm broke with full force. Somewhere, a breezeway door slammed so hard the entire house shook. Then papers fluttered under her bed. Curious, he knelt and pulled them out.

To his amazement, he discovered dozens of watercolors, all of himself, all ripped in two. He was trying to shove the entire collection back under the bed, when he heard her light footsteps at the doorway.

"Oh, my God," she said. "I forgot about those. Don't think... I mean... They don't mean anything!"

"Right."

You just painted picture after picture of me with violent, vivid brushstrokes. Then you shredded them all. For no reason.

"You obviously weren't too happy with me," he muttered.

"I really don't want to talk about it."

"Did you paint anything else…besides me?"

"A few birds."

"How many?"

"Not so many. One actually." She turned away as if uncomfortable with that admission.

Obviously, she was just as uneasy about her feelings for him as he was about his obsession with her.

"Why don't we drink our tea and go back to the yacht," he said brusquely.

"Fine with me."

"I shouldn't have pulled those pictures out," he said.

"We said we were going to forget about them."

"Right. We did." So, while he'd been obsessing about her absence, maybe she'd done a bit of obsessing herself. He took a long breath.

They sat on the porch drinking tea as the gray fury of the storm lashed the island. Now that he wanted to leave, the weather wasn't cooperating. To the contrary. Monstrous black waves thundered against the beach while rain drummed endlessly against the metal roof. No way could he trust his small tender in such high seas.

"Looks like we're stuck here for the duration," he said. So much for distracting himself from his bride anytime soon.

She nodded, her expression equally grim. "Sorry I suggested coming here."

The squalls continued into the night, so for supper she

heated a can of beans and opened cans of peaches and to-matoes. Happily, she produced a bottle of scotch that she said she kept hidden.

"We have to hide liquor from the pirates," she told him with a shy smile.

"Pirates?" he asked.

"We call anyone who lands on the island pirates. We leave the house open so they don't have to break in. Because they will if we don't."

"So, you're not entirely unaware of the dangers of being here all alone?"

"Jim's here."

"Right. Jim."

Quinn poured himself a drink and toasted good old Jim. Then he poured another. When he'd drained the second, she began to glow. Her smile and eyes looked so fresh and sparkly, he saw the danger of more liquor and suggested they go to bed.

"Separate bedrooms, of course," he said, "since that's what you want."

Nodding primly, she arose and led him to the guest bed-room. When she left him, he stripped off his shirt and lay down. She wouldn't leave his thoughts. He remembered her brilliant eyes lighting up when she saw him hauled safely onto *Pegasus.* He remembered how shyly she'd blushed every time she'd looked at him in his office, when she'd faced him down to ask him not to marry her sister. He remembered her breasts in the skimpy T-shirt she'd worn today and her cute butt and long legs in her white shorts as she'd raced him across the deep sand back to the house.

With the scotch still causing visions of her to warm his blood, he couldn't sleep for thinking of her on her narrow bed in the next room. Would she sleep curled in a ball like a child or stretched out like a woman? Was she naked? Or in her bra and panties? Did she desire him, too?

Remembering all the things she'd done to him in his loft in San Antonio, he began to fantasize that she was in the bed with him, her long legs tangled with his. That got him even hotter.

If only they were on board the yacht so he could hide out in his office on the upper deck and bury himself in paperwork. Here, there was nothing to think about but her lying in the bed next door.

At some point, he managed to fall asleep only to dream of her. In his dream, she slipped as lightly as a shadow into his bedroom. Slim, teasing fingers pulled back his sheet. Then, calling his name in husky, velvet tones, she slid into bed beside him. Her eyes blazed with the same fierce passion he'd seen when she'd realized he was safely back on board the yacht, away from the shark's teeth.

His heart constricted. Was this love? If it wasn't, it felt too dangerously close to the emotion for comfort. Even in his dream he recoiled from that dark emotion. Love had ruined his life and the life of his father. Hadn't it?

Then, in the dream, she kissed him, her sensual mouth and tongue running wildly over his lips and body while her hands moved between his legs and began to stroke. Soon he forgot about the danger of love and lost all power to resist her.

Lightning crashed, startling him. When his eyes flew open he heard the roar of the surf. He was alone in a strange, dark bedroom with sweat dripping from his long, lean body onto damp sheets, aching all over because he wanted to make love to his forbidden wife.

She was driving him crazy. On a low, frustrated groan, he hurled himself out of bed and stalked onto the breeze-way in the hope that the chill, damp wind whipping through the screens would cool his feverish body and re-store his sanity.

"Quinn!" came Kira's soft, startled cry, the sexy sound setting his testosterone-charged nerves on high alert.

He whirled to face her just as a bolt of lightning flashed. Her hair streaming in the wind, she leaned against a post some ten feet away, in the shadows. Momentarily blinded from the lightning, he couldn't make her out in the dark-ness. Imagining the rest of her, his blood notched a degree hotter.

"You'd better get back to your room," he rasped.

"What's the use when I couldn't sleep even if I did? Storms like this are exciting, aren't they?"

"Just do as I said and go."

"This is my house. Why should I do what you say, if I prefer watching the storm…and you?" she said in a low, breathless tone.

"Because if you plan to keep me in a separate bedroom, it's the smart thing to do."

"Used to giving orders, aren't you? Well, I'm not used to taking them. Since I'm your wife, maybe it's time I taught you that. I could teach you a lot…"

Thunder rolled, and rain slashed through the breeze-way furiously, sending rivulets of water across the concrete floor.

"Go," he muttered.

"Maybe I will." But her husky laughter defied him. "Then, maybe not."

When she turned, instead of heading across the breeze-way toward her bedroom, she unlatched a screen door behind her and ran onto the beach. As she did, a blaze of white fire screamed from the wet black sky to the beach.

Hell! She was going to get herself fried if he didn't bring her back.

"Kira!" he yelled after her.

When she kept running, he heaved himself after her, his bare feet sinking deeply into the soft, wet sand and crushed shells as he sprinted. Sheets of rain soaked him through within seconds.

She didn't get more than twenty feet before he caught her by the waist and pulled her roughly into his arms. She was wet and breathless, her long hair glued to her face, her T-shirt clinging to her erect nipples.

Quinn closed his eyes and willed himself to think of something besides her breasts and the light in her eyes. But as the cold rain pounded him, her soft warmth and beauty and the sweetness of her scent drew him. He opened his eyes and stared down at her. Slowly, she put her arms around him and looked at him as she had in his dreams, with her heart shining in her eyes.

Laughing, she said, "Have you ever seen anything so wild? Don't you love it?"

He hadn't deliberately stood in the rain or stomped in a puddle since he'd been a kid, when his dad had encouraged him to be a boy, as he'd put it. Hell, maybe that was his loss. Maybe it wasn't right for him to control himself so tightly.

As the torrents washed them, he picked her up and spun her crazily, high above his head. Then he lowered her, slowly, oh, so slowly. He let her breasts and tummy and thighs slide against his body, which became even harder in response to hers.

If only she'd stop looking at him with such fire in her eyes… She made him crave a different kind of life…. One of brightness, warmth and love.

"Kiss me," she whispered, pressing herself into his rock-hard thighs, smiling wantonly up at him when she felt his impressive erection.

So—she wanted him, too.

Kissing her so hard she gasped, he plunged his tongue into her mouth. The rain streamed over their fused bodies and the lightning flashed and the thunder rolled. He knew he should take her inside, but she tasted so good that, for the life of him, he couldn't let her go.

He would regret this, he was sure. But later. Not now, when she smelled of rain. Not when the wild surf roared on all sides of them. Not when his blood roared even louder.

Tonight, he had to have her.

Eleven

When he stripped her and laid her on the bed, she closed her eyes. With her face softly lit by an expectant smile and her damp hair fanning darkly across her pillow, she looked too lovely and precious for words.

"I wanted you to come to me… Even before…you appeared in the breezeway," she admitted, blushing shyly. "I know I shouldn't have…but I just lay on my bed craving you."

"Imagine that. We're on the same page for once."

"I don't want to want you…"

"I know exactly how you feel."

Thank God, he'd thought to stuff some condoms into his wallet before they'd left the yacht—just in case. Thinking about them now made him remember the first time—the one time he'd failed to protect her—and the little clock ticking in the back of his mind ticked a little louder.

She could be pregnant.

Part of him hoped she *was* pregnant…with a son. His son… No, *their* son. A little boy with dark hair who he could play ball with as his father had played with him. They would call him Kade. Quinn would come home, call his name, and the boy would come running.

Foolish dream.

Stripping off his wet jeans and Jockey shorts, he pulled the condoms out of his wallet and laid them on the bed-side table. Still thinking she could very well be pregnant and that he wouldn't mind nearly as much as he should, he stroked the creaminess of her cheek with his thumb. When her eyes sparked with anticipation, he kissed each eyelid and then her smiling mouth.

"Such tiny wrists," he said as he lifted them to his lips. He let his warm breath whisper across her soft skin. "Your heart is beating faster than a rabbit's. So, you did want me…my darlin'. Feed my bruised ego—admit it."

She laughed helplessly. "Okay—I'm tingling in so many places, I feel weak enough to faint."

He touched her breasts, her slender waist, the thatch of silken curls where her thighs were joined. He pressed his lips to all those secret places so reverently that his kisses transcended the physical.

"Better." He smiled. "I told you that you'd change your mind about sex." Triumphantly, he skimmed his mouth along her jawline. With each kiss that he bestowed, she claimed another piece of his heart.

"That you did. Are you always right? Is that how you became so rich?"

He kissed her earlobe, chuckling when she shivered in response.

"Focus is the key in so many endeavors. It only took a day, and I didn't once try to seduce you, now, did I?"

"Stop crowing like a rooster who's conquered a henhouse! I see you brought plenty of protection…which means you intended this to happen."

"I was hopeful. I usually feel optimistic about achieving my goals." He trailed the tip of his tongue along her collarbone.

She moved restlessly beneath him. "You're rubbing it in, and I said don't gloat." When he licked her earlobe again, she shuddered, causing a blazing rush of fire to sizzle through him. "Just do it," she begged.

"Why are you always in such a hurry, sweet Kira?"

Because she was unable to take her eyes from his face, she blew out a breath. Except for clenching her fingers and pressing her lips together, she lay still, as if fighting for patience.

"After all," he continued, "for all practical purposes, this is our wedding night."

Her quick scowl made him wonder why the hell he'd reminded them both of the marriage he'd forced her into.

Before she could protest, he kissed her lips. Soon her breathing was deep and ragged, and it wasn't long until she was quivering beneath his lips and begging him for more.

Her hands moved over his chest and then lower, down his torso and dipping lower still. When her fingers finally curled firmly around the swollen length of his shaft, he shuddered. Soon she had him as hot and eager to hurry as she was. He was out of control, completely in her thrall.

"I bet we're on the same page now," she said huskily, a triumphant lilt in her husky tone.

"Sexy, wanton witch." Unwrapping a condom, he sheathed himself.

Compelled to claim her as his, he plunged into tight, satiny warmth. Stomach to stomach. Thigh to thigh. The moment he was inside her, she wrapped her legs around his waist and urged him even deeper.

"Yes," she whispered as a tortured moan was torn from her lips.

"Yes," he growled, holding her even closer.

Then, some force began to build as he stroked in and out of her, his rhythm growing as hard and steady as the surf dancing rhythmically against the shore. His blood heated; his heart drummed faster. When he fought to slow down, she clung tighter, writhing, begging, urging him not to stop—shattering what was left of his fragile control.

With a savage cry, he climaxed. She felt so good, so soft, so delectable. Grabbing her bottom, he ground himself into her, plunging deeper. As she arched against him, he spilled himself inside her.

She went wild, trembling, screaming his name, and her excitement sent him over the fatal edge he'd vowed never to cross. Walls inside him tumbled. He didn't want to feel like this—not toward her, not toward any woman.

But he did.

Long minutes after he rolled off her, he lay beside her, fighting for breath and control.

"Wow," she said.

Even though sex had never felt so intense before, he didn't trust his feelings. Why give her any more power than she already had by admitting them? But though he confessed nothing, her sweet warmth invaded him, soothing all the broken parts of his soul.

She sidled closer and touched his lips with feverish fingertips, her eyes alight with sensual invitation. As she stroked his mouth and cheek teasingly, desire sizzled through him. He was rock-hard in another instant.

No way in hell would one time suffice. For either of them. With one sure, swift movement, he slid nearer so that his sex touched hers. When she stared up at him hungrily, he kissed her brow, her eyelids and then the tip of her pert nose. Then he edged lower, kissing her breasts and navel. Spreading her legs, he went all the way down, laving those sweet forbidden lips that opened to him like the silken petals of a warm flower. The tip of his tongue flicked inside, causing her to moan.

"Darlin'," he said softly. "You're perfect."

"I want you inside me. So much."

He wanted that, too, so he eased into her, gently this time, and held her tight against him. How could she feel so wonderful in his arms? So right? Like she belonged there, always, till the end of time? How could this be? She was Earl's daughter, a woman he'd coerced into marriage.

"How can this be?" she asked, her words mirroring his dark thoughts.

He took his time, and when it ended in violent, bitter-sweet waves of mutual passion, he felt again the inexplicable peace that left no space for hate or thoughts of revenge. He simply wanted her, wanted to be with her. He didn't want to hurt anything or anybody she loved.

"You're dangerously addictive," he whispered against her earlobe.

Her sweet face was flushed; her lips bruised and swollen from his kisses.

"So are you," she said with a tremulous smile even as her wary eyes reminded him that she hadn't married him for this. "This wasn't supposed to happen, was it? You didn't want this connection any more than I did."

"No…" His mood darkened as he remembered she didn't believe this was a real marriage.

His old doubts hit him with sweeping force. Tomorrow… if it would make her happy, he'd swear to her he'd never touch her again. But not tonight. Tonight, he had to hold her close, breathe in her scent, lose himself in her…dream of a different kind of life with her.

Just for tonight she was completely his.

Hugging him close, she sighed and fell asleep. Beside her, he lay awake for hours watching her beautiful face in the dark, longing and…wishing for the impossible.

When Kira awoke, her arms and legs were tangled around Quinn's. She'd slept so well. For a fleeting instant she felt happy just to be with him.

Last night he'd made her feel precious and adored. Until…the end. With a frown, she remembered how tense and uncertain he'd seemed right before he'd crushed her close and she'd fallen asleep in his arms.

How could she have thrown herself at him? Begged him? He was determined never to love again. Sex, even great sex, would not change his mind.

Despite regrets and misgivings, the gray morning was beautiful. Rain was falling softly, scenting the island with its freshness. A gentle breeze whirred in the eaves while dazzling sunlight splashed the far wall with vivid white.

Had she been sure of Quinn's love, it would have felt romantic to be nestled so warmly in his strong arms. She would have reveled in the sensual heat created by his breath stirring her hair.

But wrapped in cocoonlike warmth with him when she knew he couldn't ever care for her only aroused longings for forbidden things like friendship and affection.

He was going to break her heart. She knew it.

Slowly, she shifted to her side of the bed. Careful not to wake him, she eased herself to her feet. When he smiled in his sleep, she couldn't help thinking him the most stunningly handsome man she'd ever seen.

He looked so relaxed. So peaceful. Last night, he'd taken great care to make her happy in bed. Longing to brush his thick hair away from his brow filled her. Because of what they'd shared, she simply wanted to touch him.

No… She had to remember his experience. He was probably just a great lover and had taken no special pains with her.

Fearing she'd accidentally awaken him if she didn't stop gaping at his virile, male beauty, she tiptoed onto the breezeway where salty air assaulted her. When her tummy flipped violently, causing a brief dizzy spell, she sank against the doorjamb.

After a deep breath, the dizziness loosened its hold. She wasn't sick exactly, but her face felt clammy and she was queasy in a way she'd never been before.

Alarmed, she swallowed. Shakily, she smoothed her damp hair back from her face.

Again, she remembered that Quinn hadn't used a condom their first time in bed. In her head, she began to count the days since her last period, which she already knew was a little late. It was time…past time…for her period to start…and under the circumstances, her odd light-headedness made her anxious.

What if she were pregnant? How would Quinn react? He had not married her because he loved her or wanted a family. Quite the opposite. He'd used protection every single time since that first lapse. She'd never want to force him to stay married to her because of a baby. She wanted love, acceptance. Making their marriage of convenience a permanent situation was the best way to guarantee she'd never find it.

Quickly, she said a little prayer and decided not to borrow trouble just yet. Why upset him until she knew for sure? Still, no matter how she denied it, a seed of worry had taken root.

By the time Quinn had awakened, yanked on his jeans

and called for her, Kira had had her first cup of coffee and felt almost calm enough to face him. As she sat on the front porch, she watched the last gusts of the storm whip the high waves into a frenzy and hurl them against the shore.

At the sound of his approaching footsteps her belly tightened. Then she reminded herself there had only been one lapse…so there really wasn't much danger of pregnancy, was there?

"Kira?"

Concentrating on the angry seas, she wondered how soon the waves would calm down enough for them to leave. When she heard Quinn turning away from the porch, maybe because she hadn't answered, and stomping around somewhere inside the kitchen calling her name, she sensed he was out of sorts, too.

The door behind her creaked.

"Why didn't you answer when I called you?" His low voice was harsh, uncertain. "Avoiding me, are you?"

She didn't turn around to look at him. "Maybe I didn't hear you."

"Maybe you did."

"The seas are still so high, it may be a while before we can leave," she said.

"I see. After last night, you're too embarrassed to talk about anything but the weather. Are you blaming me because I didn't stick to our no-sex deal?"

Hot color climbed her cheeks. "No. I know that what happened was as much my fault as yours."

"But you don't like it."

"Look, what I don't like is being bullied into this marriage in the first place."

"Right."

"If you hadn't forced me to marry you, we wouldn't be

trapped on this island together. Then last night wouldn't have happened."

"Okay, then. So, am I to assume from your mutinous expression that you want to go back to our no-sex deal?"

Why were men always so maddeningly literal? All she wanted was a little reassurance. Instead, he'd launched into the blame game.

Well, she wasn't about to admit she'd craved him last night or that she'd enjoyed everything they'd done together. Nor would she admit that despite everything, she still wanted him. That the last thing she wanted was their no-sex deal. To admit any of that would prove her irrational and give him too much power over her.

When she sat staring at the stormy gulf in silence, he squared his shoulders. "It's too bad the waters are so rough and you're stuck with me, but if we've waited it out this long, I don't intend to push our luck by trying to take the tender out when we could capsize. I'm hungry. Do you want to share that last can of pork and beans with me for breakfast or not?"

The mere thought of canned pork and beans made her mouth go dry and her tummy flip. Within seconds, she began to perspire.

"Or not," she whispered, shaking her head fiercely as she inhaled a deep breath to settle her stomach.

"Are you all right? You look a little pale," he said, stepping closer. "Sick almost."

"I'm fine," she snapped, turning away so he couldn't read her face.

"I wasn't too rough last night, was I?" he asked, the genuine concern in his low tone touching her.

"The less said about what happened the better!"

With a weary look, he nodded. "I talked to my captain via satellite phone. *Pegasus* held up well under the rough seas and squalls. The crew had a bit of a bad night, but other than a case or two of seasickness, all is well."

"I'm glad."

"Look, for what it's worth, I'm sorry I reneged on our bargain and made love to you."

She knotted her hands and unknotted them.

"I took advantage."

"No, you didn't! I was the one who ran out in the storm and lured you after me!" She jumped up. Hugging herself, she walked over to the window. "I'm sure any man would have done the same."

"Look, I'm not just some guy you picked up off the street who is out to get what he can get."

She whirled on him. "Whatever you may think because of that night we shared in San Antonio, I don't do one-night stands, either!"

"I know that. I believe that. I wouldn't have married you otherwise."

"I wonder. Did anything besides my last name really matter to you?"

His face went cold. "I'm your husband. Last night I knew what you wanted and what you didn't want. But in the end, it didn't matter."

"You told me you'd have me in your bed in no time, and you did. So why don't you chalk up another win for your side in your little plan to get revenge against my father."

"Damn it. Because that's not how I feel about it! Or about you!"

"Don't romanticize what happened! We were bored and trapped. Big deal. It's over."

"The hell it is."

"Ours is only a marriage of convenience."

"Do you have to constantly remind me of that?"

"Why not, if it's the truth?"

"Is it? Does it have to be?"

"Yes! Yes!"

He was silent for a long moment. "If that's really how you feel, I won't sleep with you again. You can have your marriage of convenience—permanently. I hope it makes you happy!"

His cold announcement chilled her. Not that she was about to let him see how hurt she felt.

"Great! Now that that's settled, go! Eat your beans and leave me alone!"

"All right. And after I eat them, I'm going out. For a walk. To check on the tender. And I won't be back till the storm's over."

"Great! Perfect!"

When he slammed out of the porch and stalked toward the kitchen, her stomach twisted sharply. She felt ill, really ill. Clutching her stomach, she ran out the back door so he wouldn't see, knelt on the damp sand in the lightly falling rain, and was sick.

She *was* pregnant. She just knew she was.

His strides long and quick because he was anxious to get as far from the house—and from her—as fast as he could, Quinn stalked down the beach toward the dock. As his heels thudded into the deep sand, his head pounded viciously. Their quarrel had given him the headache from hell.

How different he felt now than he had when he'd first woken up. The air had smelled so fresh. He'd lain in bed, his eyes closed, drinking in a contentment he hadn't known in years. Then, he'd reached for her and discovered cool sheets instead of her warm, silky body, and some part of him had gone cold.

He didn't regret his harsh words because she'd smashed

his heart. He didn't regret the sex, either. She'd been sweet, and she'd felt too good—so good that just thinking of her naked and writhing in his arms, her shining eyes big as she'd begged for more had him brick-hard all over again.

When he saw the dock up ahead and the tender riding the waves, he felt intense relief.

He wasn't used to second-guessing himself or feeling the slightest guilt or confusion after sex. In his whole life he'd never awakened beside a woman who hadn't wanted him. Quite the opposite. They always clung, wanting more than he could give. Then he'd be the one to pull away. With her, he felt different. That's probably why he'd been fool enough to marry her.

From the moment Kira had shown up in his office to beg him not to marry her sister, he'd changed all the rules he'd lived by for so long. She'd tangled his emotions into a painful knot.

For some insane, ridiculous reason, he wanted to please her. He'd actually hoped she'd be happier with him after last night, so her obvious misery this morning ate at him all the more.

In his frustration, he broke into a jog. His marriage be damned. The sooner he ended this farce of a honeymoon and got back to business the better.

From now on, their marriage would be as she wished— all for show. He'd ignore the hell out of her except when there were in public.

When he reached the dock, he grabbed the stern line. After snugging the tender closer, he sprang on board.

Crafted of teak for the turbulent waters of the North Sea, she was an efficient, self-bailing craft. Maybe that was why she hadn't sunk. Also, the dock was on the leeward side of the island and in a well-protected cove.

He started the engine and smiled grimly when it purred

to life. Once he made sure the tender was sound, he shut it off, sat down and let the wind buffet him.

In no mood to return to the house or to his wife, he kept an eye on the distant horizon. As soon as the seas calmed, he'd take his bride home and get back to work. He'd lose himself in negotiations with the European Union and forget all about Kira.

His marriage was turning out to be the last thing from convenient, whatever Kira might say to the contrary.

Twelve

Quinn spoke to her as little as possible now.

If Kira had wondered how long Quinn would pretend to be interested in her, she had her answer and was miserable as a result.

No sooner had they returned to San Antonio than he'd made it clear he intended to live as he had before his marriage—working nearly every waking hour.

"The EU deal is going to command my full attention, so I won't be around much for a while," he'd said.

"Fine. I understand."

"Jason will come promptly at ten every morning to take care of you and the house."

"Jason?"

"My houseman. He's at your command. You'll find him highly competent."

Quinn had ensconced her in his fabulous loft apartment, and yes, he'd given her the master bedroom. Now she slept alone in the vast bed they'd shared that first night. As for himself, their first evening home, he'd packed a suitcase and moved his things into a second bedroom. Then he'd politely bid her a terse good-night, gone to bed early and left for work the next morning hours before she'd woken up.

That first morning Jason, a much older man, who was thin-lipped and skeletal, had greeted her so haughtily in the kitchen, she'd felt she was invading his territory.

"I'm Jason," he'd said with a vague sneer in his upper-class tone. "I'm here for whatever you need, cleaning, shopping, cooking—anything. It is my duty and privilege to please you, madam."

Madam?

"Wow! I'm really not used to being waited on. I can't think of a thing for you to do. I mean, I can pour my own cereal out of a box, can't I?"

"Cereal?" He scowled briefly. "Would you prefer an omelet?" he'd suggested with a contemptuous lift of his brows.

"Well, why not," she'd whispered, sensing they were getting off to a bad start. She wanted to be agreeable, yet she despised herself for giving in to him when he was supposed to be serving her. The man made her feel more out of place in Quinn's home than she'd felt before.

Jason had cooked a very good ham-and-vegetable omelet, and she'd dutifully eaten it. Then she'd rushed off to Betty's restaurant to help out while one of the waitresses was away, and the kitchen smells had bothered her way more than usual.

The rest of the week followed the same pattern with Quinn leaving early and returning late. Jason cooked her breakfast and made her dinner, and she began to feel grateful for his presence since it meant she wasn't totally alone.

Since Quinn was gone all the time, she might hardly have noticed she was married if she hadn't missed him so much. She was on her own, as she had been before her marriage, but because her husband was a man she found exceedingly attractive, she felt rejected and constantly unsettled. If he was home behind his shut door, she thought of him every minute.

When he was gone, she felt lost. With every passing day she grew more acutely sensitive to odors, which made her increasingly worried that he'd made her pregnant. She wanted to talk to Quinn about the situation, but she dreaded the conversation, especially now that he was so intent on avoiding her.

On the eighth day of their return, when her period still hadn't started and she was queasier than ever, she called her doctor and made an appointment for the next morning. She'd agreed to take her mother to a routine chemo treatment the same afternoon.

Jaycee had called her earlier in the week, begging her to pick up their mother for her appointment as a favor because escorting her mother for treatment made Jaycee so sad.

"So, how's it going with Quinn?" Jaycee had asked after Kira agreed.

"Fine."

"Fine? Hmm? Well, they do say the first few months are an adjustment."

"I said we're fine."

"I know you don't believe this, but he cares about you. He wanted to marry you."

"Right."

"He bought you that beautiful wedding dress, and you should have seen him when you were gone and nobody knew where you were."

"Well, he's ignoring me now," Kira confided.

"Did you two have a fight?"

She didn't answer.

"If you did, and I think you did, you need to find a way to kiss and make up."

"Why bother to make up, if we have no future?"

Kira changed the subject to her cat, Rudy, and asked if Jaycee minded keeping him a while longer. "I don't want him attaching himself to Quinn…if we're just going to break up."

"He's only a cat."

"Rudy's sensitive."

"And Quinn's not? If I were you, I'd worry more about your husband."

She was; she just wasn't going to admit it.

When Jaycee hung up, Kira had marked her mother's appointment on her calendar. She was glad to have something other than Quinn and her possible pregnancy to concentrate on.

Hours later, she was in bed that night with her light out when she heard Quinn at the door. Throwing off her covers, she started to go out and greet him. Then, pride made her stay where she was.

Wishing he'd knock on her door, she counted his approaching footsteps as he walked across the great room before he made his way down the hall.

When he paused at her door her heart beat very fast. But after a minute, he resumed walking to his own bedroom.

When his door slammed, a strangled sob rose in her throat. With a little cry, she got out of bed and ran to her window. Staring out at the brilliant city, she imagined other married couples, happier couples, slipping into bed together, snuggling close, talking about their day or their children, taking such blissful marital pleasures for granted.

Suddenly, Kira felt as lonely as a butterfly trapped in a child's glass jar.

Pulling on her robe, she wandered out into the great room. Baby or not, she could not live like this, with a husband who didn't want her.

Behind her, she heard a floorboard creak. Whirling, she caught her breath at the sight of Quinn standing barechested in the dark. His shadowed eyes looked haunted.

"You okay?" His low, harsh voice made her shiver. She wanted to be held, loved and crushed against him.

"I'm fine. And you?"

"A little tired, but the deal with the EU seems to be coming together. I'll be going to London for a few days."

"Oh."

"A car's coming for me at 5:00 a.m. Don't worry. I'll be careful so as not to wake you."

How could he be so obtuse? Was he just indifferent? Or was he still angry with her for their harsh exchange on the island?

She wanted to scream at him that he should kiss her goodbye properly. She wanted to drive him to the airport herself. But she kept such foolish thoughts to herself, and he only stared at her from the dark with his intense, burning gaze. She thought he was watching her, waiting—but for what?

Jaycee had advised her to kiss and make up. But how? To what purpose, when he so clearly had his mind on more important things?

After a few minutes of staring at each other in stony silence, he said good-night.

The next morning, when she heard the front door close behind him, she got up. Throwing away all pride, she rushed from her room into the foyer that was filled with crimson light, managing to catch up to him as he waited for the elevator.

"Sorry to wake you," he murmured, concern in his eyes.

"Don't be. I had to say goodbye and wish you a safe journey, didn't I," she whispered, surprised that she could sound so calm, so normal when she felt so incredibly depressed. "I'll miss you."

His dark brows arched warily. "Will you now?"

"I will," she said.

After another long moment spent considering her, he sighed and drew her close against his long, hard body. "I'll miss you, too." He paused. "Sorry about the last week or so."

"I'm sorry, too."

"Habib will call you later and give you all the numbers where I can be reached. I'll think of you in London. I really will miss you. You know that, don't you?" he murmured.

Would he really?

Wrapping her closer, he kissed her hard. She clung to him, probably revealing more of her real feelings than was wise. Then the elevator pinged, and he was forced to let her go or be late. Holding her gaze, he picked up his suitcase and strode through the doors.

She couldn't turn away or stop looking at him or take even one step toward the loft until the door shut.

Pregnant! Needing a moment to take in that news, Kira clenched the steering wheel of her Toyota as she sat in the parking lot of the medical complex and kneaded her forehead with her knuckles.

After a brief exam, the doctor had ripped off his latex gloves and confirmed she was pregnant.

"How do you know? You haven't even tested me."

"When you've been doing this as long as I have, young lady, you just know."

Within minutes, a pregnancy test administered in his office confirmed his opinion.

After the office visit, she felt both numb and tingly as she sat in her car. Biting her lip, she pulled out the slip of paper where she'd written all the numbers Habib had given her earlier. After calculating the time difference between the U.K. and Texas, she grabbed her cell phone and started dialing. Then she stopped. Quinn was probably extremely busy or in an important meeting. Her news would distract him from what was all-important to him—the deal. Better to share the news with him in person when she was sure she had his full attention and could gauge his reaction.

Still, her heart felt as if it was brimming over. She was bursting to tell someone…who would be every bit as excited as she was.

Mother. Suddenly, she was very glad she would be taking her mother to treatment today. Who better to confide in than her precious baby's grandmother? Nobody adored babies, anybody's babies, more than her mother did. Her mother would be happier about this news than anyone, and goodness knew, with all she was going through, she needed a cheerful future to contemplate.

"Oh, my dear," her mother gushed, setting her flowered china teacup aside and seizing Kira's hand in both of her thin ones. Kira had waited until after her mother's treatment, when they could sit down together at Betty's, to share the news.

How weak her mother's grasp felt, even if her eyes were alight with joy.

"Such wonderful news! The best ever! Unbelievable! And it was so easy for you two! And so soon!"

A fierce rush of pride swamped Kira. Never had her mother been so pleased with her. Such rapture had always been reserved for Jaycee's accomplishments.

"Have you told Quinn yet?" her mother asked.

"I started to call him. Then I thought I'd wait…until he comes home, until he's not so distracted."

"So, I'm the first!" Her mother beamed so brightly she almost looked as she had before the illness. Her grip strengthened. "I'm going to beat this thing and live for a very long time. I have to…if I'm to see my darling grand-baby grow up."

Kira's gaze blurred, and she had to turn away to hide her emotion. She felt exhilarated and proud, and a big part of her pleasure had to do with the fact that for once she'd trumped Jaycee.

Oh, why hadn't she ever felt sure of her parents' love?

The river sparkled beside their table outside Betty's. Kira was thrilled her mother's fighting spirit was intact and that she felt reasonably strong. But most of all, she couldn't help being glad that she'd been the one to make her mother so happy.

"Your father will be just as excited as I am. He's very up on Quinn's successes in London, too. So this will be a doubly great day for him."

"Oh, so he's already heard from Quinn?" Kira whispered, feeling more than a little hurt that Quinn had called her father and not her.

"Yes, and it sounds like things are going very well," her mother replied. "Am I to assume by the way you're biting your lip that *you* haven't spoken to him?"

"He texted me, saying he'd arrived in London safely. I'm not hurt. Not in the least."

After studying her for a long moment, her mother looked

dubious. "Well, I'm sure he'll be so happy to hear your exciting news."

Would he be? Oh, how she hoped so, but her doubts soon had her biting her lower lip again.

"Don't do that, dear. How many times have I told you that biting your lip like that chaps your beautiful mouth?"

"When I was a child, Mother!"

"Well, just the same, I know you want to be beautiful for Quinn when he comes home, now, don't you?"

"Right. I do." She glanced at the muddy green river and tried to focus on a white duck. "Frankly, I'm a little worried about telling him. You know…we didn't marry under the best of circumstances."

"I wish you wouldn't make so much of that. I really think it means something when a couple gets pregnant so easily," her mother said almost enviously.

"What are you saying?"

"Sometimes it doesn't work that way… Earl and I had a terrible time getting pregnant with…with you. But let's not go there."

Did she only imagine the shadow that passed over her mother's thin face?

"Is anything wrong, Mother?"

"No, dear."

But her mother looked away and something in her manner and stiff posture rang alarm bells inside Kira. When the silence between them lengthened and grew more strained, she was sure her mother was worrying about something.

"What's wrong? Have I upset you?"

Her mother stared at her, hesitating. "I guess…it's only natural that your news would stir up the past."

"When you were pregnant with me?"

A single tear traced down her mother's cheek. "No…"
She clenched her napkin.

"Did the doctor tell you something when you were alone
with her that has you upset? Bad news of some kind?"

"Dear God, no!" Her mother took her hand. "No. It's not
that. It's nothing like that. It's about you…" Her mother's
eyes filled with some unfathomable emotion. "I was never
pregnant with you."

"What?"

"I…*we* tried so hard, your father and I, to have a baby.
So dreadfully hard. You know how I am. I took my temperature all the time. Ten times a day. But I didn't…I couldn't
get pregnant…no matter what I did. We went to so many
specialists, and they told us that it was my fault, not your
father's. Some hormone imbalance. And then…we never
told anyone, not even you, the truth."

"What truth?" Under the table Kira's hands fisted so
tightly her nails dug bloody crescents into her palms.

"I couldn't conceive, so, in the end, we adopted."

"What?"

"You're adopted. Please don't look so upset! I could
never have had a daughter of my own as wonderful as you.
You've always been so sweet. Like now. Coming with me
for my treatment when poor Jaycee couldn't bear it. She
hates thinking of me being sick. She's too much like me,
you see. I'm strong in some ways, but weak in others. Until
now, I could never admit, not to anyone, that you weren't
my biological child. It represented my biggest imperfec-
tion as a woman."

"Oh, my God." Kira felt overwhelmed, hollow. Suddenly
she remembered all the little things that had never added
up in her life. The rest of her family members were blond
and blue-eyed, while she had dark eyes and hair. She was

tall and slim, while her mother and Jaycee were more petite and curvy.

She'd never been as interested in style or fashion as they were. She'd been wired more emotionally and hadn't thought as logically as they did. Maybe this was why she'd always felt as if she hadn't belonged in her family. Maybe she'd always sensed this huge falsehood in her life.

"I felt like such a failure," her mother continued. "As a woman. For not being able to conceive a child. And then suddenly, inexplicably, when you were two years old, I became pregnant with Jaycee…without even trying. When she was so perfect, so gorgeous, I felt I'd achieved something grand by giving birth. But really, having you was always just as big an achievement. Only I never appreciated it until now. Illness like this can change you, make you wiser somehow.

"I was silly and so unsure when I was young. I know I haven't always understood you, but you are very precious to me."

Kira could say nothing. She was as overwhelmed as a stage actress in a drama who'd forgotten all her lines. Her mind had gone blank.

"I'm so glad you have Quinn. We all suffered so much when Kade died right after selling the company to us. Your father loved Kade like a brother. And then, all these years later, to have Quinn take over the company at the best possible moment for us was a fortunate irony. And now this baby. This wonderful baby will make everything right again. I just know it will.

"I'll get well, and you'll be happy with Quinn. You'll quit…doubting you belong together because you'll have this baby to love together. Nothing can bring a couple closer than a child."

"If only life were that simple."

"Sometimes it is."

Kira couldn't think about her adoption and what it meant right now. So she focused on finding out more about Quinn's past.

Squeezing her eyes shut, she reopened them. "Mother, why did Quinn blame Daddy for his father's death?"

"Your father and Kade Sullivan created Murray Oil. Well, back then it was Sullivan and Murray Oil. Esther Sullivan was extravagant, but Kade adored her. Of course, he was always borrowing from Earl, always needing more... because of her, you see. Esther's needs were insatiable. In time, Kade began to gamble on the side and play the market. For years he was lucky, but then one day his luck ran out.

"When money went missing at the company, from accounts he was responsible for, your father asked him some pointed questions. Kade got angry. The money was found eventually, but the misunderstanding had caused a rift between them.

"Kade said he wanted out, so Earl bought him out. But when times got better and the stock price took off, Kade got hard feelings and started drinking and bad-mouthing your father, especially to Quinn, I think. Around that time, Esther divorced Kade and took whatever he had left.

"Not too long afterward, Earl made a deal that tripled the worth of Murray Oil. Kade claimed the deal had been his idea and wanted compensation, so he sued. He lost the suit, and Quinn discovered his father's body in his shop off the garage. Supposedly Kade had been cleaning his shotgun and it went off. Accidentally. But who knows? Not that Kade ever seemed like the kind of man who'd kill himself. In fact, your father definitely believes it was an accident.

"Oh, my darling, let's not talk of such depressing things.

I much prefer to think about my future grandbaby. Do you want a boy or a girl?"

"A little boy," she whispered. "A little boy with blue eyes who looks just like Quinn and Kade."

"So, you're beginning to love him a little."

With all her heart. Yet she wasn't ready to admit that, not even to her mother.

But her mother saw the truth. "I told you so," she said triumphantly. "And no wonder. He's everything any woman with half a brain would want in a husband."

Not quite everything. He could never return her love, Kira thought.

Thirteen

Quinn remained in London for a week, during which time Kira ached for him. She didn't know how she could miss a man who'd worked so hard to ignore her before he'd left, but she did.

Then, suddenly he sent her a brief text informing her of his flight information for the next day. He said he'd hired a driver to pick him up. Then, right before he boarded his plane, he called her cell while she was still asleep. When she didn't answer, he left a message saying he'd called to remind her of a company party they were attending that evening an hour after his flight was scheduled to land.

So, there would be no private time together his first night home.

"You can call my secretary to find out what to wear," he'd said over the phone. Then his voice had lowered. "Missed you…worse than I thought I would," he'd whispered before ending the call.

Damn. Damn. Damn. What rotten luck that she'd missed his call. What else might he have said if they'd actually talked? She replayed his message several times just to hear his mesmerizing voice say he'd missed her.

A lump formed in her throat. Why had she muted her phone before laying it on her bedside table?

Dialing his secretary, she asked what she should wear to the party.

"It's formal, but Mr. Sullivan did tell me to suggest you wear something red."

"Why red?"

"He didn't say. The deal he pulled off with the EU will have far-reaching consequences for Murray Oil, hopefully positive. Since he's returning in triumph, the party's important to him. I'd suggest you go with his color choice, in case it fits with a bigger plan."

Her heart thumping wildly, Kira took off early from Betty's to indulge in a shopping spree with her mother in search of the perfect sexy red dress. Then she rushed home, with her low-cut scarlet gown and a pair of new heels, so she could take special pains getting dressed.

After the party, if Quinn was in a good mood, she would tell him she was pregnant.

At six, while she was combing her hair, his driver called to tell her Quinn's plane had just landed. "I'll have him home soon."

"Can I please talk to him?"

"He's on the phone. Business. But I'll tell him to call you as soon as he finishes."

When Quinn's key turned in the lock, Kira hurried to the door to greet him. His luggage thumped heavily on the floor. Then he strode through the foyer with his phone still pressed to his ear.

His voice rang with authority as he stepped into the living room. When she met his hard, dark eyes, she saw the shadows of weariness under them. Even if he hadn't bothered to call her from the car, she was so thrilled he was home, her heart leaped with pure joy.

"Gotta go," he said abruptly. "We'll wrap this up in the morning." He flipped his phone shut and stared at her. "Sorry about the phone call. Business."

"Of course. I understand." She smiled tremulously.

His mouth curved, but his smile played out before it reached his eyes.

She wanted to rush into his arms, and it was only with great effort that she remained where she was. No matter how eager she felt, she would not throw herself at him.

"You look pale," he said. "Thinner. Are you okay?"

She hadn't been eating as regularly due to her morning sickness, but she couldn't tell him that. At least, not now.

"I'm fine," she whispered.

"Right. Why is that answer always your first line of defense?"

She didn't know what to say to him. If only he would take her in his arms and kiss her, maybe that would break down the barriers between them.

His eyes burned her, and his hands were clenched. Was being married to her so difficult for him?

"I like the dress. It becomes you," he murmured.

She blushed, pleased.

"I bought you something." He tossed a box onto the sofa carelessly. "Open it and see if you like it." He spoke casually, as if the gift was a token and nothing more.

When he turned sharply and walked down the hall to his bedroom, she felt a sickening sensation of loss. How foolish she'd been to dream they might have a new beginning.

Sinking onto the sofa, she opened the black box and let

out a pleased cry when a necklace and earrings of rubies and diamonds exploded in fiery brilliance. He'd tucked his business card inside the box. On the back of it, scrawled in bold black ink, she read, "For my beautiful wife."

Tears filled her eyes as she hesitantly touched the necklace. She quickly brushed the dampness away. The necklace was exquisite. Nobody had ever given her anything half so lovely.

In the next breath, she told herself the gift meant nothing. He was wealthy. It was for show. He'd bought the jewels to impress Murray Oil's clients, stockholders and employees. He'd probably had someone pick them up for her. The gift wasn't personal.

"Do you like it?" Tall and dark, he stood in the doorway looking gravely handsome in his elegant black suit.

"It's too beautiful," she whispered. "You shouldn't have, but thank you."

"Then stand up, and I'll help you put it on. You have no idea how many necklaces I looked at. Nothing seemed right until I found this one."

"You shopped for it yourself?"

"Indeed. Who could I possibly trust to select the right gift for my bride? The wrong necklace could overpower you."

He let her secure the earrings to her ears before he lifted the necklace from the black velvet box and fastened it around her neck.

At the warmth of his fingertips against her nape, her skin tingled and her heart beat wildly. Was it possible to have an orgasm from sheer longing?

"With your dark hair, I thought rubies would become you, and they do," he said, staring so long at the sparkle on her slim neck his gaze made her skin burn. "I imagined you wearing them and nothing else."

In spite of herself, she giggled. *This was more like the homecoming she'd fantasized about.* In another moment, he would kiss her.

He stepped back to admire her and shot her an answering grin. Why, oh, why hadn't he kissed her?

She pursed her lips, touched her hand to her throat.

His face grew guarded again; his lips set in that firm line she'd come to dread. Instead of taking her in his arms, he backed away almost violently. "Shall we go?" he said, his tone rough and deliberately impersonal.

Cut to the quick, she didn't dare look at him as she nodded. During the short drive, he didn't speak to her again.

As soon as they arrived at the party, he put his arm around her as executives and clients rushed up and surrounded him, all clamoring to congratulate Quinn on his successes in London.

Black silk rustling, Cristina was among the first who hurried to his side. Barely managing a cool smile for Kira, she placed a bejeweled, exquisitely manicured hand on Quinn's cheek with practiced ease and kissed him lightly.

"I'm *so* proud of you," she gushed in a low, intimate tone. "I knew you'd pull it off. See—everybody loves you now. Worries over."

Clearly, he'd taken the time to inform *her* personally of his successes.

"So the deal went well?" Kira whispered into his ear when the lovely Cristina glided away.

He nodded absently as he continued shaking everybody's hand.

"Why didn't you tell me?"

"You know now, don't you?"

"But I'm your wife…"

"Unwillingly, as you keep reminding me. Which is why

I've been working hard not to burden you with too much attention."

Stung, her eyes burning and her heart heavy, she turned away. Why did it hurt that he saw no need to share the things that mattered to him when she'd known all along their marriage was for show?

She was sure he had a duty to mingle, so she was surprised when Quinn stayed by her side. When she noticed a dark-skinned man talking animatedly to her family, she asked Quinn who he was.

"Habib."

"The man you were talking to after we made love that first time?"

He nodded. "I thought you two had met…at the wedding."

"No, but we've talked on the phone this past week. Why did he think you should marry Jaycee instead of me?"

"Whatever he thought, he was wrong. What difference does it make now?"

"My mother told me today that I was adopted."

When Quinn's blue eyes darkened, she sensed that he knew more than he wanted to let on.

"Something you said that morning made me wonder if you and he somehow knew that," she persisted.

He stiffened warily.

"I thought that if you had known, maybe you assumed my family cared more about her…and maybe that was why Habib concurred with my father that she was the better choice…?"

"Habib's research did indicate a partiality on your father's part for Jacinda."

Her chest constricted. That truth was one of the reasons being loved in her own right by her husband was something that was beginning to matter to Kira more than anything.

"I preferred you from the first," he countered.

He kept saying that. Could she dare to believe him?

"Doesn't that count for something?" he asked.

"Our marriage was a business deal."

"So you keep reminding me."

"You only married me to make taking over Murray Oil go more smoothly, and now that you've made a place for yourself, your need for me is at an end."

"I'll decide when my need for you is at end. What do you say we end this depressing conversation and dance?" He took her hand. "Shall we?"

"You don't really want to dance with me— I'm just—"

"Don't put yourself down," he growled as he pulled her into his hard arms. "You're my wife."

"So, dancing with me at the company party is expected?" she said.

"I suppose." His grip strengthening, he smiled grimly down at her. "Did it ever occur to you that I might want to dance with you even if it wasn't expected?"

She was aware of people watching them and reminded herself that he was only dancing with her to make the guests believe their marriage was real.

From a corner, her laughing parents and a smiling Jaycee watched them, too. Looking at them, so happy together, Kira felt left out, as usual. Even being in Quinn's arms, knowing she was pregnant with his child, gave her no joy. How could it? Had he touched her other than for public viewing, or shown her any affection since he'd returned? Their marriage was a business deal to him, and one that wasn't nearly as important as the one he'd just concluded in London.

"Quit thinking dark, mutinous thoughts, and just dance," he whispered against her ear. "Relax. Enjoy. You're very beautiful, you know, and I'd seize any excuse to hold you in my arms."

Despite her determination to resist his appeal, his words, his nearness and his warm breath against her earlobe had her blood beating wildly.

She knew it was illogical, but being held in his arms reassured her. Soon she almost forgot dancing with him was just for show. Everyone in the gilded room blurred except her handsome husband.

They didn't speak again, but his eyes lingered on her lips as the music washed through her. Did he want to kiss her? She wanted it so much, she felt sick with longing. Surely he knew it. If so, he gave no indication, and, after a while, all the spinning about began to make her feel dizzy and much too hot.

She didn't want to be sick. Not now…not when he was finally holding her, when he seemed almost happy to be with her. Still, she couldn't take another step or she'd faint.

"I need some air," she whispered.

"All right." He led her round along the shadowy edges of the room until they came to a pair of tall French doors that opened onto a balcony overlooking the sparkling city. Gallantly, he pulled her outside. The night was mild, pleasant even. Once they were alone, his grip around her tightened in concern and he pressed her close.

"You look so strained and pale. Are you sure you're okay?"

She gulped in a breath of air. And then another. "I'm perfectly fine," she lied, believing that surely in a minute or two she would be.

"Obviously, even being in my arms is an ordeal."

"No!"

"You don't have to lie. I know well enough that I've given you ample reason to dislike me."

"I don't dislike you."

"But you don't like me. How could you? I was your father's enemy."

"Quinn—"

"No, hear me out. Since the island, I've kept my distance in order to make our marriage less onerous to you. I know I pushed you into this situation too hard and too fast, and I took advantage of you the night of the storm. I'm not proud of that. But do you have any idea how difficult it's been to stay away from you ever since?

"I wanted to give you your precious space and time to get used to our arrangement. I prayed that a week's separation would give me the strength to resist you when I returned," he muttered. "So, I didn't call you from London, and when I came home, I tried to be the cold husband you desire. But after our days apart, when you looked so ethereal and beautiful in your flashy red dress, my vow not to touch you drove me crazy. God help me, ever since the first day I saw you at your parents' ranch, you've obsessed me."

"But I don't desire a cold husband. I've wanted you, too," she whispered, wishing her feet felt a little steadier beneath her. Despite the fresh air, she was beginning to feel light-headed again.

"You have?"

Whatever encouragement he sought in her eyes, he found. Instantly, his lips were on hers, but when he crushed her closer, holding her tightly and kissing her, her dizziness returned in a sickening rush.

"I've wanted you so much," he murmured. "Missed you so much. You have no idea. Darlin', tell me you missed me, at least a little?"

Her heart beat violently even as she gulped in another breath. "Of course I did," she managed to say even as his dear face blurred and the walls of the building and the twinkling lights beneath them whirled dizzyingly like bright colors dancing in a kaleidoscope.

She willed herself to be strong, to fight the dizziness. "I did… But there's something I have to tell you, Quinn. Something…wonderful."

Little blue stars whirred. *Not good.* On the next beat the bottom dropped out of her tummy, and try as she might to save herself by gulping in mouthfuls of air, she couldn't get her breath.

"Quinn—"

Her hands, which had been pushing frantically against his hard chest, lost their strength. She was falling into a heavy darkness that was hot and swirling and all-enveloping.

The last thing she saw was Quinn's anxious face as his arms closed around her.

Fourteen

When Kira regained consciousness, Quinn was leaning over her in a small room, pressing a cool rag to her brow. To his right, a tall blond man with an air of grave authority had a finger pressed to her wrist while he studied his watch.

"Dennis is a doctor, and he wants me to ask you if…if you could possibly be pregnant," Quinn said.

"I wanted to tell…you. First thing… I really did."

"What?"

"Yes!" She blushed guiltily as Quinn stared down at her. "Yes. I'm pregnant. "I…I think that's why I got too hot while we were dancing. I've been having morning sickness while you were gone."

"That's why you were so pale. Why didn't you call me? Or tell me when I got home?" Quinn's hand tightened on her arm, and his expression grew grim. "Because you were unhappy about the baby? Were you planning to end the pregnancy without telling me?"

"No!" she exclaimed, horrified.

Quinn turned to the doctor and grilled him about her condition. The man quickly reassured him that her pulse and blood pressure were just fine. Still, he advised that she see her own doctor the next day, just to make sure.

"We're going home," Quinn said. "You're going to bed. No wonder I thought you looked thin. You should have told me."

"I was going to…"

"When?" he demanded so coldly she couldn't answer him.

That was the last word either of them said until they reached his loft. In the car, he gripped the steering wheel with clenched fists, while his profile seemed fashioned of unyielding granite. Never once did he look her way. Deliberately, he shut her out. The walls between them thickened and grew taller. Would she ever be able to reach him again?

Once inside the loft, he lingered in the crimson shower of light by the door while she fled to the master bedroom.

Alone in the vast room, she stared at the bed they'd shared. Silently, she kicked off her heels and pulled off the red dress and then slipped into a frothy white nightgown.

This wasn't the way she'd imagined telling him about the baby.

The rubies on her neck felt heavy, unbearable, but when she went to undo the clasp, her fingers shook too badly for her to manage it. The weight on her heart was even heavier. How could he have thought, even for one second, she might want to end her pregnancy? How could she go to bed when heartbreak was suffocating her?

She had to talk to him, to at least try to make things

right. Without remembering to grab a robe, she raced to the huge living room. It was empty, so she tiptoed back down the hall to his bedroom door, which he'd shut against her. She called his name, softly at first. When he didn't answer, she knocked.

His door swung open and he stood before her, his powerful, bare-chested body backlit by the lamp on his nightstand. He looked so glorious, she caught her breath. For a long moment, she could only stare at his bronzed muscles with bemused fascination. He was so fit and hard. If only she could throw herself into his arms and tell him she loved him and his baby.

But she knew he didn't want her love.

"I want this baby, and I was going to tell you," she whispered.

She watched his magnificent muscles cord as he pushed the door wider. "When?" he muttered roughly, disbelieving her.

"Just before I passed out at the party. I wanted to tell you in person, and... It was just that I was scared," she continued breathlessly. "I—I...couldn't believe you'd want my baby, too."

"Our baby," he corrected in a tight tone. "Couldn't the baby give us something more positive to build on?"

"How? If you regret marrying me. And blame our child for trapping you into a permanent involvement with a woman you don't want.

"Quinn, if you'd planned to dissolve our marriage after your takeover of Murray Oil, you don't have to stay with me because of this. I hope you know that. This doesn't have to change the businesslike nature of our arrangement."

He sucked in a breath. "Damn it. Are you ever going to quit telling me what I feel?"

"But isn't that...how you feel?"

For a long moment he was silent. "Would you listen to me for once, instead of being so sure you've got me pegged?"

"Yes. All right."

After another lengthy interval, his expression softened. "I guess I'm a little scared by your news," he said simply.

"Because you know our marriage isn't real?"

His mouth tensed. "No! Because babies are a lifetime commitment. Because they are so little…and so helpless. Because they know how to turn their parents into doting sots—and they do it with charm, in no time flat. Anything could happen to a baby." He caught her hand, and when she didn't struggle, he pulled her into his arms. "Or to you… while you're pregnant. I couldn't bear it." He kissed her brow.

It was bliss to be in his arms.

So he didn't love her, couldn't love anybody. But he cared. She was sure he cared, at least a little. He was holding her as if he did.

"But nothing will happen because we'll take good care of the baby…and me," she said reassuringly.

"My father was strong, and he died. We're all only a heartbeat away from death." There was so much grief and passion in his voice she felt hot tears sting the back of her eyelids.

"Which is why we have to live each moment to the fullest," she whispered. In a burst of tenderness, she raised her fingertips to stroke his temples in consolation. "We don't have a second to waste. We might as well be dead if we're afraid to live." To love, she wanted to add.

Quinn's arms tightened around her. He lowered his face and this time it was her mouth he sought. When he found it, he kissed her long and deeply. She opened her lips and sighed. She'd wanted him to kiss her like this for hours, days. Maybe that was why she couldn't help shivering in delight and giving him everything—all her love, even her soul—when she kissed him back.

"Oh, Kira…" For an endless time, he couldn't seem to stop kissing her. Then, suddenly, he let her go and jerked free of her embrace.

"Forgive me. I forgot—you don't want me pawing you. That's what made you sick, earlier." His dark face was flushed and his breathing ragged.

"No… I told you… I've had morning sickness. Only sometimes it's not just in the morning."

"Go to your own room. We can talk tomorrow." Even as his harsh rejection wounded, his eyes continued to hungrily devour her.

He wanted her. He was pushing her away *because* he desired her so much. And because she'd made him promise not to sleep with her.

She'd been wrong, impossible from the first. She'd missed him while he was away. She was carrying his child.

Everything had changed for them.

If she had to beg, she would.

"Don't make me sleep alone tonight," she pleaded. "Because I won't sleep. I'll just lie there…wanting you."

"I won't sleep, either. Still, in the morning you'll regret it if you don't go." His expression darkened. "Like you did before…on the island."

But she hadn't regretted it. He had.

"I don't think so," she said. "You did say we should focus on the positive…for the baby's sake. Am I right?"

His sensual mouth quirked ever so charmingly, and the heat in his gaze soon had her bones melting.

"How do you make me break every rule that allowed me to survive during my long, dark years of grief?"

"I get that you don't want to love anybody ever again.

Especially not me," she whispered. "But I'm not asking for your love tonight."

When he would have protested, she sealed his lips with a fingertip. "I'm not asking for anything you can't give. I just want to be with you."

"My father loved my mother too much, and…she destroyed him…when she left. I can't help thinking you're just waiting for the right moment to walk out."

Don't you know how much I love you? Don't you know that if only you loved me, I would never leave you?

Her knees were so weak with desire, she could barely stand. No way did she possess the courage to voice her true thoughts. She was afraid they would only drive him further away.

Her hold on him was tenuous, and only sexual. She had to accept that, use it and hope that someday she could build on that foundation.

Reaching toward him, she splayed her fingertips against his massive chest. Flesh and bone and sinew felt solid and warm beneath her open palm. When she ran her fingers over his nipples and through the dark hair that matted his torso, he groaned, which pleased her.

"Kira. Darlin'." On a shuddering sigh, he pulled her close and teased her lips and jawline with his mouth and tongue.

Lifting her, he carried her to the bed. There, he slid off his belt and slacks and pushed her nightgown down her shoulders. As it pooled onto the floor, he pulled her against him and pushed inside her slick satin warmth. Riding their mutual passion, they let it carry them like a charging black steed, faster and faster, until they soared together in torrid surrender. Afterward, as she held on to him, her sated body melted into his.

"You've ruined me," he whispered.

"Whiner," she teased.

"Seriously. I'll never be able to move again," he said.

She laughed. "Sure you will. And it better be sooner than you think. Because I'm going to be wanting more… very soon. You've neglected me…you know."

"Have I now? And whose fault was that, darlin' Kira?"

For an entire hour, he held her against his body as if she was precious to him. When she kissed his rough cheek, his throat, his nipples, he muttered huskily, "You weren't kidding, were you?"

"I've missed you."

"Slave driver."

But he smiled and ran his hands through her hair as he pulled her close.

This time his love was sweeter, and slower, and afterward, when he kissed her belly gently, he showed her that his intense passion included their precious child.

"So, you want my baby, do you?" he whispered.

"So much, too much," she admitted in a breathless whisper as she pressed his dark head against her flat stomach. "More than anything. In fact, I hope the baby's a boy and that he looks just like you."

He laughed in husky delight and nuzzled her tummy with his feverish lips. "Be careful what you wish for. He'll be a handful, I assure you."

"I can't wait."

When he held her close like this and was so teasingly affectionate, she could almost forget he didn't love her, that he never could. She could almost forget how inadequate and uncertain she'd always felt.

Almost…

He was a handsome billionaire, who could have any woman he wanted. What could she do to hold him?

Nestled in his arms, she fell into a restless sleep and

dreamed. She was a child again, standing beside her parents as they cheered Jaycee and her basketball team to victory. Then she was sitting in her room alone. The house was empty because her mother and father had driven Jaycee to a slumber party.

Older now, Kira was walking across the stage at Princeton where she'd graduated with honors. As she posed for photographs, she smiled brightly through her disappointment. None of her family was in the audience because Jaycee had a conflicting high school event. The picture was all they'd have to remember this huge milestone in Kira's life.

"Remember to smile," her mother had commanded over the phone. "You never smile." A pause. "Oh, how I wish I could be there to see you graduate!"

"Couldn't Daddy stay with Jaycee?"

"You know your father. He's no good at those high school functions without me."

The dream darkened into a nightmare. Quinn was standing in a shower of crimson light, holding Cristina against his long, lean body. "I have to marry *her*, don't you understand? I don't want to. You're the one who's special to me. Don't ever forget that my marriage to her is strictly business. You're the woman who really matters. Who will always matter. Nothing will change between us. You'll see."

Then he kissed Cristina as those awful words repeated themselves in her mind. "Strictly business…"

Kira woke up crying that phrase even as Quinn wrapped his arms around her and held her close.

"Hush. It's okay, baby. You were only dreaming."

Was she? Or were her dreams where she faced the harsh truths she denied when awake?

"I'm fine," she murmured, pushing him away. "You

don't have to comfort me. I can take care of myself—just like I always have. I didn't ask you to love me—did I?"

"No, you damn sure didn't."

Strictly business.

God, if only Quinn could feel that way, too, maybe then he'd survive this nightmare.

As soon as Kira's breathing had become regular again and Quinn was sure she was asleep, he'd tossed his own covers aside and shot out of bed.

Groping clumsily for his slacks on the dark floor, he yanked them on and stalked out of the bedroom in bare feet. When he got to the bar, he splashed a shot of vodka into a glass.

Strictly business.

Damn her! Not that he didn't feel sorry for her, because he did. Even now, her stricken cries echoed in his mind. She was no happier than he was.

He'd been right to think she'd regret the sex. So, why the hell had she slept with him when he'd given her an out?

He'd never figure her out. She might regret what had happened, but he couldn't. She'd been too sweet, and he'd craved her too desperately. Hell, it embarrassed him to think of how needy he'd felt all week without her in London.

Frowning as he stared into his glass, he remembered how he'd grabbed his cell phone at least a dozen times in his eagerness to call her, only to shove it back in his pocket. All he'd wanted was to hear her soft voice. Without her, he'd felt cut off, alone, alienated in a city he usually enjoyed.

Once in San Antonio, he'd rushed home. And when he'd seen her, he'd wanted nothing except to sweep her into his arms and kiss her endlessly. But she'd been pale and with-drawn.

Every day his obsession for her increased. If she could not reciprocate, they were shackled together on the same fatal course his own parents had traveled. He would not endure that kind of marriage.

His father had given his mother everything, and it hadn't been enough.

He would not make the same mistake.

Fifteen

Quinn's side of the bed was ice-cold.

Nothing had changed.

He was gone.

It wasn't the first time Kira had woken up alone in Quinn's bed, but this morning, she felt needier than usual. Maybe because of what they'd shared the night before, or maybe because of her bad dreams, she wanted a good-morning kiss. And maybe breakfast together punctuated with a lot more kisses.

But he'd left her for work, which was all-important to him. Hadn't business been the sole reason he'd married her?

To him, last night must have been about sex and nothing more. She'd known that, hadn't she? Still, as she lay in bed, her body sore from making love, she felt lonely. Would it always be like this?

Stretching, she rolled onto his side of the bed where his

scent lingered and hugged his pillow. Then, realizing what an idiot she was, she hurled his pillow at the wall. It struck an etching, which crashed to the floor.

Footsteps in the corridor brought a quick blush to her face.

"Mrs. Sullivan? Is that you? Do you need my assistance?" Jason sounded so stiff and formal, she cringed. She wanted her husband, not some uptight houseman with high-class British airs.

"I'm fine," she cried.

How was she going to get from Quinn's room to hers in her sheer nightie without Jason seeing her wrapped in a blanket? Such an encounter would be embarrassing for both of them.

When five minutes passed without another sound, she cracked the door. There was no sign of him, so she ripped a blanket off the bed, covered herself and shot down the hall on flying tiptoes. Once inside her bedroom, she bolted the door.

As she dressed, taking her time because it was hours before she needed to be at Betty's, she turned on the television. Murray Oil and the EU deal were all over the news.

Both the local news channels and the national ones were full of stories about Quinn's heady successes. In too many shots, a beaming Cristina stood so close to Quinn the pair seemed joined at the hip. Why hadn't Quinn told her that Cristina had gone to London with him?

Cristina worked for him. Surely he'd taken other executives. It was no big deal.

But in her fragile mood, and after her dream last night, it felt like a big deal to her.

You can't blame a man for something you dreamed!

Maybe not, but she still had to ask him about Cristina and his reasons for taking the woman to London. So, when the phone rang, she rushed to pick it up, hoping it was Quinn.

"Hello!" she said a little too brightly.

"Kira? You don't sound like yourself."

The critical male tone was very familiar. Still, because she was focused on Quinn, it took her a second to place the voice. Then it came to her: Gary Whitehall, her former boss.

"Hi, Gary."

"Are you still looking for a job?"

"I am," she said.

"Even though you're Quinn Sullivan's wife?"

"Yes, even though. He's a very busy man, and I love doing what I'm trained to do."

"Well, Maria is retiring because she needs more time to help her daughter. The minute she told me she wanted to play grandmother, well, naturally, we all thought of you."

She lifted a brow. *And Quinn.*

"You could have your old job back… Although, like I said, I wasn't at all sure you'd be interested now that you're *the* Mrs. Sullivan."

"Well, I am, so…this is wonderful news."

"Then you'll make yourself available for a meeting? No hurry, though. Don't want to pressure you."

"I'm available. In fact, I'm free for an hour or two this afternoon."

They agreed upon a time and hung up.

The call boosted her mood until she remembered how Quinn had rushed off to work this morning without even a goodbye. Until she remembered what a gorgeous couple he and Cristina had made on television. They were both so stylish and good-looking. They had business concerns in common, too.

With an effort, she quit thinking about Cristina and refocused on Gary's offer. She was glad Gary had called, even if it was her marriage to Quinn that had made her more attractive as a job applicant.

On a whim, she decided to call Quinn and run the job idea by him just to see what he'd say.

Oh, be honest, Kira, you just want to hear his sexy voice and distract him from Cristina.

Kira made the call, only to be deflated when his secretary told her, "I'll have him return your call. He's in a meeting."

"With whom?"

"Cristina Gold. They're taking a last look at the contracts for the EU deal before everything is finalized."

Don't ask a question if you don't want the answer.

"Would you please tell him…that I'll be on my cell."

"Are you all right, Mrs. Sullivan?"

"I'm fine," she whispered as she hung up.

Perfectly fine.

Clutching the phone to her breast, she sank onto her bed. She didn't feel fine. She felt more uncertain than ever.

Leave it alone. Cristina works for him. That's all there is to it. Go to Betty's. Do the interview with Gary. Forget your stupid nightmare.

But being pregnant had her feeling highly emotional. She couldn't leave it alone. She had to see him. After last night, she had to know how he felt.

Dressing hurriedly, she was in his office in less than an hour. The same beautiful blonde secretary who'd greeted her on her first visit greeted her again, more warmly this time.

"Mr. Sullivan told me you two are expecting a baby. He sounded so happy about it. Congratulations."

"Thank you."

"Would you like coffee? Or a soda?"

"I just want to talk to my husband. He didn't call me back, and since I was in the neighborhood…"

"I'm afraid he's still going over those contracts."

"With Miss Gold?"

The young woman nodded. "I'm afraid the documents are long and very complicated. A mistake could cost millions. Miss Gold is one of our attorneys, you see. She had several concerns."

"Please tell him I'm here."

After the young woman buzzed him, she looked up almost immediately. "He says he'll see you. Now."

Intending to lead her down the hall, she arose, but Kira held up a hand. "I remember the way."

When Kira reached his office, Cristina was just exiting with a thick sheaf of documents. She tossed Kira a tight smile. Behind Cristina, Quinn leaned negligently against the doorjamb.

When he opened the door, Kira said, "I hope I'm not interrupting."

"Glad that meeting's over. And doubly glad to see you." He shut the door. "I needed a break."

Despite the welcoming words, when their eyes met, she felt a sudden unbearable tension coming from him.

"Sorry I left so early this morning, but I had a couple of urgent texts."

"From Cristina?"

"One was. Unfortunately, I still have a lot of balls in the air related to the EU deal," he said.

"No problem."

"You look upset." His voice was flat.

"I didn't realize Cristina went to London with you… until I saw some of the news coverage on television."

A cynical black brow lifted. "I took a team of ten. She

was part of the team. She's very talented at what she does, or I never would have hired her."

"Not only is she talented, but she's beautiful, too."

He stood very still. "I imagine her looks are part of why she made it into so many of the TV shots. Look, there's no need for you to be jealous of her...if that's what this is."

"I'm not."

"I'm married to you, and whether you believe it or not, that means something to me."

What did it really mean if he could never love her?

"Since you obviously want to know more about Cristina and me," he began in the maddening, matter-of-fact tone of a lawyer presenting his case, "I'll clarify our relationship. We dated briefly. The press gave our romance more attention than it deserved.

"Then she broke up with me—for another man with whom she's still seriously involved. At the time, she complained I never had time for her. He did. Naturally, I was angry, but since then I've realized she was right."

"A vengeful man might have held what she did against her," she said coolly. "Why did you hire her?"

"We worked together on several projects before we dated. She will do a lot for Murray Oil."

"So, as always, business is all-important to you? Does nothing else ever matter? Not even your own injured feelings?"

He shrugged. "They weren't that injured. I got over her pretty quickly."

Would he get over Kira and be this matter-of-fact about it? At the thought, Kira cringed.

"Business will always be an important part of my life. I don't deny that. It's part of who I am. I hired her...before I met you." He paused. "What is it you want from me this morning, Kira?"

"Right. I'm interrupting you. You're a busy man. You probably have many more important meetings to get through today. All those balls in the air. And here I am, your pregnant, overly emotional wife needing reassurance."

He studied her warily. "What do you want, Kira?"

Why couldn't she be as cool and logical as he was? Because everything in her life was out of balance. She was pregnant and feeling needy. There were too many unanswered questions in their relationship, and she was still reeling from the discovery that she'd been adopted.

She wanted to belong somewhere, to someone. She wanted to matter to *Quinn*. If she'd been more important to him, wouldn't he have kept her in the loop while he was gone? Wouldn't he have shared more details concerning his oil deal?

"I guess I want the impossible," she blurted out. "I want a real marriage."

"Now you want a real marriage, when all along you've said that's the last thing you want? Last night you woke up crying from some dream, apparently about me, demanding 'strictly business.' You pushed me away as if you wanted nothing to do with me. If I give you space it's wrong. If I push myself on you it's wrong."

"I know I'm not making sense," she said. "Our marriage was never based on love, mutual understanding or anything that makes up a true partnership. I guess I'm upset because…because I don't know… I just know I can't go on like this!"

"As soon as I complete this deal, I'll have more time…"

"How will that matter if you don't want the same kind of marriage I do? Now, maybe because of the baby and finding out I was adopted, I have this huge need for things to be right between us. I want more. I've wanted more my whole life. I don't want to feel left out anymore. Most of all, I want to count to my husband."

"If you wanted to belong in this marriage, then why did you tell me from the first that you didn't want to sleep with me?"

"I guess to protect myself…from ever feeling like I feel now—needy…confused. I knew this marriage was only a business deal for you. I didn't want to get my heart broken," she whispered.

"What are you saying?"

"What we have isn't enough. Not for me…or for you."

"You're pregnant. We can't just walk away from each other. It's not about you and me anymore, or even Murray Oil. We have a child to think about now."

"That's all the more reason I don't want us trapped in a loveless marriage. I want a husband who can love me. I want my child to grow up in a loving home. After the deal you just made, the executives at Murray Oil trust you. You don't need to be married to me anymore. You can divorce me and date somebody who understands you, someone who can make you happy…someone like Cristina."

"Damn it. I don't want a divorce. Or Cristina. Like I said—if you'd ever once listen to me—she's practically engaged."

"But you don't love me…"

"Well, I damn sure don't love anyone else. And I'm not lusting after anybody else. I'm focused solely on you! You're very important to me, Kira. Vital. Still, it's true that I'm not sure I'll ever be capable of loving anyone—even you. Maybe I've been hard and dark and driven for too long."

"Well, I want a man who will commit his heart to me, or I want out."

"Okay," he said in a tone that was cold, infuriatingly

logical and final. "Now that our marriage has served its purpose, you want out. Well, I don't want out, and I'm not ready to let you go. But if that's what you want, I won't hold you against your will any longer."

"What?"

"I'll give you what you say you want. You're free to leave. But understand this—I intend to take an active role in raising our child."

"Of course," she whispered, feeling shattered.

"Then so be it," he said.

He stared at her, waiting for her to walk out the door, and, for a brief moment, his guard fell. She saw longing and pain flash in his eyes.

Suddenly, she realized just how much she'd wanted him to fight for her, for them.

After stumbling blindly out of his office, she sat behind the wheel of her car, clenching her keys in her hand. All her life she'd wanted someone to fight for her, someone to put her first. She'd had a right to push for more from her marriage.

He wasn't willing to fight for her as he'd fought for his oil deal in London, so she would do the fighting.

She would fight for her self-respect, and she would teach their child to fight for his, too.

Kira had been in no condition to be interviewed by Gary the afternoon she'd parted from Quinn, so she'd rescheduled.

Two miserable days later, she still didn't feel strong enough, but here she sat, facing Gary across his wide, cluttered desk in his flashy corner office that overlooked the museum grounds and the busy street that fronted the modern building.

If only she could stop thinking about Quinn and how

bereft she'd felt ever since he'd agreed to end their marriage.

Concentrating on Gary, who wasn't the most fascinating man, was difficult. Lately, everything had been difficult. Returning to Quinn's gorgeous loft, packing the beautiful clothes that she would no longer need and then moving back into her cramped apartment with her dead plants and resentful cat had been full of emotional hurdles.

Rudy wouldn't sit on her lap or use his scratching post. Only this morning he'd peed on her pillow just to show her how much he resented being abandoned.

"Quit feeling sorry for yourself! I'm the one who got married and pregnant...and separated," she'd yelled at him.

Swishing his tail, he'd flattened his ears and stalked indifferently to his bowl where he'd howled for more tuna.

She tried to pay attention to Gary, she really did, but her mind constantly wandered to her miserable new separated state and to Quinn and how cold he'd been right before he'd watched her walk away.

Suddenly, she found Gary's droning insufferable and longed to be anywhere else, even home alone with her sullen cat. If she didn't interrupt Gary, he might easily rant on for another half an hour.

"Gary, this is all very fascinating, but I need to ask a question."

He frowned.

"Is this job offer contingent on me remaining married to Quinn?"

"What?"

"Let me be blunt."

His mouth tightened. "You do that so well."

"Quinn and I have separated. Do you still want me for this job? "

His face fell. "Separated?" Flushing, he pushed himself

back from his desk. "Well, that does change things." Recovering quickly, he ran a nervous hand through his hair. "Still, I want you to work here, of course."

Her voice was equally silky as she leaned toward him. "*Of course.* I'm so glad we understand each other."

A few minutes later he hastily concluded the interview. "I'll call you," he said.

She left, wondering if he would.

As she stood on the curb outside the museum, about to cross the street, Jaycee called her on her cell.

"How are things going?"

"I've been better," Kira replied. "The interview with Gary went okay, I guess."

"And Rudy?"

"He peed on my pillow this morning."

"Well, you abandoned him. He's still mad at you."

"I guess. Hold on—"

Pressing the phone against her ear, she looked both ways to cross the street. But just as she jumped into the crosswalk a motorcycle made a left turn, going too fast.

She felt a surge of panic, but it was too late. In the next moment, she was hurled into the air.

It was true what they said about your life flashing before your eyes.

She saw Quinn's darkly handsome face and knew suddenly, without a doubt, that she loved him.

It didn't matter that he could never love her. Or maybe she knew, on some deep level, that he must love her, too— at least a little.

She remembered all the times he'd looked at her and she'd felt her soul join to his.

She'd been an idiot to walk out on the man she loved, to

abandon a man so afraid of love that he denied what was in his own heart. He needed her.

She wanted to get up and run back to his office. She wanted to beg him for another chance. But when she tried to sit up, her body felt as if it were made of concrete.

Someone knelt over her, but she couldn't see his face.

"Quinn," she cried. "I want Quinn."

The man spoke, but she couldn't hear what he said.

Then everything went black.

"A Jerry Sullivan is here to see you," Quinn's secretary informed him crisply. "Says he's family."

"Show him in," Quinn ordered in a dull voice as he set the lightning whelk Kira had given him back on the shelf. "He's my uncle. He'll want coffee with cream and sugar."

Uncle Jerry didn't wait for Quinn's secretary to return with his coffee before he pounced.

"Sorry to interrupt you, but I just heard you separated from your beautiful wife. I'd ask you to tell me it isn't true, but since you look like something my dog dragged in from the gutter, I won't bother."

"Good to see you, too, Uncle J."

"What the hell did you do to drive her away?"

"I never should have married her in the first place."

"If you let her go, you'll be making the biggest mistake of your life. You've already wasted too many years of your life alone."

"Let me be, why don't you?"

"You're still in love with her. I can see it!"

"The hell I am. Did anybody ever tell you to mind your own business?"

"Sure. You. Plenty of times. Good thing I've got better sense than to listen to the likes of an upstart nephew who doesn't have a clue about what's good for him."

"I think some men are better off single. And I'm probably one of them."

"Bull. I saw the way you were with her. You're like your father. He was the most loving man I ever knew."

"And what did it get him—other than a broken heart and an early grave?"

"You're not your father. Kira's not Esther. Kira's the real thing. Esther was a beautiful woman who knew how to play your dad. And, yes, your dad foolishly loved her with all his heart—just like he loved you. But when you get down to it, even when you're wrong about the people you love, loving is still the best way to live. That's why we still miss Kade. He loved us all so much!"

"My father killed himself because my mother left him."

"You'll never make me believe that! Kade wouldn't ever deliberately walk out on you. You were everything to him. His death was an accident."

"Uncle Jerry, thanks for coming by."

"Great. Now you're giving me the brush-off."

"I know you mean well...but I'm a grown man—"

"Who has the right to screw up his life royally and who's doing a damn good job of it."

"If you've said your piece, I've got work to do."

"You've always got work to do! Maybe it's time you got a life." Uncle Jerry smiled grimly. "Okay, I'll leave you to it, not that it's any fun watching my favorite nephew walk out on the best thing that ever happened to him."

"I didn't walk out on her! Damn it! She left me!"

"So, quit sulking, and go after her!"

"If only it were that easy!"

"Trust me—it is. The only thing stopping you is your damn arrogance."

"Get the hell out of here!"

Holding a silver tray with a coffee cup, Quinn's secretary pushed the door open and would have entered except Quinn held up a hand. "Uncle Jerry won't be having coffee after all. He's leaving."

For some time after his uncle had gone, Quinn sat in his office and seethed. Slowly, as he cooled down, everything the older man had said began replaying in his mind. Since his father's death, Uncle Jerry was the one person Quinn had been able to count on.

Quinn walked over to the shelf where he'd placed the lightning whelk. How full of hope he'd felt when she'd given it to him. He remembered her shining eyes, her glowing beauty.

Turning away, he grabbed his cell phone. For a long moment he just held it.

Quinn didn't just want to call Kira for his own selfish reasons. He was genuinely worried about her and the baby. The longer he went without talking to her, the more worried he grew. Would it be so wrong to call just to make sure she and the baby were all right? Would it? Even if they never got back together, she was the mother of his future child.

Swallowing his pride, he lifted his phone and punched in her number. As he waited for her to answer, his gut clenched.

Then, on the third ring, a man answered.

"I want Kira," Quinn thundered. "I need to speak to my wife."

"Sir, I'm so sorry. I'm terribly afraid there's been an accident…"

The man introduced himself as someone working at the local hospital. He said something about a motorcycle hitting Kira and that Kira had been taken to his emergency room by ambulance. After getting the specifics, Quinn hung up and was grabbing his jacket and on his way to the door, when Earl Murray rang his cell phone.

Quinn picked up on the first ring. "I just heard Kira's been hurt."

"Apparently, Jaycee was talking to her when the motorcycle hit her… I don't know anything else."

"Then I'll meet you at the hospital," Quinn said. His heart was in his throat as he bolted out of his office in a dead run, praying he wouldn't be too late.

Sixteen

Quinn had never been as scared in his life as he was when he stood over Kira watching the IV drip clear liquid into her veins. Her narrow face had the awful grayish tint Quinn had seen only one time before—on his father's face as he'd lain in a pool of his own blood.

"Tell me she's going to be all right. Tell me the baby's all right."

"I've told you," the doctor repeated patiently. "Apparently, she was thrown onto the pavement, but seems to have suffered only a concussion and a few bruises. After a night or two of rest, she and the baby will be fine. She's one lucky young lady."

"You're sure?" For some reason, the facts weren't sticking in Quinn's head as they usually did.

"As sure as I can be under the circumstances."

"When will she wake up?"

"Like I told you before—soon. You just have to be patient."

An hour later, the longest hour of Quinn's life, her long lashes fluttered. Sensing that she was struggling to focus on him, Quinn gripped her hand and leaned forward.

"Kira… Darlin'…"

"Quinn… I wanted you to come. I wanted it so much."

"Kira, you're in a hospital. You're going to be okay. The baby, too."

"I love you," she said softly. "I was such a fool."

Rather than terrifying him, those three words brought a rush of joy.

"I love you, too. More than anything." He squeezed her hand tightly. "So much it scares the hell out of me."

It had only taken her admission to make him brave enough to admit his own feelings for her.

With glistening eyes, she laughed softly. "You really love me?"

"Yes. Maybe even from the first moment I saw you. I just didn't know what had hit me." He paused. "Jaycee's here, along with your parents. We've all been so scared for you and the baby. Half out of our minds."

"They're all here, too?"

"Of course we're here," her father roared.

Kira smiled radiantly up at them. "It's almost worth getting hit by a motorcycle to have all of you all here… together, knowing…knowing that you love me."

They moved closer, circling her bed. Holding hands, they smiled down at her. "Of course we love you," her father said. "You're our girl."

"You gave us a terrible scare," her mother said. "You're very important to all of us."

"I'm so happy," Kira whispered. "I've never been happier."

"By the way," her father said, "your old boss called and said you'd better get well soon because you've got a big job at the museum waiting for you. So, no more waitressing…"

Kira smiled weakly. "I guess that's good news…but not nearly as good as all of you being here." Her grip on Quinn's hand tightened as she looked up at him. "I never, ever want to let go of you again."

"You won't have to."

Quinn needed no further encouragement to lean forward and kiss her. Very carefully, so as not to hurt her, he pressed his mouth to her lips.

As always, she gave her entire being to him, causing warmth and happiness to flow from her soul into his.

She was everything to him. He would love her and cherish her always, or at least until the last breath left his body.

"Darlin'," he whispered. "Promise me you'll never leave me again."

She nodded. "Never. I swear it. Like I said, I was a fool."

Circling his neck with her hands, she brought his face down to hers and kissed him again.

Epilogue

One Year Later
July the Fourth
Wimberley, Texas

Kira looked across the green lawns that sloped down to cypress trees shading the sparkling river. The air stirring through the leaves was warm, while the water was clear and icy.

Kira couldn't believe her happiness. Ever since that afternoon in the hospital, when she'd awakened to Quinn and her family gathered around her bed, her happiness had grown a little every day.

Despite the pain in her shoulder and back, she'd seen the love shining in all their eyes.

Love for her.

Had it always been there? Whether it had or not, all her doubts about herself, about Quinn, about her adoption, had vanished. She'd simply known that she mattered—to all of them.

She belonged.

Knowing she was truly loved, her confidence had grown in every aspect of her life, including in her career as a curator. Naturally, Gary had been thrilled that she was to remain Mrs. Sullivan. Quinn had thrilled him even more by being most generous to the museum, stipulating with every donation that his wife be in charge of the funds.

This lazy summer afternoon on the grounds of the Sullivans' new weekend home on the Blanco was perfect for a July Fourth celebration that included friends, family and business associates. The star of the show was only a few months old.

Thomas Kade Sullivan fulfilled his mother's most fervent hopes as he sat on his red-and-blue quilt by the water, holding court. He shook his rattle while Aunt Jaycee laughed and held up a stuffed bunny rabbit. With his brilliant blue eyes, Tommy Kade was every bit as handsome as his father.

Off to one side, a band played as their guests took turns swimming in the cool waters or serving themselves barbecue.

Quinn left the men he'd been talking to and walked up to her. Grinning down at her, he circled her with his arms. Contentment made her feel soft and warm as he held her close. Never had she dreamed she'd feel this complete with anyone.

She smiled at the sight of her mother ordering the caterers about. With her illness in remission, her mother was her old formidable self. When Vera had been well enough for Kira's dad to leave her at home, Quinn had made a place for him at Murray Oil.

"Murray Oil's too big for one man to run," Quinn had said when Kira had tried to thank him.

Life was good, she thought as her husband brushed his lips against her cheek. Very good.

"Happy July Fourth," Quinn said.

"The happiest ever."

"For me, too. Because you're in my life," he murmured huskily. "You're the best thing that ever happened to me... besides Tommy Kade. And you're responsible for him, too."

"Stop. We're at a party. We have to behave."

"Maybe I don't want to behave."

He drew her away from the crowd into the shade of the towering cypress trees. Once they were hidden from their guests, he wrapped her in his arms and kissed her long and deeply.

"I love you," he whispered. "I love you, and I always will. We have a real marriage, now—wouldn't you agree?"

The most wonderful thing of all was that she knew it and accepted it—down to her bones—because she felt exactly the same way. "I would! And I love you, too," she murmured. "Oh, how I love you."

* * * * *

A BABY FOR
THE BOSS

MAUREEN CHILD

To Sarah and Dan—
Ten years is something to celebrate
As we celebrate the two of you every day
We love you

One

"I don't trust her." Mike Ryan drummed his fingertips on his desktop and glared at his younger brother.

"Yeah," Sean said on a laugh. "You've made that clear for months. What *isn't* clear is why. She's a terrific artist, meets her deadlines, is easy to get along with and a hell of a baker—she's always bringing goodies in for everyone. So how about you tell me what Jenny Marshall ever did that you're so against her."

Scowling, Mike gritted his teeth and shifted his gaze to the view out his office window. Even in Southern California, January gardens looked a little grim. The backyard of the Victorian mansion that served as Celtic Knot Gaming's office boasted dry, brown grass, leafless trees and empty flower beds. The sky was studded with gray clouds and a cold wind swept in off the ocean to rattle those bare tree limbs.

Still, looking at that dismal view was better than draw-ing up a mental image of Jenny Marshall. As unwilling as he was, though, that picture of her flashed across his brain. She was a damn munchkin, only standing about five foot two, but that tiny body was really packed well. She had curves that made Mike's mouth water every time he saw her—especially since he already knew just what those curves looked like *naked*. One more reason he tried to avoid running into her.

Her short blond hair was a mass of curls that ended at her jawline, stirring up a grown man's idle daydreams into fantasies of hot, sweaty nights. Instantly, he forced his mind away from the images of naked Jenny and in-stead thought of her eyes. As blue as the sky, bright with lies—and once, glazed with passion—for him.

Okay, that's enough of that, he told himself firmly.

"I've got my reasons," he muttered, not bothering to look at his brother again.

Sean had no clue that Mike and Jenny had met long before she was hired at Celtic Knot and there was no reason for that to change.

"Fine." Sean blew out a breath. "Always were a hard-head. Anyway, doesn't matter what the reasons are. You, me and Brady already decided this."

"Brady's in Ireland."

"Yep," Sean said, then added, "ain't technology great? You do remember the meeting we had over webcam? The one where we *all* decided who would do which hotel?"

"I remember."

"Good. Because Jenny's in her office right now, work-ing on the designs for the River Haunt hotel." Sean met his brother's gaze. "She's already coming up with some great stuff. If we switch designers at this stage, it's going to slow down everything. Besides, Jenny's good. She *earned* this."

Mike scowled and bit back any further argument because it just wouldn't do any good. Sean was right: the plans had been made. He couldn't change them now. All of the artists for the company had already been assigned their work schedules. Most of them were finishing up the graphics for the next game to be released in the coming summer. So Jenny was the only logical choice.

Didn't mean he had to like it.

But there were deadlines to meet and no one knew that better than Mike. He, his brother and their friend Brady Finn had begun this gaming company when they were still in college. Their first game had been short on art and long on mystery and action. It had taken off faster than any of them had hoped and by the time they graduated from college, they were all millionaires.

They'd plowed their money back into the company they called Celtic Knot and within six months had released a bigger, more sophisticated game. They built a reputation for action games based on ancient Irish legends and superstitions, and their fan base swelled.

They'd bought this old Victorian in Long Beach, California, as their home base and hired the very best computer programmers, and digital and graphic artists.

They'd won awards and had legions of fans waiting for the release of their next game. And now, they were growing in another direction.

They were buying three hotels and revamping them into perfect role-playing venues for guests. Each hotel would be modeled after one of their top-selling games. The first, Fate Castle, was in Ireland. The modifications had just recently been completed and the hotel would be open and welcoming guests in March. The second, River Haunt, was in Nevada on the Colorado River and was just waiting for Mike to step up and get the renovations moving forward.

But how the hell could he do that while working one-on-one with Jenny Marshall? Answer: he couldn't. But he wasn't prepared to go into all of the reasons why with Sean. Instead, he'd simply go to Jenny. Convince her to back off this project. She was probably in no more hurry to work with him than he was with her. If she went to Sean herself and asked to be replaced, there wouldn't be a problem. Mike would offer her a raise. Or a bonus. A woman like her would jump at a chance for that—and he'd be able to get on with the hotel transformation.

"Meantime," Sean said, loudly enough to snap Mike's attention back to the moment, "I'm still talking to the toy company about the line of collectibles they're proposing based on our gaming characters."

"What do the lawyers say?" Mike asked.

"Plenty," Sean admitted. "And most of it I can't understand. I swear they teach these people to speak in tongues when they're in law school."

"Agreed. How much did you get out of it?"

Sean crossed his legs, ankle on knee. "Enough to know that if they up their offer on the licensing fee, this could be a really good thing for us."

"I don't know… Toys?"

"Not toys. Collectibles," Sean corrected. "I called Brady this morning and he's on board. So think about this, Mike. At the next gaming convention we not only have the games to push, but the collectibles. We can spin that off to board games even, for people not interested in video games."

Mike laughed shortly and leaned back in his chair. "There aren't many people uninterested in games."

"Okay, true. But we're pushing into the hotel industry, giving people a chance to live their favorite games. We could take that another step," Sean said, slapping one hand down on Mike's desk. "We can sponsor our own conventions."

"What?" Surprised, Mike just stared at him.

Sean grinned. "Think about it. Hell, Comic-Con started out small and look at them now. We could hold Celtic Knot Con—an entire convention centered around our games and products. We can host tournaments, offer prizes. Costume contests. Hell, we could run a contest offering a contract to whoever comes up with the best new beast to use in one of our games."

"Did you go surfing this morning?"

Sean stopped. "What's that got to do with anything?"

"That water's cold, probably froze a few brain cells."

"Funny."

"Don't you think we've got enough going on right now? The latest game came out in December, and the sequel to 'Fate Castle' hits this summer, not to mention the hotel business."

"Okay, we're busy," Sean allowed. "We want to *stay* busy, we have to keep thinking, expanding. Our business is based on the fans. On the way they feel connected to the scenarios we create. If we give them more, offer them other ways to connect, to feel a part of the world they love, that can only benefit us."

Mike thought about it for a minute. He could see the enthusiasm on his brother's face and knew that Sean was at least partly right. Continuing to build their brand would only solidify their position in the marketplace.

The castle hotel in Ireland already had a waiting list six months long and they hadn't even opened yet. That told Mike there was a huge market for just what Sean was describing. And little brother was right about something else, too.

"We'll talk to Brady about your convention idea—that may be a good way to go."

"Whoa." Sean grinned. "This is a moment. Maybe I should hunt up a photographer."

Mike laughed. "Okay, fine. I think you're onto something. On the collectibles, I'm on board. Tell the lawyers to work up the company's licensing offer and then we'll sign."

"Already did," Sean said.

"Sure of yourself, weren't you?"

"Damn right."

Amused, Mike said, "Okay, well, you're right about the other stuff, too. The role-playing, the contests. Ireland's too hard for a lot of people to get to. The grounds on the hotel in Nevada aren't big enough for us to hold tournaments on any kind of real scale. So the hotel in Wyoming will have to be the base for that kind of growth."

"Just what I was thinking," Sean said. "It's on a hundred and fifty acres, with lakes and forests. It's perfect for the kind of thing I'm talking about."

"Then it's handy you're in charge of that one, isn't it?"

"Also what I was thinking," Sean said with a quick, smug smile.

It was the smug part that had Mike suggesting, "You should go to Wyoming. Check it out in person."

Sean snorted. "Sure. That'll happen. It's *January*, Mike. It's snowing there. Like crazy cold snowing." He shivered. "No, thank you. Look, we bought the property in Ireland by checking it out online and that worked great."

"Yeah, but—"

"I've talked to the Realtor, had her make videos of everything. The inn itself needs a lot of work, but the property is perfect and that's more important, right?"

"Yeah, but—"

"You take care of yours and I'll take care of mine. No worries, I'll go look around in a few months, *before* we start the design stage." Sean stood up and looked down at Mike. "Right now, though, I'm dealing with the big Game Con in Chicago next month. And I've got the art on 'Banshee Screams' to oversee. I'll get to Wyoming," he said. "But it can wait until summer…" Shaking his head, he laughed and headed for the door. "A surfer. In the snow. Yeah. That'll work."

Mike frowned after him. Brady was happy as hell, working and living in Ireland with his wife and new baby son. Sean was busy making plans to be a happy, surfing megalomaniac. So, it was only Mike staring at nothing but trouble. It would take at least six months to refit the Nevada hotel. And since he couldn't find a way to get her off the project, that meant a hell of a lot of time spent with Jenny Marshall.

A woman who had already lied to him once.

Yeah. This was gonna be great.

Jenny Marshall poured herself a glass of white wine and sat down in an overstuffed chair, ordering herself to relax. But she didn't take orders well, not even from herself. Curling her feet up under her, Jenny looked out the window at the neighbor kids playing basketball in the driveway across the street.

The duplex she rented was old and small. Built in the 1940s, it sat on a narrow street a few blocks from the beach. The rent was too high, but the place itself was cozy, close to work and less generic than some cramped apartment. Here, she could garden and go to block parties and buy Girl Scout cookies and football pizzas from the kids who lived on the street. Here, Jenny felt that she was…connected. A part of things. And for a woman alone, that feeling was priceless.

She took a sip of her wine and shifted her gaze to the front yard, where bare trees clattered in the wind. Twilight fell over the neighborhood in a soft lavender glow and lamplight began blooming in her neighbors' windows. Relaxation still eluded her, but with everything she had on her mind that really wasn't a surprise.

Between her work on the upcoming game from Celtic Knot and the designs she was working on for the River Haunt hotel, there was plenty to think about. She did love her job and was grateful for it. Especially since one of her bosses would like nothing better than to fire her—or to see her drop into a black hole and simply disappear.

She frowned into her glass and tried to ignore the pain of regret that clutched at her heart. It hadn't been easy, working with Mike Ryan for the past several months. Every time they were in the same room together, she felt hostility coming off him in waves so thick it nearly choked her. The man was hard-hearted, stubborn, unreasonable and…still the one man who made her insides quiver.

She lifted her glass of wine in a toast to her own stupidity.

Seriously, hadn't she learned her lesson more than a year ago? When they met that night in Phoenix, it had been magic, pure and simple. And, like any good fairy tale, the magic had lasted exactly one night. Then Prince Charming had turned into an ogre and Jenny's proverbial glass slippers were flip-flops again.

It had all started out so well, too. The night before a big gaming convention in Phoenix, Jenny had met a tall, gorgeous man with a wicked smile and eyes as blue as a summer sky. They had a drink together in the bar, then had dinner, then took a walk and finally had ended up in her room at the convention hotel. She'd never done that before—gone to bed with a man she barely knew. But that night, everything had been…different. From the moment she met Mike, she'd felt as if she had somehow only been *waiting* for him to walk into her life. Which, she could admit now, was absolutely ridiculous. But that night… Jenny had allowed her heart to rule her head. She'd given in to the rush of attraction, that *zing* of something special that she'd only ever felt for him. And by morning, Jenny knew she'd made a huge mistake.

Sighing, she laid her head against the back of the chair, closed her eyes and drifted back to the moment when the floor had opened up beneath her feet. The morning *after* the best night of her life.

Mike pulled her close and Jenny laid her head on his chest, listening to the steady beat of his heart. Her body was loose and languid from a long night of loving. Dawn streaked the morning sky with pale rose and gold and she was nowhere near wanting to get out of bed.

This was so unlike her, she thought, smiling to herself. She didn't do one-night stands and never with a veritable stranger. But she couldn't regret any of it. From the moment she'd met Mike, she'd felt as if she'd known him forever. She didn't even know his last name, yet she felt closer to him at that moment than she had to anyone else.

"Really hate to move from this spot," Mike said, "but I've got to get down to the convention floor early."

"I know. Me, too." Jenny cuddled in closer. "My uncle needs me to set up his booth. He can't get here until tomorrow, so..."

Mike ran one hand up and down her back and his fingertips felt like tiny sparks of heat against her skin.

"Yeah?" Mike asked, his voice low and slow and lazy. "Who's your uncle?"

"Hmm?" She was nearly hypnotized by the slide of his fingers and the deep rumble of his voice. "Oh. Hank Snyder," she whispered. "He owns Snyder Arts."

Mike suddenly went still. His hand dropped from her back and she felt a hard shift in the lovely little glow they'd been sharing. Then there was a physical shift as Mike pushed to a sitting position and rolled Jenny right off his chest.

She plopped onto the bed and stared up at him. "What?"

"Hank Snyder?" Mike jumped out of bed and stood staring down at her with a wild, dark gleam in his eyes, sharp as a knife blade. With the morning light streaming in through the window behind him, he looked like a naked avenging angel.

The haze in her mind was clearing and a cold, sinking sensation opened in the pit of her stomach. Slowly, she sat up and tugged the blankets over her breasts. Pushing one hand through her hair, she shoved blond curls out of her eyes and met his hard gaze with a look of confusion. "What's wrong?" she asked. "Do you know my uncle?"

He snorted. "Wow. That's really good. The little hint of innocence in your voice? Nice touch."

Completely confused now, she shook her head. People should not be expected to be coherent in the morning before several cups of coffee. "Innocence? What?"

"Oh, drop it," Mike snapped and stalked across the room to snatch up his clothes. He dragged them on as he talked, flicking her quick, icy glances. "Gotta say, you were good."

"What are you talking about?" The sheet where he'd been lying only a moment ago was rapidly cooling and she shivered in response. "Good at what? You're not making sense."

"Sure. You're confused." Mike nodded. "You know, I bought the whole act last night, but trying to keep it up now, when I know who you are, is only pissing me off."

She didn't have the first clue what he was so angry about, but her own temper was beginning to boil in self-defense. How could they have gone from lovemaking, to snuggling, to spitting ice at each other all in the blink of an eye?

"Will you just tell me what's going on?"

"What I don't get is how you knew I'd be in the bar last night." He pulled his long-sleeved white shirt on and buttoned it with an almost eerie calm that belied the fury in his voice and eyes.

"I didn't know—heck, I didn't even know I was going to be in the bar last night until just before I went in."

"Sure. Your uncle," Mike said, nodding. "He had to have planned all this for you anyway."

"What does Uncle Hank have to do with us?"

He laughed but there was no charm or humor in it. "Everything, sweetheart, and we both know it. Snyder

Arts has been trying to get us to incorporate their pro-grams into our games for the past year and a half." His gaze dropped to her chest, then lifted to her eyes again. "Looks like Ol' Hank finally decided to pull out the big guns."

Every word Mike said echoed weirdly in her mind until at last, Jenny understood what he meant. What he was accusing her of. Anger leaped into a full boil in the pit of her stomach. Her heart pounded crazily and she felt as if she couldn't catch her breath. Her mind racing, Jenny practically leaped out of bed, preferring to meet her accuser on her feet. She held the blanket up in front of her like a shield that could somehow protect her from the ice in his eyes.

"You think my uncle sent me here to have sex with you?" God, she could barely force the words past her tight throat. "So I could convince you to use his arts program?"

"That about sums it up," Mike said flatly.

Jenny's brain burned. She was torn between insult, fury and complete humiliation. Instantly, images of the night before streamed through her mind like a movie on fast-forward. She saw him, over her, staring into her eyes as his body claimed hers. She saw herself, straddling him, taking him deep inside her. And she felt in that flash of heat the pleasure, the sense of completion his every touch caused. Then the mind movie ended abruptly, and she was here, in this sunlit room, staring at a stranger who now knew her body intimately, but her heart and soul not at all.

"Who the hell do you think you are?" she asked, voice trembling.

"Mike Ryan."

She staggered at the name. Mike Ryan. One of the owners of Celtic Knot. Jenny knew their work, knew the art and graphic design that went into every one of their games. She'd admired them for years, had hoped to one day work for them—which wouldn't happen now. Not only did he clearly think she was a spy—and oh yes, a whore—but she couldn't imagine herself working for a man who made snap decisions with zero thought behind them.

"Uh-huh," he said, nodding as if he'd just had every one of his suspicions verified. "So you do know me."

"Now," she said. "I didn't last night. Not when I met you. Not when we..." *She pushed one hand through her hair and kept clutching the blanket with the other. Best not to think about everything they'd done because she'd do something completely stupid like blush, for heaven's sake. With her fair skin, the moment she was embarrassed, her cheeks lit up like a red light at an intersection.*

"And I'm supposed to take your word for that," he said.

Her gaze sharpened and narrowed on him. "It seems you don't need anything but your own suspicions to make up your mind. You've already decided who and what I am, why should I argue with you over it?"

"You know, playing the outraged innocent isn't nearly as convincing as the seductress I met last night."

She sucked in a gulp of air and fed the flames burning in her belly. "You arrogant, conceited, smug bastard."

One dark eyebrow winged up and a look of pure male amusement tugged at the corners of his mouth. "Doing better now. The outrage almost looks real."

Her heart pounded so hard in her chest it was a won-

der he couldn't hear it. She half expected her heart to crash right through her rib cage. "This isn't an act, you jackass. Think about it. I didn't seduce you. You approached me in the bar. And nobody forced you into my bed. As I remember it you came willingly enough."

"Several times," he said, playing on her words just to irritate her further.

It worked.

"That's it. I don't have to listen to any more of your paranoid ramblings. Get out of my room." She swung one hand toward the door and stabbed the air with her index finger.

He grabbed his black jacket off a nearby chair and shrugged it on. "Oh, I'm going. No worries there. I wouldn't stay if you begged me to."

"That's not gonna happen."

He snorted again, a particularly annoying, insulting sound. Striding across the room to the door, he stopped before he opened it and looked back over his shoulder at her. "Tell your uncle I said nice try, but no cigar. Celtic Knot won't be doing a deal with him no matter how many attractive nieces he tosses into my bed."

Jenny picked up a wineglass from the room service tray they'd shared the night before and hurled it at him. He was through the door and out before the glass shattered against the wood to lie in splinters on the floor.

Jenny sighed and took another sip of her wine. She hadn't thought to even see Mike Ryan again, but then six months later, his brother, Sean, had offered her a job that was simply too good to pass up. The chance to work on the kind of art she loved was worth the risk of being around Mike every day. And frankly, by being on-site every day, she was silently telling Mike Ryan that what he'd done hadn't hurt her. Hadn't crushed her. Of course that was a big, fat lie, but he didn't have to know that. Working at Celtic Knot was a dream that only occasionally became a nightmare when she was forced to deal with Mike.

Of course now, the nightmare would be a 24/7 thing for the next few months. Yes, she was excited about being the artist to design the murals for the River Haunt hotel. But having to work one-on-one with Mike was going to make it all so much more grueling than it should have been. Still, she wouldn't back off. Oh, Jenny knew that Mike wanted her off the project, but this was too big an opportunity for her to turn tail and run. Especially, she reminded herself, since she'd done nothing wrong.

He was the one who had plenty to apologize for. He was the one who'd insulted her, humiliated her and then stomped off without so much as listening to her side of the story.

So why should *she* be the one to pay a price?

The knock on her door interrupted her thoughts and she told herself, if it was a salesman, she'd buy whatever he was selling out of simple gratitude.

She opened the door and stared up into Mike Ryan's blazing blue eyes. Without waiting to be invited in, he pushed his way past her and marched into her apartment with all the determination of Grant taking Richmond.

With little else to do but accept the inevitable, Jenny closed the door. "Well, do come in," she said, every word dripping with sarcasm. "Make yourself at home."

Features grim, eyes the color of a lake frozen over, he said, "We need to talk."

Two

Mike stopped in the middle of the room, turned and just looked at her. She wore a pale green T-shirt and faded, curve-hugging jeans with a hole at the knee. Her small, narrow feet were bare but for the pale pink nail polish. Her hair was a rumpled mass of tumbling blond curls and her wide blue eyes were fixed on him warily. She looked good. Too damned good, and that was part of the problem.

Stuffing both hands into his pockets, just to keep from reaching for her, Mike deliberately looked away from Jenny and glanced around the small living room. His gaze picked out the details even as his brain reminded him not to let her distract him. Great body, beautiful eyes and kissable lips notwithstanding, he had come here for a reason and he had to keep his focus.

The duplex was old, probably one of the original beach

cottages built in the late 1930s. Jenny's home was well kept, casual and welcoming. There were overstuffed chairs covered in a flowery fabric and a love seat boasting yellow and blue stripes. Several small tables and standing brass lamps were scattered about the room, shining puddles of golden light onto the scarred but polished wood floors and the few rugs that broke up the space. The walls were painted a soft green that reminded him of spring. There were framed paintings and photographs clustered together in no discernible pattern and on one wall, there was a mural.

His gaze caught it and held. Obviously, Jenny had painted it herself and Mike had to admit that whatever else she was, the woman was also immensely talented. The mural was a scene straight out of a fairy tale—or an Irish legend. A forest, just waking up to daylight. Fog drifted across the landscape in thin gray wisps, sunlight speared through the trees to lie in a dappled pattern on the leaf-strewn ground. There was a hint of a flower-laden meadow in the distance and in the towering trees were fairies, delicate wings looking as if they would flutter any minute.

Damn it. He hated that she was this good.

"Why are you here, Mike?" Her voice was soft, but the glint in her eye was anything but.

Good question. Mike knew he probably shouldn't have come here—they hadn't been alone together since that night in Phoenix—but he had run out of options. He couldn't tell Sean why working with Jenny was a mistake—because damned if he'd let his little brother know that he'd once been taken for a ride. In more ways than one.

But Jenny knew why this wouldn't work. All he had

to do was get her to tell Sean she didn't want the job of designing the art for the new hotel. And if Jenny herself requested that she be let out of the project, Sean wouldn't object.

Time to get to the point so Mike could get the hell out of this too-small house where her scent seemed to hover in the air for the express purpose of tormenting him. "I want you to back out of the hotel job."

She didn't even blink. "Interesting. Well, I want to be three inches taller and have smaller boobs. Looks like we're both doomed to disappointment."

Why the hell she would want smaller breasts was beyond him, but not the point. "We both know that working together for months is a bad idea."

"Agreed." She crossed her arms over her chest, pushing her breasts higher. "Maybe you're the one who should quit. Switch hotels with Sean. I *like* Sean."

"Leave Sean alone," Mike ground out.

Her oh-so-casual pose evaporated and she threw her hands high in frustration. "Please. Now you're afraid I'm going to be paid to seduce Sean?"

"I didn't say that." Thought it, maybe. Said it, no. All right, he admitted silently, he hadn't even thought it. Not really.

"What exactly *are* you saying, Mike?" She plopped both hands on her hips and the movement tightened the fabric of her shirt against the aforementioned breasts. *Distractions*, Mike told himself. *Pay no attention.*

"I'm saying leave Sean out of this," he said. "It's between you and me."

"Fine. Then *you* tell Sean he should take over the River Haunt and you do the Wyoming place."

"No." He wasn't ready to admit defeat yet. He could

still find a way to convince Jenny that this was an impossible situation and that it was up to *her* to back off.

She shrugged again, and walked past him slowly enough that the scent of her vanilla perfume flavored the breath he took and held as she made for the chair by the wide window.

"So, since neither one of us is willing to drop out of this project, I guess we're done here," she said, plopping into the chair and lifting her wineglass for a sip.

"We are far from done." Through the window behind her, he saw the street was dark, with the dim glow of lamplight shining through a neighbor's drapes.

January nights at the beach could be cold, but here in this tiny duplex, Mike felt only the heat of being near her again. Her hair shone, her eyes glittered and her mouth curved up at one corner when she spoke. She was enjoying this, he thought, and a part of him liked that about her.

Jenny Marshall didn't back down for anyone. He'd seen her go head-to-head with older, more experienced artists, defending her designs and techniques. She held her own in meetings and wasn't afraid to fight for her vision of things. But as much as he admired those traits, he wished she wasn't currently turning her admirable qualities on *him*.

"Mike, you don't want to work with me and I don't want to work with you. But we're stuck with each other." She lifted one shoulder in a half shrug. "We'll have to make the best of it."

"Unacceptable." Shaking his head, he looked away from her because the damn lamplight made her hair shine like burnished gold. He never should have come here. It had been a bad idea and if he were smart, he'd leave right now since their argument was getting them exactly nowhere.

As he sifted through dozens of pretty much useless thoughts, his gaze fixed on the magical forest mural. It was dark, mysterious, but with the fairies in the limbs of the trees, there was a sense of playfulness amid the darkness and the longer he looked at it, the more fairies he spotted. Hiding behind leaves, beside rocks, in the water of a fast-moving stream. It was hypnotic, mystical.

He shifted to look at her. "Damn good work," he blurted, before he could stop himself.

"Thanks." Surprise flitted across her face, then vanished. "But if you're wondering, I didn't *steal* that scene from any of Celtic Knot's games."

He fired a look at her that had been known to make stone-hearted business rivals quake. Jenny wasn't fazed. "I didn't say you stole it."

"Not yet," she told him, pausing for another sip of wine. "I'm sure you'll get to it. I know very well what you think of me."

"Do you blame me?" he countered. Mike pushed one hand through his hair, then scrubbed that hand across the back of his neck. Ever since he met her, this woman had had the ability to tangle him up into knots. Even knowing she was a damn liar hadn't taken away the rush he'd felt every time he thought of her.

At work, he kept his distance, knowing it was best for everyone. Coming here, into her place, being alone with her in the lamp-lit dark was dangerous. He knew it, and still he didn't leave. Instead, he took a single step toward her and stopped because her scent clouded his mind and he couldn't afford to addle his brain any more than it already was.

"That's not a fair question," she answered. "You made up your mind about me in an instant and never once listened to any side but your own."

"What other side *was* there?" he countered. "Hell, your uncle is still running Snyder Arts."

"Oh, for God's sake," she snapped, setting her wineglass onto the table with a harsh click.

"Tell me I'm wrong."

"How can I? He does own Snyder Arts. He doesn't own me."

"He's family." Mike shrugged.

"Yeah, and he thinks enough of me that he's never asked me to do what you continue to imply I've already done." She sucked in air, then blew it out. "Sean's never questioned my integrity."

"Sean's more trusting than I am."

"News flash," she muttered, then asked, "Would you lie and cheat for your family?"

"No, I wouldn't." Mike had grown up knowing exactly what kind of damage lies could do. As a kid, he'd promised himself he'd avoid lies and the people who told them. That's why he couldn't trust Jenny. First time he met her, she'd lied. No going back from that.

Her eyes flashed. "But you assume I would."

"Don't have to assume a damn thing," he reminded her.

"My God, you have a thick head." She huffed out a breath. "At least come up with a *new* crime to accuse me of. I didn't use you then. I'm not using you now."

"I'm pretty sure every thief claims innocence."

She pushed out of her chair, stalked toward him and was forced to tip her head back to meet his eyes. "Name me *one* thing I've stolen. Give me *one* reason you have the right to call me a thief."

"Fine," he said, staring into her eyes until he could actually see her anger churning and burning. "You haven't stolen anything that I know of. Yet. You're a prethief."

"Then why haven't you fired me or told Sean to?"

"I do my own firing," he said. "And if I ever have proof that you've betrayed us, then I will fire you so fast your head will spin. Suspicion isn't proof."

She laughed shortly and shook her head. Then she took a long step back, and folded her arms beneath those magnificent breasts. "Boy, you're really reaching. Being a prethief is like being prepregnant. Or prepublished. All that means is you're *not* something. Like I'm *not* a thief, so I'd appreciate it if you'd quit throwing accusations around that you can't back up."

Damn, the angrier she was, the hotter she got. Bright spots of color dotted her cheeks and her blue eyes were flashing dangerously. What did it say about him that her temper only fueled the need inside him?

Most of the women in his life agreed with him, smiled coyly, flirted outrageously and in general made sure they were pleasant company. Jenny didn't give a damn about any of that. She had an opinion and wasn't afraid to share it and that was just as sexy as the way her eyes glittered.

And sexy wasn't the point.

"We both know what's going on here, Jenny," he argued. "You might not want to admit it—and who could blame you—but the fact is, your uncle owns a company that would like nothing better than to have a contract with Celtic Knot. You meet me 'accidentally,' go to bed with me and try to convince me you're not colluding with your uncle?" She opened her mouth to argue, but he rushed on before she could. "Then months later, you come to work for us, grab a job as head designer."

"I didn't 'grab' anything," she snapped. "Sean came to me and offered me the job."

He'd never told Sean about his time with Jenny. Maybe if he had, his younger brother wouldn't have hired her in the first place. Which, Mike was forced to admit, would have been a damn shame. As much as she managed to irritate him, she was a hell of an artist.

"Sean asked, but you took it." He tipped his head to one side and studied her. "So the question is, why? You miss me? Or are you some kind of corporate spy now?"

"Now I'm a spy? Wow," she said, slowly shaking her head. "Paranoia reaches new heights."

He snorted. "I'm not paranoid if you really are a spy."

"You're amazing."

"So it's been said."

She threw her hands up. "There's no talking to you. So think whatever you want," she told him, voice as icy as her eyes were hot. "You have from the beginning."

"Right. When we met at the gaming con in Phoenix. Another coincidence?" His eyebrow lifted. "You just happened to be at my hotel?"

"Or," she countered, "you arrogant jackass, *you* happened to be at *my* hotel."

Surprise almost had him laughing. Almost. But she was too furious and he was too sure he was right. There was nothing funny about being cheated. Lied to. Old memories of his mother crying, his father shamefaced, rose up in his mind, and Mike deliberately quashed them. Not the time or the place for memories, other than the ones he and Jenny had created the first time she'd lied to him.

"Right. I went looking for you that night."

"You're the one who approached me in the bar," she reminded him. "Not the other way around."

"You were beautiful. And alone." And somehow she had looked insulated, cut off, as if she'd been alone so long that she hadn't expected anything else from her life. Intrigued, Mike had watched her sip a single glass of wine for nearly an hour, as bar patrons came and went. As the bartender flirted with her and she ignored him, apparently oblivious to her own allure.

Mike wasn't unaware, though. She was tiny, making a man want to step up and be her protector. She was beautiful, making a man want to see her smile to know what that smile would do to her eyes. And she had so many curves in all the right places, *any* man would have wanted to get her out of the short red dress and high, needle-thin heels she had worn.

How the hell could he have resisted her?

She flushed at the unexpected compliment and he watched, fascinated, as a stain of deep rose filled her cheeks. She looked away from him then as if hoping to regain her sense of balance. He knew how that felt because damned if he didn't feel off his game every time he was around her.

"Look," she said, her voice cool and even, "the past is done. All we have now is the present and the future." Lifting her gaze to his, she said, "I'm not walking away from the hotel project. Not only is it my *job*, but it's going to be fun."

"Not how it looks from where I'm standing," he muttered.

"Well that's how I'm looking at it. So you can either deal or switch hotels with Sean."

"You don't make the calls in *my* business," he pointed out, irritated that she could try and order him off his own damn project.

"Sean put me in charge of the art design," she argued. "Not you. If you have a problem with that, talk to him."

"I did." He pushed one hand through his hair and started pacing, more to get away from the scent of her than because he needed to move. "But he doesn't know what happened in Phoenix so he doesn't get it."

"So tell him," she shot back. "If you're so sure I'm a thief and untrustworthy, tell him and let him fire me."

"I'm not telling him that I let myself get used by a woman who looks more like one of the fairies she paints than she does a damn spy."

"Wow. Thief and spy," she mused. "I'm really notorious, aren't I?"

"Why the hell else would you come and work for my company if it wasn't to be a spy for your uncle? You had to know that we'd be thrown together and clearly that thought didn't bother you. The only answer I can come up with is you're still trying to use me—now *us*, for your uncle's sake." That one question had been simmering inside his brain for months. Ever since the day he'd walked into the graphic design room and seen the woman he hadn't been able to stop thinking about sitting at one of the computers.

Damn it, he *wanted* her to convince him he was wrong, that his thoughts were baseless. He wanted to know that she really was the woman she'd seemed to be when he first met her.

"Listen up, you unbelievably suspicious…*man*. I took that job in spite of you, not *because* of you. Sean offered me a great position doing something I'm damn good at and I should have turned it down because I might see *you*?"

"I don't buy it. I think I'm the reason you took the job," Mike said, his gaze spearing into hers from across the narrow room. "You were hoping to get me into bed again."

Her head jerked back as if she'd been slapped. Gulping a deep breath, she muttered, "You pompous, arrogant... You know, sex with you wasn't *that* good."

He laughed shortly. "Now I know you're lying. It's amazing what a talent you have for it."

"Get out," she said flatly, holding up both hands toward him as if warding him off. "Just get out of my house and go away. Far, far away."

Mike shook his head.

"That night we had was incredible," he said. "And I know you felt the same way."

"Please."

His body churning, his brain racing, Mike stalked back to her, grabbed her and pulled her in close. "Since you asked so nicely..."

He kissed her, drowning in the taste and scent and feel of her. Not since that hot, amazing night in Phoenix had Mike felt so completely *right* about anything. She squirmed halfheartedly against him for a second or two, as if she might actually try to deny what was happening between them as thoroughly as she'd lied about their past.

But then the moment was gone, hesitation evaporated and she wrapped herself around him, arms locked about his neck, her short, shapely legs hooked around his waist. His hands dropped to the curve of her behind and held her there, tight against the erection straining and pulsing with the need to be buried inside her.

Had he known what would happen when he'd decided to come here tonight? Had he guessed that he wouldn't be able to deny himself—as he had for months—the sheer glory of her body? Didn't matter, he told himself as his tongue swept into the heat of her mouth. Nothing mattered but the now. The feel of her surrounding him, pulling him deeper.

No other woman had ever affected him like this. It was as if his brain and his body weren't even linked. He knew this was a bad idea, but his body just didn't give a damn. All it wanted…needed was her. One more night of being in her, on her, under her.

He tore his mouth free of hers, then shifted to taste her at the pulse beat in her throat. Her heart hammered in time with his own.

"Mike…" She sucked in a gulp of air and shivered in his arms when he nibbled at her skin. "We really shouldn't do this—"

"Yeah, I know," he whispered against her neck. "Do you care?"

"No."

"Good." His grip on her tightened and she ground her hips against him, her heels digging into the small of his back. He groaned and hissed in a breath. "You're killin' me here."

She lifted her gaze to his and a slow, sensual smile curved her mouth. "Killing you, not really the plan."

"There's a plan?"

That smile widened as she leaned in and kissed him. "Oh, yeah."

He shook his head. "I don't know why…"

"Why what?" she murmured, then gasped as his hands kneaded her behind.

"Why it's *you* who does this to me," he said on another groan as his mind shut down and his body simply took the lead.

"Ditto," she whispered, then kissed the side of his neck, trailing her lips and the edges of her teeth along his skin.

"Oh, yeah." He held her tighter to his groin. "Bedroom. Where?"

"Down the hall," she whispered, her breath blowing hot against the dampness of his skin. "Hurry."

"On that." Thankfully, her place was so small, it didn't take him long to carry her into the bedroom. Like the rest of the apartment, the room was tiny. A double bed, covered by a brightly colored quilt, stood against one wall. Pale yellow curtains were parted over a window that opened onto the backyard where a soft, violet glow heralded twilight.

A narrow cushioned chair sat alongside the bed, and the dresser on the opposite wall boasted a wide mirror that reflected the two of them as Mike dropped her onto the mattress.

He stretched out over her, braced himself on his hands at either side of her head and bent to kiss her. Jenny's hands scraped up and down his arms as her mouth fused to his. God, she tasted good. Almost as good as she felt.

Quickly, he pulled her shirt up and off, then sent it sailing to a corner of the room. With just her lacy white bra standing between him and what he most wanted, Mike couldn't wait. He flicked the clasp open, then slid the straps down her arms. His gaze locked on the feast that was Jenny Marshall. He groaned and bent his head to take first one hardened nipple and then the other into his mouth.

Her hands fisted in his hair, holding him to her as his teeth and tongue lavished attention on those full, beautiful breasts. She came up off the bed when he suckled her and the groan that shot from her throat seemed to roll around them, echoing off the walls and ceiling.

Not enough, his brain screamed at him. *More. Take more.*

He dropped his hands to the snap and zipper of her jeans and undid them quickly. With her help as she wriggled eagerly beneath him, he scraped the worn denim down her legs, taking the flimsy scrap of lace panties with them. Then she was there before him, naked, willing, as desperately hungry for this as he was, and Mike couldn't wait another second to claim her.

"Too many clothes," she muttered as she ran her hands over his chest in frantic strokes, unbuttoning his shirt as she went, tearing at the tiny white buttons, muttering, "I hate buttons, why are there so many buttons?"

"No more buttons," he said tightly as he shrugged out of his shirt and tossed it over his shoulder. "I'll make a note."

"Good, good." Her fingers stroked his skin then and each tiny stroke of her nails felt like fire dragged over flesh, burning, branding.

He took a breath and held it, calling on every ounce of control he'd ever possessed, knowing it wouldn't be enough. If he didn't have her soon, the top of his head would explode. But Mike dragged it out. It had been too long since he'd had his hands on her and he wanted to savor the moment.

He ran his hands down her body, breast to the heat of her and back up to her breast again. He explored every curve, every line, and with each caress he gave her, she reached for him, fingers grabbing at his shoulders, trying to pull him in closer, tighter. Her hips arched and rocked when he dipped one hand to the heart of her and cupped her heat.

"Mike!" Her head dug back into the mattress as she lifted her hips into his touch. "If you don't get out of those slacks and come to me soon, I—" She broke off, dragged in air and whimpered when he drove first one finger and then two into her damp heat. "Mike, please!"

He worked her, driving himself and her to the edge of control and beyond. It took everything he had to keep from giving her just what she wanted. Just what he wanted. But first, he would torment them both. It had been a long year and a half.

His thumb brushed over that one tiny bud of sensation and the deliberate caress had her shout his name. Again and again, he touched her, deeply, outside, inside, across that sensitive piece of flesh until she groaned and whispered broken pleas for a release that he kept just out of reach. Her eyes glazed over, her body continued to twist and writhe, chasing a climax he refused to give her too early.

Then he couldn't bear it anymore. Pulling away from her, he stood, stripped out of the rest of his clothes and kept his gaze locked with hers as he did. She licked her lips, rocked her hips again in silent invitation and held up her arms to welcome him.

"Almost," he murmured and she groaned again, frustrated. Until he knelt on the floor and dragged her body toward him. When she was close enough, he covered her heat with his mouth and felt the crash of the climax that slammed into her. She reached down, held him to her as her body convulsed. His tongue flicked over her, into her and he tasted her as she exploded, crying out his name over and over like a mantra designed to prolong the pleasure rocking her.

When she was limp and her gasping breaths were shuddering in and out of her lungs, he joined her on the bed and she rolled into his arms. One leg tossed across his hip, she brushed the tip of him against her heat and Mike almost lost it. Then she slid her hand down and her fingers wrapped around his hard length, working his flesh as expertly as he had hers.

He hissed in a breath, squeezed his eyes shut for a moment and then opened them again to look down into hers. "Tell me you've got condoms."

"Yeah, oh, yeah. Bedside drawer." She wiggled her hips, grinding her body against his. "Hurry."

"Right." Mike didn't think about why she had condoms. About the other men she must have invited into her bed. None of that mattered now. All that was important was this moment. He grabbed a condom, tore it open and sheathed himself, then looked back to the woman waiting for him.

She was like a damned nymph, straight out of one of the fantasy games his company designed. Like one of her drawings—blond curls rumpled, blue eyes heated and languid all at once, curvy body lush and waiting for him.

"Now, Mike. I need you inside me, now."

"Yes, now." He pushed deep into her heat with one long stroke. Her body bowed beneath him, her legs hooked around his waist, pulling him tighter, deeper. He stared into her eyes, eyes that held what seemed to him the mysteries of the universe, and watching her, took what she offered. He rocked his body into hers, over and over, setting a breathtaking rhythm that she raced to meet.

Again and again, they parted and came together, each of them driving the other higher, faster. He heard her ragged breathing, felt the frantic slide and scratch of her nails at his back. The race for completion was all. They looked into each other's eyes, fierce now, impatient for what they knew was coming.

"Mike," she cried, gasping. "Oh, Mike!"

She grabbed his shoulders and held on as wave after wave of sensation crashed through her body, making her tremble and shudder violently in his arms.

He watched her eyes flash with satisfaction only seconds before his own body splintered and jolted into a wild pleasure that left him feeling jagged and shaken. Locked together, the two of them slid over the edge, riding the thunder and crash of completion. And willingly, Mike tumbled into the dark, locked in the arms of the one woman he couldn't have.

Three

Dawn crept into the room and stretched out long, golden fingers across the bed where Jenny lay beside Mike. For more than a year, she'd thought about him, wished things had been different, wanted him. And now he was here, sleeping in her bed, and she knew that as the sun rose, their time together was running out.

Nothing had changed between them. Not fundamentally. They hadn't settled the issues that had separated them for so long before falling into bed—they'd simply ignored them in favor of the desire arcing in the room like summer lightning. Basically, they'd taken a long time-out. She smiled to herself at the thought.

Turning her head on the pillow, she studied Mike, using the moment to really look at him while he was completely unaware. He didn't look young and innocent in his sleep, she thought. He looked sexy. Dangerous. Like the hard man he was. And yet… She curled her fingers into her palm to keep from reaching out, stroking his beard-shadowed jaw.

Jenny's heart took a slow tumble. Pitiful, she told herself with a heavy, inward sigh. How could she feel so much for a man who thought of her as a thief and worse? And why did she *care* what he thought about her?

"You're thinking too loud." He opened his eyes and stared at her.

"A lot to think about," she said just as quietly.

"I suppose," he agreed, one corner of his mouth lifting into a seductive smile. "But we don't have to think about it right this minute, do we?"

Under the blanket, Mike reached for her and slid one hand along her curves. Jenny held her breath as his hand glided up from her hip, along her ribs to cup her breast. She sighed when his thumb brushed across her nipple. No, they didn't have to think. Didn't have to let this night end just yet. The sun was coming up and soon enough, they'd have to face the real world again. The world where the two of them stood on opposite sides of a wall Jenny had believed would never be breached.

But for now…

"No," she said, moving into him, "there's no rush to start thinking."

He kissed her and as she fell into the swirl of sensations, Jenny put everything else out of her mind.

An hour later, though, she knew it was over. Even with his weight pressing her into the mattress, even with his body deep inside hers, she felt Mike pulling away from her. As physically close as they were at that moment, there was a distance between them that lovemaking couldn't bridge. All this time with him had actually managed to do was enforce the lines separating them. To make things worse, now it would be even harder to work with him over the coming months.

He rolled to the side and went up on one elbow. Shooting a quick glance at the window and the rays of sunlight peeking through, he shifted his gaze back to her and said, "I should go."

"Yeah." Jenny looked at him and sketched this view of him into her memory. Hair mussed, a shadow of whiskers and that amazing mouth of his quirked into a rueful smile. If she'd had any sense at all, instead of trying to build a memory, she would have been attempting to put this time with Mike out of her mind completely.

She wasn't sure where they would be going from here, but she knew that whatever connection they'd found, however briefly, was gone. Over.

"Look," he said, gently pushing her hair back from her face, "last night was—"

"A mistake, I know," she finished for him, since it was easier to say it than to hear it.

He frowned, rolled off the bed and grabbed his clothes, pulling them on while he talked. "Can't really call it a mistake since it was something we both wanted."

How did he do that? she wondered. He was right there, within reach, and yet he'd pulled so far away that he might as well have been in a different city. A cold ball of regret dropped into the pit of her stomach.

"Last night didn't change anything, Jenny."

She nearly sighed because she knew exactly where this conversation was headed. "I know, you don't trust me."

"You lied to me the first night I met you."

"I didn't lie," she argued tiredly. God, she hated having to defend herself over and over to a man who refused to see past his own suspicions. How could he sleep with her, make love with her and not have the slightest clue who she really was? "Since I've worked for Celtic Knot, haven't I done a good job? Have I ever let anyone down? Doesn't that count for something?"

"Yeah, it does," he said shortly. "You know it does. But it can't change the past." His features tightened and his mouth thinned into one grim line as he held up one hand for peace before she could respond.

"Let's not," he said. "You have done good work for us, Jenny. That's why we've got a problem now. You're the logical choice to do the work on the River Haunt hotel, but if we have to stay on the project together it's going to be more difficult than it has to be."

Shaking her head, she only stared at him. Difficult? Like going into the office every day and feeling him watching her warily? Like knowing that he was waiting for her to screw up? To prove that she was exactly the liar and cheat he took her for?

She pushed off the bed and quickly snatched her robe off the end of the bed. They weren't going to argue about the past, fine. But she was more than ready to fight for the present and her own future. And damned if she'd do it naked. Slipping the robe on, she belted it tightly, then shook her hair back and turned to face the man who continued to haunt her. "It's not a problem for me, Mike. I'm going to do a hell of a good job on that hotel. And it doesn't have to be difficult if you'll just trust me to do what I'm best at."

For a second she thought he might argue that point, but instead, he blew out a breath and shoved one hand through his hair. "All right. We do the hotel. We do the job. Then we're done."

Eager, wasn't he, to push her aside and keep her there? But even he had to realize that he'd said pretty much the same thing about being done with her more than a year before. And yet, here they were, facing each other across yet another rumpled bed.

Still, it's what she wanted, Jenny reminded herself. A chance to prove herself on the hotel project without being at war with Mike, because it really would make things harder. So why, she wondered, did she suddenly feel so terrible now that he was offering her just that? She scrubbed her hands up and down her arms as if to chase away the bone-deep chill crawling through her, but it didn't help.

"We keep…this," he said, waving one hand at the disheveled quilt and the still-warm sheets, "between us and do what we have to do."

Another secret, then, Jenny thought. But probably better that the people at work didn't know what was going on between them. Since even *she* wasn't sure what exactly it was they shared, beyond the burn and desire.

Nodding, she asked, "Do we shake hands on it?"

For the first time that morning his lips curved in a half smile. "I think we can do better than that."

He walked up to her, cupped her face between his palms and bent his head for a kiss. His mouth was firm, soft and left hers all too quickly. She really was an idiot, Jenny thought as her insides jumped and her heart galloped. The kiss meant nothing. *She* meant nothing to him and oh, boy, was that a hard thing to acknowledge. But she knew it was only hunger that burned between them, nothing more. Yet she looked into his eyes and found herself wishing things were different. Wishing for—

"I'll see you at the office?"

"Yeah," she said abruptly, cutting off her own thoughts before they could lead her down completely ridiculous paths. "I'll be there."

"All right, then." He turned away to grab his jacket off the floor. Shrugging it on, he looked back at her and said, "In honor of this new cooperation between us, I'd like you to go to Laughlin with me in a week or so. Check out the new hotel. I want to walk the property, get a feel for it before we start the renovations."

"Good." She forced a smile that she hoped looked more convincing than it felt. "It would be good for me to get an on-site idea for the placement of the murals."

"Okay." He tugged the jacket into place. "We'll go out a week from Monday. Figure to stay at least overnight. I'll have Linda make reservations at the River Lodge."

Her stomach jittered. Laughable really, because what virtue was she suddenly so worried about? But the two of them were practically combustible, so was it really wise to invite more temptation? "Overnight?"

He shrugged. "We'll take the company jet into Vegas, and drive into Laughlin from there. I want enough time to explore the place. Staying over is the only solution."

"Right." Overnight. Did that mean they'd be sharing a bed again? Was he expecting that? Well, if so, he was doomed to disappointment. Jenny wasn't going to let this spiral into an affair that would leave her broken and miserable when it ended. Better to end it now. And much better to let him know just where she stood on this before they went any further.

"I won't be sleeping with you again."

One dark eyebrow winged up. "I didn't say you would be."

"Just saying," she went on, shaking her head, "I'm not interested in an affair and I'm not going to keep sleeping with my boss."

A dark scowl marred his face briefly. "This wasn't about boss and employee. It never was."

She shivered under his steady stare, but lifted her chin to ask, "Then what was it about, Mike?"

"Need," he said simply, biting the single word off as if it tasted bitter.

There it was. Plain and simple. He didn't care about her, Jenny told herself. Probably didn't much like her. He certainly didn't trust her. She hated to admit that he was right about this, but she knew that hunger had drawn them together and then that same vicious desire had pulled them back in when they'd both believed it was done between them.

So no more. Of anything. They would have to work together for the next few months and sex—especially *great* sex—just complicated everything.

Over the next few days, Jenny almost convinced herself that nothing had happened between Mike and her. She spent her days concentrating on the art ideas for the new hotel. Using the photos and 360-degree videos provided by the real estate company, Jenny laid out her plans for the work to be done. But she couldn't really be sure of anything until she saw the place firsthand.

"Have you got the sketches for 'The Wild Hunt' done yet?"

She glanced up from her computer screen to look at Dave Cooper, the new head of graphic design. When her old supervisor, Joe, had left to take a job with one of the big Hollywood studios, they'd all missed him. But Dave had slid right into the position as if he'd always been there.

"You'll have them by tomorrow," she said. The next game they were working on was already taking shape and so far, Jenny loved doing the art for it. A wild hunt, complete with faery warriors, pookas and the supernatural beings that hunted them. No doubt, it would be another winner for Celtic Knot and she really enjoyed being a part of it.

"I think you'll like them." She'd been refining her sketches for the past few nights, polishing them so no one could say she'd neglected this project in favor of the art for the new hotel.

Dave grinned, eased one hip against the edge of her desk and pushed his glasses higher up the bridge of his nose. In his late thirties, he looked like a typical computer geek—tall, thin, with big brown eyes behind thick, black-rimmed glasses. He had a generous smile and a puppylike enthusiasm for the work. "I always like your stuff, Jen. I read your notes on the ideas you have for the drawings and I think they'll be great."

He was so nice, Jenny thought. It was a damn shame that all she felt for him was friendship. Life would have been much easier if only she'd been attracted to someone like Dave.

"Thanks." She smiled at him. "I'm glad you stopped by. There's something else I'd like to run past you."

"Yeah? What's up?"

"You know in 'The Wild Hunt,' there's the magical wolf terrorizing the village?"

"Yeah." Joe grinned wider and nodded his head eagerly. "Early renderings are awesome. Eric Santos worked it so that when the wolf transforms into a Black Knight, he retains the teeth and the yellow eyes. Truly excellent."

Eric did great work. He had an eye for detail that skipped most artists as they usually looked at the big picture and left the so-called inconsequential bits for the interns to fill in or expand on. Eric didn't work like that, though, and neither did Jenny, so she had a lot of respect for him.

"Sounds really great," she said, meaning it. "Can't wait to see it. But what I wanted to ask you about is, I've got this idea for another hero in the game program."

He frowned a little, clearly puzzled. "Another hero? We've already got Finn MacCool as the hero. He's the ancient Irish warrior. What're you thinking?"

Actually, she'd done a lot of thinking in the past few days. Trying to keep her mind busy and off Mike Ryan, Jenny had indulged herself with searching out Irish myths and playing with possible story lines. She'd even turned a few sketches into an abbreviated storyboard to pitch to Sean and Mike at some point. But her idea for "The Wild Hunt" was just a little something extra and if she ran it by Dave first, he'd let her know if it merited being presented to the Ryans.

"I was thinking that even a legendary hero like Finn MacCool could use a little help."

"Okay." Dave pushed his glasses up higher as they slid down his nose. "What've you got?"

"I was thinking it might be a nice twist to have a Wise Woman in the mix."

"Wise Woman?"

"You know, it's what they called witches back in the day."

He laughed. "Really? Interesting. Okay. Tell me."

Encouraged by the way he was giving her his complete concentration, Jenny started talking. Reaching into her top desk drawer, she pulled out a few sketches she'd made the night before. Handing them to Dave, she talked while he looked through them.

"She can live in the village. Almost like an Easter egg surprise, she wouldn't be activated unless the gamer hit a certain point on the quest."

Jenny paused, waited and was rewarded when Dave said, "Keep going."

"Okay." Tapping one finger on a storyboard of "The Wild Hunt," she said, "Here, in the timeline of the story, Finn finds a sword in a cave at the base of the cliffs. The gamer has to collect twelve rune clues to free the sword."

"Yeah…"

"Well, I was thinking, what if we laid down fifteen rune clues? Twelve to free the sword and allow the gamer to take Finn into combat with the wizard. *But*, if he finds all fifteen, then he unlocks the Wise Woman. She could help Finn defeat the forest demons and—"

"Be a love interest that maybe we could carry over into the sequel," Dave finished for her, studying the sketches of the witch. "That's excellent, Jenny. It adds another layer and rewards the gamer for collecting all of the runes." Nodding to himself, he added, "Game rules say twelve unlocks the sword, fifteen unlocks magic." He laughed to himself again and kept nodding. "Yeah, that'd be great. We make three of the runes really difficult to find so that players have to work for it if they want the extra. Most will just go for twelve and the sword, but the hard-core gamer will want to go for the magic. I like it." He lifted his gaze to Jenny's and added, "You should take this to the Ryans. Get their okay. They'll love it."

"Um…" she said, pleasure sliding away at the thought of talking to the Ryan brothers together. Sean would be okay. He was nice, reasonable and he liked her. Mike on the other hand… "Why don't you do it? You're the head of my department."

He looked surprised. "It's your idea, Jenny, and it's a great one."

"Yeah, but—"

"Don't be dumb," he said and dropped the sketches onto her desk. "Sean's in Mike's office. You can pitch it to both of them at the same time. The sooner you get this to them the better. Programmers will need more time to set up the extra layers."

"I know, but—"

Dave chuckled a little. "Since when are you shy? Come on, take your idea to the bosses, impress the hell out of 'em."

Still shaking his head, he wandered off to check on a couple of the other artists. Jenny watched him go, then dropped her gaze to the Wise Woman sketches. It *was* a good idea, damn it. And if she and Mike weren't…she didn't know what they were exactly, but if they weren't in such a weird space, she'd have no trouble at all taking her ideas to the Ryan brothers. They were always open to the employees coming to them with suggestions.

She was the head artist now, so she shouldn't be wary of facing her bosses. This was her job, and hadn't she made a point out of telling Mike that nothing was going to stop her from doing her job?

Nodding to herself, she gathered up her sketches and headed out of the office.

* * *

Mike and Sean were going over the figures sent by the collectibles company. "The licensing fee is good, but did you take a look at their latest batch of figurines based on that kids' movie?"

"Yeah," Sean said with a wince. "I admit, they're not great."

Mike snorted. "'Not great' covers a lot of territory. This can be narrowed down to crappy."

"Okay, yeah." Sean tossed the pictures back on his brother's desk. "If they couldn't get the talking frog and the Princess Knight right..."

"Exactly," Mike agreed. "Those are easy. What'll they do to our banshees, warlocks and Irish warriors?" Shaking his head, he continued, "Brady and I both went along with this idea of yours, Sean. But if this is what the collectibles are going to look like, I don't know if it's a good thing."

"True." Sean crossed his legs, propping one ankle on his knee. "There are other companies we could try."

"Is it worth it?"

"I think so," Sean countered. "If we get into the collectibles market, it's going to push our name recognition even higher and affect game sales. We could pull in gamers who haven't tried us yet."

Mike frowned and tapped his fingertips against the desk. It was hard to keep his mind on business. Even now, while his brother continued to talk about his plan, Mike's mind drifted to the woman working on the floor above him.

Three days since his night with Jenny and he'd hardly been able to shake thoughts of her for five minutes at a stretch. He'd convinced himself that spending the night with her had been a wise choice. A way to not only ease the ache for her but a chance to push away the memories of that one night in Phoenix.

Well, that had worked, but now it was memories of a night in Long Beach that tormented him. Rather than getting her out of his mind, that night had only entrenched her there.

"Are you listening to me?" Sean demanded.

"What?" Mike scowled and shot his brother a hard look. "Yeah. Sure."

"Uh-huh." Sean smirked at him. "What did I just say?"

"Collectibles. Gamers. Blah, blah. Pretty much what you've been saying for months."

"Right. So what's going on with you?"

"Nothing," Mike said, picking up a pen and twirling it idly between his fingers. "I'm busy."

"Yeah," Sean said, "me, too. So what's going on?"

"Who're you all of a sudden?" Mike asked. "Mom?"

"Hah. If I was Mom I'd get an answer to my question."

True. Peggy Ryan was tough and had a way of getting her family to confess all. Which, Mike reminded himself, wasn't always a good thing. She'd once pried truths out of her husband that had changed the way Mike felt about his father forever. It was the day that Mike learned how much damage liars and cheats could do.

And that thought steeled his spine and firmed his resolve to get past whatever it was he was feeling for Jenny. Liars had no place in his life and damned if he'd forget that.

As if his thoughts had conjured her, a perfunctory knock on the open door announced her presence. Mike looked at her, his gaze locking with hers, and he felt a fast jolt of awareness tangled up with a bone-deep need that just never seemed to drain away. "What is it?"

She blinked at the brusque tone, then deliberately looked away from him to Sean. "I had an idea I wanted to run past you. For 'The Wild Hunt.'"

Sean glanced at Mike, then shrugged and said, "Sure, Jenny. Come on in."

He waved her into a chair and she sat, still avoiding looking at Mike directly. "I was talking with Dave, showed him a few sketches, and he said I should bring it to you guys."

Mike watched her lips move, heard her voice, but couldn't concentrate on what she was saying as she explained her idea for a new character to drop into "The Wild Hunt." Instead, his brain insisted on dredging up images from the other night. How the hell could he focus on work with rich, sexual memories flooding his brain and torturing his body?

"Those are great," Sean was saying. He leaned close to Jenny to look at the sketch she held and a flash of irritation shook Mike in response.

Why the hell did Sean have to practically drape himself over Jenny's shoulder to get a look at her sketch pad?

"Let me see," he said abruptly, breaking up what looked to him like a too-cozy scene.

Sean passed the drawings over and said, "I think she's onto something. I like the idea of a powerful woman coming to the aid of the beleaguered hero." He grinned. "Might get more female players out of it, too."

Nodding, Mike scanned the drawings and once again was forced to admit just how talented Jenny Marshall really was. The sketches weren't complete, more of a bare-bones idea for a new character, but even at that stage, he could see the beauty that would pop through when it was finished. The witch was tall, powerful, magical, a perfect addition to the game cast.

He slanted a look at Jenny and found her watching him, waiting for whatever he was going to say. And in her eyes, he saw resignation, as if she was expecting him to shoot down her ideas. Well, hell, he might have some issues with her, but he wasn't an idiot.

"This is good work."

"Wow, high praise," Sean muttered and earned a quick, grateful grin from Jenny.

Mike ignored a new flash of irritation and kept talking. "I'll keep the high praise for when I see the fleshed-out ideas. But for now, I agree. It's a good addition to the game."

A slow, pleased smile curved Jenny's mouth and everything in Mike warmed, softened. The effect this woman had on him was dangerous. And it didn't seem to be dissipating any.

"Thank you," she said simply. Her eyes shone with a deeper gratitude that only Mike was aware of. It made him feel like a damn bully to know that she had fully expected him to shoot down her ideas just because they were hers.

He handed the sketches back and turned to his brother. "What do you think? Can we come up with a new story line and get it to the writers by the weekend?"

"Probably," Sean said, then shrugged. "But what's the rush?"

Mike slanted a look at Jenny. "Because Jenny and I are headed to Laughlin to check out the new hotel. We're leaving on Monday. Be gone a couple days."

She shifted a little uneasily in her chair and Mike

caught the motion. He could only hope Sean hadn't. Sometimes, Mike's little brother saw too damn much.

"Well, then," Sean said and stood up. "I'll talk to the writers, get them to amend the script. Meanwhile," he added, "if you could finish out those sketches, that'd be great, Jenny."

"I can have them to you in an hour," she said, rising and heading to the door.

"Great. You want to start on the storyboard changes now, Sean?"

"Should we call Brady before making a final decision?"

Mike thought about it, then scrubbed one hand across the back of his neck. "No. We'll tell him about it at our next conference call, but he'll be on board."

"Okay." Sean headed out. "I'll get the stuff together."

"Be right there," Mike called after him. When they were alone, he stood up and asked, "Leaving Monday work for you?"

"Oh," Jenny said, giving a quick look over her shoulder as if to make sure the hallway behind her was empty. "So you *are* going to ask me? I thought you were just handing out a royal decree."

Mike grimaced and stuffed his hands into his pants pockets. "We talked about going to the hotel."

"Yeah, but you didn't give me a specific date," she countered. "And I was supposed to have dinner with my uncle on Monday."

Everything in Mike fisted at the reminder of Hank Snyder, her uncle and the owner of Snyder Arts.

"You don't have to make that face," she told him. "You might not like my uncle," Jenny added, "but I love him. He's my family."

"That's the problem, isn't it?"

"For you, yes."

A couple of people walked down the hall, their voices raised in argument.

"Zombies have to die when you cut their heads off."

"In real life, not in the gaming world, hello?"

"We have to at least try to be realistic, don't we?"

"You want realism, then our zombies have to eat brains, not just bite people…"

Their voices faded as they went into the break room and shut the door after them. A moment later, Jenny chuckled. "Zombies in real life." She looked up at Mike, the smile still curving her mouth. "We have weird lives."

All he could see was that smile and after a second or two, he returned it. "Yeah, I guess we do. So. Monday?"

"I'll be ready," she said, all trace of amusement disappearing. "Should I meet you here?"

He shook his head. "I'll pick you up at nine. We'll take the company jet to Vegas."

"Okay." She took a breath, blew it out. "Now, I'd better go see about finishing the images of my Wise Woman."

Mike crossed the room and propped one shoulder against the doorjamb. Watching her go, he wondered if, when all this was done, seeing her walk away from him would be his clearest memory.

Four

"I'll only be gone overnight, Uncle Hank."

"With *him*," Hank Snyder muttered under his breath.

Jenny sighed and let her head fall back. It was Monday morning; Mike would be here in a few minutes and she still had to finish packing. But as her uncle went on a long-winded rant, she realized having to listen to this was her own fault.

She never should have confessed to her uncle what Mike had accused her of a year ago. But in her defense, she had really been upset, and Hank had dropped by her apartment just when she was in the middle of a good rant. So instead of shutting up, she'd spewed everything at the feet of the man who'd raised her.

Naturally, his first instinct had been to go to Celtic Knot and punch Mike Ryan in the mouth. Thankfully, she'd talked him down from that. But he hadn't forgiven and he hadn't forgotten. In fact, Hank had tried to talk her out of going to work for the Ryan brothers on the principle that she should simply stay the hell away from Mike altogether. But Jenny had refused, then and now, to let Mike Ryan's presence dictate how she ran her life and career.

"He is my boss," she finally said.

"Doesn't have to be," Hank told her, and Jenny's hand fisted around her phone. "You could come to work for me. You know that."

Snyder Arts was a small company with an excellent arts program. The program itself simplified digital and graphic arts design and implementation. They sold retail and to companies looking to refine their own graphic art departments. Which is why Hank had tried to make a deal with Celtic Knot in the first place. He'd thought—and *rightly*, Jenny acknowledged—that his program would streamline the gaming company's art and design division.

And since Jenny now knew *both* companies well, she understood that if Mike weren't so hardheaded, even he would have to admit that her uncle's program would make the work easier for his own artists. But Mike being Mike, he would never let himself see that. Especially since he believed that Hank had tried to use Jenny to worm a contract out of Mike.

She sighed and leaned against the bathroom door. "I do know that, Uncle Hank. And I appreciate it. Really. But I'm not interested in R & D or in sales and marketing. I'm an artist and I'm good at what I do."

"You're the best, honey," he said on a belabored sigh. "I just don't like you being upset is all. And I really don't like you having to deal with a man who thinks so little of you."

"It doesn't matter what Mike thinks of me personally," she said, though in her head she was chanting, *Liar, liar, pants on fire.* "I like my job. And this trip to Laughlin will be fast and all business. I want to scope out the hotel in person so I can start planning the murals."

"Never could argue with you once you had your mind set on something, could I?"

Jenny smiled. "Nope."

"Fine, fine. You just be careful and you let me know when you're home safe."

"I will." Then Jenny listened as her uncle talked about what was happening at Snyder Arts. His R & D department was coming up with some interesting things. Jenny knew how important his company was to him. Until she had come into his life and he had taken over as her guardian, that company had been his entire world.

But the main point in all this was Hank didn't need a deal with Celtic Knot to make Snyder Arts profitable. Their bottom line was very comfortable. Okay, not billionaire comfy, but still. It was laughable that Hank would have needed her to coax Mike into some kind of deal even if it hadn't been insulting on the face of it. Snyder Arts didn't need Celtic Knot and Mike had to know that, in some part of himself. He was just so down-to-the-marrow suspicious and hard, he'd never admit it.

While Hank talked, she smiled to herself and quickly packed away her hair products and makeup, zipping them into a small purple bag. She walked into the bedroom, tucked the bag into her suitcase and sat on the edge of the bed.

Now she was packed and ready to go. Well, as ready

as she could be. Two days alone with Mike would be either a misery or wonderful—and that would turn into misery later. The man wanted her, that was plain enough. But he didn't want to want her and she had no idea how to get past that. Or even if she should try.

Jenny had spent a lifetime knowing that she wasn't wanted. Heck, her own parents had walked away from her and never looked back. She was twelve when they decided they didn't really want the burden of a child and were bored with being parents. They'd dropped her off with Hank, her mother's older brother.

Hank was a widower who had buried himself in his company at his wife's death. Barely home back then, he'd had to shift his entire life around to accommodate Jenny. And she'd known it. She'd tried to be as invisible as possible so that he, too, wouldn't decide to walk away.

Even as a kid, Jenny had known that Hank didn't really *want* her. Taking her in had simply been the right thing to do. But Hank had always been kind and supportive, and she was still grateful to him for so much.

"You're not listening," Hank said with a short laugh.

Caught, she said, "I'm sorry, Uncle Hank. My mind wandered."

"That's fine. I know you're getting ready to leave."

True. Mike would be arriving any minute. Well, there went the knots in her stomach, tightening viciously enough that it was hard to breathe.

"I'll just remind you to be careful."

"I will, promise." Jenny glanced out the window, saw Mike's car pulling up and said, "I've really gotta go."

Her uncle hung up, still muttering direly. Jenny tucked her phone into her pocket, zipped her suitcase closed and told herself to relax. Not that she was listening, but she had to try. Outside, Mike stepped out of his car, looked at her apartment and for just a second, Jenny felt as if he were looking directly into her eyes. That was stupid of course, but it didn't change the zip of heat that raced through her.

This was probably a mistake. Two days. Alone. With Mike Ryan.

No way this was going to end well.

Traveling with a gazillionaire was eye-opening.

Even at the small airport in Long Beach, people practically snapped to attention for Mike Ryan. Baggage handlers hurried to stow the overnight bags they both carried, then the pilot stepped out onto the stairway to welcome them aboard personally.

Once they'd boarded the private jet, Jenny curled up in a buttery-soft leather seat and sipped at the fresh coffee served by a friendly attendant. Mike concentrated on work, staring so hard at the screen of his tablet, Jenny was almost surprised he didn't burn a hole through it. But left to herself, she watched the clouds and enjoyed the all-too-short flight.

In less than an hour, they were landing in Las Vegas. There again, people scrambled to make Mike's life easier, smoother. A rental car was waiting for them and after forty minutes on a nearly empty highway flanked on either side by wide sweeps of desert, they were in Laughlin, Nevada.

Laughlin was sort of the more casual, fun, younger sister of Las Vegas. There were plenty of casino hotels, but there was also the Colorado River. In the summer, the town was booming with water-skiers and boaters and everyone looking for a good time on the water. Then the hot desert nights featured riverside dining or visits to the casinos where top-name acts performed on glittery stages.

Jenny had been there before, though the last time had been five years ago for a bachelorette party. Remembering, she smiled. That party was the reason she'd had condoms in her bedside drawer a week ago when Mike had shown up at her apartment. As a party favor, the condoms had seemed silly at the time, but now, Jenny could appreciate the gesture because without them, she wouldn't have had that spectacular night.

The town had grown a lot in five years. There were new casinos springing up everywhere along with housing developments and shopping centers just out of sight of the big hotels.

In late January, the weather was cool and the river ran high and fast. Jenny stood on the shore and looked upstream toward the heart of the city where big hotels lined the Riverwalk—a wooden boardwalk that stretched the length of hotel row. At night, she knew, there were old-fashioned streetlights sending out a golden glow along the walk. There were restaurants and bars, where a couple could sit and talk and look out over the water.

The Ryans had made a good choice in building their hotel here. All in all, Jenny told herself, if she had a choice, she would come to Laughlin instead of Vegas. It was smaller, friendlier and offered a variety of things to do.

She shrugged deeper into her navy blue jacket as a hard, cold wind carrying the sharp tang of sage blew in off the desert. There were clouds on the horizon promising a storm, but for the moment, the sky was a bright blue and all around her, trees dipped and swayed in the wind. Jenny walked out onto the boat dock and watched as the river churned and sloshed below her.

"It's a good spot."

She turned her head into the wind to look back at the shore. Mike was headed her way, hands tucked into the pockets of his black leather jacket.

Nodding, Jenny shifted her gaze to the river again. "I was just thinking that. There are so many trees on the grounds, you could almost forget you're in the desert."

"Yeah, now," he said, a chuckle in his voice as he came closer. "Wait until summer."

She smiled. Temperatures in the desert regularly topped out at one hundred twenty and more during the summer. But as the locals liked to say, *It's a dry heat.* "Agreed. But you can go in the river to cool off."

"Or the hotel pool," he said as he joined her at the edge of the dock.

"True."

Upstream, there were flat-bottom boats, owned by the hotels, taking tourists for river rides. The windows and gold trim on the hotels winked brightly in the sunlight. But here, standing in the shadows of the nest of trees edging the river, it was as if they were alone.

"I wonder why the previous owners couldn't make the hotel work," she mused aloud. "It's a great spot. Wonderful views, plenty of trees, a gorgeous pool—"

"No gambling."

She looked at him. "What?"

"The hotel." Mike squinted into the sun. "The old owner didn't approve of gambling so the hotel didn't offer it." He shrugged. "A hotel with no casino in a gambling town isn't going to survive. Plus, he didn't have smoking rooms, either."

"That's important?"

"Again, a gambling town. People come here looking to relax, throw a little money down a rat hole…" He looked at her. "They're not interested in being snubbed because they smoke. Or if they can't find a slot machine anywhere on the premises."

"Good points." He was always thinking and she shouldn't have been surprised to know that he'd done his homework on the previous owner's failures and come to his own conclusions. Mike Ryan always had a plan. "So, you'll have gambling?"

He gave her a fast grin. "Not a regular casino, no. But we'll have some custom-made slot machines if people are interested. Based on the game, of course."

"Of course." She smiled and looked up at him. He was so tall, so broad shouldered. His dark hair ruffled in the wind and his blue eyes were narrowed on the distant view, as if he was staring off into a future that lay waiting for him to conquer it.

Oh, she really had to stop.

"Still," Mike said, grabbing her attention again, "the River Haunt isn't going to be your standard hotel. It's being designed to appeal to gamers—not gamblers."

"Gamblers like games, too."

"Yeah," Mike said. "But they're more interested in risking their money for the chance of a big reward. A gamer wants to beat his time, beat the game." He turned and looked back up the rise to the hotel that now belonged to Celtic Knot. "The people who come here are going to be looking for the experience. The opportunity to pretend they're a part of the game they love. Gambling doesn't have anything to do with that."

"But you'll have a few slot machines just in case."

He winked at her. "Doesn't hurt to cover all bases."

Pleasure rushed through Jenny at that friendly wink.

She liked this. They were talking. About important things, and he hadn't taken a single shot at her yet. No insults, no disapproval. Maybe it was being away from their everyday routine, but whatever the reason, she was enjoying it. And maybe, she thought, these two days with Mike wouldn't be as hard as she'd thought they would be.

"I'm guessing you'll have smoking rooms, too, then," she said with a smile.

"Absolutely," he said. "I'm not going to cut anyone out of coming to the hotel." He shook his hair back when the wind tossed it across his forehead. "It's ridiculous for any business owner to discriminate against possible customers."

"Agreed," she said. Half turning, she looked back at the hotel sitting at the top of a low rise.

It was old, but sturdy. Paint that had once been a deep brick red had faded in the sun until it looked almost pink. The building sprawled across the property but Jenny knew that compared to the rich new hotels farther downriver this place was small. Only a hundred and fifty rooms, the soon-to-be River Haunt hotel would be exclusive and that would appeal to the gamers who would flock here.

There was a wide porch that swept along the front of the building, and floor-to-ceiling windows provided a great view of the river and the purple smudge of mountains in the distance. The now pink paint was peeling and the plain boxlike structure wasn't exactly appealing, but she knew that Mike would be changing it all up. The rehab wouldn't go fast, but she could imagine it all as it would be in a few months.

Like the setting of the "River Haunt" game, the main building would be made to look like a weathered, deserted cabin. A cabin where ghouls, ghosts, zombies and other assorted supernatural beings assembled and tormented the gamers who fought to defeat Donn, Lord of the Dead.

The guests at the River Haunt hotel would be treated to rooms and suites decked out with top-of-the-line gaming systems, flat-screen TVs and enough gaming tokens and symbols to make them feel as though they were a part of their favorite game. The latest Celtic Knot hotel was going to be huge.

"It'll be a lot of work," Jenny said thoughtfully.

"It will."

She turned and flashed him a quick smile. "But it's gonna be great."

"Damn straight."

His gaze locked with hers and for one bright, amazing moment, Jenny felt like they were a team. In this together. And in that impossibly fast heartbeat of time, she really wished it were true.

They were making the most of their two days in Nevada.

Mike spent hours with his contractor, Jacob Schmitt, going over the plans for the River Haunt. The two of them walked the hotel, checking out the rooms and talking to the skeleton staff who remained on-site.

Mike appreciated good work and loyalty, so when he was given the opportunity to keep on some of the hotel employees, he did. He wasn't a soft touch, though, so in interviews with the hotel manager, and the heads of the other departments, he'd quickly weeded out the people who were simply dead weight.

Maybe the previous owner's standards had been lax,

but Mike had no intention of paying people to do nothing. But he was also ready to pay top money for the right kind of employee. Which was why he'd fired the previous manager and promoted that man's assistant, Teresa Graves.

Teresa was a middle-aged woman with a no-nonsense attitude and an unerring ability to cut through the bull and get the best out of the people who worked for her. With his new manager's help, Mike wanted to keep the skeleton crew in place during the transition. He didn't want the hotel sitting empty and deserted while it was being rehabbed. It seemed like too much of an invitation to vandals and or thieves.

Having people there was important enough that he was offering bonuses to the workers who were willing to actually *live* in the hotel so that someone besides the security people he'd hired were around 24/7. With a working kitchen, a pool and plenty of guest rooms to choose from, it was no hardship for those who chose to stay. Plus, they were paid enough that they didn't have to look for another job while waiting for the hotel to reopen.

"I figure we'll do the pool last," Jacob said as they walked through the main lobby and out onto the sun-splashed deck. "Leave it as is so your people can use it while we work. And this way, with all the construction going on, we don't risk breaking up the new tiles you wanted in the pool surround."

Mike studied the architect's line drawings for a long moment.

"That's a good idea," he said finally. "Pool's going to be the last thing we need done anyway."

"Yeah, and these tiles we'll be laying in the deck and surround aren't something we want scratched up." Jacob yanked his battered blue ball cap with a faded Dodgers patch off his head and rubbed the wild scrub of gray hair that sprung up as if freed from prison. "Just like you wanted, the tiles actually look like rough wood—gives the feel of the forest floor."

Mike glanced at the man and smiled. "You know the 'River Haunt' game?"

"I should," the other man said. "My son plays the damn thing every chance he gets." Chuckling, he added, "I swear, I hear banshees wailing in my dreams."

"That's good to hear, too," Mike said, and gave the other man a friendly slap to the shoulder.

"I'll bet." Jacob Schmitt turned slowly to take a look around the property. "This is a perfect spot for what you're wanting. My opinion, the last owner didn't make enough of what he had. But his loss—your gain."

"That's what I think, too."

"You know, my son's already nagging at me to bring him to the hotel for a long weekend."

Mike followed the other man's gaze and realized that he was anxious to get this hotel up and running, too. He couldn't wait to see how it all came out. "Tell you what," Mike said. "You bring the job in on time and on budget, you and your family can stay a week, on us."

The older man's bushy gray brows shot high on his forehead as he gave a wide smile. "My son will think I'm a god."

Mike laughed. "Anything I can do."

Eager now, Jacob pointed to the sketch of the pool area. "You can see this wall behind the pool will be a series of ledges, each of them planted with flowering plants that will trail down to the edge of the pool itself."

Mike listened as he looked at the ink drawings, bringing it all to life in his mind. He had a good imagination and used it to mentally change the plain, kidney-shaped pool into the fantasy spot he wanted.

He could almost see it. A waterfall would cascade at one end of the pool and behind that waterfall would be a swim-up bar where guests could be served as they hid behind a froth of water. There would be lounge chairs in deep forest green and tables that looked like the twisted limbs of ancient trees. The flowering vines Jacob described would be a curtain of green in the desert heat. It was a very good representation of the kind of scenery found in the "River Haunt" game.

Hell, Mike thought he could practically hear the groaning zombies approaching. He'd like to show the sketches to Jenny, get her opinion. After all, she was here to work, he reminded himself. But she was inside, scouting out the right places for the murals she would design and paint.

"I've expanded the dock," the contractor said, getting Mike's attention again, "so you'll have room for both of the boats you're planning for."

"That's good. We want to offer late-night cruises as part of the experience."

"It's pretty out here at night," the contractor said with a nod as he lifted his gaze to look around. "Far enough away from hotel row, you can see the stars like you never would in the city."

"Yeah?" It had been a long time since Mike had even taken the time to look up at a night sky. But it was part of the whole experience his guests would have. "What did you think of the idea for the animatronics?"

Jacob chuckled and tugged his hat back into place. "I

think it's gonna scare the hell out of your guests," he said. "But I suppose that's why they're coming here, isn't it?"

"It is." Mike nodded to himself and glanced toward the riverbank that stretched along the front of their property. Plenty of thick, high bushes and trees to hide the mechanics of the banshees and river specters who would be made to move in and out of the shadows as the gamers drifted by on the water. He could practically see how it would play out and he was anxious to get it all going.

"We're working with the engineers to make the housings for the creatures to move on as well as the shells they'll retreat to so they're protected from the elements," Jacob said.

"You can hide the housings well enough they won't be seen?"

"Absolutely."

It all sounded good. Hell, perfect. With any luck at all, the hotel would be finished and ready to welcome guests by summer. Hot desert nights, dark skies, perfect for scaring the hell out of people.

"I've got the best crew in Nevada," Jacob assured him. "We'll get it all done just the way you want it."

Nodding, Mike said, "I'll be making trips out to check on things, but Ms. Graves, the new manager, will be the point person on this. You go to her with any issues if you can't get hold of me. She'll make sure I'm kept up to date."

"I'll do that, and don't worry, it's going to be something special when it's done."

"Agreed," Mike told him, then turned back to the hotel. "Let's go through the kitchen work that needs doing. I want to hear about any potential problems."

"Well," Jacob said as he fell into step beside him,

"we've got a few of those, too. But nothing to be worried about."

Mike only half listened as they headed inside. He had researched every aspect of this rehab. He knew Jacob Schmitt would deliver good work done at a fair price. He knew Teresa Graves could be trusted to keep on top of the day-to-day issues that were bound to crop up. And he was sure that the security company he'd hired would protect his property.

Of course, the only thing he wasn't sure of in all this was Jenny. He hadn't seen her since the conversation on the dock hours ago. Probably best to keep a distance between them, but damned if he didn't want to go find her. Talk to her. Look at her.

And more.

Yeah, not going there.

"Right, Jacob. Let's get back to work."

Five

Jenny's imagination was in overdrive. She'd brought her ideas for murals with her and she'd spent the past two hours walking the halls and the big rooms on the main floor, plotting just where she'd put them.

The restaurant was perfect for a wide mural on the back wall. She would paint it as if there was a path leading from the room into the forest itself. Sort of a trompe l'oeil, giving the guests in the room the feeling that they could simply step into the painting. Of course, being gamers, they would know what lurked in that forest, she thought with a smile, so maybe they wouldn't want to follow the path.

On the opposite wall, there were tall windows, displaying the view of the tree-laden yard and the river beyond. Those she would surround with deep green vines, twining down the wall to pool on the floor.

She took a deep breath and simply sighed at the pleasure of having so many blank canvases just waiting to be turned into fantasies. Her hands actually itched to take hold of her brushes. God knew, she loved her job, but having the opportunity to paint rather than generating images on a computer was just…fun.

Grinning, she left the dining room and walked into the lobby. She had a great idea for the main entrance to the hotel and knew that it was only because she'd been here to see it in person that the thought had occurred to her. She wanted this painting to make a statement. To show the gamers and other guests that from the moment they walked into the hotel, they were stepping into another realm.

The lobby area was another big, gorgeous space that only needed some attention to really wake it up and make it special. And Jenny was just the artist to do it. There were a few crewmen in the room already, tearing out the old reception desk. It was white and sterile and too contemporary-looking for what the Ryans had in mind, so it had to go.

"Excuse me," she said and waited until one of the men turned to look at her to ask, "who do I speak to about the color of paint I want on this entry wall?"

"Oh, that'd be Jacob." A guy in his thirties with big brown eyes, a heavy mustache and deeply tanned skin smiled at her, touching off a dimple in one cheek. "I think he's in the kitchen with the boss."

"Okay, thanks." She started that way, but stopped when the man spoke again.

"You're the artist, right? Jenny?"

Jenny turned to face him. "That's right."

"Nice to meet you. I'm Rick."

He really was cute and that dimple was disarming. His jeans were worn and faded, and his white T-shirt strained over a build that was truly impressive. And Jenny was pretty sure Rick knew exactly how good he looked. There was something in his stance—as if he were posing for her admiration—and in the knowing gleam in his eyes that told Jenny he was used to women curling up at his feet and staring up at him adoringly.

Hard to blame them.

"Hi, Rick," she said. "Good to meet you, too. I'm going to be doing the murals for the new hotel. Well," she hedged, "not me all on my lonesome. It would take me ten years to do all of them myself.

"But I'm doing the designs and supervising the artists we'll bring in to finish the job."

He nodded as if he cared and she knew he didn't. Please. Were most of her gender really so easily manipulated by a gorgeous face and the appearance of interest in what they were saying?

"So what color do you want for that wall?" he asked.

She glanced at the wall in question. It was the first thing you saw when you walked into the hotel. Right now, it was cream colored, with sun stains from where framed paintings had once hung. But when Jenny was finished with it, it was going to be…mystical.

When she spoke, she wasn't really talking to Rick-With-Dimples. Instead, she was describing her vision to herself, sort of putting it out into the universe.

"Deep purple," she said, tipping her head to stare at the blank space as if she could see the wall changing color as she spoke. "I want it the color of twilight just before darkness falls. There will be stars, just barely appearing in the sky, with dark clouds streaming past a full moon, making them shine like silver." She sighed and continued, "There'll be a forest beneath the stars and moonlight threading through the trees. And in the shadows, there will be the hint of yellow eyes, red eyes, staring out at you, and you won't be sure if you see them or not.

"But the night will draw you in, make promises, and you'll dream about that forest and the eyes that follow you as you walk."

She fell silent and was still staring at the blank wall when she heard Rick say, "Damn, lady, you're a little spooky, you know that?"

She laughed, until Mike's voice came from right behind her.

"You have no idea."

Whipping around, she looked up into Mike's eyes and noticed the all-too-familiar flare of anger. Well, for heaven's sake, what had she done *now*?

"Don't you have work to do?" Jacob asked Rick and he immediately left, doing his best to look busy.

"Thanks for the tour, Jacob," Mike was saying. "We'll meet up here again tomorrow."

"I'll be here," the older man said, with a nod acknowledging Jenny. "You make a note on the paint colors you want where, miss, and I'll make sure the painters get the message."

"Thank you. I'll have them for you tomorrow, then."

"That's good." Jacob looked back at Mike. "The crew starts on the main floor in the morning. You and I can look at the upper floors and talk about what you want."

"See you then." Mike took Jenny's elbow and began steering her toward the front door.

She pulled free though, because A, she wasn't going

to be dragged around like a dog on a leash. And B, she needed her purse.

"Just wait a minute," she snapped and marched across the front room like a soldier striding across a battlefield. Snatching up her black leather bag, she slung it over her shoulder and stomped right back to Mike. "*Now* I'm ready."

He gritted his teeth. She could see the muscle in his jaw twitching and she almost enjoyed knowing she had the ability to irritate him so easily. Of course, she'd enjoy it even more if she knew what exactly she'd done to make him walk as if there were a steel spike between his shoulder blades.

Without waiting for him, Jenny walked out the front door, down the overgrown walk and stopped at the passenger door of the shiny red rental car to wait.

He looked at her over the roof of the car and demanded, "What the hell were you doing?"

"My *job*," she shot back, then threw the door open and slid inside.

He did the same, slammed the key home and fired the engine. Neither of them spoke again on the short drive to the hotel where they'd be spending the night.

When they got there, Mike turned the car over to the valet and Jenny was inside the hotel before he caught up to her. Again, he took hold of her elbow and pulled her to a stop.

"Will you quit doing that?" Her gaze shot from his hand on her arm up to his eyes.

"Quit walking away from me."

"Quit being a jerk and I'll quit walking away."

"You make me nuts," he grumbled.

"I think you were born that way," she said, "but Sean

seems perfectly reasonable, so it's probably not hereditary."

All around them, tourists swarmed through the lobby and into the casino. Bells, whistles and loud bursts of laughter played backdrop to their hurried, angry whispers.

"I'm not having this conversation here."

Jenny flinched at the cold, sharp edge of his voice. "I'm not having it at all."

"Yeah you are. We'll talk about it upstairs. Your room or mine?"

"Ha!" She laughed shortly. "Despite that charming invitation, I think I'll pass."

"We talk privately," he said, lowering his voice until it was a hush, "or we do it right here in the middle of the damn hotel."

"Fine. Upstairs. My room because I want to be able to tell you to leave."

He snorted, took her elbow in a grip firm enough she couldn't shake him off and steered her to the bank of elevators. One of them opened instantly as soon as Mike stabbed the call button. The two of them stepped into the open car as soon as it emptied and were joined by a half-dozen other people.

The elevator was crowded and the piped-in music was straight out of the 1980s. Mirrors on the walls made it seem as if there were fifty people crammed together, but the only person Jenny really looked at was Mike. He was at least a head taller than anyone else and in the mirror, his gaze shifted to hers and held. The car stopped, people got off, got on, and then they were moving again. Conversations rippled around them, but Jenny hardly heard them. All she could focus on was the glint in Mike's eyes and the grim slash of his mouth. Finally, though, they hit the eleventh floor. Jenny stepped off and Mike followed after.

The hallway was dimly lit and narrow, and with Mike right behind her, felt even tighter. She reached her door, slid the card key through the slot and opened it. Jenny'd left her drapes open, so afternoon sunlight swamped the room as she walked to the bed and tossed her purse down on it.

Mike closed the door and was walking toward her when she turned to face him.

"What the hell was that all about?"

"What was what about?" Jenny threw both hands high and then let them fall.

"You and the carpenter." Mike bit the words off. "When I walked into the lobby, you were flirting and he was drooling, so I ask again, what the hell was that about?"

Sincerely stunned, Jenny gaped at him for a second or two. "Flirting?" she repeated as anger bubbled and churned in the pit of her stomach. "I was talking about *paint*. About the mural I want on the wall in the lobby."

"Yeah, I heard the end of the performance." Mike cut her off with a wave of his hand. "Deep, breathy voice going all dreamy and soft. Hell, you had that carpenter standing there with his mouth open and his eyes bugging out."

"Dreamy? Soft?" Had she really sounded like that, she wondered, then shook her head to dismiss the question. Didn't matter if she had, Jenny thought. She hadn't been flirting, she'd been sort of lost in her own vision.

Mike inhaled sharply and said, "You sounded just like you did when you woke up in my arms."

Now it was her turn to drag a deep breath into her lungs. Reminding her of their most recent night together wasn't playing fair. "You're wrong."

He took a step closer, grabbed her upper arms and pulled her up against him. Jenny's heart leaped into a gallop and as he was holding her so tightly to him, she felt his heart raging in the same rhythm.

"I know what I heard," he said, staring down into her eyes. "What I saw."

She fought the natural impulse to wrap her arms around his waist and hold on. To go up on her toes and kiss him. To feel that rush of incredible sensations one more time. Instead, she reminded herself just how little he really thought of her. Of the fact that he didn't want her—it was only desire driving his reactions.

"I wasn't flirting," she told him. "But even if I had been, what business is that of yours? You're my boss, Mike, not my boyfriend."

"I am your boss," he agreed. "And I don't want you playing with the crew. I want them focused on the work, not you."

Stunned all over again, Jenny demanded, "Can you hear yourself? Do you even realize when you're being insulting? I mean, is it just instinct or is it deliberate?"

"Insulting? I walk into a room in my new hotel and find you practically salivating over some guy with a tool belt and a set of dimples, and I'm insulting?"

"You are, and what's worse is you don't see it," Jenny said and slapped both hands against his hard chest to shove her way free. He let her go. Taking a few steps away from him just because she *really* needed the distance right now, she faced him and said, "I'm here to do my job, Mike. You're my boss, not my lover."

"I remember it differently."

She flushed. *Damn it*. Jenny could actually feel heat race into her cheeks and could only hope that with the sunlight behind her, her face was in shadow enough that he wouldn't notice. "A couple of nights together doesn't make you my lover. It makes you…"

"Yeah?"

"A mistake," she finished. "Isn't that what you yourself called that first night? Oh, *and* the last one we spent together?"

He shoved both hands into his pockets and stared at her with an intensity she could feel. "I did. It was. That doesn't mean I enjoy standing by, watching you work some other poor guy into a frenzy."

"I had no idea I had so much power," Jenny said, shaking her head in disbelief. "Didn't realize I was so oblivious, either. I didn't see Rick—"

"Hmm. First-name basis already, huh?"

She ignored that and punched home what she most wanted to say. "I didn't see Rick in a frenzy—but you surely were."

"I was angry, not in a frenzy."

Was he jealous? Was it possible that Mike Ryan had seen her talking to Rick and had felt territorial over her? If he had, what did that mean? "Really. Angry that I was 'flirting' with someone other than you?"

"That you were flirting on the job, that's all," he said, and pulled both hands from his pockets to fold his arms across his chest. "Don't read more into this than there is."

"I don't think I am," Jenny said, moving close to him again. This was the weirdest conversation she'd ever had. Just a week or so ago, she'd pledged that she wouldn't be sleeping with Mike again. She already knew that this was a ticket to disaster. That the man had believed her to be a thief. Maybe he still did, she couldn't be sure. And yet, here she was, surrendering to the very need and hunger that had led her to his bed in the first place.

No. She couldn't. Not again. She would not allow herself to willingly walk right into more pain. With that thought firmly in place, she stopped where she was, looked up at Mike and said, "We're not going to do this again. I won't go to bed with you again."

"I didn't ask you to."

Now she smiled sadly. "Yeah, you did. In everything but words."

"Now you're a mind reader?"

"I don't have to be," Jenny told him and took a breath, hoping to ease the gnawing inside her. "I just know what happens when the two of us are alone together."

Seconds ticked past and the silence was heavy with a kind of tension that nearly vibrated in the air. Jenny held on to the ragged edges of the control that was rapidly slipping out of her grasp. If he pushed back, if he kissed her, then she'd be lost and she knew it.

"Damn it," he finally said in a gruff whisper. "You're not wrong." His gaze dropped from her eyes to her lips and back again. "I saw you with the carpenter and… Never mind. Like you said, none of my business."

Jenny nodded and said, "Let's just forget today, okay? We'll get the job finished tomorrow, then go home and things will get back to normal."

His blue eyes flashed with emotions that came and went so quickly, she couldn't identify them all, and maybe that was for the best.

"Normal." He nodded sharply. "Fine. We can finish

up at the new hotel by noon, probably. Then we'll head home and forget the whole damn trip."

Her heart gave a tug that unsettled her, but Jenny only forced a smile, keeping that small sliver of pain to herself. He wanted to forget the whole trip. Forget being with her, even that way-too-short moment they'd shared on the dock, where they'd talked like friends—or maybe more.

Forgetting wouldn't be easy, Jenny told herself, but it was the one sure path to sanity. Holding on to what she felt for Mike—feelings she didn't want to examine too closely—was only going to add to the misery later on. She had to find a way to let go of what-might-have-beens and focus instead on the cold, hard facts.

The man she wanted didn't want her beyond the nearest bed.

And that just wasn't good enough.

"So," Mike said, interrupting her thoughts, "I'll see you in the morning, then. Nine o'clock. Be ready to go to work."

"I will be." Once he was gone, Jenny dropped to the edge of the bed like a puppet whose strings had been cut.

This would be so much easier if only she didn't care.

Mike spent the evening working in his suite. He figured if he kept his mind busy with figures, budgets, plans for the future of their company, he'd have no time to think about Jenny. Or how she'd looked when he heard her describing the painting she wanted to do. He wouldn't hear the magic in her voice or see the interest in that carpenter's eyes when he watched her.

And he wouldn't keep seeing the look on her face when he had acted like some kind of demented comic-strip moron by accusing her of flirting with the guy. Hell, even if she had been, like she said, it was none of his damn business. But it sure as hell felt like it was. He'd hated watching that other man so focused, laser-like, on Jenny's face. Hated that he'd blamed *her* for whatever *he* was feeling.

"I don't know what's going on here," he muttered darkly, "but I don't like it." He'd always been in control. Of his feelings, his emotions—until Jenny. And what that meant, he didn't have a clue.

Mike scrubbed one hand across his face, pushed out of the desk chair and walked to the terrace. When his cell phone rang, he dragged it out of his pocket as he opened the sliding door and stepped into the teeth of a cold desert wind.

He glanced at the screen, then answered. "Hi, Mom."

"Hi. How's Vegas?"

"Laughlin."

"Same diff," she said and he could almost see her shrugging. "Sean told me you're out there inspecting the new hotel. What's it like?"

He dropped one hand on the iron railing, squinted into the wind and looked down to watch the river below froth beneath the hulls of flat-bottom boats taking tourists on a short ride. Neon fought against the stars for supremacy and won. On the Riverwalk, golden lamplight sifted onto the people strolling in and out of the shadows beside the river.

"It's run-down and sad right now, but I think it'll come together."

"Of course it will," his mother assured him. "My sons always do what they set out to do."

Mike smiled to himself.

"Sean says Jenny Marshall has some great ideas for

the artwork, too." She paused for a moment. "He says you and Jenny are there. Together."

"Does he?" Shaking his head, Mike ignored the blip of interest in Peggy Ryan's voice. He had to wonder if all mothers were as determined as his own to see her children married, with kids.

"Yes, he told me that you and Jenny would be working together for months on this new hotel…"

"Don't start," he warned her, amusement softening his words.

"Well, why shouldn't I?" she demanded with a huff. "You're not getting any younger, you know. And I've met Jenny. She's a nice girl. Talented. Pretty, too."

All true, he thought. She was also smart, opinionated, desirable and oh, yeah…untrustworthy. He scowled and remembered how cozy she'd looked with the damn carpenter today.

"Mom…"

"You can't fault a mother for hoping," she said, cutting him off before he could tell her to dial it back.

"Not interested in getting married, Mom," he said flatly. And she should know why, but he'd learned over the years that Peggy Ryan wanted nothing more than to forget the day that had changed everything for Mike.

There was a sigh in her voice when she said, "Fine. You are so hardheaded. Just like your father."

His frown deepened, but he didn't say anything. His mom didn't notice, or chose not to notice, because she rushed right on.

"I wanted to remind you, your dad's birthday is next week, and I want you and Sean both to show up, okay?"

Mike took a breath and blew it out. No way to avoid it and he knew it. But he never really looked forward to spending time with his father. It was...awkward. Uncomfortable.

Not that it had always been. Up until the year Mike turned thirteen, he'd thought of his father as his hero. Big, strong, with a wide smile and a kind nature, Jack Ryan was the kind of father most kids dream about. Jack had taught both of his sons to surf. A Little League coach, he'd spent hours at batting cages with them.

But the year he was thirteen, Mike had discovered that the father he idolized was also a liar. And that discovery had colored his image of his father ever since. He hadn't been able to forget or forgive. Jack had tried to close the distance between them many times, but Mike couldn't do it.

Memory was sometimes a hard thing and the images from the day when his father tumbled off that pedestal were as clear now as they had ever been.

"Oh, Mike," his mother said on a sigh, "I'm so sorry. You can't possibly know how sorry I am."

Mike stiffened. "You didn't do anything wrong, Mom."

"Yes," she argued. "I did. And I truly wish I could take it all back. Change that day."

"Yeah, well, we can't do that." Mike's hand tightened around his phone. "So let's just leave it in the past, okay?"

"I really wish you would, sweetie," Peggy said, then sighed again. "But fine. For now, I'll move on."

"It's appreciated."

"But I want you at your father's birthday dinner, Mike. No excuses. Sean's already promised to be here."

Of course he had. Sean didn't know what Mike did. He'd never told his younger brother about their father's fall from grace. Protecting Sean? Maybe. And maybe it was just that the thought of even more people knowing was too hard to take. Either way, though, Sean remained in the dark and that's how it would stay.

"Fine. I'll be there," he said, knowing his mother wouldn't stop until she'd gotten him to agree.

"Thanks, sweetie. We'll see you then." She paused. "Oh, and say hi to Jenny for me."

He hung up on her laughter. Shaking his head, he leaned his forearms on the terrace railing and watched the people below. Then he saw her. Jenny. Everything in him fisted as he watched her walk, alone, through the night, moonlight and neon playing in her hair.

Six

Normal was relative.

Jenny reminded herself several times during the following week that she and Mike were supposed to be back to "normal." And she supposed they were. For them.

The first day back, they stayed out of each other's way. But soon enough, work made that ploy impossible. While Jenny continued to work on the sketches of the Wise Woman for "The Wild Hunt" game, she was also going over her plans for the paintings at the new hotel. She'd taken so many pictures of the place, it was easy enough to figure out what she wanted where—it was simply time-consuming.

Then Mike got bogged down with calls from the contractor and plumber and electrician and the work on the game wasn't getting done, so Jenny volunteered to help. With her handling the Nevada hotel, it gave Mike time he needed to work with Sean and the marketing department on the cover design and the publicity campaign designed to push the game during release week.

Naturally, Jenny spent a lot of time in Mike's office fielding phone calls that she then had to tell him about, so they ended up spending hours together every workday. Yet what should have made them closer was instead highlighting the tension building between them.

Like now, Jenny thought as she sat down in front of Mike's desk. He was on the phone with one of the bloggers who posted about Celtic Knot, so Jenny had a minute to indulge herself in watching him.

His features were stony—his businessman face, she thought. Cool. No-nonsense. Unforgiving. His voice was clipped as he told the man what he wanted and expected, and Jenny had no doubt the blogger would do whatever Mike said. He had a knack for getting his way.

And for just a second, she wished *she* was his way.

Then he hung up and she forced her mind out of the lovely little daydreams it preferred and back to the business at hand.

"So, what've you got?" he asked, idly flipping a pen over and over between his fingers.

"Jacob says the painters can start next week," she said, checking her tablet and scrolling down to tick off information she had to give him. Jenny had spoken to the lead contractor so many times that week, she was beginning to think of the older man as family. "He also says the hotel employees you have living on-site have been helping the construction crew—lifting and toting mostly, but Jacob says they're really doing a lot to keep the work on schedule."

"Interesting," Mike admitted. "That wasn't part of our deal."

"Apparently, they got bored with just waiting for the new hotel to open." She shrugged and suggested, "They don't need to go out and find a new job, so maybe they're willing to help out, get the hotel open that much quicker. According to Jacob, they're doing a lot of the scut work, freeing up the crew to do the rehab."

Nodding, Mike said, "Make a note of the names of the guys who are doing the helping. We'll make sure they're paid for the extra work."

"Already done," she said.

He smiled and tossed the pen to the desk. "I like self-starters, people who are willing to step in and do what needs doing without being asked. Keep their names handy. We'll look at promotions when the hotel's up and running."

"I've got the list for you and the departments they worked in at the old hotel. I figured you'd want to do something like that."

"Impressive," he said with a nod of approval. "Are you sure you're an artist, not an admin?"

Surprised at the compliment, Jenny laughed. "Oh, artist, for sure. I don't mind helping you with this stuff, but if I had to keep track of everyone in the free world every day, it would drive me crazy."

"It does," Mike admitted. "I've been riding herd all week on bloggers, beta testers, the marketing guys and the design team working on the game cover. Sean hates the cover, I'm okay with it, but since neither of us is *happy* with it, they've got to go back to square one."

"What're they putting on the cover?"

"The forest, hints of a warrior stepping out from the trees, full moon…"

"Sounds a lot like the cover for 'Forest Run.'"

"Yes! That's exactly what I said." He shook his head, jumped up from his chair and paced to the window overlooking the yard and the blue, cloud-studded sky. "We need it different enough that people won't think they've already got it and similar enough that they know they'll be getting the same kind of fantasy they've become accustomed to."

"Hmm…" Jenny's gaze tracked him as he shifted impatiently from foot to foot at the tall window. If her gaze also dropped briefly to enjoy the view of his very nice behind, who could blame her? "What if we did something with the Wise Woman and the warrior together on the cover?"

He looked at her over his shoulder. "Go on."

"Maybe lightning flashing in the sky." Jenny closed her eyes briefly and could almost see it. "Magic shooting from her fingertips, wind lifting her hair, light gleaming off the warrior's sword…"

"I like it," he said, voice softer that it had been.

Jenny opened her eyes and looked into his and for a second or two convinced herself that she saw something…special. Then the moment was gone again because really, she shouldn't torture herself like that anyway.

"I'll give your ideas to the design team."

"Thanks," she said, pleasure making a warm knot in her chest.

"Hey, it's nice to talk to someone who doesn't need constant monitoring. Sometimes all I want to do is skeet shoot my cell phone."

"Understood. Completely." Didn't need to be monitored? Did that mean he was actually starting to trust her? *No,* she told herself, *don't get crazy.*

Going back to her tablet, Jenny continued. "We might as well finish this up. The engineers are on-site, working on the mechanisms for the river ghosts and ghouls. They say it'll take a couple months to get everything to be perfect, but again, according to Jacob, the engineers are excited."

"Okay, what else?"

"After all the positive stuff, there's a downside."

"Naturally," Mike said on a sigh. Easing one hip down onto the corner of his desk, he waved a hand. "Let's hear it."

"Jacob—wow, I've talked to him a lot this week—says there's a problem with the pipes."

"Great. What kind of problem?"

"The kind that means laying down new pipe. Mainly, the problem is the kitchen and the pool area. He says they'll probably last another five years, but after that, you'll need to redo the whole thing."

He laughed shortly, a scrape of sound with no trace of humor behind it. "Brady redid an entire fifteenth-century castle and those pipes were fine. I'm in charge of a hotel built in the 1950s and it's crap. What's up with that?"

Jenny shrugged. "Apparently castle pipes are made to last?"

"Apparently. Okay, what else does Jacob say?"

She winced a little. "He says to remind you that if you wait to do it, you'll have to pull out all the new tiles in the pool surround and take out a wall in the kitchen to get to everything. He suggests you do it all now."

"Of course he does," Mike said on a laugh. Then he

sighed and rubbed the back of his neck. "How the hell did we not find out about this problem during the inspection?" he muttered.

"Jacob says it's impossible to find stuff like this until you start getting beneath the surface." Jenny took a breath. This was going pretty well. They were in the same room and not sniping at each other. All she had to do was keep the focus on work and they'd be okay.

Of course, looking at him, it was hard to keep *thinking* about work. What she wanted to do was reach up and smooth his hair off his forehead. Step closer and feel his arms come around her. Lay her head on his chest and listen to his heartbeat.

And oh, dear God, she was sliding into a pool of something warm and tempting and way too dangerous. With that thought firmly in mind, she lifted her chin and stuck to business. "He says they didn't find the problems until they ripped out the kitchen floor to lay down a new subfloor before the tiles."

Mike nodded thoughtfully but didn't speak so she kept going.

"It's like all those rehab shows on HGTV. Couples buy this great house and they're redoing it and they find hideous things under the floor and behind the walls." She shuddered. "Makes you want to build new and avoid any old houses like the plague."

One dark eyebrow lifted and his mouth quirked. "Your apartment is an old one," he reminded her.

"Don't think I don't worry about that every time I see the people on TV finding mice and who knows what behind the walls." She shook her head hard and shivered again. "I try not to think about it."

"Don't blame you." Briefly, his eyes were warm,

nearly friendly. Then it was as if a shutter dropped down and suddenly, those blue eyes were cool and dispassionate again.

Jenny smothered a sigh.

"Jacob's right," Mike said finally. "We do the work now, make sure it's right. I want this hotel to be top-of-the-line all the way. No holding back. I'll call him, take care of it."

"Okay, good."

"Anything else?" He reached behind him for a bottle of water. Uncapping it, he took a long drink.

Jenny swallowed, too. Ridiculous that watching a man taking a drink could make her palms sweaty. Clearing her throat, she checked the tablet again. "Oh. Yeah. I talked to the interior designer you hired to furnish the hotel. She's not sure if you want contemporary furniture or something more—and I quote here—'antiquey' for the bedrooms."

"Antiquey?"

She shrugged. "Her word. I told her I thought you'd want something that feels old, almost otherworldly if she can manage it, but that I'd talk to you to make sure."

"You're right," he said and pushed off the desk. "I'll talk to her, but yeah, that's just what I want. Nothing fancy or fussy, but solid, heavy pieces that could be from the past or from the fantasy world we're re-creating."

"I think that's perfect."

Again, his mouth curved slightly and Jenny's heart did a slow tumble in her chest. It was ridiculous just how susceptible she was to this man.

"Good to know you agree," he said. "Because I need you to go with me to look at some furnishings. The designer's going to do most of it. She'll text me pictures of what she finds for approval, but Brady told me about a few places near here that had some great stuff he actually bought and had shipped to Ireland for the castle."

"He had stuff shipped? All the way to Ireland?"

"Well," he said, smiling a little, "not really. He had the movers stack it on the company jet and we flew it over ourselves. Still, would've been easier to buy it all there, but he found some nice stuff. Told me to check it out."

"Okay, when do you want to do that?"

"Next week's fine. We've still got plenty to arrange before then and…" he paused. "Aren't your new drawings of the Wise Woman due in tomorrow?"

"Yeah, they're nearly ready," she said, feeling a slight twinge of guilt. Usually, she turned her work in early, but she'd been so busy with everything else…

"If you need an extra day or two, don't worry about it." He walked closer. "I know you've been busy, picking up the slack on the hotel work."

"I don't mind helping."

He looked down at her. "And I appreciate it."

Her mouth was dry; her heart was pounding. She stared into his blue eyes and felt heat slide through her in a thick rush. Just being close to Mike was enough to weaken her knees—and her resolve. This was so not a good idea.

A quick knock sounded on the door and Sean walked in, already talking. "Hey, Mike? You're not going to believe what—" He stopped, looked from one to the other of them and asked, "Am I interrupting something?"

Mike took a single long step back, shook his head and said, "No. We were finished. Weren't we?"

Jenny shifted her gaze from Sean back to Mike and saw in his eyes that whatever had been looming between them was gone now. Probably a good thing, she acknowledged silently, but oh, she really wished Sean hadn't shown up.

"Yes," she said, when she found her voice, "we're finished."

And as she left the brothers alone, she thought those words had an eerie finality to them.

"Interesting," Sean mused as soon as Jenny had slipped off down the hall. He turned to look at his brother. "Something you want to share with the class?"

"No," Mike said shortly, hoping that Sean would let it go. But of course he didn't.

"I knew there was something going on between you two."

"You don't know anything about it," Mike insisted and walked around his desk to sit down.

"Oh, please. Am I blind?" Sean laughed and dropped into the chair opposite his brother. "That was an almost-kiss moment."

"Butt out, Sean."

Ignoring his brother, Sean continued. "Things were tense as hell between you guys before you went to Laughlin. When you came back it was tenser." He paused. "More tense? Whichever. You know what I mean."

"Yeah, I do, and I wish to hell you'd get what I mean when I tell you to back off."

"Oh, I get it," Sean assured him. "I'm just not listening. So tell me. What's with you and the oh-so-delicious Jenny Marshall?"

Mike's gaze snapped to his brother's. "Watch it."

"Oooh," Sean mused, grinning now. "Territorial. A good sign."

Well, walked right into that, didn't you? Mike's brain whispered.

"Damn it, Sean, stop." Mike tapped a few keys on his laptop, hoping to look too busy to sit and talk to his brother. "What did you come in here for in the first place?"

Still grinning, his brother eased off. "I wanted to tell you about the Wyoming property."

Mike frowned. "A problem?"

"Not with the place itself," Sean told him. "The sale went through, it's all ours. My problem is with the contractor."

"I'm having some issues there myself," Mike said, thinking about all the problems involved in getting a hotel up and running.

"Yeah, but your contractor's a guy. You can talk to a guy."

"Who's yours?"

"Supposedly the best one in the area. A woman. Kate Wells." Sean shook his head, jumped from the chair and paced the short distance to the window. "It's the middle of the damn winter and she wants to get started on the inside of the hotel. Says why waste time? Says she can't have the crew out working in the snow, but her schedule's clear now, so she wants to take her guys inside and start the renovation early."

"That's a problem?" Mike leaned back in his chair and tried to keep his mind on Sean's issues. Not easy when Sean was right about the almost-kiss moment. Seconds ago, he'd been about to—what? Kiss Jenny? Grab her, hold her? Close the office door and lay her down across his desk?

Damn it. Now he was hard and hot and it was even more difficult to focus on Sean.

"Sounds like a good plan to me," Mike said. "I like that this Wells woman has a good work ethic. Eager to get started, get a jump on things. Hell, she could have half of it done by the time the snow melts."

"Yeah?" Sean turned to look at him, exasperation clear on his face. "To get her started, I have to go the hell out there and work with her on the plans. Go through the hotel, see what's what, just like you did in Laughlin."

"Ah." In spite of everything else that was crowding his mind, Mike had to smile. "That's what this is about. You don't want to go to Wyoming."

"Of course I don't," Sean snapped. "There's *snow* there. Lots of it. Have you looked outside *here* today?" He waved one hand at the window behind him. "Blue skies, puffy white clouds, *sun*. It's almost eighty today. You know what it is in Wyoming? I do. I checked. It's twenty-eight. That's the *high*."

Mike chuckled and at his brother's glare, tried his best to muffle it and failed. "It's not forever, Sean. You go out, do the work, come back. At the most, you'll miss a few days of surfing. You'll survive."

"Thanks for the support," his brother muttered. "I'd have to take one of the artists to look the place over for murals, too. Hey." His face brightened. "Think Jenny'd be interested in a quick trip to snow country? Her sketches are great, she'd probably be a big help—"

"No." Mike cut him off before he could get going. Damned if he was going to sit back and have Jenny fly off to Wyoming with Sean. They'd be alone on the plane, at the hotel… No.

"Well, that was decisive."

"Just get one of the others to go with you."

"Not going to be easy to coax someone off a beach and into a snowbank."

"We've all got our problems," Mike told him, and instantly, his mind shot back to Jenny.

The problem there was he couldn't stop thinking about her, wanting her, needing her. And he knew damn well that there was no place in his life for her. He already knew that she was a liar. Okay, fine, she hadn't lied *lately*. But that didn't mean a damn thing. All it told him was that more lies were coming. When? What kind? And how the hell could he be so damn interested in a woman he *knew* he couldn't trust?

Sean came back, sat in the chair again, braced his forearms on the desk and leaned in. "Talk to me, Mike. What is going on with you? What's the deal with Jenny?"

Tempting to confide in Sean, but at the core of it, Mike wasn't a big sharer. He kept his thoughts, his emotions, locked down tight. Not many people got past the wall he'd built around himself. He loved his brother, but there were some things a man just didn't discuss. With anyone.

Shaking his head, Mike scraped one hand across his face. "Nothing I want to talk about, okay?"

Sean watched him for a long minute before saying, "All right. But I'm here when you want to talk. Remember that."

"I will."

"Okay," Sean said. "You're going to Mom and Dad's tonight, right? Not backing out?"

From one problem to another. Mike had considered blowing off his father's birthday dinner. He didn't need the aggravation piled on top of everything else going on. All he needed was to stoke the fire burning at the back of his brain. But if he didn't show up, his mother would make him pay. Somehow. Didn't seem to matter how old you were, your mother retained power over you. And Peggy Ryan had no difficulty wielding that power.

"Yeah, I'm going."

"Wow, feel the enthusiasm."

Mike glared at him. "I'm going. Should be good enough."

"You keep saying things that make me want more information," Sean told him, leaning back in his chair. He kicked his feet up and crossed them on the corner of Mike's desk. "You don't want to talk about Jenny. How about you tell me why you're always pissed at Dad."

"Not going there, either."

"You are not an easy person to have for a brother," Sean told him with a shake of his head. "You've got more secrets than the CIA."

"And the nature of a secret is, it's not talked about."

"That's what you think," Sean countered. "You know I could find out. I could just go to Mom."

"Don't." He didn't want his mother reminded of old pain. Didn't want her to have to tell her other son the things she'd inadvertently told Mike so many years before.

"Just 'don't'? That's all I get? What the hell, Mike? You've been at war with Dad for years and you won't say why." Sean braced both hands on the edge of the desk. "If you know something I should, then tell me."

Mike studied his brother for a long minute. During that short period of time, his brain raced through the familiar scenarios he knew he would be facing over dinner. Strained conversations, his mother trying to be overly bright and happy, his father sending Mike covert glances.

It wouldn't be pleasant. Wouldn't be easy. But he would play the game for his mother's sake.

As far as his little brother went, though, there was just no reason for Sean to have to battle the same emotions that Mike did when the family was together. "Sean, believe me, you don't want to know. So just let it go, all right?"

For a second or two, Sean looked as though he'd argue, but finally, he nodded and stood up. "Fine. But try to remember. I might be your younger brother…but I'm not a kid you need to protect."

Maybe not, Mike thought, but there was no reason to shatter his illusions, either.

A few hours later, Jenny jolted out of the movie she was watching when someone knocked at her door. Wearing her flannel sleep pants and a white tank, she was curled up on the couch with a bowl of popcorn and a glass of wine. Not working. Trying not to think. Just immersing herself in a few harmless explosions on the television.

She wasn't expecting anyone, so naturally, her very excellent imagination conjured up images of roving pirates, rabid serial killers or maybe even an escapee from a mental institution, all crowded together on her tiny front porch.

She wasn't the nervous Nellie type, but when she was alone at night, she often thought about getting a dog. A big one. But for now, she got up, looked out the curtains and sighed, both relieved and annoyed.

Mike.

At least he wasn't a marauder, but why did he have to show up when she looked hideous? No makeup, her hair a messy tumble of curls and wearing her *Star Wars* flannels? And what did it matter? she asked herself. He'd made it clear he wasn't interested, so let him see the real her…flannel jammies and all.

She opened the door and looked up at him.

"You don't ask who it is before you open a door?" he demanded, blue eyes flashing.

"Wow. Hello to you, too."

"Come on, Jenny. You're a woman living alone. Be smart."

"I looked out the window and saw you."

"Oh, that's all right, then."

"Thanks very much." One hand on the open door, one on the jamb, she asked, "What are you doing here, Mike?"

"Honestly," he said, "I don't know. Just had dinner with the family at my folks' house and didn't want to go home yet. I drove around for a while and ended up here."

Fascinating.

He wore a black jacket over a white shirt, open at the collar, with black jeans and boots that looked as if they'd seen a lot of miles. His hair had been ruffled by the wind and his eyes looked…empty. His features were tight, his shoulders tense, and Jenny thought he was on the verge of leaving. She didn't want him to.

"Do you want a glass of wine?" she asked.

His gaze fixed on hers. "That'd be good. Thanks."

Polite, but distant. That, plus a little outright suspicion, she was used to. Tonight, though, there was a sadness about him that she'd never seen before and Jenny felt a flicker of worry she knew he wouldn't appreciate.

He stepped inside, and she closed and locked the door behind him.

"You were at your parents' house, you said. Are they okay? Sean?"

He looked at her. "Yeah. They're all fine."

She tipped her head to one side and studied him. "You're not."

He laughed shortly and scraped one hand along his jaw. "I don't like being read that easily, but no, I guess not."

It was the first time she could ever remember seeing Mike Ryan vulnerable in any way. Normally he was so in charge, so much the stalwart head of a billion-dollar company, that seeing his features strained and closed off was unsettling. She'd rather have him raging at her than see him looking so lost.

"I shouldn't have come here—" he said abruptly.

But he had, Jenny told herself. For whatever reason, he'd been upset and he'd come to *her*. That had to mean something, didn't it? "Stay. Take off your jacket. Sit down. Have a glass of wine, Mike."

It took a moment or two, but he finally nodded and said, "Okay, thanks."

He shrugged out of his jacket and draped it across the back of a chair, then looked around the room as if seeing it for the first time. It wasn't his first visit, though. He'd been here before. The night they'd— Whoops. Probably not a good idea to think about that right now.

Mike stood in the middle of the small living room, glanced at the popcorn and her wineglass and then shifted his gaze to hers. "Movie night?"

She shrugged. "I just wanted to relax, you know. A lot going on right now…"

"Tell me about it." He sat on the couch, took a handful of popcorn and watched the movie playing out on the screen.

She went to the kitchen to get him that wine, then walked back to the living room and handed him a glass of chardonnay. He took a sip, gestured with the glass toward the TV and asked, *"Die Hard?"*

She smiled and sat on the other end of the couch. "It's my feel-good movie. You know, Christmas, good guys beating the bad guys…"

"And lots of stuff blowing up."

"Exactly." She grinned and sipped her wine.

"I didn't know you liked action movies."

"There's a lot you don't know about me."

"And some I do," he said, a frown flattening his mouth.

"Or think you do," she countered. She wasn't a liar and a thief, and she felt that somewhere inside him, he knew that or he wouldn't have been sitting on her couch.

"Touché." He nodded, glanced at the television again. "One guy going against a whole crew."

"To save his wife," she said with a satisfied sigh. "It's romantic."

He chuckled. "Romance and bombs?"

"Works for me."

His gaze shifted to the flannel pants she wore. "Darth Vader pajamas?"

She grinned. "They're cozy." And were a gift from her uncle Hank, but she doubted he'd want to hear that.

"I don't know what to think about you, Jenny," he said.

"Good. I'm glad. That means you're not entirely sure you should think what you used to think because now you think your thinking might have been wrong."

He blinked at her, then shook his head. "I actually followed that."

Turning his head again, he stared at the television. In the flickering light, darkness passed over his features, highlighting the shadows crouched in his eyes.

"Why are you really here, Mike?"

Slowly, he looked back at her. "You know why."

There was that wild flutter and rush of anticipation moving through her stomach again. She took a swallow of wine to ease her suddenly dust-dry throat, then set the glass on the table in front of her.

Jenny knew exactly what he was talking about. She'd felt it in the office today. Before Sean came in, there had been a slow, simmering burn between Mike and her, and that fire was still there, hot as ever. Acting on it would be a huge mistake. But *not* acting on it was driving her crazy.

"Yes," she said softly, holding his gaze with her own. "I know."

"So the question is," Mike asked, voice low and deep and intimate, "do you want me to leave?"

"No."

"Thank God." He set his glass down and reached for her.

Pushing the popcorn out of the way, Jenny went into his arms; all the while her mind called out a warning she refused to heed. She didn't want to be wise. Didn't want to be smart. She wanted Mike and that just wouldn't change.

But it was more than that, she admitted silently as Mike's mouth claimed hers. She leaned into him, opened to him, and felt the heat within build into something that was both wilder and more…steady than anything she'd ever known before.

Her breath caught, as understanding dawned. Her mind spun and she clung to Mike because he was the only steady point in her universe.

She loved Mike Ryan.

Her brain went into overdrive in the span of a single heartbeat. The months of working at Celtic Knot, watching Mike work with young artists, encouraging them. Seeing his dedication to his work, his brother and friend. Knowing that he didn't trust her, but having him give her the opportunity to work on his hotel in spite of it all.

He didn't trust her.

Didn't love her.

There was misery lying in wait, and Jenny knew it. But her whole life had been spent wanting the very feelings that were crashing down around her right now.

So she'd risk the pain to have this one moment—even if Mike never knew what was shining in her heart.

Seven

A few days later, Mike was at his desk when the video chat bell on his phone went off. He hit Answer and his brother's face appeared on the screen.

"I hate Wyoming."

Mike laughed. Sean looked haggard, on edge. His eyes were narrowed, whisker stubble covered his jaws and the scowl he wore looked as if it had been permanently etched into his face.

"Don't hold back, tell me how you really feel."

"Funny." Sean glanced over his shoulder, then back into the camera. "It hasn't stopped snowing since I got here. There's like three feet of snow piling up out there and it's still coming down. I don't think it'll ever stop."

"Sounds cold."

"Hah! Beyond cold. Beyond freezing. I'm wearing two sweaters *inside*."

Chuckling, Mike asked, "What's it like when you're not bitching about how cold you are?"

Sean sighed then grudgingly admitted, "It's pretty. Lots of trees. Lots of open land. And who knew the sky was so big when you get out of the city?"

Mike smiled. He'd discovered that for himself when he and Jenny were in Laughlin. Of course, allowing Jenny into his mind meant opening himself up to the memories that never really left him. Her smile. Her eyes. The feel of her skin against his. The soft sigh of her breath as she surrendered to him. Stopping in at her house after work, spending the evening watching movies, making love, talking about the work, the hotel. Talking about everything except for the fact that he couldn't trust her.

Pushing those thoughts away, he asked, "What's the hotel itself like, Sean?"

"Big. Cold. Empty." Sean blew out a frustrated breath and pushed one hand through his hair. "But the bones are good. A lot of work to do to turn it into a 'Forest Run' fantasy."

"And is Kate Wells up to the task?"

"To hear her tell it," Sean muttered. "Anyway, there's a hundred and fifty guest rooms and they all need work."

"If we go with your idea to hold our own game con on the property, we'll need more rooms. Are there other hotels close by?"

"No. We're ten miles from the closest town and it's got two B and Bs and one motel right off the highway."

It was Mike's turn to frown. "Sean, we can't go with a big conference if there's nowhere for people to stay." He took a breath and spoke again before Sean could suggest camping. "And don't say people can pitch tents."

Sean laughed. "Just because I like camping doesn't

mean I want strangers staying all over the property. Anyway, there's a bigger city about twenty-five miles from here, with more hotels and Kate—the contractor—had another idea on that, too."

"What's she thinking?" Mike picked up his coffee and took a long drink.

Sean's frown deepened. "Is that a cappuccino? You bastard."

"I'll enjoy it for you."

"Thanks." Shaking his head, Sean said, "Kate thinks we should put in some small cabins, behind the main lodge, staggered back into the forest. Give people more privacy, a sense of being out in the open…"

Mike nodded, thinking about it. "It's a good idea."

"Yeah, I know."

"Yet you don't look happy about it."

"Because she was so damn sure she was right," Sean told him. "It's hard agreeing she was."

"Sounds like you're having a great time," Mike said with another deliberate sip of his hot coffee.

Sean's eyes narrowed into slits. "This woman is the most hardheaded person I've ever dealt with and that includes *you*."

"As long as she does good work, that's all you should care about."

"Yeah, yeah. She wants to get her crew in here next week and start in on the rehab and I don't see a problem with it." He paused and ran one finger around the collar of his black sweater. "As long as I can oversee it from California."

"Okay, but since you didn't take any of the artists with you, what'll she do about the painting we'll need done?"

"Come on," Sean said. "I couldn't bring an artist out

here when everyone's doing the final run on 'The Wild Hunt.'"

True. It was bad timing all the way around, really. Sean had had to get to the next hotel and every artist in the company was focused on the finishing touches of the game that would be released next.

"Anyway," Sean continued, "how hard is it to leave walls blank? They can paint it white or something and then when we bring the artists in, they can change it to whatever."

"That'll work. You still coming home tomorrow?"

"That's the plan, thank God," Sean said. "Kate's outside, bringing her truck around. Naturally, it's still snowing."

"If it makes you feel any better, it's seventy-five here today."

"Great. Thanks. That just caps it." A door slammed somewhere. Sean looked to one side and shouted, "What?"

"What is it?" Mike asked.

"Karma probably," Sean told him, his expression disgusted. "Kate just heard on the truck radio that the pass down the mountain is closed. I'm snowed in."

Mike tried not to, but his brother looked so furious and frustrated, he couldn't hold back the laughter. Even as Sean gave him a dirty look, Mike held up one hand and tried to stop laughing. "Sorry, sorry."

"How is this funny?" Sean demanded. "I'm trapped in an empty hotel with a crabby contractor and a mountain of snow outside the door."

"Clearly," Mike said finally, "it's only funny from California. But have you got food, heat?"

"Yeah," Sean said, then spoke to someone in the room with him. "Come here for a minute. Meet my brother."

A second or two later, a woman popped onto the screen. Pretty, with a heart-shaped face and a wide mouth, she had black hair and eyes as blue as Sean's. She was wearing a baseball cap pulled low on her forehead and what looked like a heavy green sweater.

"Hi, I'm Kate and you're Mike," she said, words tumbling over each other. "Nice to meet you, but we don't have a lot of time to talk. There's firewood outside, we need to bring it in before the rest of the storm hits. Don't worry, though. There's plenty of food since I make sure my crew is fed while they work and we've been out here this last week taking measurements and getting ideas about the work."

"Okay." Mike threw that word in fast, thinking he probably wouldn't have another chance to speak. He was right.

"The storm'll blow through in a day or two and the plows will have the pass cleared out pretty quickly, so you can have your brother back by the end of the week."

"Okay…"

Sean grabbed the phone and told Kate, "I'll be right there to help. Yeah. Okay." When he looked back at Mike, he was shaking his head. "I was this close—" he held up two fingers just a breath apart "—from getting outta Dodge. Now I don't know when I'll get out. Tell Mom not to worry and don't bother calling me. I'm going to shut off the cell phone, conserve power."

"Okay." In spite of the fact that he'd been amused only a few minutes ago by Sean's situation, now Mike wondered. "You sure you'll be all right?"

Sean laughed now. "I'm the outdoors guy, remember? There may not be any waves to surf out here, but I'll be fine. I've been camping in worse situations than I've got here. At least we have a roof and plenty of beds to choose from. I'll call when I can. Just keep a cappuccino hot for me because I'll be back as soon as I can."

"I will. And, Sean?" Mike added, "Don't kill the contractor."

Smirking, Sean said, "I make no promises."

Two weeks later, Jenny was fighting a resilient flu that just refused to go away.

Every morning her stomach did an oily slide toward rebellion and every morning she fought it back. She was simply too busy to let some determined bug knock her flat. So she went to work, forced herself to eat and by evening was usually feeling if not great, at least better. Until the next day when it would all start again.

Hunched over her tablet, Jenny made notes on the hotel murals, then shifted files and added a few more finishing touches on the Wise Woman sketches for "The Wild Hunt." The witch was great and the addition to the script had really given the game that extra punch.

She'd even played the beta game the day before herself just to see how difficult it really was to find the extra runes that would free the witch. It was a challenge. So she knew the hardcore gamers among their fans were going to love it.

Yawning, she shut down that program and called up the list of artists and painters she'd developed. She'd need to hire at least three or four people to help her with the murals and would have to check out their qualifications first.

Sunlight slanted in through the windows of the graphic arts department and all around her conversations and ripples of laughter rang out. Fingers hit keyboards, rock music played softly from one of the cubicles, and here and there in the room people bent their heads together to go over the work.

None of the distractions bothered her because Jenny was used to working with background noise. She'd never yet met an artist who did their best work in sterile silence. So while her friends and colleagues worked the games, Jenny went to artists' websites.

She looked at portfolios, studied techniques, then checked the artists' bios and read about their backgrounds. Artists were usually solitary people, but she needed those who could work with others and take instruction. That was the hard part and she knew it. Most artists treasured their own vision of whatever they were working on at the time and didn't much care for someone else coming in and telling them what to do next.

But in this case, whoever was hired had to be willing to go along with the plans for the murals and portraits. They had to stick to the creative brief that Jenny was still finishing and not waste time arguing over the direction of the project.

She yawned and scrolled through the bio of a Nevada artist who specialized in fantasy paintings. His work was stellar but the smugness of his bio convinced Jenny he wasn't a team player.

"Next," she muttered and closed the page before moving on to another name on her list. She only needed to find one more artist and then she could get moving on the actual painting on-site.

"Hey, Jen—"

She looked up and smiled at Casey Williams. New to the company, Casey was a talented intern. She'd only worked at Celtic Knot for a couple of months, but she'd slid right into the mix as if she'd always been there. About twenty-five, Casey was married with a baby son. She had long dark hair that lay in a single braid across her shoulder. Her T-shirt was bright red, her jeans were a faded gray and her flip-flops revealed the green polish on her toes.

"What's up, Casey?" Jenny smothered another yawn behind her hand.

"Dave wants to know if you've finished tweaking the Wise Woman—"

"Yes, just a few minutes ago. I'll email the file to him."

"Cool. And I just want to say, I love your vision of her." Casey's hands were gripped together at her waist. "I saw the prelim sketches and they're amazing. It was a great idea to include her as a surprise for gamers. But the images are what really grabbed me. She's powerful and beautiful and— You don't look so hot."

Jenny laughed shortly. And here she thought she'd been so good about covering up how miserable she felt. "Thanks."

"No." Casey backtracked fast. "No, I mean, you look like you still don't feel well."

"Actually, I really don't," Jenny said, shaking her head, then regretting the abrupt motion because it wobbled her already unsteady stomach a little. For days, she'd been dragging around the office, trying to concentrate on the work even while her body continually reminded her she should be home in bed.

"Um…" Casey glanced around her, as if checking to make sure no one could overhear them. Then she sat down on the edge of a chair and leaned in closer. "I know we don't know each other very well yet, so this is probably out of line. But you've been feeling sick for a week or more now, right?"

"Yes..." Jenny said, wondering where this was going.

"I know this is none of my business." Casey took a breath and then let it go. "But I know the signs because I lived them myself a year ago."

Confused, Jenny asked, "What're you talking about? What signs?"

"Is it possible," Casey asked gently, "that this isn't the flu? That maybe you're pregnant?"

Shock held Jenny in place for a slow count of ten. Her mind, however, was racing. Thinking. *Counting.*

"Oh, my God." Panic rose up and choked off the nausea in the pit of her stomach. She did some fast calculating again, running through the numbers, the weeks, the possibilities. And ended up wheezing for air.

"Yeah," Casey whispered, nodding in understanding, "that's what I thought."

Oh, God, how far out of it was she that another woman was the one who had to tell her she was pregnant? How had she missed this? But even as she asked herself that, she knew the answer. She hadn't figured it out because she hadn't wanted to. Her relationship with Mike was so...tricky, a pregnancy was going to change everything.

Casey was still talking; excited, comforting, worried, Jenny couldn't be sure. All she really heard was a buzz of sound from the other woman. It was as if Jenny's head were filled with cotton, muffling everything but the pounding of her own heart.

Pregnant? By her *boss*?

It was more than possible, she knew. Instantly, her mind dragged up images from over the past few weeks. Incredible sex, sharing moments with Mike that she wouldn't trade for anything. They'd used protection of course, but no contraception worked 100 percent guaranteed. Would Mike believe that, though? No, he wouldn't.

Oh, God.

She blinked and the office came back into focus. She looked at Casey, and saw the woman's encouraging smile. All around her, life went on as usual, with no one but Casey aware that Jenny's world had just taken a major shift. She took a breath, tried to calm down, but that wasn't going to happen. Not until she knew, for sure. She could suspect she was pregnant, but until she knew without a doubt, she wouldn't be able to think clearly. Wouldn't be able to face Mike, with this suspicion simmering in her bloodstream. She had to know. Now. Suddenly, she couldn't sit there a moment longer.

Jenny grabbed her purse out of her desk drawer, then lunged to her feet. "You know, I really think I should just go home early."

"Are you worried?" Casey asked gently. "About how your boyfriend's going to take the news? I was nervous before I told my husband." She smiled to herself. "There was no reason to be. He was excited. Happy."

Mike wouldn't be. But Jenny couldn't say that because no one in the office knew she and Mike were together. Oh, this just got more and more complex.

Still, she forced a smile she didn't feel and lied to the nice woman still watching her. "I'm sure you're right and he will be. But right now, I think I just need to lie down for a while."

"That's a good idea," Casey said and stood up, too. "Take care of yourself and if you need anything—" She shrugged. "Call me, okay?"

"Sure. I will. Um, thanks, Casey."

"No problem. Drive safe."

Drive, Jenny told herself as she left the office and headed for the parking lot. Straight to a drugstore where she'd buy a few pregnancy tests and take them all. For the first time in her life, she was actually hoping she had the flu.

She didn't.

An hour later, Jenny looked at the five test strips lined up on her bathroom counter. Every last one of them was positive. She hadn't trusted one kind of test, either. She'd bought different ones, tried them all. And they all proved her suspicions right.

"I guess that's it, then," she murmured, lifting her gaze to her own reflection in the bathroom mirror. "I'm going to have a baby. Mike's baby."

Both hands covered her flat belly as if cradling the child within. She waited, meeting her own eyes in the mirror, trying to decipher the myriad emotions racing through her. Sure, panic was in there, but it wasn't uppermost in her mind. First and most important, there was *excitement*.

This wouldn't be easy, she admitted silently, but nothing great ever was. There was a lot to think about, to plan for. First, of course, she had to tell Mike. She wouldn't even try to keep this from him, even knowing how he was going to react.

Her heart hurt as she thought about the confrontation that would come soon. He'd never trusted her and this news was going to convince him that he had been right about her all along. She still had to tell him that she was carrying his child. Even if he wanted nothing to do with her afterward. Even if he walked out and never looked back.

She took a breath to steady herself, but the twinges of pain still squeezed her heart. Mike wasn't going to be happy. But Jenny was. There had never been a future for her and the man she loved, but now when he walked away, she would have something of him, forever. A baby. Her own child. Her own family. Someone to love. Someone who would love her.

She hadn't planned this, but now that the baby was here, she wouldn't change it, either.

"I promise, I want you," she whispered, voice soft with wonder as her palms stroked her belly. "You'll be loved and you'll never have to worry about me walking away. About being left alone. You'll be safe, I swear it."

She lifted her chin, stiffened her spine and resolved then and there that no matter what Mike said, what he tried to make her feel, she wouldn't lose this excitement. This sense of pure joy that was already whipping through her like lightning strikes. She hadn't expected this pregnancy, but she would never regret it.

She would give this child the life she had always wanted. It would grow up loved and secure and it would never, ever doubt its mother's love.

Jenny took a steadying breath and tried to steer her celebratory thoughts back down into more immediate concerns. Like facing Mike—and the possibility that she would have to change jobs. Even if he didn't fire her and who knew, he very well might, working at Celtic Knot over the next few months could be very uncomfortable.

But before she made any decisions, she had to tell Mike.

Jenny watched her reflection wince. That conversation wasn't going to be pretty. He would never believe she hadn't planned this pregnancy. And any semblance of warmth that had sprung up between them over the past few weeks was going to dissipate.

She hated knowing that. Hated understanding that her time with Mike was going to end. But not only did she love the man, she *knew* him. So she had to prepare herself for the fact that once he knew the truth, all of her fantasies would be over.

When her cell phone rang she went out to answer it. Seeing Mike's name on the screen didn't even surprise her. Of course he would call when she was thinking about him. Of course she wouldn't have time to get used to this staggering news before having to tell him and weather the inevitable fallout. But maybe it was better this way. Worrying over the coming confrontation would only tie her up in knots anyway.

Steeling herself, she answered. "Hi, Mike."

"Jenny, are you all right?" She closed her eyes at the sound of his voice. At the concern ringing in his tone. "Casey says you went home sick."

Sick. Well, technically, her stomach was still feeling a little iffy, but it was so much more.

"I'm okay, but, Mike," she said, mentally preparing herself for what was to come, "we have to talk."

An hour later, Mike stood in her living room staring down at the five test sticks she'd laid out on the coffee table. Brain burning, heart pounding, Mike stared at the evidence in front of him and still couldn't quite bring himself to believe it. He took a few deep breaths, willing himself to calm down, to beat back the sense of betrayal and suspicion that slapped at him.

"Pregnant?" He shifted his gaze to the woman across

the room from him. Her blond hair curled around her head. Her blue eyes were wide and shone with an innocence he couldn't trust. She wore those silly flannel pants and a yellow tank top that bared her shoulders and hugged her generous breasts. His gaze dropped to her belly briefly as he tried to imagine a child—*his* child—nestled inside.

He couldn't do it.

"How the hell did that happen?"

Her eyebrows lifted. "Really?"

He pushed both hands through his hair and scrambled for patience. "I know *how*, so don't get cute. But we used a condom. Every time."

"I know," Jenny said, wrapping her arms around her middle almost defensively, "but nothing's a hundred percent."

"Well, they damn well should be," he argued. What the hell as the point of using a damn condom if they didn't do their job? "Unless..." Mind clicking along, racing down dark, twisted, tangled roads, he said, "You had those condoms in your drawer."

"So?"

He didn't answer that question. Instead, he turned and stalked into her bedroom, tore open the drawer and grabbed one of the condoms still there. Had they been damaged somehow? Had she found a way to sabotage them so... He saw the date stamped on the bottom of the foil.

"What're you doing?" Jenny asked as she came into the room behind him.

"I thought maybe you'd done something to these," he muttered, turning to look at her, still holding the damn condom. "I don't know, poked holes in them with a needle or something."

She gaped at him. "Are you serious?"

He ignored that, just as he paid no attention to the look of astonishment on her face. She wasn't an innocent and he should have remembered that before allowing himself to slide into an affair that could only end badly. "Turns out you didn't have to. How the hell long have you had these things?"

She blinked in confusion, then said, "What does that have to do with anything?"

"Just answer the question."

Frowning at him, she said, "They were party favors at a bachelorette party I went to five years ago."

"Five years." Nodding, he curled his fingers around the condom package and squeezed.

"Does that matter?"

A short, sharp laugh shot from his throat. "Yeah. It matters. Especially since they *expired* five years ago." He couldn't believe this.

"What do you mean?" She practically pried his fingers apart to snatch the packet from him. "Condoms can *expire*?"

"You thought they lasted forever?"

"No," she said, "I never thought about it. Why would I? It's not like they have to be refrigerated or anything. Who would expect they could go bad? They're in their own little foil packs for heaven's sake."

"That's just perfect," he muttered and thought back to the first night with her here, at her house, and how damned grateful he'd been that she had condoms on hand. He'd never checked them out. Never thought to make sure they were good.

He scrubbed both hands across his face and told himself this was what he got for going against his own instincts. He'd wanted her. Had to have her. Even knowing that she was a liar. Now he was paying the price for following his own needs.

"It's probably why your friend gave them away as party favors," he muttered darkly. "Because they were no good, she got 'em cheap."

"But why would you hold on to them?"

"I didn't think about it," she said with a shake of her head. "I just tossed them into the drawer and never gave it another thought."

"Perfect," he muttered, scraping one hand across his face.

"You knew they were no good," he said, voice deep, dark. Anger bubbled in his gut until it was a thick, hot brew that spilled through his veins. "You knew what would happen if we used them and you were good with that, weren't you?"

"Are you serious?"

"Damn right, I'm serious." He crowded in on her, forcing her to back up until her legs hit the mattress and she plopped down onto it. "This was all a setup, wasn't it? Right from the beginning."

"What *all* are you talking about?" she demanded, glaring up at him. "You mean, you coming to my house, willingly going to my bed? That *all*?"

"Us meeting in Phoenix. You coming to work at Celtic Knot. It's all been building to this, right? Why the hell else would you come to work for me after what happened when we met?"

"You are seriously paranoid," she snapped, tossing her hair out of her eyes so she could glare up at him.

"Right. I'm paranoid, but you're pregnant, so maybe I'm not crazy, huh?" He leaned over her until their faces were just a breath apart. The smell of her invaded his senses and threw gasoline on the fire inside him. Even furious, even staggered by her news, Mike could admit to wanting her. To needing her. And that fried him.

"All you needed to do was get me in here, to use the damn useless condoms so you could get pregnant." He was so angry, the edges of his vision were blurred. His breath came fast and hard, his heartbeat thundered and desire tangled with fury until his whole body practically vibrated.

She shoved at him and he backed up just far enough for her to clamber off the bed and gain her feet again. "My God, do you really think you're that great a prize? Do you know how many times you've insulted me by calling me a thief? And that's supposed to endear you to me somehow?"

"Yet you slept with me anyway and here we are," he reminded her, in spite of the sparks flashing in her eyes.

"You're right," she said, sarcasm dripping from her words. "How clever I must be. And psychic as well to *know* that the great Mike Ryan would one day deign to visit my little apartment. Would allow me to seduce him with my trickery and feminine wiles. How brilliant of me to have faulty condoms so I could fool him into impregnating me. My God, I'm *amazing.*"

It sounded ludicrous even to him, but Mike couldn't let it go completely. His mind worked, with two opposing voices shouting, demanding to be heard. But the calm, cool, rational part of him was buried beneath the facts he couldn't forget. She'd lied to him the first time he met her. She'd come to work at his company in spite of that.

She'd wormed her way onto his hotel design team. She'd made herself *important*. But he'd kept her on. Hadn't told Sean to fire her. Why? Because she had gotten into his blood whether he'd wanted her there or not.

Now she was pregnant.

He looked down at her and the flash in her blue eyes did nothing to ease the anger bubbling and frothing inside him. It didn't help to know that even as furious as he was, he could still look at her and need her.

"No matter what you think," she said tightly, "I didn't trick you. I didn't set up a *trap* to catch the mighty and elusive Mike Ryan."

"Well, since you're so honest," he ground out, "I'll just believe you, okay?"

"You should but you won't," she told him, shaking her head, sending those curls that drove him crazy into a wild dance about her head. She underlined each of her words with a determined tap of her index finger against his chest. "Do you really think I would trap a man who doesn't want me? I've got more self-respect than that, thanks."

Jenny stood there facing him, chin lifted, eyes narrowed and hot with banked fury. She looked beautiful and strong, and it took everything he had to fight the urge to grab her and pull her in close. Jenny Marshall got to him like no one else ever had and he hated admitting that, even to himself.

Shaking his head, he took a mental step backward and told her, "It's not going to work. You're not getting money out of me and I won't marry you."

Her head jerked back as if he'd slapped her, but she recovered fast, he had to give her that.

"I don't want *anything* from you. As for marrying me?

Who asked you to?" she demanded and whirled around. She left the bedroom, walked into the living room, and he followed because what the hell else was he going to do?

She stopped in front of the windows and with the last of the sun's rays silhouetting her in gold, she looked at him and said, "I wouldn't marry you on a bet, Mike. You think I'd actually trap a man who doesn't want me into a marriage that would be a misery? No, thanks. I don't need you to take care of me or my baby, Mike."

Now it was his turn to feel insulted. Whatever he did or didn't feel for Jenny, she was carrying *his* kid and she'd better get used to that from the jump. "You can't keep my child from me, Jenny, so don't even try."

"Who said I would?" Shaking her head, she said, "You keep putting words in my mouth. So why not just stop trying to think for both of us? Telling you about the baby was the right thing to do. If you want to see our child, that's your choice. But you don't call the shots here, Mike, and I think you should leave."

He didn't want to. But staying here angry wouldn't help the situation any. He needed some air. Needed to think. But when he walked out of her house and heard the door slam shut behind him, Mike acknowledged that the real problem was that he needed her, too.

Eight

"You're pregnant?"

Jenny sighed and waited for her uncle to finish ranting. Right after Mike left, she had driven south to her uncle's house on Balboa Island. She'd needed…support, and she'd known she'd find it here. At least, she would once her uncle was finished calling down curses on Mike Ryan's head.

Her gaze tracked the older man as he paced around his living room. Just as when she'd told Mike about the baby, she'd come expecting this exact reaction. The man had never forgiven Mike for accusing Jenny of trying to use him. And this situation wasn't making her uncle any fonder of Mike Ryan.

"He turned on you, didn't he?"

Jenny winced and her uncle saw it. His gaze narrowed and his features tightened into lines of fury.

"I knew it. That son of a bitch."

She sighed a little.

"When you told him about the baby, he accused you of trying to trap him into marriage, didn't he?"

Well, she could lie to her uncle or she could tell the truth and confirm his opinion of Mike. Jenny thought about it for a second, then decided she didn't need to protect her baby's father. "Yes, he did."

"Still thinks you're trying to wangle a deal for Snyder Arts?"

"I guess," she said on a sigh.

"Idiot," Hank muttered.

Before he could get going again, Jenny started talking. She wanted to say something that she should have said years ago. "Uncle Hank…"

The tone in her voice must have alerted him to a change in subject. He looked at her, concern shining in his eyes. "What is it?"

Lamps on the tables tossed golden light around the room. Outside, lights in homes and boats flickered in the darkness. This was home. Had been since she was a girl. And the comfort she felt here was something she was still grateful for.

She smiled a little. "I wanted to tell you something. When I first realized I was pregnant, I thought about all the responsibilities lying ahead. And I understood how you must have felt when my parents foisted me off on you."

"When they—"

"I just want you to know that I don't blame you for not wanting me, back then. I mean," she hurried on as Hank's forehead furrowed and his eyes narrowed, "I was twelve and you were alone and had your life and I was a—"

"Gift," Hank finished for her while she searched for the right word. "You were a gift," he repeated as if making sure she understood exactly how he felt. "My sister and her husband were fools then and they're fools now—wherever they are. They didn't know what they had in you."

Stunned silent, Jenny could only watch him as he approached and cupped her face in his big hands.

"You opened up my life, Jenny. Of course I wanted you. You're my family. You've been a joy, always. You're my *daughter* more than my niece. And now, you've given an old man something to look forward to—you're going to make me a grandfather."

Her vision blurry from behind a sheen of tears, Jenny could only look up at the one steady presence she'd known her whole life.

"No more of this not-wanting-you stuff, okay?" he asked. "Don't you ever even think it. Understand?"

She nodded because she didn't trust herself to speak. Her heart was too full to allow for mere words to explain what she felt.

"Good," he said with a sharp nod. "We've got that settled once and for all. But as for Mike Ryan…"

"Uncle Hank, this isn't all on Mike. I'm a big girl—"

"You're too trusting and he's a man used to taking what he wants. That's the issue here," Hank muttered darkly. He paced again as if he couldn't stand still another minute. "Thinks because he's richer than Croesus he can just call the tune everyone's supposed to dance to."

Jenny rolled her eyes and he saw that, too.

"I'm wound up and I know it," he said, "but with reason."

"I appreciate it, really I do," Jenny told him and

walked across the comfortably furnished and oh-so-familiar room to his side.

Nothing in this house had changed in decades. There were comfy chairs, heavy tables and a stone-faced fireplace. The cream-colored walls were covered with paintings by local artists—and a few of Jenny's early works. He had a housekeeper who'd been with him for thirty years and ran the house like a general his battalion.

"You're going to have the man's baby, Jenny. He should offer to marry you. It's what's right—not that Mike Ryan would know that."

She blew out a breath as she looked into the older man's worried eyes. Uncle Hank was tall and lanky, with thick gray hair, steely blue eyes and a stubborn jaw that was now set as if he were ready to bite through a box of nails. He had been the one steady influence in her life and he was the only family she really had. Her parents had disappeared from her life so many years ago, Jenny had no idea if they were living or dead. Hank, though, had always been there for her.

Even though, despite what he had just said, she couldn't imagine it had been easy for him to take on a twelve-year-old girl out of the blue.

She had known even then that she was his duty. She hadn't believed he'd really wanted her—why would he? His life was simple, uncomplicated. Why would he take on a twelve-year-old with abandonment issues voluntarily? But he'd taken her in, cared for her, seen her through school and dating, and even hired Jenny for her first real job as a summer intern at Snyder Arts. Hank had been the one to give her pastels and inks and sketch pads. He'd seen her raw talent and encouraged her to grow it. She would always owe him for that and for so much more.

"I don't need him to marry me," she said softly, laying one hand on her uncle's arm.

"'Course you don't, but he should have offered, damn it, not made you feel like a cheat or worse."

"I don't want a man who's forced to marry me because of circumstances." She remembered the look on Mike's face before he left. The harsh words they'd thrown at each other, and though it tore at her to admit it, Jenny knew that it was over between them. A low, throbbing ache settled into her heart and she had the distinct feeling that it would be there with her forever.

"So you'd have said no if he'd asked?"

"Yes," she said and knew he didn't really understand. In Hank's world, a man took care of his responsibilities. But what he didn't get was that Jenny didn't want to be the duty Mike picked up and carried under duress. If he didn't love her and want her, she didn't want him, either.

She still loved him, though, damn it. Even hearing his accusations hadn't been enough to kill off her feelings. Did that make her crazy or just stupid? She didn't know. All Jenny could hope was that the love she felt for Mike would slowly fade away.

Besides, she hadn't really been surprised when Mike didn't want her. No one ever really had. Until today, she would have said that not even her uncle had wanted her.

And she would never allow her child to feel that way.

"Mike Ryan." Hank shook his head and gray hair sproinged out around his head until he looked like a taller, more handsome Albert Einstein. "What were you thinking, honey? You know that man isn't to be trusted."

"Funny," she mused. "He says the same about *me*."

Hank stabbed his index finger toward her. "That tells you everything you need to know about the man. You're the most honest person I've ever known. If he can't see that, it's a lack in him, not you."

Warmth trickled through her. "Thanks, Uncle Hank."

"You don't have to thank me for the truth, honey," he said, shoving both hands into his pockets. "And I'm sorry to be carrying on so, but it just pops my corn that the man has taken advantage of you this way."

Jenny's mouth quirked. He sounded as if he thought she was a vestal virgin tempted out of her temple by Blackbeard.

"Uncle Hank…"

"Fine, fine." He lifted both hands. "You're a grown woman and you don't need your old uncle spouting off when you've got plenty to think about on your own."

"Thank you, though," she said, putting her arms around his waist. "For the outrage. For the support. For loving me."

True to form, Hank stiffened a little, as he always had. Hugs seemed to flummox him a bit, as if he wasn't quite sure what to do in response. And Jenny had often wondered what his late wife had been like. If she'd lived, would he be more comfortable with displays of emotion? He gave her a few awkward pats on her shoulder, then eased her back so he could look into her eyes.

"Are you all right with this?" he wanted to know. "I mean, you're healthy? You're going to be okay?"

"I'm fine and yes, I'm going to be great." She smiled. "I want this baby, Uncle Hank."

"Then I'll do whatever I can to help you, honey."

She smiled again. Hank wasn't the most outwardly

affectionate man, but he was loyal and kind and dependable. If he made a promise, he kept it.

"What're you going to do about your job?" he asked.

"To tell you the truth, I don't know." She bit at her bottom lip as she thought about it. "Working with Mike for months will be impossible now. Especially once word gets out around the office—and it will—that I'm carrying his child."

Hank frowned and looked as though he wanted to say something else, but he kept his silence and Jenny went on.

"But I'm not going to do anything about it right now. I've got the hotel in Nevada to finish."

"You're still going to do it?"

"Absolutely," she told him. Not only was she too invested in the project to give it up now, but being in Laughlin working would keep her from having to deal with Mike every day. "It's a fabulous opportunity and I don't want to give it up. I've got the whole thing planned out and letting someone else take it over is just impossible."

"Always were stubborn," he muttered.

"Wonder where I got it," she countered and went up on her toes to kiss his cheek.

He looked pleased but baffled.

"Come on in and eat, you two. Dinner's going cold on the table."

Jenny looked over at Betty Sanders, housekeeper, cook and, as Uncle Hank liked to call her, his nemesis. She was short and thin, disproving the theory that a great cook had to be big. She wore jeans and a sweatshirt and had her long gray hair in a braid wrapped around the back of her head like a halo.

Jenny appreciated the offer, but she wasn't all that hungry, either. "Thanks, Betty, but—"

"If you're going to have a baby, you're going to feed it. Now come in and sit down." Betty had helped raise Jenny and had run Hank's house and life for too long to stop now.

"Might as well," Uncle Hank said with a shrug. "You know she won't quit hounding you until you do."

"True." Jenny walked with him into the dining room, glad to be here in the home she'd loved growing up. Out the windows was a view of Balboa Bay, with beautiful houses lined along the shore and boats tied up at the docks.

When she first came here, Jenny had spent a lot of time down on the dock, watching the boats sail past, wondering if her parents would come back, if Hank would send her somewhere else. She'd felt lost and alone until the day her uncle had come out, sat down beside her and said, *If you're going to be spending so much time out on the dock, I'd better teach you how to sail.*

He took her out on his boat that very afternoon and for the first time in her life, she'd felt the amazing freedom in skimming across the water's surface, feeling the wind stream through her hair. He'd let her steer the boat, putting his big hands over hers on the wheel and explaining the harbor and the neighborhood that was now hers. That's when she'd understood that she was there to stay. Hank had given her everything in that one afternoon.

At the round oak table in the dining room, all three of them sat down and dug into the hearty bowls of home-made potato soup. While they ate, they talked, and Jenny was glad her uncle seemed to be calming down.

"There's just no point in worrying over what is," Betty

said, with a warning look at Hank. "Jenny's fine and she'll keep being fine with or without a man."

"'Course she will," Uncle Hank shot back. "That's not the point."

"It's exactly the point," Betty argued. "Why would you want her to have a man who doesn't really see her for who she is?"

"I want him to do the right thing, is all."

"The right thing is to walk away if you can't care."

Jenny felt as if she were at a tennis match. Her head swiveled back and forth as she followed the heated conversation that swirled around her as if she wasn't even there. Through the windows, she could see tiny white patio lights strung across the pergola, blinking like fireflies.

"I'm just saying she shouldn't have to do all of this alone," Uncle Hank muttered with a nodding glance at Jenny.

"She's not going to be alone," Betty snapped. "She's got us, doesn't she? We don't count?"

Jenny smiled, reached out and covered Betty's hand with her own. Betty was right. She wasn't alone. She had family. A family that Uncle Hank had given her. She grabbed for her uncle's hand, too, linking the three of them.

"She's right, you know," Uncle Hank told her, with just a touch of discomfort. "You've got us. For whatever you need."

"Thank you," she said, as warmth spread through her. He'd given her a real gift today. He'd let her know that her early fears in childhood hadn't had a basis in reality. He had wanted her. Still did. And now, he was making another choice, Jenny thought. A deliberate one, to once again be there—not just for her, but for her baby.

"Jenny," Betty said, giving her hand a quick pat, "you should think about moving back home."

"What?"

"That's a good idea," Uncle Hank piped up. "Never did like the idea of you living alone."

"Nonsense, why shouldn't she live alone?" Betty countered. "You're living in the dark ages, Hank. What I'm saying is, with a baby coming, she should come back home where she will have all the help she needs."

Both of them turned to look at Jenny, waiting for her response. Though she really appreciated the thought, Jenny wasn't ready to give up her little apartment and go running back home. Maybe that would change later on, when the baby's due date was closer, when she began to worry about being able to handle everything on her own.

But for now... "Thanks," she said, meaning it completely. "I appreciate that a lot, really." She looked from one to the other of them. "But I'm fine for now. I have my work and my own space."

Betty and Hank exchanged a knowing look, then her uncle turned to her. "Okay, but..." He paused and with an embarrassed shrug added, "You should remember that you've got a home here. People ready to help."

Jenny's eyes filled with tears but she blinked them back because she knew if she cried, Uncle Hank would panic. Instead, she squeezed his hand and whispered, "Thank you, Uncle Hank."

He squeezed back briefly. "No need to thank family."

Betty gave a loud sniffle, then snapped, "All right, now, that's enough of that. Soup's getting cold and, Jenny, you need to eat. That baby doesn't need a skinny mama."

Smiling to herself, Jenny did as she was told.

* * *

Mike spent the next few days at home. He couldn't go to the office because there, he'd have to deal with Jenny and he needed some damn time to come to grips with what had happened.

A baby.

Because of faulty condoms, he was going to be a father and he couldn't quite wrap his head around that one simple fact. Mike had never considered having children. To his mind, being a father meant being married and he'd never do that. Never give another person the ability to cut him off at the knees. To bring misery and—

Hell.

He left the silence of the house and stalked across the stone patio that led down a wide sweep of lawn toward the cliff. Beyond those cliffs was the Pacific and as he stared out at the ocean, glittering brightly beneath the morning sun, he squinted to see the handful of sailboats skimming the water. Closer to shore, there were a few surfers waiting for a decent wave.

The sound of the ocean reached him and the steady pulse of water against rocks seemed to steady him. He'd bought this house mainly for the view. It was too damn big for a man alone and he knew it, but until today, the quiet and the…emptiness really hadn't bothered him much.

Now, though, he looked at the pristine backyard and pictured a swing set there. He turned and stared at the shining windows and imagined Jenny in one of them, smiling down at him as she held their child in her arms.

Shaking his head, he rubbed his eyes and told himself he was just tired. Not surprising since he hadn't gotten much sleep over the past few days. How could he when memories of Jenny kept intruding? He saw her as she was the night he'd come to her after a miserable dinner at his parents' house. In her flannel pajama bottoms and slinky tank top. Saw her eyes as she leaned into his kiss. Heard her sighs as he entered her.

"How the hell is a man supposed to sleep when his own mind is working against him?" he demanded of no one.

"It's a bad sign when you talk to yourself."

Mike spun around to see Sean strolling out of the house and down the patio toward him. "When did you get back?"

"Last night," Sean said, shaking his head. "It was a hell of a storm. Kept us locked down for way too long." He tipped his head back, stared up at the blue, sunny sky and sighed. "It's good to be back in the sun. Man, I thought I'd never get warm again."

Mike gave him a halfhearted smile. It shamed him to realize he hadn't given Sean a thought in days. His own brother trapped in a snowstorm and he hadn't wondered once how he was doing. But now, it was good to steer his brain in a different direction. "You didn't kill the contractor, did you?"

Sean shot him a look, frowned and said, "No. Didn't kill her."

Mike frowned, too. "Something going on there?"

"Not a damn thing," Sean told him, then changed the subject abruptly. "I don't want to talk about Kate Wells, all right? Went by the office this morning. Glad to see everyone got the final changes in on 'The Wild Hunt.'"

Huffing out a breath, Mike realized he hadn't paid attention to that, either. One of their biggest games getting ready to roll onto the assembly line and he hadn't bothered to dot the i's and cross the t's.

"Jenny's Wise Woman character turned out spectacularly. Dave showed me the final sketches. That woman is talented."

"Yeah." Mike turned his face into the wind. Jenny was talented. And beautiful. And exasperating. And *pregnant*.

Sean was still talking. "Linda told me you haven't been in to the office in days. You sick or something?"

"Or something," Mike said. "You want some coffee?"

"Got a cappuccino on the way over." Sean grinned. "It was worth waiting for. But you're stalling. What's going on, Mike?"

He shoved his hands into the back pockets of his faded jeans and rocked on his heels. He hadn't told anyone about Jenny. About the baby. If Brady had been here, instead of in Ireland, Mike might have spilled the whole thing. But now, Sean was here and he found he needed to say it all out loud.

"It's Jenny," he said, looking at his brother. "She's pregnant."

A second or two ticked past as Sean simply stared at him, a befuddled expression on his face. Then a slow smile curved his mouth and he said, "I *knew* there was something going on between you two. And there's a baby? That's great, right?" He rushed across the patio and gave his brother a brief, hard hug. "I like Jenny a lot," he said, stepping back and grinning. "And everybody's noticed the red-hot chemistry between you two."

Mike went still. He'd been sure that what was between Jenny and him was a secret. Private. "Everybody noticed? You mean people at work know about—"

"Well, they don't *know*, but sure, there's been some talk." Sean shrugged. "Mostly the women. They really notice the stuff that sails right over most guys' heads."

"Great. That's great." Just what he wanted. All of his employees knowing about his private life, speculating, maybe even making bets on what would happen next.

"What's the problem?" Sean asked. "It's not like it would have stayed a secret for long. Not with Jenny pregnant. And here's another question. If she's pregnant, why is she out working on the hotel in Laughlin and you're not with her?"

"She's in Laughlin?"

"Yeah. Linda says she went out yesterday. She didn't want to take the jet, so she drove, hauling all of her paint supplies with her." He paused. "And you didn't know anything about this, did you?"

"No." Mike wasn't happy about it, either. She could have told him she was driving out alone to Laughlin. He thought about that long, lonely road through the desert. Hell, there were sections where you could go for *miles* with nothing but sand on either side of your car. "She didn't tell me."

"Why wouldn't she?"

Mike snapped his brother a hard look. "None of your business."

"What'd you do, Mike?"

"I didn't *do* anything," he argued, feeling defensive even though he knew there was no reason for it.

"Yeah? The woman you're crazy about is pregnant with your kid and you look like you want to punch somebody." Sean tipped his head to one side and said, "Why don't you spill what's really going on?"

"She did this on purpose," he muttered.

"Wow. She *forced* you to have sex with her?" Sean snorted. "You poor guy."

"Shut up, Sean."

"Do you get how ridiculous you sound? Get over yourself, Mike. She didn't trick you. Or trap you. Hell, you're not that great a prize."

"Thanks. So glad you're home." Mike scrubbed one hand across the back of his neck and remembered that Jenny had said the same damn thing to him not so long ago. But you'd think his own brother would be a little more supportive.

"Come on, Mike. Condoms leak. Nothing's perfect." Sean slapped Mike's shoulder. "So you gonna marry her or what?"

"No, I'm not marrying her."

"Why the hell not?" Sean threw both hands high, clearly exasperated. "She's gonna have your baby and you're obviously nuts about her."

"I need more coffee." Mike walked away from his brother to the glass-topped table at the edge of the patio. There, he poured a cup of coffee from the thermal hot pot his housekeeper had brought out. He took a sip and let the heat slide through him.

"What's going on?" Sean followed him. "I can't believe you won't marry her. This is your kid we're talking about, Mike. Marrying her is the right thing to do and you know it."

His head was pounding, brain racing. Sean's haranguing wasn't helping with the headache throbbing behind his eyes. He hadn't slept, hadn't been able to think clearly in days, and now he'd found out Jenny was in Laughlin—without bothering to tell him.

"What do you think Mom and Dad'll have to say when they find out?"

"They should understand better than anyone." Mike's gaze shot to his brother's and before he could stop himself, he was blurting out the secret he'd held since he was thirteen. "I'm not marrying anybody, you understand? I won't risk being lied to, cheated on. You think I want to take a chance on ruining my own kid's life?"

"What the hell are you talking about?"

Too late to pull it back now, Mike told his brother about the day his own image of the perfect family had been shattered. "When I was thirteen, I came home from baseball practice and found Mom crying," he said tightly. "I was worried, thought maybe Dad had been in an accident or something."

"What was it?"

He could still remember it all so clearly. Sunshine pouring through the kitchen window. His mom sitting at the table, head in her hands, crying. He'd never seen her cry before and it scared him.

Mike set his coffee cup down, crossed his arms over his chest and said, "She grabbed me into a hard hug and she told me that Dad had cheated on her. That she found out he'd been out with some woman."

"No way." Sean's eyes went hard and cool and flat.

Mike knew how he felt. Back then, it had seemed to Mike as though the floor had opened up beneath him. He'd worried about his mom, wondered if his dad would ever come home again. Would they get a divorce? Who would he live with? A thirteen-year-old kid shouldn't have to think about any of it. Shouldn't have to learn so suddenly that his parents were flawed. Human.

"She never would have let any of it slip if I hadn't

caught her in a vulnerable moment," he said, and knew it for truth since his mom had apologized over and over again over the years. "Dad lied. To her. To us. He was a liar and a cheat and ever since that day, I can't be around him without remembering our mother crying."

Sean looked away toward the ocean and Mike finished. "I won't get married, Sean. I won't put my faith in someone only to be lied to and cheated on. Not gonna happen. I won't risk my kid being destroyed by lies."

After a moment or two, Sean turned his head to look at him and Mike read the fury in his brother's eyes.

"You had no right," Sean said tightly. "No right to keep this from me. I'm a Ryan, too."

"Why the hell should you feel as crappy as me?" Mike argued. "You didn't have to know and a lot of the time I wished to hell I didn't know."

"And you make the choice for me, is that it? You decide what I should know, what I should think?"

"That's not it," Mike said.

"Sure it is," Sean snapped. "You don't even see it, do you? You've been mad at Dad for years for lying. Every time you talk about Jenny, you call her a liar, say you can't trust her. But you've been lying to me since we were kids.

"So what's the difference, Mike? Are you the only one who gets to lie? Do you get to decide which is a good lie and which is bad?"

Mike had never thought about it exactly like that until now and he didn't know what he could say to the accusation. His father's lies had destroyed Mike's image of a happy family. Mike's own lies of omission were to protect Sean from the same hurt Mike felt.

And yet today, Sean was slapped with not one, but two sets of lies.

"You ought to take a good look at yourself, big brother," Sean said quietly. "Whatever was between our parents back then? They fixed it. Healed it. In case you hadn't noticed, they're still together, stronger than ever."

Truth could hit as hard as lies.

"So don't kid yourself. This isn't about Dad. Or Jenny. This is all on you, Mike. You're the liar now." Sean turned and walked away, stalking across the patio and into the house.

Alone in the yard, Mike felt the ground he'd built his life on tremble beneath his feet. Sean was right, he realized. Which meant that Mike was wrong. About a lot of things.

Nine

Laughlin in February was pretty.

The summer heat was still a few months off and the river was quiet but for the inevitable tour boats and an occasional Jet Ski. There were a lot of snowbirds in town, older people coming in to escape snow country with a few months in the desert. Tourists were always there of course, and every day, pontoon boats full of visitors to the city slowed to watch the progress being made on the River Haunt.

True to his word, the contractor, Jacob Schmitt, was keeping to schedule. He had men working on both the hotel facade and the interior, where Jenny spent most of her time. There was the constant drone of saws and the slamming of hammers, not to mention shouted conversations and laughter ringing out all around her.

But she was still glad she'd come. Being in the desert, away from the office for a while, had been a great idea. In Nevada, she didn't have to deal with the worry of having to face Mike again so soon after their confrontation. It hurt, knowing that their connection was over. But it would be even more painful if she had to see him every day. To be reminded of what they might have had.

No, what she needed was a little space, a little time, to get used to the idea that she was going to be a single mother.

She'd always wanted to have kids—lots of them. But in her secret dreams, she also had a husband who loved her. That little dream wasn't going to come true, though. Remembering the look on Mike's face when she told him she was pregnant was enough to convince her of that. Even if she didn't also have the memory of him accusing her of trying to trap him into marriage.

Pain and anger twisted into a knot that sat like lead in the pit of her stomach.

"He really is an idiot," she muttered, swiping a paintbrush loaded with deep violet paint across the entryway wall. Why couldn't she have fallen in love with someone—*anyone*—else? Why did Mike Ryan have to be the only man for her?

Jenny sighed and finished covering the wall with the paint she'd chosen for the biggest impact. Once it was dry she'd lay out the lines for the forest, the moon and the hints of figures she wanted lost in the trees. It would take a few days, but that was okay with her.

She had driven out here with a plan to stay for at least a week. Heaven knew there were plenty of hotel rooms to choose from and she wouldn't be lonely, either. Not with the security people and the hotel employees staying here, as well.

Besides, being on-site, she could oversee the other artists she'd hired to help with the murals. There were three of them, all talented, but artists were temperamental people and just as likely to go off plan and add their own visions to a design. But that couldn't happen here. The designs had all been approved by Mike, Sean and Brady already, so there was no deviating from them.

"Hey, Jenny!"

She looked up at the friendly shout. Tim Ryerson, one of the hotel employees, stood at the front door. "What's up, Tim?"

"Some of us are going into town for lunch. You up for it?"

They were all being so nice to her, but what Jenny really wanted was quiet and some time to herself. "Thanks, but I think I'll stay here and get started on the dining room mural."

"You're allowed to have fun, too, you know," he said with a sad shake of his head.

"Thanks, but for me, this *is* fun."

"Okay, then." He shrugged good-naturedly. "Can we bring you back anything?"

"A burger," she said quickly. "And lots of fries."

She was starting to get her appetite back—at least in the afternoons—and she wasn't sure if that was a good thing or not. She was so short that if she kept eating like this, by the time the baby was born, she'd look like a soccer ball.

"You got it. Later."

Once he and the others had gone, the hotel fell into blessed quiet. Lunchtime was the one time of the day she could count on a little peace. Even the crew's ever-playing radio was silent as the men left to get something to eat. She had the place to herself for the next hour and Jenny relished it.

Leaving the main wall to dry, she walked into the dining room and studied the long partition that separated the room from the kitchen. She'd have Tony and Lena work this wall, setting out the characters and scenery from the "River Haunt" game that would bring the room to life. Christa could work on the vines that would trail around the windows at the front of the room. If they all worked together, they could knock this out in a few days and move upstairs to the hallways. According to the plans, there would be vines, flowers and a banshee or two in each of the long halls, and haunting trees, bent in an invisible wind, painted on to the elevator doors.

She looked around the dining room and saw it as it would be when finished. As in the castle in Ireland, this dining hall would consist of long, banquet-style tables and benches, forcing guests to intermingle during meals. The gamers who came here would huddle together, talking scores and routes and walk-throughs of the game itself.

Guests who were unfamiliar with the game would soon be drawn into the fantasy world of Celtic Knot and the plush environment of the hotel. Once again, Jenny was impressed by the foresight of the Ryans and Brady Finn. By expanding their company into other realms, they were going to build the brand that was already becoming known around the world. To have a small part in this expansion was both exhilarating and sad. Because she knew without a doubt that this project would be one of her last for Celtic Knot.

In the quiet, her mind drifted to thoughts of Mike and she wondered what he was doing. If he even knew she was gone. And if he would care. If only he'd trusted her. Believed in her. Her heart ached when she remembered the expression on his face when he learned about the baby.

He'd come to her concerned that she wasn't feeling well and then left her, convinced that she was trying to use him. How could it all turn so bad so quickly? Why couldn't he see that she loved him? That if given the chance, the two of them and their child could have something wonderful? Was he so hard, so accustomed to shutting down his heart to keep possible pain at bay that he couldn't risk it for a chance for happiness?

Her own pain blossomed in her chest until it squeezed her heart and she had to force herself to stop thinking of what-ifs and of Mike, because there was no help there. Nothing was going to change and it was best if she got used to that as soon as possible.

Patting her belly, Jenny whispered, "Don't worry, baby. We're going to be okay. You'll see." She got back to work, pushing thoughts of Mike and her up-in-the-air life to the back of her mind. Time enough to worry when she was lying awake all night.

Mike almost called Jenny. Twice. And each time, he hung up before the call could connect. He was still on edge after having Sean ream him, so it probably wasn't the best time to talk to her anyway. But she was there. In his thoughts. In his soul.

She was off in the desert and hadn't bothered to tell him. Because when she told him about the baby, he'd turned on her.

That shamed him, but now, with Sean's temper still burning his ears, Mike admitted that it was past time to settle a few things that had been guiding him for years. He drove to his parents' house, determined to finally talk to his mother about what had happened so long ago. To figure out if that one day, that one secret, was worth steering his entire life by.

The house looked the same as it always had. No matter how successful he and his brother had become, Jack and Peggy Ryan hadn't allowed their sons to buy them a bigger place in a more upscale neighborhood. They preferred staying in the house where they'd raised their family, where they knew their neighbors and where every room held a memory. On this familiar street, houses were well cared for, yards were neat and nearly every driveway sported a basketball hoop.

Mike parked the car, then let himself in the front door, yelling to announce his presence. "Hey, Mom! It's me!"

The house was quiet but for the low murmur of the television, set to a 1960s music channel. He walked through the living room, past the neat kitchen and into the den, and still didn't find her. "Mom?"

"Mike, is that you?"

Relief shot through him as he turned to watch her approach. Her light brown hair was in a tangle and she was tugging at the hem of a pale pink shirt.

"You okay?" he asked, since she looked harried and a little nervous.

"Fine. You just caught me in the middle of something." Then his mother *blushed*.

Mike suddenly had the feeling that he'd walked in on something he'd rather not think about. "Look, I'll come back another time and—"

"Don't be silly," his mother said, already walking.

"Come into the kitchen. There's coffee and I made cookies this morning."

If she was willing to pretend she hadn't blushed, Mike could do it, too. "Sold."

"Good, good," she said, smiling now as she smoothed her hair. "Come and tell me why you stopped by. Is everything all right?"

"That's a good question."

"Sit down," she ordered when they were in the bright, sunny yellow kitchen. She poured coffee, set it in front of him, then brought a plate of cookies to the table, as well. Holding a cup of coffee, she sat down opposite him and said simply, "Tell me."

How many times over the years had he sat at this table with a plate of cookies in front of him and his mother listening to whatever problem he'd brought her? It was at this table where he'd found her crying. Where his life had taken that abrupt turn from innocence into suspicion. It was only fitting, he supposed, to be sitting at this table again while making the attempt to turn back.

So he told her about Jenny, about the baby, about Sean now knowing what happened all those years ago and how pissed his little brother was to find out he'd been lied to for years.

"What about Jenny?" his mother asked. "She's pregnant with your child. Do you love her?"

Mike shook his head. Of course she would zero in on that part of the story. "Another good question."

He pushed up from the table, walked to the counter, then turned around, bracing both hands on the granite countertop behind him. "But for right now, that doesn't even matter."

"Michael Patrick Ryan," his mother said, drawing a reflexive wince from her son, "love is *all* that matters."

"How can you say that, Mom, when—" He shook his head. "When you were cheated on. Lied to."

"That's it. I've had enough." Peggy stood up, pointed at the kitchen table and ordered, "Sit down. I'll be right back."

He did as instructed mainly because he was too tired to keep standing. If he didn't get some sleep soon, he'd go through life a zombie.

When his mother came back, she was dragging his father with her. Jack's hair was messy and he was trying to button his shirt as he was pulled in his wife's wake. And suddenly, Mike knew exactly what his parents had been doing when he dropped by. And yeah, he'd rather not think about that. Didn't matter how old you got, nobody wanted to imagine their parents having sex.

Mike stiffened and he noticed that Jack Ryan did the same. His father was an older version of himself, with sharp blue eyes, and a sprinkling of gray at his temples. The two of them were still so uncomfortable with each other over something that had happened twenty years before. But damned if Mike knew how to get past it, get over it.

"Both of you sit down right now," Peggy said and crossed her arms over her chest until her men complied. Then she looked from her husband to her son before saying softly, "Mike, I've tried to talk to you about this before, but you never wanted to listen. I could have *made* you hear me out, but your father wouldn't allow that." She spared Jack a glance and a smile. "He wanted you to come to us yourself when you were ready. Frankly, I thought it would never happen."

"Mom…"

"I never should have burdened you with what I felt that day," Peggy said. "But you came home early from practice and found me, crying, and somehow it all came out. And I hope you know that if I could wipe it from your mind, I would."

"I know all that, Mom—" He shot a look at his father, who looked every bit as uncomfortable as he felt. "We don't have to talk about it again."

"That's the problem," Peggy said, pulling out a chair and taking a cookie that she began to crumble between her fingers. "We've never talked about it." Her gaze softened as she looked at Mike. Then she took her husband's hand and threaded her fingers through his. "Mike, you were just a little boy, so you don't remember, but back then, your dad's business was in trouble."

Jack picked up the thread and Mike looked at his father as he spoke. "It's not an excuse but we were under a lot of pressure and instead of talking to each other about it—" he paused and smiled sadly at his wife "—we each closed down, shut each other out."

"We were wrong. We handled it all badly. But it takes two to make or break a marriage, Mike. So you were wrong to blame only your father all these years. We both made mistakes. We both nearly lost something most people never find."

Mike heard them, saw how together they were on this, but he couldn't let go. Turning to face his father, he said quietly, "You lied. You cheated."

"I did lie," Jack said. "I was hurt, worried about my family. Feeling like a damn failure and as if I were alone in the mess and missing your mother because we weren't talking to each other anymore."

"Oh, Jack…"

He squeezed her hand and then looked at Mike again. "I did lie, I give you that. And I cheated, too, I guess, but not the way you mean."

"What?"

Jack sighed. "The woman your mother heard about— I did take her to dinner. We talked. She listened to me, laughed at my jokes, made me feel important." He shook his head. "Stupid. It was stupid, but I didn't sleep with her, Mike." Jack's gaze met his son's squarely. "I never touched another woman from the day I married your mother."

Peggy spoke up then. "Instead of being there for each other, your dad and I pulled apart until we were each so far from the other, it was as if we were two strangers living in this house together."

Jack lifted their joined hands and kissed her knuckles. "What's important is that we found each other again before it was too late."

"I don't even know what to say," Mike muttered. For twenty years, he and his father had sidestepped each other, neither of them willing to talk about the thing that had put a wedge between them.

"Why didn't you tell me?" he asked.

"Because you wouldn't have believed me," Jack said.

"I guess that's true enough," Mike admitted. So much time being angry, letting old pains rule his life, believing that no one could be trusted because he had looked at a situation he didn't understand through the eyes of a wounded thirteen-year-old boy.

"The point is, honey," Peggy said, "you've been using your father as an excuse to keep everyone at a distance. You're protecting yourself from being hurt by not letting anything at all touch you." She shook her head. "That's no way to live, sweetie."

She was right, Mike thought. He had been using his father's betrayal as a way to keep everything and everyone else at a distance. And even with the walls he'd erected around his heart, Jenny had found a way in.

"You never should have been aware of that bump in our marriage," Peggy said. "And it breaks my heart to see the two of you so far apart."

Mike looked to his father and in the older man's eyes, he saw the same sorrow, the same sense of loss that Mike had felt for years. Now he was forced to do some serious thinking. Sean's words still echoed in his head as he thought back on all the years of sitting in a position of judgment, so sure he was right and everyone else was wrong. He had shut down emotionally. At the ripe old age of thirteen, not knowing anything at all about the world or what adults had to do to survive, he'd made a decision that had affected his entire life.

He had been a kid making a child's decisions, and he had allowed those decisions to rule him. If he'd once come down off his throne of righteousness and actually *talked* to the people around him, maybe this tightness around his heart could have been eased years ago.

"What happened wasn't your fault," his father said carefully. "You were a boy and you reacted how you had to at the time."

"Yeah," Mike said, rubbing his eyes to ease the throbbing headache settled behind them. "But I never let go of that decision. An angry, scared, thirteen-year-old boy chose that day to believe that no one could be trusted."

His father reached out and laid one hand on Mike's shoulder, and the heavy, solid strength of that touch seemed to ease away the last of that long-ago boy's resolve. He looked at his dad and said simply, "I'm sorry."

"You don't have to be," Jack told him. "Parents aren't supposed to give their kids burdens to carry. And I did that to you. I hurt you, your mother, all of us. It's something I'll never forgive myself for."

Peggy sniffled and swiped tears off her cheeks. "It's been long enough, hasn't it?" she asked. "Can we all let it go now and be the family we should be?"

Mike looked at his mother, still holding her husband's hand as she watched her oldest son with worry and hope at war in her eyes. The old hurts and fears and convictions dropped away, slipping into the past where they belonged, and Mike let them go. He felt as if a weight had been lifted from him and it surprised him to realize just how heavy that burden had been.

"Yeah," he said, smiling first at his mother and then at his father. "I'd like that."

Jack grinned, slapped Mike's shoulder again and then looked at his wife. Peggy gave him a watery smile in return then reached for her son's hand and held it tightly. "Good. This is good."

She was right about that. It was good, to get past pain and anger and betrayal. But his father wasn't the only one he'd judged. Mike thought back to that night in Phoenix when he'd spotted a beautiful blonde in a conference hotel bar. He remembered the rush, the pull toward her, and he remembered the next morning when he'd become judge, jury and executioner without once giving her a chance to explain.

Then those memories morphed into his last image of Jenny, at her house when he accused her of trying to trap him into marriage. He'd done the same damn thing to her all over again.

"Sean's right," he muttered. "I am an idiot."

"What's wrong, honey?"

He lifted his gaze to his mother's and sighed. "A lot. I've got some thinking to do. About Jenny. The baby." He stopped, smiled. "And you guys will have to get used to the idea of being grandparents."

"Oh, my goodness," Peggy exclaimed with a laugh. "With all the tumult I almost forgot that Jenny's pregnant!"

"Grandfather?" Jack asked.

"This is wonderful news!" Peggy jumped to her feet and wagged her finger at her son. "I'm making a fresh pot of coffee and you, mister, are going to tell us everything."

Jack picked up a cookie and handed it to him. "Congratulations. I hope you do a better job of it than I did."

Mike shook his head and took a bite of the cookie. He'd already made mistakes and his child wasn't even born yet. "You didn't do so badly, Dad. But for me, I swear I don't know what the hell I'm doing."

Jack laughed. "Welcome to parenthood. None of us know what we're doing, Mike. And even trying our very best, we all make mistakes. The trick is to keep trying to fix them."

Mike found Sean in his office the next morning. He'd thought about this all night, had worked out just what he wanted to say. But looking into his brother's unforgiving stare threw him for a second. The two of them had always been close, but now, there was a wedge between them that Mike himself had put there. So it was up to him to tear it out.

"You were right."

Surprised, Sean waved him to a chair. "Always a good start to a conversation. Continue."

Mike laughed and sat down. "I've been protecting you since we were kids," he said thoughtfully. He'd had all night to consider this situation from every angle. And no matter how he looked at it, he came off badly. That didn't sit well with him. "It got to be a habit."

"Okay," Sean said, acknowledging that with a nod.

"But it was wrong to lie to you all those years." Mike sighed, leaned forward and braced his forearms on his thighs. "Whenever you asked me what was wrong between me and Dad, I brushed it off. Covered it up, telling myself you were better off not knowing. So, yeah. I made that call and I shouldn't have. You've been grown-up a long time, Sean, so shutting you out was the wrong call, but you should understand why I did it."

"You're really not very good at apologies, are you?"

Grumbling, Mike admitted, "No."

"Well, points for effort anyway," Sean said.

"Thanks." Mike nodded and told him, "I stopped by the house yesterday. Saw Mom and Dad. We talked."

"And…?"

"And," Mike said with a rueful smile on his face, "I apparently interrupted an afternoon quickie."

"Oh, man!" Laughing, Sean covered his eyes with one hand. "I didn't need to know that."

"Hey, you're the one who doesn't want me lying to him."

"Discretion, man. There's a difference between lies and discretion. Look it up."

Glad things were smoothed out between his brother and him, Mike chuckled. "The point is, we finally straightened everything out. I think things will be all right now, between me and Dad."

"Good to hear." Sean sat forward, folded his hands on the desktop.

"They know you know," Mike said. "I told them that I talked to you about it."

"Great. When you decide to be honest, you go all out, don't you?" A half smile curved Sean's mouth. "Guess I'll be having a talk with them, too, now. But as long as they're good together, happy together, I'm fine with it. It's all their business, Mike. Not mine. Not yours."

"When did you get so rational?"

"When I grew up," his brother said. "You missed that, I think."

"Yeah, looks like." Mike frowned. "I think I missed a lot."

"Ah, now we get to the important part of the conversation. Jenny."

Shooting his brother a hard look, Mike said, "You'll butt out of what happens to our parents, but I'm fair game?"

"Hell, yes." Sean grinned. "So, have you talked to her?"

"No." He still hadn't called, because talking to her on the phone wouldn't be enough. He had to look into her eyes, read what she was thinking, feeling.

"Don't you think you should?" Sean asked. "She's pregnant with your baby."

"I don't need reminding," Mike said and hopped out of the chair. Walking to the wide window on the far wall, he looked out at the garden and didn't see a thing. How could he, when his mind was filled with images of Jenny.

"Maybe you do." Sean waited until his brother looked

at him again to continue. "You've been in charge of things so long, you've forgotten how to just be Mike."

"That's ridiculous."

"Is it? You talk to Jenny like she's your employee…"

"She is."

"She's more, too," Sean said. "And it's the *more* you're not getting. To get what you really want out of all of this, you're going to have to get humble."

Mike snorted. "And you think you know what I want?"

"Yep," Sean mused. "Don't you?"

Yeah, he did. He wanted Jenny. In his house. In his bed. He wanted to wake up in the morning reaching for her and have her curl up against him. But "humble" wasn't the way to get it.

"You can't just march up to Jenny and order her to forgive you," Sean said.

"It's the easiest way," Mike mumbled.

"Yeah, if you want to tick her off even more."

He might have a point, but Mike didn't want to think about it. "Can you handle things here at the office for a few days?"

"Sure," Sean said. "Why?"

"Because," Mike said, "I'm going to Laughlin."

"It's about time," Sean told him.

Early the next afternoon, Jenny stood back from the wall to take an objective look at the finished painting. It was just as she'd imagined it. Hints of danger hidden among the trees, moonlight filtering through the leaves to dapple on the overgrown ground. A river wound through the back of the painting like a silver snake, a moonlit, watery path that only the brave would dare follow. The painting was vaguely menacing and intriguing and set just the right mood for the River Haunt hotel.

The other artists were doing a great job on the murals and already the dining room motif was coming together. Another day or two and they could move upstairs. While the construction crew were mostly huddled in the kitchen finishing the cabinets and the new countertops, Jenny walked through the lobby into what used to be the lounge.

Here, the plan was to have clusters of furniture scattered throughout and several game-playing stations set up, with four-flat screen TVs that invited guests to dive into Celtic Knot games. There would be a bar on the far wall where a battered old piano now stood and one section of the room would be set up with wide tables so guests could also play the role-playing board games as well.

It was going to be a gamer's paradise, she told herself with a smile. And that wasn't even taking into account the midnight pontoon rides on the river, where animatronic banshees, ghouls and hunters would lunge from their hiding places onshore. It was all going to be amazing.

Jenny hated knowing that she'd have to quit her job at Celtic Knot. She enjoyed being a part of something so fresh and interesting and fun. But working with Mike now was just impossible. She couldn't see him every day and know she'd never have him. So she'd do her best on this project and then she'd walk away, head high. And one day, she promised herself, she'd come to the River Haunt hotel as a guest, just so she could see people enjoying what she'd helped to build.

Sighing, she stopped at the piano and idly stroked a few keys. She hadn't really played since she was a girl and Uncle Hank had paid for the lessons she'd wanted so badly. That phase had lasted more than a year, Jenny remembered, and then she had discovered art and playing the piano had taken a backseat.

For an old instrument, the piano had good tone and as her fingers moved over the keys in a familiar piece from her childhood, the music lifted into the stillness. She sat down on the bench, closed her eyes and let her troubled thoughts slide away as she listened only to the tune she created.

Mike found her there. A small woman with a halo of golden hair, sitting in a patch of sunlight, teasing beautiful music from a piano that looked as old as time.

His heart gave one quick jolt in his chest. Damn, he'd missed her. Everything in him was drawn to her. How had she become so important to him in so short a time? She was talented, brilliant, argumentative and beautiful, and he wanted her so badly he could hardly breathe. Now that he was here, with her, he wasn't about to wait another minute to touch her.

Wrapped up in the music that soared around her, she didn't hear him approach. When Mike laid both hands on her shoulders, she jumped, spinning around on the bench, eyes wide.

"You *scared* me."

He grinned at the glint in her eyes. He'd even missed her temper. "I didn't mean to sneak up on you, but with the music, you couldn't hear me. I didn't know you played piano."

"I told you before, there's a lot you don't know about me."

"Yeah, I guess you're right," he said, and pulled her

up from the scarred wooden bench. "But there's plenty I do know."

"Like what?" she asked, taking one short step backward.

"Like," he said, closing the gap between them, "you're so stubborn you're probably getting ready to quit your job at Celtic Knot."

Clearly surprised, she asked, "How did you know that?"

"Wasn't hard to figure out, Jenny. You think it'll be too hard for us to work together now."

"I'm right and you know it, Mike."

"No. You're not," he said, and watched hope bloom in her eyes. Sean had been wrong. All Mike had to do was lay out his plan and she'd see that it was the best thing for everyone. "I think we should work together and more. We both want our baby. We have great chemistry. Passion."

His hands came down on her shoulders and he drew her closer. Looking down into those blue eyes of hers, he said, "We forget about the past. Let it all go and just move on from here. We're going to get married, Jenny. It's the right thing to do. For all of us."

He waited, for her to smile at him, go up on her toes and kiss him. He wanted the taste of her in his mouth again. It had been days and he felt as if it had been years. All she had to do was say yes.

"No."

She was screwing up a perfectly good plan. Staring down at her, he blurted, "Why the hell not? You're pregnant, remember?"

She laughed shortly. "Yes, I remember. And I won't marry you because you don't love me. You don't trust me. Passion isn't enough to build a marriage on, Mike.

And I won't risk my baby's happiness on a marriage doomed to failure."

"It's not doomed."

"Without love it is," she said, shaking her head. Laying one hand on his forearm, Jenny continued. "It's *our* baby, Mike. I would never try to keep you from him. Or her. But I won't marry a man who doesn't trust me."

Then she kissed him.

And left.

Ten

Jenny had a stalker.

For the next few days, every time she turned around, Mike was there. He carried her paints and insisted on getting her a chair if she so much as yawned. Only that morning, when she climbed a step ladder to add a few silvery cobwebs to a naked tree on an elevator door, he'd snatched her off the darn thing and carried her to her room. In spite of her loud protests. The man had appointed himself her caretaker whether she wanted one or not. It was annoying and endearing at the same time.

She didn't want to get used to this kind of treatment, though. Firstly because she was perfectly healthy and able to take care of herself. But mainly because she knew it was all for show. He was trying to schmooze her into marrying him on his terms.

But she couldn't do it. Couldn't give up her fantasies of a loving husband and settle for a man who didn't trust her, didn't love her. Passion was a poor substitute for real love.

"Jen, what do you think of this?"

Jenny popped out of her thoughts and focused instead on the job at hand. "What've you got, Christa?"

The other artist was tall and thin, with black hair cut close to her scalp and a penchant for wearing eye-searing colors. She was also fast, talented and eager to please.

"I was thinking about adding in a few of the Death Flowers among the vines here at the windows."

"Death Flowers?" Jenny repeated with a smile.

Christa shrugged. "I admit, I love the 'River Haunt' game. I play it with my fiancé all the time."

"Do you win?"

"Not so far," she admitted, "but I keep trying. Anyway, you know the bloodred flowers that have fangs? I thought if it's okay with you, I'd add a few of them here on these vines. I mean, they're not on the original design so I wanted to run it by you before I did anything."

The dining room was nearly finished. The far wall was complete and the forest scene was spectacular. Though she'd had a few problems with one of the artists, she couldn't fault the work. Jenny looked up at what Christa had done so far. The vines were thick and lush, wrapped around the edges of the windows and down to the bottom of the wall where a few of them even pooled on the floor. "You've done a great job here, Christa."

"Thanks," she said, stepping back to check out her own work. "I'm really grateful for the opportunity."

Jenny looked up at her. As short as she was, she pretty much looked up at *everyone*. "The flowers are a fabulous idea. I love it."

Christa grinned.

"Use your own eye for placement. Seeing your work, I trust your judgment."

"That is so cool. Thank you, Jenny." Christa's features lit up in pleasure.

"You know, when this project's finished, if you're interested, I'll talk to Dave Cooper, he's the head of the graphic arts department for Celtic Knot. I'm sure he could use an artist like you." She paused. "If you're interested."

"Seriously? Interested?" Christa laughed, then scooped Jenny up for a tight hug. "That would be like my dream job."

When she was on her feet again, Jenny grinned at the other woman's enthusiasm. "You could probably work from here, but Dave might ask you to move to California."

"Not a problem," Christa swore, lifting one hand as if taking an oath.

"What about your fiancé? Would he be willing to move for your job?"

Christa smiled. "He loves me, so sure. Of course. Plus, he's a writer, so he can work anywhere."

"Then I'll talk to Dave and let you know what he says."

"Thank you, Jenny. I mean it. This is just the ultimate thing that could have happened."

"You're welcome. But for right now, concentrate on the Death Flowers."

"They'll be the most bloodthirsty blossoms in the universe when I'm done with them," Christa vowed, and immediately bent to her paint palette.

Sure what she was feeling was etched on her features, Jenny was grateful that the other woman had turned away. She heard Christa's words echoing in her mind. *He loves me. So sure. Of course.* Envy whipped through her like a lash, leaving a stinging pain behind. Christa was so certain of her fiancé. So confident in his love and support. And Jenny yearned to know what that feeling was like.

Sighing, she watched for a few minutes as Christa laid out quick sketches for placement of the flowers. It was nice to be able to help someone so talented. Someone who'd already proven herself to be a team player. Jenny was sure that Dave would jump at the chance to bring aboard such a skilled artist. Especially since he'd be needing someone to take Jenny's place once she turned in her resignation. Oh, that thought hurt. She loved her job. Loved being a part of the magic of imagination. But she had to give it up. For the sake of her own sanity.

Jenny left the main floor and took the stairs to the third. She couldn't take the elevators, since they were shut down temporarily so the paintings on the doors could be completed. Wanting to take a quick look at the hallway up here, Jenny walked slowly, checking the progress of the artwork.

On the third floor, there were werewolves sprinting along the wall, muscled bodies ripping through ribbons of fog as they gazed out at the hall as if staring at those who walked past. Jenny admired the art even as she shivered at the images. Not exactly the kind of thing designed to promote an easy night's sleep. But then again, the gamers who would flock to this hotel would love the imagery. Then they would slip into their hotel rooms and play the games on the top-of-the-line gaming systems.

She smiled to herself, then gave a quick glance to the antiqued brass wall sconces, shaped to give the illusion of torches. A dark blue carpet runner stretched the length of the hallway, covering the center of the wood-grain ceramic tiles. It was a good idea, she thought, for the flooring. Giving the feel of wood while offering the much-easier-to-care-for tile.

She headed back to the staircase and then walked down to the second floor to peek at what the other two artists were doing with the banshee/ghost halls. When she found them, the artists were in a heated discussion and didn't even notice her approach.

"The banshees all have white hair," Lena shouted. "Have you ever played the game?"

"I'm an artist, I don't waste my time playing video games," Tony argued. "And what difference does it make if a banshee has black hair? They're not *real*, you know."

"No," Jenny said loudly enough to interrupt their argument. "Banshees aren't real, but they are integral to the game you're supposed to be replicating here."

He sighed heavily, dramatically, as if to let her know how put-upon he was to be questioned by anyone about his artistic decisions. Jenny had known when she hired the man that he was going to be difficult. But the sad truth was, his talent had won him the job. She'd run out of names of local artists and had had to take a chance on him being willing to play by the rules stated. It looked as though she'd made a bad call.

"Artistically speaking, a black-haired banshee will pop more from the cream colored walls," he argued.

"You jerk," the other artist countered. "If you knew anything about shadows and highlighting, you'd know how to make that white hair stand out. It's supposed to be otherworldly, not like a photo shoot for a fashion magazine."

"What you know about art," he shouted, "could be printed on a business card with room left over for a Chinese menu."

"I know enough to do what I've been contracted to do," she said.

Jenny's head ached. They'd had the same problems with Tony while finishing the mural in the dining room. He wanted things done his way—too bad for him, he wasn't in charge. Holding her hands up for quiet, Jenny felt as if she were refereeing a fight between second-graders. "That's it. Lena, thanks, you're doing a great job. Just get back to it, okay?"

With muttered agreement, the woman did go back to work, throwing one last fulminating glare at the man smirking at her.

Jenny lowered her voice when she spoke again. There was no need to humiliate the man, but she wasn't going to be ignored, either. "Tony, you agreed when you signed on to this project to follow the planned art designs."

"Yes, but—"

"And," Jenny said, a little more loudly, "whatever you think of video games, the guests who will be coming to this hotel know these games like the backs of their hands."

Tony sighed heavily again. "If you'll only let me show you what I mean—"

"So," she said, overriding him again, "you will either do what you agreed to do, or you can pack up your paints and leave."

Insulted, he jerked his head back and glared at her. "You can't fire me."

"Oh, yes," a deep voice sounded from behind her. "She can."

Jenny looked over her shoulder, unsurprised to see Mike coming up behind her. The man was always close at hand these days.

"Mr. Ryan…"

Mike shook his head and continued speaking to the artist. "But allow me to repeat it so you'll understand. Either follow the planned design, or leave and we'll send you your last check."

"I'm an artist," Tony said hotly, lifting his chin with its wispy goatee. "If all you want is someone to fill in the lines with color, you don't need an artist. You need a child with a box of crayons."

"Your choice," Mike said. "Thanks for your time."

Clearly outraged, the man flushed darkly, then spun around to pack up his supplies, muttering all the while. From the corner of her eye, Jenny saw Lena do a little hip-shaking happy dance at the other artist's exit and she smiled.

"Well, that was fun." Jenny looked up at Mike. "I was handling it, you know."

"I saw and you were doing a great job." He smiled at her and Jenny's foolish heart gave a hard thump in response. "Any reason why I shouldn't help out when I can?"

"I suppose not," she said, but inside, she whispered that it wasn't a good idea for her to learn to depend on his help. Because it wouldn't always be there.

"Lena, are you all right here on your own?" Jenny asked.

"Are you kidding?" She laughed. "With Tony gone, it'll be like a vacation."

"Great. I'll send Christa up to help you when she finishes in the dining room."

"Fab, thanks. Oh, boss?"

Jenny and Mike both answered, "Yes?" Then Mike waved one hand as if telling Jenny to take it.

"I had an idea I wanted to run by you."

"Shoot."

Another grin from Lena. "I was thinking, what if I drew out one or two of the banshees so that their arms are stretched across the door—you know, so their clawed hands look like they're reaching for the guest opening their door…" She bit her lip and waited for a decision. She didn't have to wait long.

"That's a great idea," Jenny said and glanced at Mike. "What do you think?"

Nodding, he said, "I love it. Good thinking, Lena."

"Thanks."

"And your banshees look like they stepped right out of the game, I appreciate that," Mike added.

"Hey," Lena said, "I love that game!" When she turned to go back to work, humming to herself, Jenny and Mike headed back down the hall.

"The elevators are turned off, so we have to take the stairs."

"Yeah," Mike said, "I know. But I don't like you climbing up and down those stairs every day. What if you tripped and fell?"

"What am I, ninety?" Jenny shook her head and laughed to herself. "You're being ridiculous, Mike."

"I'm being concerned, Jenny," he said, pulling her to a stop just inside the stairwell. "I care about you. About our baby."

Care was such a pale word. It was pastel when what she wanted was bold, primary colors.

"I appreciate it, but we're both fine and I've got to

get downstairs to finish the main-floor elevator doors. We're one artist short now." She started for the stairs, but Mike was too quick for her. He scooped her up into his arms and Jenny huffed out a breath of exasperation.

He was smiling at her, holding her, and though she wanted nothing more than to hook her arms around his neck and hold on, she knew she couldn't. "You're not playing fair, Mike."

"Damn right, I'm not," he agreed, walking down the stairs with her held close to his chest. "I've told you how it's going to be between us, Jenny. I'm just giving you time to get used to the idea."

Later that night, the construction crew was gone for the day and most everyone else had headed into Laughlin for dinner and some fun. In the quiet darkness, Jenny went out onto the pool deck by herself, eager for a little solitude. It had been days now since Mike showed up at the hotel and it looked as though he had no intention of leaving anytime soon. Didn't he know that by staying, he was making this whole situation so much harder on her?

"Of course he does," she whispered wryly. "That's his plan, Jenny. He's trying to make you crazy enough that you'll agree to marry him, even though you know it would be a mistake."

Oh, God, she was so tempted to make that mistake.

Shaking her head at her own foolishness, Jenny sat down on the edge of the pool, took off her shoes and dangled her feet in the warm water. It was still cool in the desert at night, so she enjoyed the mix of a cold wind brushing over her arms and the warm water lapping at her legs. Lazily kicking her feet through the water, she leaned back on her hands and stared up at the night sky.

"Beautiful," she said to no one. With no light pollution here, the stars were brilliant and there were so many of them. It was like a painting, she thought and instantly, her mind drifted to just how she would capture that scene on canvas, though she knew she would never be able to do it justice.

"It is, isn't it?"

Jenny sighed and tipped her head down to watch Mike come toward her. Her time alone was over and though she knew that spending time with Mike was only prolonging the inevitable, she relished the hard thump of her heart at the sight of him. She'd thought he went into town with the others, but she should have known better, she told herself now.

He took a seat beside her, dropped his bare feet into the water and looked up at the sky. "Being in the city, you never see this many stars," he said, voice low, deep, intimate. "You forget how big the sky really is."

Jenny knew he hadn't come out here to talk about the stars. "Mike..."

He looked at her and in the shadowy moon and starlight, his blue eyes looked dark, mysterious. "I talked to Dave today," he said, surprising her. "He says you quit your job as of this project's completion."

Jenny had hoped he wouldn't find out so quickly. Turning in her resignation had cut at her. She loved her job and would miss everyone there, but she'd felt obligated to give Dave as much time as he might need to cover her absence. "I had to."

"No, you didn't," he mused quietly, sliding his bare foot along her leg, giving her chills that had nothing to do with the cool night air. "Dave also said you recommended he hire Christa full-time."

She shrugged. "He'll need someone to fill in for me when I'm gone. Christa's good. Talented, but willing to take direction."

"If you think she'll work out, that's good enough for me."

Pleased that he thought so highly of her suggestion, she smiled briefly. "Thanks for that."

"You could have stayed with the company, you know." He tossed a quick glance at the sky, then shifted his gaze to hers again. "Could have pulled the the-boss-is-my-baby's-father card."

She stared at him, shocked. "I would never do that."

His gaze moved over her face as he slowly nodded. "Yeah, I'm getting that. I'm beginning to get a lot of things."

"Mike," she said, hoping to make the situation perfectly clear between them. "Quitting my job was the right thing to do. For both of us. Working together every day would just be too hard. Besides, I don't need your money to take care of my baby. I don't need the Ryan name to make sure my future's secure—"

"What *do* you need, Jenny?"

Oh, wow, that question had too many answers. Too many pitfalls should she even try to tell him what was in her heart, her mind. So she smiled and said softly, "Doesn't matter."

"It does to me," he said.

Tipping her head to one side, she looked at him and asked, "Since when, Mike?"

"Since I woke up and started paying closer attention." He took her hand and smoothed his thumb across the back, sliding across her knuckles until she shivered at the contact. "I want you, Jenny. More than anything else in my life, I want you with me."

Her breath caught in her chest and her heartbeat quickened until it fluttered like a deranged butterfly. To be wanted. It had been the driving force in her life since she was a child. But now, she knew it wasn't enough. *Want* wasn't *love*.

"You do for now, Mike," she said quietly. "But what about in five years? Ten?" Shaking her head, she continued, "Want, need, passion, they're all good things. But without love to anchor them, they fade and drift away."

"They don't have to." He gripped her hand even tighter. "Love is something I've avoided, Jenny. Too big a risk."

She could see what it cost him to admit that, but with her heart hurting so badly, she couldn't tell him that she was all right and that she understood. "It's worth the risk, Mike. Because without love, there's nothing."

"Need is something. Want is something."

"But not enough." Sadly, she pulled her hand free of his, swung her legs out of the water and stood up. Looking down at him, she took a breath and braced herself to give him the hard truth she was only just accepting. "We have a child together, Mike. But that's all we have."

She walked back to the hotel and stopped in the doorway to look back at him. He was alone in the starlight, watching her, and it took everything Jenny had to keep walking.

Two days later, things were still tense between Mike and her. She had hoped that after their last conversation at the pool, he would give up and go home. He had to know that nothing was going to come of this. They each needed something from the other that they couldn't have. Jenny needed Mike to love her. To trust her. Mike needed her to settle for less than she craved.

Her time here at the hotel was almost done. Most of the paintings were completed now and what was left, Christa and Lena could finish on their own. Jenny couldn't stay much longer. Because Mike refused to leave her side, she had to be the one to leave. She had to get some distance from him before she did something stupid like rush into his arms and accept whatever crumbs he was willing to offer.

The cacophony of sound at the hotel was familiar now and Jenny half wondered if the silence of her apartment once she was home again would feel stifling. Between the men talking, the tools buzzing and crashing, and the roar of Jet Skis on the river, it was hard to hear yourself think. But in her case lately, maybe that was a blessing.

"Jenny! Jenny, where are you?"

Up on the second-story landing, Jenny was just adding a few finishing touches to the naked tree sprawled across the elevator doors when she heard that familiar voice booming out over the racket.

"Uncle Hank?" she asked aloud. Setting her paintbrush aside, she quickly went down the stairs and spotted her uncle, Betty right beside him, taking a good look around the front lobby.

"There she is," Betty shouted over the construction noise and used her elbow to give Hank a nudge in the ribs for good measure.

The older man's face brightened as he grinned and came toward her.

"Uncle Hank, what're you doing here?"

To her surprise, the usually stoic man gave her one hard hug, then let her go and beamed at her. "Well, Betty and I wanted to see what you were doing out here. Take a look around and see what's what."

"Darn fool, we could have caught a plane," Betty said, scraping her hands across her tangled hair. "But no, he insisted on driving so he could try out his new toy."

"No point in having a new car if you're not going to drive it," Hank pointed out.

"New car?" Jenny looked out the front window and saw a shiny red convertible. She couldn't have been more surprised. Though he was a wealthy man, Hank had been driving his classic Mercedes sedan for twenty years, insisting he didn't need anything new when that one ran just fine. Shifting her gaze back to her uncle, she asked, "That's yours?"

"It is," he said proudly.

"Like to froze me to death, driving out here with the top down the whole way," Betty muttered.

"No point in having a convertible if you keep the top up," Hank argued.

Jenny just laughed. It was so good to see them; she was enjoying their usual banter. But she had to ask, "You didn't drive all the way out here just to look at my paintings, did you?"

"Well," Hank hedged, "that's part of it, sure." His eyes narrowed on something behind her and without even looking, Jenny knew who was coming up beside her. Her uncle's features went cold and hard as Mike stopped alongside Jenny.

"Mr. Snyder," Mike said with a nod.

"Ryan." Hank gave him another narrow-eyed stare, then shifted his gaze to Jenny, ignoring the man beside her completely. "Jenny, I came to tell you I've sold Snyder Arts."

"What?" Stunned and in shock, Jenny stared at the man who'd raised her. First a convertible, now *this*? His company had been Uncle Hank's life. He lived and breathed the business, dedicating himself to building Snyder Arts into a well-respected, multimillion-dollar firm. She couldn't imagine him without it. "Why would you do that? You loved that business."

Still ignoring Mike, Hank moved in on her and dropped both hands on her shoulders. "I love *you* more," he said and Jenny received her second shock of the day.

He'd never said those words to her before and until that moment, she hadn't been aware of how much she'd wanted to hear them.

"Uncle Hank…"

"I see tears," he blurted and warned, "don't do that."

She laughed and shook her head. "I'll try. But tell me why."

"Main reason?" he said, sliding an icy glance toward Mike. "So no one could accuse you of being a damn spy for me."

"Damn it," Mike muttered from beside her.

Jenny hardly heard him as she stared into her uncle's sharp blue eyes. Oh, God. Guilt reared up and took a bite of her heart. He'd given up what he loved to prove something to Mike and it was all for her sake. "You shouldn't have done that," she whispered.

"It was time," Hank said, pausing long enough to glare at Mike.

"There's more to it than that," Betty interrupted, her

clipped tone cutting through the sentiment that was suddenly thick in the air.

Stepping in front of Hank, Betty looked at Jenny and said simply, "It was long past time he sold that business. Haven't I been trying to get him to live a little before he dies?"

"Who said anything about dying?" Hank wanted to know.

"Nobody lives forever," Betty snapped, then focused on Jenny again. "With the company gone, we'll both have time to help out when the baby comes. We can both be there for you, Jenny. And that's the important thing. Family stands for family. You understand?"

"I do," Jenny said and reached out to hug the woman who had always been a constant in her life. Heart full, she looked at the older couple and realized that she'd always had family—she'd just been too insecure to notice. Now, she couldn't understand how she had ever doubted what these two amazing people felt for her.

"Now, you just show us around," Hank said, letting his gaze slide around the lobby and briefly rest on her entry wall painting. "Let us see what all you've done here, then you can quit this job and come home with us where you belong."

She opened her mouth to speak, but Mike cut her off.

Speaking directly to Hank, he said, "I know you've got no reason to trust me, but I need a minute with Jenny."

"Mike—" She didn't want more time alone with him. Didn't think she could take much more.

"I think you've said plenty already," Hank told him.

"I agree with Hank," Betty said, lifting her chin imperiously.

"Please," Mike said, looking at Jenny directly, catching her off guard with the quietly voiced plea.

In all the time she'd known him, Jenny had never heard him say *please* to anyone. And that one simple word decided it for her.

To her uncle, she said, "I'll be back in a minute." Then she turned, walked into the game room, which was currently unoccupied, and waited for Mike to join her.

With so much happening, Jenny's heartbeat was fast, her mind spinning. She hardly knew what to think. Her uncle selling the company, her quitting her job, having a baby. And now Mike, wanting to talk again when they'd already said both too much and too little to each other.

She tried to calm the jumping nerves inside her by focusing on the view out the window. The desert landscape was softened by the trees swaying in a soft wind. Jenny focused her gaze on the purple smudge of mountains in the distance and tried to steady her breathing.

"Jenny?"

She turned to face him and her heart raced. He looked—unsure of himself. Something she'd never seen in Mike Ryan. That realization shook her. She wouldn't be persuaded, in spite of her instinctive urge to go to him and hold on until she eased whatever was bothering him.

"I feel like an idiot," he muttered, scraping one hand through his hair.

"Not what I expected to hear," she admitted.

"Oh." He laughed, but there was no humor in the sound. "There's more." He took a step closer, then stopped, as if not trusting himself to get within reach. "I can't believe your uncle showed up out of nowhere," he muttered.

"You're upset about Uncle Hank coming to see me?"

"Not the act," he said, "just the timing."

Now she was really confused.

"You should know that I was wrong about you. Right from the beginning, I was wrong and I think somehow I knew that, I just couldn't admit it," he grumbled in irritation. "Just like I know I've loved you from the first moment I saw you in that bar in Phoenix."

Suddenly unsteady, Jenny reached down and grabbed the back of a chair for support. *He loved her.* She hadn't thought to ever hear those words from him. Only yesterday, that confession would have had her glowing in happiness. Now, though, it was too late. "Mike—"

"Just hear me out," he said, moving in close enough to touch her. To hold her. Hands at her waist, he spoke more quickly now, as if afraid she'd stop listening. "I'm asking you to marry me, Jenny. Not *telling* you, *asking* you. It's not for the baby's sake, or convenience or any other damn reason except that I love you. I want to go to bed with you every night and wake up beside you every morning." His eyes locked with hers and she read the truth there and wished, so wished he had said all of this sooner.

"You're it for me, Jenny," he confessed. "Maybe that's why I fought it so hard. Seeing your future spilling out in front of you can be…overwhelming. But the thing is, no matter how I looked at the future, you were there." His hands tightened on her waist and the heat of his touch slipped inside her. "There is no future without you, Jenny. There is no *me* without you."

Her mouth worked, but anything she might have said was choked off by the river of tears crowding her throat.

"I need you to believe me, Jenny," he said urgently. "I love you. I trust you. Please marry me."

Oh, God, it was everything she'd ever wanted. The

man she loved was giving her the words she'd yearned to hear and it was too late. How could she ever believe in him when it had taken her uncle selling his company to make him believe in her? What kind of irony was it that she was given exactly what she longed for and couldn't have it?

Disappointment rose up inside her and she couldn't keep it from spilling out. "No, Mike, I won't marry you. I can't. You're only saying this now because Uncle Hank gave you proof your suspicions about me were wrong."

"No, that's not true."

She shook her head wildly. "I wish you had said all of this before Uncle Hank arrived. It would have meant everything to me."

"This is what I meant about Hank's timing. I was going to talk to you tonight." He shook his head and laughed ruefully. "I had it planned. Moonlight, seduction, romance…"

"Mike, you're just saying this now, to try to make it better."

"No, damn it." He scowled. "You're wrong. I believed before today. It was that talk the other night, out at the pool?" He pulled her tight as if expecting her to make a bolt for escape. "It was then reality crashed down on me. When you said you didn't need me. Didn't want my money. When you made me see that you're not the kind of woman who has to *trap* a man into anything.

"You're one of the strongest women I've ever known. You're beautiful, talented. You're kind and funny and you don't take any of my crap."

She laughed, but it hurt her throat, so she stopped short.

"You're everything to me, Jenny. You have to believe me."

"I want to," she admitted. "So much."

He smiled, just one brief curve of his mouth. "Then let this convince you." Digging into his pants pocket, he pulled out a small deep blue velvet box.

Jenny's eyes went wide and she sucked in a gulp of air and held it. He was telling the truth, she thought wildly. He'd already had a ring for her when Hank showed up. It was real. It was staggering.

Mike flipped the top of the box open, and showed her a canary yellow diamond, glittering in an old-fashioned setting that seemed to Jenny as if it were made especially for her. "When did you—"

"Yesterday," he said. "After our talk the night before last, I drove into Vegas, found the best jeweler in the city and got this ring for you." He lifted her chin with the tips of his fingers until her teary eyes met his. "I knew, before your uncle showed up, that I love you. I trust you. I need you, Jenny. I always will."

"Mike…" Her bottom lip trembled.

Taking her left hand in his, he slid the ring onto her finger and sealed it there with a kiss. "Say you'll take the ring, Jenny. And me."

It was a gift, Jenny told herself. A gift from the universe, because suddenly she had everything she'd ever wanted most in her life. She looked up into his beautiful eyes and saw her own love shining back at her.

"Jenny?" he asked, a half laugh in his voice, "you're starting to worry me…"

"There's no need, Mike. I love you. I have since that first night in Phoenix." She went up on her toes and kissed him lightly. "I'll take the ring. And you. And I promise I will love you forever."

"Thank God," he whispered and pulled her in close.

His arms wrapped around her, her head nestled on his chest, she heard him say, "You are the best thing that has ever happened to me, Jenny Marshall, and I swear I will never let you go."

Epilogue

A few months later, the wedding was held at the Balboa Pavilion. Built in 1905, the Victorian-style building was on the National Register of Historic Places, and a California landmark. The grand ballroom boasted dramatic floor-to-ceiling windows that provided a spectacular view of one of the largest small-yacht harbors in the world.

Candles flickered on the linen-draped tables scattered around the wide room. Yellow and white flowers decorated every surface and cascaded over the front of the bride-and-groom table. And tiny white fairy lights sparkled and shone on every window as the day wore down and night rushed in.

"It was all perfect," Jenny mused, leaning back against her brand-new husband.

Mike's arms wrapped around her middle, his hands

tenderly cupping the bump of their child, and he dipped his head to kiss the curve of her throat. "It was, and you are the most beautiful bride ever."

Jenny did feel pretty in her white off-the-shoulder dress that clung to her bosom and waist, then fell in a soft swirl of skirt to the floor. Mike, of course, was gorgeous: tall, handsome and looking as though he'd been born to wear a tux.

"I love you," she whispered, tipping her head back to look at him.

"Never get tired of hearing that." He grinned, kissed her and swore, "I love you, too. And I'm going to show you how much every day of our honeymoon."

A slow, knowing smile curved her lips. "You haven't had a vacation in years. I can hardly believe we're taking a week in Ireland *and* a week in London."

"And," he teased, "another week in Tuscany."

"Really?" Jenny turned in his arms and hugged him. "You didn't tell me!"

"Surprise!" He grinned down at her and said, "An artist really should tour Italy, don't you think?"

"Absolutely." Jenny couldn't possibly be happier, she thought. A man who loved her, a baby on the way, a job she loved and so many friends who had come to wish them well.

"Maybe we'll look around, see if we can find a spot we like, buy a place of our own there."

"Seriously?" He shrugged. "Why not? We can take the kids there every summer."

"*Kids?*" she repeated, still grinning.

"Well, we're not gonna stop at one, are we?" He patted her belly and she caught his hand and held it in place, linking the three of them.

"No, we're not," she agreed, then leaned back against him and watched their guests dance on the wide wooden floor beneath thousands of tiny white lights.

"Your uncle and Betty look like they're having fun," he said, giving a nod toward the dance floor.

Jenny smiled to see Hank and Betty dancing together, alongside Mike's parents. The four of them had hit it off well enough that they were all planning a trip to wine country together. Their family was big and growing, Jenny thought, and she couldn't be happier.

"You two should be dancing," Brady said as he and Aine approached. Their infant son had stayed home in Ireland with Aine's mother, and though of course they were worried about leaving him, they were also enjoying the little break from parenthood.

"Why aren't you?" Mike asked with a laugh.

"We're about to," Brady assured him with a slap on the shoulder. "But first, we wanted to say happy wedding, happy life and good luck with the baby."

"Thanks," Mike said and pulled his oldest friend into a hard, one-armed hug.

"What's all this?" Sean asked as he walked up to join them. "People partying without me?"

"Where've you been?" Mike demanded. "You disappeared like an hour ago."

"On the phone with the contractor from hell," Sean muttered, glaring down at the phone so he didn't see the amused glances Mike and Brady shared.

"How is the very efficient Kate?" Brady asked.

"Driving him crazy," Mike offered.

"Hey, you try dealing with a know-it-all," Sean quipped.

"We do it all the time," Aine said, with a grin for Jenny.

"She's right," the new bride agreed.

"All right, enough of the insults." Brady pulled his wife onto the dance floor and her delighted laughter spilled out in her wake.

"Can I dance with the bride now?" Sean asked.

Mike strong-armed him out of the way. "Get your own girl.

"You owe me a dance, Mrs. Ryan," Mike said and spun Jenny into his arms and then around in a tight, fast circle.

"Sweep me away, Mr. Ryan," Jenny said and laughing, she wrapped her arms around his neck and held on tight. While the music played and the night wore on, joy shone as brightly as the fairy lights in the darkness.

* * * * *

FROM ENEMIES
TO EXPECTING

KAT CANTRELL

One

Logan McLaughlin hated losing. So of course the fates had gifted him with the worst team in the history of major league baseball. Losing had become an art form, one the Dallas Mustangs seemed determined to master. Short of cleaning house and starting over with a new roster, Logan had run out of ideas to help his ball club out of their slump.

Being the team's owner and general manager should be right up his alley. Logan's dad had run a billion-dollar company with ease and finesse for thirty years. Surely Logan had inherited a little of Duncan McLaughlin's business prowess along with a love of baseball and his dad's dot-com fortune?

Ticket sales for the Mustangs' home games said otherwise. A losing streak a mile long was the only reason Logan had agreed to the ridiculous idea his publicist had put forth, otherwise, he'd never have darkened the door of a reality game show. As last-ditch efforts went, this one took the cake.

But, as his publicist informed him, Logan had run out of charity golf tournaments, and they hadn't helped drive ticket sales anyway. Short of winning games—which he was working on, via some intricate and slow trade agreements—he needed to get public support for his team another way. Now.

Exec-ution's set teemed with people. Logan stood in the corner nursing a cup of very bad coffee because it was that or rip off someone's head due to caffeine withdrawal. He should have stopped at Starbucks on the way to the studio, but who would have thought that an outfit that asked its contestants to be on the set at 5:00 a.m. wouldn't have decent coffee? He was stuck in hell with crap in a cup.

"Logan McLaughlin." A pretty staffer with an iPad in the crook of her elbow let her gaze flit over the other contestants until she zeroed in on him standing well out of the fray. "Care to take a seat? We're about to begin filming."

"No, thanks. I'll stand," he declined smoothly with a ready smile to counter his refusal.

Chairs were for small people; at six-four, 220, Logan hadn't fit in most chairs since eleventh grade. Plus, he liked being able to see the big picture at a glance.

A soft-looking middle-aged man in a suit nodded at Logan. "Thought I recognized you. I'm a Yankees fan from way back. Used to watch you pitch, what, ten years ago?"

"Something like that," Logan agreed easily.

The Yankees had let him go eight years ago, but who was counting when the career he'd poured his heart and soul into ended in a failed Tommy John surgery? His elbow still ached occasionally, just in case he didn't have enough reminders that his days on the mound were over.

"Man, you were great. Sorry about the arm." The man shook his head. "Shame you can't get any of your starters shaped up. The Mustangs could use a guy with your skill."

Yeah. Shame. Logan nodded his thanks. He tossed his crap in a cup into a trash can and crossed his arms over the void in his chest that owning a baseball team hadn't filled. It was getting harder and harder to convince himself that his glory days were not behind him.

Winning games. Ticket sales. Merchandise sales. These were things that would fix that void. And when he won *Exec-ution*, sports news outlets would have something to do with his name besides dragging it through the mud.

The staffer called a few more people to take seats around the boardroom table. A photograph of the downtown Dallas skyline peeked through the faux window behind the table. Crew members buzzed around the cameras, and a few tech guys sat behind glass in a control room, wearing headsets. The host of the show sat at the head of the table, hands carefully laced in front him, with perfectly coiffed hair and a bogus TV smile.

"Let's have a good show!" The staffer melted away, and Well-Coiffed Guy launched into his spiel.

"Hi, everyone! I'm Rob Moore, your host for *Exec-ution*, where executives compete in two-person teams in an entrepreneurial challenge designed to showcase the ability to run a business. The winners get one hundred thousand dollars for charity. Losers? Executed!"

Logan rolled his eyes as the host smacked the table with his trademark chopping motion. So cheesy.

A commotion caught everyone's attention. A dark-haired woman strode onto the set with the pretty staffer dogging her heels.

Logan promptly forgot about the smarmy host and fake boardroom in favor of watching the real show—the dark-haired woman walking.

She moved liked an outfielder with a batter's home run in the works: fast, purposeful and determined not to let that ball go over the wall. Maybe she could teach his guys a few things about how to hustle.

The closer she got, the more interesting she became. A wide stripe of pink ran down the left side of her hair. The right side had been shorn close to her head in an asymmetrical cut that made Logan feel off-kilter all at once. Or maybe that was due to her thick, black Cleopatra-style eye makeup, which was far sexier than it should be.

She had everyone's attention exactly where she wanted it—on her. A woman dressed in a slim-fit, shocking pink suit cut low enough to allow her very nice breasts to peek out clearly expected people to no-tice her.

"Sorry I'm late," she offered the host. Her throaty voice thrummed through Logan in a way he hadn't been *thrummed* in a very long time. Not since his pitching days, when baseball groupies had been thick on the ground, which he'd taken advantage of far less than he could have.

This lady in pink had the full package, and then some. For some other guy.

Logan avoided packaged women like the plague, as they often came with nasty surprises once you unwrapped them. He liked his women simple, unaffected and open, a younger version of the best woman he knew—his mom.

Didn't mean he couldn't appreciate a gorgeous woman with a sexy voice.

Pink Lady drew even with Logan, electing to stand despite open seats at the table and ice-pick heels on her feet that couldn't be comfortable.

"I tried to explain that we'd already started filming," the staffer told Rob Moore in a hushed voice that carried across the whole set. "She barged in anyway."

"It's okay," the host said with a crafty smile. He waltzed over to them, his gaze cutting back and forth between Logan and the lady in pink at his side. "Oh, I like this. Very nice. Bad girl meets all-American boy. The viewers will love it."

"Love what?" Logan glanced down at his blue Mustangs T-shirt and jeans and then at the dark-haired woman. Moore's comment sank in. "You want us to be teammates? I don't think so."

That was not happening. But Moore had already moved on to the next couple, both of whom looked relieved with their matches.

The sinking feeling in Logan's stomach bottomed out. Pink Lady had crossed her arms under her spectacular breasts, shoving them upward so that they strained against the fabric of her suit. He averted his eyes as she started tapping out a staccato rhythm with one stiletto.

"What's wrong with being my teammate?" Her agitation pushed her voice up a notch. "You don't think I have any business savvy because of the tongue piercing. That's crap and you know it."

A…*tongue* piercing? Instantly, he envisioned exactly what skills a woman with a steel bar through her tongue might have. And they all centered on being naked. With her mouth on his flesh as she pleasured him.

Dragging his thoughts out of the gutter took entirely too much will. That's why he liked unassuming, unsexy, *uneverything* women.

"I didn't even notice that," he informed her truthfully and tried to stop himself from catching a glimpse of the piercing. "My objections have nothing to do with you."

That part was patently false. It had everything to do with the fact that she had *distraction* written all over her. He'd have to get a new teammate, no question.

For God knew what reason, she laughed, and that did a hell of lot more than *thrum* in Logan's gut.

"I have a BS meter with new batteries," she said. "Look around, honey. Everyone else has been paired. Can we get with the program?"

Logan peered down at his new teammate's fingernail, which had landed in the dead center of his chest. Then he glanced back up at her incredibly disturbing eyes. They were a shade of ice blue that seemed so much more stark and unique than they should, probably because of her eye makeup.

"I'm with the program." He reeled back the curl of awareness that her finger had aroused. "The question is, are you? I wasn't late."

"Five a.m. is an ungodly hour, and I was only fifteen minutes late. You can't hold that against me."

Yeah, actually he could. *He'd* been on time and so had everyone else. But since it did appear as if all the other teams had been set, he sighed. "Fine. You're forgiven. What did you say your industry is again?"

"I didn't. What did you say your name is again?"

The point wasn't lost on him. He'd completely abandoned civility with this pink curveball, and his mama had taught him better than that. He stuck out a hand. "Logan McLaughlin. Owner and general manager of the Dallas Mustangs."

"Sports is your thing, I see. The lack of dress-up clothes threw me." She glanced at his Mustangs shirt, and then slipped her hand in his for what should have been a perfunctory shake.

The moment her palm slid against his, a shock zinged up his arm, arrowing straight for his groin. He let it ride because it was that powerful and, God, he hadn't felt anything like it in ages. Her eyelids drifted downward a touch, and she peeked up at him from under her lashes, clearly affected by it as well.

"I own suits," he muttered, loath to release her and completely aware that he should have ended the handshake at least thirty seconds ago. "I'd rather go naked than wear one."

What was he *doing*?

Get a grip, McLaughlin. This woman was the polar opposite of his type, and flirting with her could only lead to disaster, especially since they were supposed to be focused on winning. Unfortunately, he had a feeling the disaster train had already pulled out of the station.

"Naked is my favorite, too." Her voice had dropped back into the throatiness he much preferred. That was not going to work, either. "Trinity Forrester. Yes, as in the holy trinity, the chick in *The Matrix* and the river. I've heard all the jokes, so save them."

"I guess I'm not allowed to ask if you're overly religious, then."

She smiled, leaning in close enough to share a whiff of her exotic scent that of course only added to her allure.

"If you do, you get my standard answer. 'Any man

in a ten-foot radius is expected to treat me like a goddess. You can get started worshipping me any time.'"

Oh, she'd like that, wouldn't she? His eyes narrowed.

If they were going to be teammates, they had to get a few things straight. No flirting. No throaty voices coupled with come-hither glances. Logan called the shots, and Ms. I've Heard All the Jokes had better be able to keep up. Sexy heels were optional.

The cameras had captured every word of the exchange. So far, so good.

The more the cameras tuned in to Trinity, the more times the producers would overlay her name and Fyra Cosmetics on the screen. You couldn't buy better advertising than that, and Fyra needed all the positive press it could get.

Trinity Forrester would get that press come hell or high water. Nothing could be allowed to happen to her company, the one she and her three best friends from college had built from a concept and a dream. Thanks to an internal saboteur, Fyra was struggling. As the chief marketing officer, Trinity took the negative publicity personally. It was her job to stop the hemorrhaging. *Exec-ution* was step one in that plan.

Otherwise, she'd be in her office hard at work on the campaign for Formula-47, the new product they'd hoped to launch in the next couple of weeks.

Mr. McLaughlin still had her hand in his as if he might not let go. Perfect. The more enthralled he was, the easier it would be to take charge. Men never paid attention to her unless they wanted to get her into the sack, mostly because that was the way she preferred it. Sex was the only thing she'd ever found worth doing with a man.

She smiled at Logan for good measure. He had good ole Texas boy baked into his DNA. Toss in his longish brown hair that constantly fell in his face and his casual clothes, and yeah, Logan McLaughlin was the epitome of the all-American type. Also known as a nice guy.

Nice guys were always hiding something not so nice, and she'd learned her lesson a long time ago when it came to trusting men—don't. A surprise pregnancy in her early twenties had cured her of happily-ever-after dreams when the father of her baby took off, and then a miscarriage convinced her she wasn't mother material anyway.

"Mr. McLaughlin," she murmured. "Perhaps you'd give me my hand back so we can get to work?"

He dropped it like he'd discovered a live copperhead in his grip and cleared his throat. "Yeah. Good idea."

They retrieved a sealed envelope from the show's host, and Logan followed Trinity to an area with an easel and large pad of paper for brainstorming. Her fingers itched to mark up those pristine white pages with diagrams. If that didn't jump-start her missing muse, nothing would. Though she'd tried a lot of things.

The cameraman wedged into the small area with them, still rolling. Perfect. She'd have to come up with more outrageous things to do, just to ensure the editors had plenty to work with. Coming in late had been a stroke of brilliance. And McLaughlin's face when she'd informed him he couldn't hold fifteen minutes against her…priceless. He was obviously a rule follower. Shame.

He tore open the envelope and pulled out the contents, scanning it quickly. "We have to run a lemonade stand in Klyde Warren Park. Whichever team makes the most money wins the task and avoids execution."

"Excellent." Rubbing her hands together, she then quickly sketched out her vision for the stand, filling in small details like cross-hatching to indicate shadowing. "Orange will be the best color to paint the booth. Good contrast against green, assuming we'll be in the grassy part of the park."

Her partner loomed at her shoulder, breathing down her neck as he stretched one muscular arm out to stab the pad. "What is this?"

"A sign. That says Trinity's Lemonade."

What did the man bathe in that smelled so…manly? The clean, citrusy notes spread through her senses and caught the attention of her erogenous zones, none of which had gotten the memo that she did not go for Texas boys who looked like they lived outdoors.

The man owned a sports team, for God's sake. He'd probably need a dictionary to hold a conversation over drinks, which would no doubt include beer and a hundred TVs with a different game on each one. She and Logan were ill matched for a reality game show, let alone outside one, his rock-hard pecs aside. Her fingertip still tingled from when she'd poked him, not at all prepared for the body she'd discovered under that blue T-shirt.

"Why would we call it Trinity's Lemonade, exactly?" he asked, his deep voice rumbling in her ear. "Logan's Lemonade sounds better. Starts with the same letter."

"It's alliterative, you mean," she supplied sweetly. "I understand the dynamics of appealing to the public better than you do, honey. So let's stick with our strengths, shall we?"

She stroked a few more lines across her work of art and then yelped as her partner spun her around to face him. His mouth firmed into a flat line and he towered over her even in her five-inch Stuart Weitzman sandals. Trinity was used to looking men in the eye, and the fact that she couldn't do that with Logan McLaughlin put her on edge.

"You've done a really good job of not mentioning your strengths, *darling*," he threw in sarcastically. "I run a multimillion-dollar sports franchise. What do you do, Ms. Forrester?"

"Haven't I mentioned it?" she tossed off casually when she knew good and well she hadn't—on purpose. The moment a man like him heard the word *cosmetics*, he'd make more snap judgments and she'd had enough of that.

At this point, though, she needed to impress upon him that she was in her sweet spot. "I'm the CMO at Fyra."

Blandly, he surveyed her. "The makeup company?"

"The very same. So now we're all caught up," she informed him brightly. "Marketing is my gig. Yours is figuring out which guy can hit the ball hardest. When we have a task that requires balls, I'll let you be in charge."

This lemonade stand graphic was the first inspired thing she'd done in weeks, which was frankly depressing. Her muse had deserted her, which was alarming enough in and of itself, but the timing was horrific. Fyra planned to launch its premier product in the next ninety days. Fortunately, no one knew she'd run dry in the creativity department. It wasn't like she could tell her business partners that she had a mental block when it came to Formula-47. They were counting on her.

His mouth tipped up in a slow smile that didn't fool her for a second. "In case you've forgotten, we're partners. That means all tasks require balls, specifically mine. Shove over and let's do this together."

Nice. Not only had he called her on her double en-tendre, he'd done it with a style she grudgingly appreci-ated. Which was the only reason she stepped a half inch to the right, graciously offering him room at the pad.

His arm jostled hers as he took way more space than she'd intended. The man was a solid wall of muscle, with wide shoulders and lean hips, and yeah, of course she'd noticed how well his jeans hugged the curve of his rear. That part of Logan McLaughlin was a gift to women everywhere, and she'd gotten in her share of ogling.

Without a word, he picked up his own marker and crossed out "Trinity's Lemonade," then scrawled, "McLemonade" across the sign. Oh, God. That was perfect. How dare he be the one to come up with it?

Scowling, she crossed her arms and in the pro-cess made sure to throw an elbow into his ribs. Which promptly glanced off as if she'd hit a brick wall. And now her elbow hurt.

"Fine," she ground out. "We'll go with yours. But the booth will be orange."

He shrugged, shouldering her deliberately. "I didn't have an issue with that."

The man was intolerable. Nowhere near the nice guy she'd pegged him as, and once he opened his mouth, totally unattractive. Or at least that was what she was telling herself.

"Oh, yeah? So the stuff you do have issues with—that's all getting the McLaughlin veto?" Standing her ground shouldn't be this hard, but heels coupled with the immovable mountain snugged next to her body threw her off, and not solely because it was impossible to think through the shooting pangs of awareness that she couldn't seem to get under control.

Instead of glaring, his expression smoothed out and he took a deep breath.

"Let's start over." He extended his hand.

Because he'd piqued her curiosity, she took it and he swallowed her palm with his. Little frissons of awareness seeped into her skin at the contact.

"I'm Logan McLaughlin. I run a baseball team and our ticket sales suck. My publicist insisted that this game show would be a good way to get some eyes on the team, so here I am. Any help I can get toward that goal is appreciated."

His clear hazel eyes held hers, and his sincerity bled through her, tripping her pulse unexpectedly. Well, jeez. Honesty. What would the man think of next?

"Hi," she said because that seemed to be all her throat could summon as they stared at each other, intensity burning through her. "I'm, um, Trinity Forrester. I sell cosmetics alongside three women I love dearly. Our company stepped in a negative publicity hole, so *my* publicist came up with the brilliant idea to stick me on a TV show. I'm…not so sure that was a good move."

That made Logan laugh, and the rich sound of it wound through her with warmth that was so nice, her knees weakened. Weakness under any circumstances was not acceptable. But hardening herself against him took way more effort than it should have.

Was it so wrong to let a man like him affect her? Sure he was insufferable, pigheaded and way too virtuous for her tastes, but he had a gorgeous body, a nice smile and longish hair made for a woman's fingers. He couldn't be all bad.

"Oddly enough, I was thinking the same thing," he admitted, his eyes crinkling at the corners. "But I've changed my mind. I think we can help each other if we work together. Willing to give it a shot?"

Guess that was her answer about what else he had up his sleeve—he was going to be pleasant instead of an obstinate jackass. Strictly to mess with her head, most likely.

But she needed to work with him to benefit both of their goals. She bit her tongue and slipped her hand from his. "I can give that a shot."

They put their heads together, and true to his word, Logan listened to her ideas. She considered it a plus when he laughed at her jokes. No one had to know she secretly reveled in it.

By the end of the afternoon, they'd amassed a solid four hundred dollars and change with their McLemonade booth. God knew how. They'd fought over everything: how much to charge, where to set up, how much lemonade to put in the cups. Apparently, Mr. Nice Guy only made an appearance when he wanted something, then vanished once he got into the thick of things.

Finally, the show's producer asked them to pack up and head to the studio so they could wrap up the day's shooting. They drove separate cars to the set and met up again in the fake boardroom.

This time, Trinity grabbed a seat. An entire day on her feet, most of it on grass while wearing stilettos, was not doing her body any favors.

"Welcome back, everyone!" Rob Moore called, and the teams gathered around the table.

Logan stood at the back and Trinity pretended like she didn't notice the vacant seat by her side. All the other teammates sat next to each other. Fine by her. She and her partner got on like oil and water and had only figured out how to work together because they'd had to.

"We've tallied all the sales, and I must say, this was an impressive group of teams." The host beamed at them. "But the winners are Mitch Shaughnessy and John Roberts!"

Disappointed, Trinity clapped politely as the winning team high-fived each other and jogged to the head of the table to claim the giant check made out to St. Jude Children's Hospital. That was the important thing—the money was going to a good cause.

"The winning team's proceeds were…" Rob Moore paused for dramatic effect. "Four hundred and twenty-eight dollars. Impressive!"

Oh, dear God. They'd lost by a measly twenty-five dollars? She thought about banging her head on the table, but that wouldn't put the cameras on her face with a nice graphic overlay stating her company's name. But what if there was a way to get some additional airtime? The cameras were still rolling, panning the losers as the host launched into his trademark parting comments.

"Fire up the electric chair, boys," he cried. "We've got some executions to perform!"

This was the cheesiest part of the show, which she'd hoped to avoid. She had a good idea how to do that and get some cameras on her at the same time.

Pushing her chair backward with a sharp crack, she bolted to her feet and charged over to her partner, poking her finger in his chest with a bit more force than she'd intended. But she'd gotten the cameraman's attention, and that was all that mattered.

"This is all your fault, McLaughlin. We would have won if it wasn't for you."

His gaze narrowed, and he reached up to forcibly re-move her finger from his person. "What are you talking about? This ship started sinking the second we were paired. Bad girl meets all-American boy. *Please.* What they should have called us was train meets wreck."

That struck her as such a perfect way to describe the day that she almost laughed, but she bit it back. She could admire his wit later, over a glass of wine as she celebrated the fact that she never had to see him again. "You know what your problem is?"

"I've got no doubt you're about to tell me," he offered and crossed his arms in the pose that she'd tried—and failed—to ignore all day. When he did that, his biceps bunched up under his shirt sleeves, screaming to be touched. She just wanted to feel one once. Was that so much to ask?

"Someone needs to. Otherwise, you'd walk around with that rule book shoved up your…butt," she amended, lest the producers cut the whole exchange due to her potty mouth. "Some rules are made to be broken. That's why we lost. Apply for sainthood on your own time."

His expression heated and not in a good way. "Are you saying I'm a Goody Two-shoes?"

"If the shoe fits, wear it," she suggested sweetly. "And that's not even the worst of your problems."

He rolled his eyes, fire shooting from his gaze, and she almost caved, because he was really pissed and while she wanted the cameras on them, she also felt like crap for poking at him. But when he got hot and bothered, he lost all his filters and focused on noth-ing but her.

That, she liked.

"Oh, I've gotta hear this. Please, enlighten me."

"You're attracted to me and you can't stand it." That

was like the pot calling the kettle black, though she scarcely wanted to admit that to herself, let alone out loud.

"I'm sorry, what?"

"You heard me."

Her finger ended up back on his chest. Oops. It was hard and delicious and there was something super hot about how immovable he was. Logan was solid, the kind of guy who might actually stick around when unexpected challenges cropped up. Sometimes a girl needed a strong shoulder. He had two.

"I heard you," he growled and went to smack away her finger—she'd assumed—but he crushed her palm to his chest, holding it captive with his hand. "What I meant was, that's the craziest thing you've said so far today."

The cameraman had zoomed in on their discussion. She noted the lens from the corner of her eye and nearly smiled.

You couldn't buy this kind of exposure. This time tomorrow—with her help—this clip would go viral: *Two executives melt down on the set of a reality TV show.* Viewers would see a strong woman not taking any crap from her male partner. As long as they spelled Fyra correctly, it should amp up the positive publicity and counter the negative.

"Get ready for more crazy, because not only are you attracted to me, you can't stop thinking about what it would be like to kiss me. Admit it. You're curious about the tongue piercing."

"Of course I am," he bit out, fuzzing her brain at the same time.

He was? Fascinated, she zeroed in on him, and yeah, there was a whole lot more than agitation in his expression. Logan McLaughlin, official Boy Scout of major league baseball, had never kissed a woman with a tongue piercing. And he wanted to.

Heat and a thick awareness flooded all the places between them. His heart thumped under her palm, strong but erratic, which perfectly mirrored the stuff going on under her own skin.

"What red-blooded male wouldn't be curious," he murmured. "When there's only one reason to have a steel bar through your tongue—to pleasure a man."

His eyelids shuttered for a beat, and when he opened them, his eyes held so much wicked intent, her pulse bobbled. Caught in his hot gaze, she swayed toward him, her hand fisting his shirt. "One way to find—"

His mouth captured hers before she'd fully registered him moving. And then all rational thought drained from her mind as Logan kissed her. The TV set melted away, the fascinated onlookers disappeared—none of it registered as he yanked her into his embrace.

Exactly where she wanted to be.

Logan McLaughlin was perfection under her hands, because *yes*, he was that hard all over. His back alone qualified as a work of art, defined with peaks and valleys that she hadn't ever felt on a man before. Imagine that. Something new to be discovered on a male body.

She wanted more. And took it.

Tilting her head, she deepened the kiss, and he countered instantly, swirling his tongue forward to find hers, taking command of the kiss, heightening the roar of hunger pounding through her veins. *His mouth.* God, the things it was doing to her. The things it could do.

And then all at once, his lips disappeared and she swayed forward, desperate to get them back on hers. Instead, he leaned in and nuzzled her ear.

"How'd I do?" he murmured. "Close enough to what you were going for?"

Trinity laughed, because what else could she do? "Yeah. That was perfect."

He'd been on to her scheme the entire time. Of course. What had she thought, that a man with commitment and white picket fences written all over him might actually go for a woman like her, who'd turned her independence into a shield? That he'd been as into the kiss as she had?

Never in a million years would they make sense together—unless it was fake.

This was a great place for goodbye. But for some reason, Trinity was having a very difficult time taking her hands off her partner.

Two

The next morning, Trinity entered the five-story glass-and-steel building that housed the cosmetics company she'd helped build with her marketing savvy and love of all things feminine. She still got a thrill out of the modern design and purple accents she and her three partners had selected, and the location just north of downtown Dallas was perfect for a single woman who owned an amazing condo in the heart of the city.

Cass had been making noises about moving the company to Austin. Trinity kept her mouth shut because Fyra's CEO had a very good reason for wanting to do so—her husband, Gage, lived there and they were expecting a baby together. Trinity didn't have anything against Austin, per se. But it was yet another example of something she had no control over. She hated anything that smacked of lack of control.

Plus, what was wrong with Gage moving his company to Dallas? Both CEOs ran large companies with lots of employees. Just because Gage was the man in the equation, why did that mean he automatically won the battle?

Trinity strode toward her office to the sounds of hoots and clapping. She took a moment to grin and wave. Obviously the footage of her kiss with Logan had made the rounds. The game show itself wouldn't air until later in the week, but she'd charmed the producer out of a clip of the kiss, starting it on its viral journey by posting it to her own social media accounts and tagging everyone she knew to share it.

Trinity wasn't one for leaving things to chance.

Cass had scheduled a meeting for first thing this morning, probably to get the full scoop. Humming, Trinity grabbed coffee and dug around until she found her iPad in her shoulder bag, then strolled to the conference room where Cass stood at the head of the table.

"Hey," Trinity called and repeated her greeting to Fyra's CFO, Alex Edgewood, and then to Dr. Harper Livingston-Gates, the chief science officer, whose faces appeared in split screen on a TV mounted on the wall. Both of them were participating in the meeting virtually since they'd abandoned Dallas the moment their husbands crooked their fingers.

Trinity sank into a seat and mentally slapped herself for being unkind.

Alex was pregnant with twins and on bed rest, so it made sense that she lived in Washington, DC, with her husband, Phillip, a United States senator. Harper's husband worked in Zurich, and Trinity didn't blame her for wanting to be in the same bed with a man as hot as Dr. Dante Gates, especially since they'd just figured out they were in love after being friends for over a decade.

Maybe Trinity was a little jealous that everyone else

had such an easy time with normal female things like falling for a great guy and having his support during pregnancy. And none of them had suffered a horrendous miscarriage that had left them feeling defective. Well, so what? Trinity had other great stuff in her life, like more men than she could shake a stick at.

Except lately, great men had been pretty scarce. The pitfalls of turning thirty. Made you think more about the definition of "great," and pseudo–frat boys with Peter Pan syndrome were not it. Unfortunately, that seemed to be the type she met at her usual haunts, which was fine for the short term.

She just wished she knew why that didn't feel like enough anymore.

Cass started off with a sly smile. "You and your reality show partner got pretty chummy. Do tell."

"All for the cameras, hon," Trinity assured her. God, what was with that pang in her gut? The kiss had been fake. On both sides—never mind that she'd liked how real it felt. "We were both interested in getting additional coverage. It worked."

Alex and Harper both murmured their disappointment that the story wasn't juicier.

"I know we've turned dissecting our love lives into a regular boardroom agenda item, but let's move on," Trinity insisted smoothly. "I'm sure Cass didn't call this meeting to talk about my partner on a reality game show."

"Actually, I did," Cass corrected. "We've got a publicity issue that's at the top of everyone's mind right now. After the mess with the leak and then the FDA approval fiasco, sales went into the toilet. We've got new problems daily as articles keep popping up in what feels to me like a smear campaign."

Felt that way to Trinity, too. Which was why it pissed her off so much. This was her territory. Her company. And someone was after it.

"Yeah, I'm aware. That's why I did the show, remember?"

"I'm not sure it's enough." Cass frowned. "I approved it since the publicist suggested it, but we need to move forward with launching Formula-47. When can you schedule time to present the marketing plan?"

"Next Monday?" Trinity suggested and started calculating exactly how screwed she was...since the campaign didn't exist. *Very* would be the precise amount of screwed.

It wasn't anyone's fault but hers, but then she'd never had a creative dry spell like this one, and she couldn't even commiserate with her friends. Recent personal events for all three ladies had driven a wedge between them, with Trinity on the wrong side of the married mom division.

Trinity hated it. She was happy for her friends, but sad that they'd all chosen lives so different from the ones they'd had. So different from the one she'd mapped out for herself. And she was pretty sure that was why her creativity had completely abandoned her when she needed it most.

The sketching she'd done on that pristine white pad while Logan peered over her shoulder had been a welcome flood of ingenuity. Maybe the medium was the key—she'd run out at lunch and pick up one of those easels. It could work.

She could totally get her muse to make an appearance, work straight through and have a brilliant campaign by Monday morning. Especially if the publicity from *Exec-ution* worked like it was supposed to. With that load off her mind, then she could concentrate on turning Formula-47 into a powerhouse wrinkle and scar cream that would put Fyra at the top of the industry.

Cass nodded and shifted focus to numbers, so Alex took the lead on that, while Trinity sank down in her seat to let her mind wander in hopes of jogging something passable from her subconscious. Didn't happen, but she had almost a week. No problem.

The easel and pad did not turn into a magic bullet. Neither did the marathon brainstorming session she called to generate ideas from her creative team. At four o'clock, she sent Melinda, Fyra's receptionist, to the office supply store to get a dozen more blank pads. The remains of the two Trinity had purchased at lunch lay in ripped and crumpled pieces on her office floor. She might have stabbed a couple of the papers with her Louboutin heels, but only because big jagged holes improved the package design she'd started on.

She didn't even have a product name, which meant she had no business trying to design the packaging. Her creative process required building blocks, and the name always came first, but she'd been desperate to make *some* kind of progress. Formula-47 would be Fyra's premier product and as the CMO, Trinity should and would take on the heaviest lifting. Her creative team had enough on their plates with managing the rest of Fyra's marketing juggernaut while she buried herself in this mess.

Melinda poked her head in the door. "I've got your pads. Also, Lara from Gianni Publicity Group is here. She doesn't have an appointment. Shall I send her away?"

The publicist. Great. That was exactly what Trinity needed right now—a reminder that Cass had hired an outside firm to do Trinity's job. And Lara's big contribution thus far had landed Trinity in the arms of a do-gooder Texas boy who kissed like a wicked fantasy.

Logan McLaughlin was a name she should have forgotten by now. For God knew what reason, it still rattled around in her head, heating up places that shouldn't be heating at the thought of a rugged, lean-hipped outdoorsy guy who wasn't her type.

She sighed. "No, it's okay. I'll see her."

Lara Gianni rushed into the office, long hair streaming behind her as the chic woman grabbed Trinity by the shoulders and kissed both cheeks, Italian style. "You brilliant, brilliant lady. Logan McLaughlin is *magnifico*."

"Back off. I saw him first," Trinity said drily. Was the woman reading minds now? "Why is he magnificent again? Please tell me it's because you've got good news."

The publicist laughed. "The best. Your video has already been shared over half a million times, and the response? Amazing. People love you two together. The comments are priceless. Love on the set of a TV show is brilliant marketing."

"Wait a minute. Love on a TV show? It was an entrepreneurial game show, not *The Bachelor*." The look on Lara's face gave Trinity a very bad feeling. "The public was supposed to see the name Fyra and think positive thoughts about it. That's how you sold the idea to us."

"That was before you went in a whole different direction. One I love! You're truly brilliant."

Yeah, that part was clear. What wasn't clear was what the hell Lara was talking about. "I didn't go in a different direction. We lost the game and I had to do something extra. I kissed my partner. Voilà, now Fyra is all over social media."

"No." Lara shook her head. "*You* are all over social media. They like the romance you unwittingly created. I would highly recommend continuing it."

Trinity's stomach dropped into her shoes. "Continue what? There's no romance. It was one kiss."

A hot kiss. If she'd watched the footage a couple of dozen times before she'd posted it, no one had to know.

Lara shrugged. "I suggest you figure out how to make it into more than a kiss. It doesn't have to be a real relationship so long as you get yourself photographed with Logan McLaughlin. A lot. While kissing and making goo-goo eyes at each other."

The logic of it warred with the insanity. A fake relationship strictly for publicity? She couldn't. *He* wouldn't. Yet…how was that so different than a fake kiss for the same reason? Logan had jumped on that deal like a starving dog on a steak. Maybe he'd be *really* good at pretending they were a hot-and-heavy couple.

The thought unleashed a shiver that nearly unglued her. The side benefits of such an arrangement held many interesting possibilities that she could not ignore, like enticing a nice guy into a walk on the wild side. How much fun would it be to corrupt the hell out of the all-American boy, especially on camera?

No. A long-term fake relationship was a whole lot different than one fake kiss. Her acting skills weren't that good. Except all at once, she couldn't figure out if she'd be feigning she was into him…or pretending she wasn't.

"No way. I can't do something like that."

Lara's brow furrowed as she pulled out her phone

and tapped a few times, then held it out to display a nearly all-red pie chart. "That's the click-through rate from your video to Fyra's website."

All the blood drained from Trinity's head. Seventy-five percent. *Seventy-five percent.* The click-through rate of her most successful social media campaign ever was 12 percent.

In the wake of the smear tactics someone had launched against Fyra, she couldn't afford to pass up this idea.

Looked like she'd be paying Mr. McLaughlin a visit. Tomorrow. *Hello, new boyfriend.*

Myra slapped the printed spreadsheet on Logan's desk and didn't bother to hide her smirk. "Told you that reality show would work."

Yes, it had. He didn't need his publicist to point out the double-digit increase in ticket sales. The Mustangs' entire front office had been buzzing about it since he'd walked in this morning. And he had Trinity Forrester, CMO, to thank.

Who would have thought that sizzling kiss would pay such huge dividends?

Duncan McLaughlin had never done *that* to get customers to open their wallets, but in Logan's defense, it hadn't been his idea. Yet he'd gotten on board with it pretty dang fast, at least once he'd realized the hot woman he'd been salivating over was not coming on to him. She'd simply found one last way to get the camera on them. As tactics went, he could find little to complain about.

Other than the fact that one bad-girl kiss later, he'd come to the uncomfortable realization that he could not wipe the feel of that tongue piercing from his memory.

His admin, Lisa, popped into his office, eyes wide. "Um, boss? You have a visitor. Ms. Forrester?"

Well, well. He leaned back in his chair as Myra's expression veered between intrigued and very intrigued. Logan had a feeling his own face might be doing something similar, so he schooled it before nodding to Lisa. "You can send her in. Thanks, Myra. I'll get back to you."

And then everything in the world of baseball ceased to exist as Trinity waltzed into his office, her off-kilter hair throwing him into a tailspin. God, how was that so sexy? On her, it was one more in-your-face reminder that she was a force to be reckoned with.

Today's outfit consisted of a deep purple suit with a micro skirt, black stockings that made her legs look a mile long and silver ankle breakers that he'd like better on his bedroom floor.

"Thanks for seeing me on short notice," she said.

That throaty voice. He'd underrated what it did to him when the sound slid down his spine. His blood woke up and sluiced through his veins in a rush that made him feel alive—only being on the mound had ever replicated that feeling.

Why her? Of all people? He'd *always* been on the lookout for a simple, uncomplicated woman who listened to country music and planned picnics. A nice woman to settle down with, who could have his babies and be the love of his life. That was how his dad had done it. That was how Logan wanted to do it. The fact that he'd yet to meet his fictional perfect lady was neither here nor there—she was out there somewhere.

And her name was not Trinity. He should not be attracted to her.

All at once, he remembered his manners and rose to

his feet, palm outstretched toward the love seat near the window that overlooked the ballpark, his favorite spot in the whole stadium as long as there wasn't a game in progress. Then it was the dugout until the bitter end.

Most general managers sat in an air-conditioned luxury box, but his players were slugging it out on the field, and in August, it wasn't unusual for the temperature to hit 110. The senior McLaughlin had regularly hit the trenches alongside his employees. Logan could do the same.

Instead of taking the offered seat, Trinity slid a steamy once-over all the way down his body. "You're wearing a suit. What was it you said about those?"

I'd rather go naked.

The unspoken quote hung in the air between them, dissolving into a dense awareness that answered one lingering question on his mind since that kiss—whether or not he misremembered how deeply she'd gotten under his skin with all her innuendo.

He'd recalled it perfectly.

"I'm being a grown-up today," he croaked and cleared his throat.

"Oh, yeah, I once thought about being one of those for Halloween." She shrugged with a smile that he felt in his gut. "By the way, I like you in a suit."

"What can I do for you, Ms. Forrester?"

The sooner he got her out of his office, the sooner he could get back to work. Or take a cold shower. The last thing he should do was give her an advantage, or she'd railroad him into doing her bidding before he'd fully surfaced from being whacked upside the head by all the pheromones.

"You can call me Trinity." She jerked her chin toward the desk, flinging the dark swath of hair into motion.

She hadn't colored it today, strictly to throw him off, no doubt. "Talk to me about your numbers."

He glanced at the spreadsheet Myra had thrown at him to give himself a half second. What was she fishing for? "I'm happy with the results of the viral video and hopeful that when the show airs, the upward trend will continue. How about your numbers?"

"Fantastic. So good, in fact, I'm here with a proposal."

The way she said it brought to mind closed doors, a secret rendezvous and a solid block of time to explore just how good that bar through her tongue would feel on his body. If that ever happened, she'd completely ruin him for all other women, no doubt.

His body tightened in anticipation. *Let's find out*, it begged.

"I'm listening," he said when what he should have said was *there's the door*.

"My target customers loved the video of us together. My publicist thinks we should take advantage of it and start a public relationship. Pretend that we're dating after meeting on the show."

"That's the worst idea I've ever heard. We'd kill each other before anyone believed we were a couple."

His mind ignored his instant denial and latched on to the idea, turning it over. The timing of the video coincided with the increase in ticket sales too neatly to be a fluke. What would it hurt to capitalize on the momentum?

It could hurt *a lot*. His major objection had nothing to do with the brilliance of the idea and everything to do with his illogical reaction to her every time she got within breathing distance.

And then last night, she hadn't even been in the room

when he'd let himself envision a bedtime story about finishing that kiss with her legs wrapped around his waist. Yeah, she might be the star in his current shower fantasies. It wasn't a felony. Except he'd never in a million years have guessed that today would bring her back into his orbit, especially not this way.

Her gaze glittered with calculation. "Actually, the worst idea you'd ever heard was the one where we got paired on that stupid game show. But we made that work. *Together.* It was a team effort, and we almost won. Just think what we can accomplish with a concerted effort to exploit the public's thirst for celebrity couples. I'm offering you my complete attention to boost your ticket sales."

Her negotiation skills hit all the right notes, buttering him up, stressing the goal. Worst of all? He had an urge to say yes, simply to find out what her complete attention looked like.

Was it distasteful to use this opportunity to sate his curiosity about Trinity? A better question was how long he could do it and keep his hands off her. Not long— either he'd make good on the urge to strangle her or he'd provoke her until she kissed him again.

This idea got worse and worse the longer he thought about it.

"How do you even know I'm single?" he countered. "Maybe I've got the perfect girlfriend already and I—"

"Please don't insult me, McLaughlin." She snorted. "Or yourself. You couldn't have cut the sexual tension between us with a meat cleaver. If you do have a girlfriend and you can still kiss me like that, you're not the man I assume you are."

He scowled, and not just because of her excellent point.

"I get it now." He nodded sagely. "This is a ploy to earn yourself some more camera time. Attend a few Mustangs games where the general manager's hot girlfriend would most definitely be a subject of interest."

Boldly, she contemplated him, not at all bothered by his half-assed accusations. "What if it is? Does that automatically make it a bad idea? My reasons for liking this plan have nothing to do with the reasons you should agree. Ticket sales are the only thing that matters."

Wow. He shook his head. When you called a spade a spade with Trinity Forrester, she turned over a full house. "Let me make sure I've got this straight. You're suggesting we manufacture a relationship. Date each other, be seen at some events. And the public is going to approve of this by spending a lot of money?"

"We're going to help them do that with ad campaigns heavily laced with click bait. But, yeah. Get your publicist involved. Talk to your marketing people. Let's make it a party and get some eyes on our individual brands."

Not only did everything she was saying make sense, she had a unique way of presenting it that appealed to him. That alone ruffled his nerves. "How exactly are we going to date and manage to be civil to each other?"

Like that was the biggest issue.

"Who said we were?" Her blue eyes glowed as she caught his gaze. "Part of what sizzles about us is the way we clash. It translates really well on camera. Didn't you watch the clip?"

He might have watched the video a few times, and there wasn't a good way to pretend she was wrong. Nor could he forget how arguing with her had exploded into the heat of that kiss. "So not only are we supposed to fake date, but we're also supposed to have knock-down, drag-out fights in public, too?"

That was way over the line. Logan and his temper were old enemies, and bad decisions followed when he allowed his emotions off the leash. He'd left his hot-head days behind him when he bought the Mustangs. A team owner had to play it cool, and thus far, he'd call his newfound calm a success.

Until Trinity.

She was the only person of his acquaintance who threatened his composure on a minute-by-minute basis.

She shrugged. "Let me be clear. I'll do whatever it takes to get you to agree to this. If you want me to be nice and sweet and smile at your fans, I will."

Waltzing closer, she let her fingers trail down the front of his shirt, reminding him of the last time she'd done that—right before he'd tested out kissing a woman with a bar through her tongue.

As if she'd read his mind, her gaze instantly caught fire and swept him with a thousand licks of heat as she let her eyes wander down his body in a slow perusal that almost had him squirming. But he had far more control over his body than that—any athlete worth his salt had enormous discipline. Losing his pitching arm hadn't become an excuse to sit on the couch and get fat.

"Logan," she murmured throatily, splattering his control to hell and back as his lower half went hard. "If you want me to wear leather and carry around a whip because you like the bad-girl persona that *Execution* coated me with, I would be happy to oblige. Tell me what it will take."

Now that was an interesting proposition. His imagination took off at a brisk trot, and it was nearly impossible to rein it back in. "We'd have to make it look real."

Guess it was too late to pretend he wasn't considering it.

"Sure. Lots of public kissing. Affection. Lots of making up after a good fight. Maybe you pop the question at an event with a huge diamond ring that sparkles."

Not for a thousand percent increase in ticket sales would he do something so sacred unless he meant it. "I'm not proposing to you no matter how fake it is. That's reserved for the future Mrs. McLaughlin. She deserves to be the only one to have that experience."

Something flashed in her gaze. Longing, maybe. But it was gone before he could process it and her expression hardened. "Fair enough. You play this however you want."

"You realize we have to spend time together doing things. You're going to have to pretend to like baseball. No glazed eyes when I wax poetical about Nolan Ryan."

Actually, he might do that on occasion just for fun.

"Only if you listen with rapt attention when I mention Estée Lauder," she countered with a sly smile. "I need you. Make me an offer."

"I'll think about it."

He didn't have to. There was no way he could say no. The part he had to think about was how deep this fake relationship would ultimately go. How deep he'd be willing to admit he wanted it to go. And whether he could, in fact, hold on to both his temper and his sanity while dating Trinity Forrester.

She swept from his office on a cloud of femininity and something spicy that he suspected he'd smell in his sleep for a long time to come.

Before he could remind himself of the million and one reasons it was a dangerous, horrible idea, he texted her: I'm in.

Three

Trinity sat on Logan's text message for two days. Mostly because she had no idea what to do with a fake boyfriend. Boyfriends of any sort vexed her on the whole, but one she wasn't sleeping with broke all kinds of new ground.

What did you *do* with a man outside of bed?

Should she hit a club with him? Stand at the red rope and hope someone took pictures? That seemed too chancy, and frankly, the idea of Logan McLaughlin at a techno bar with lots of smoke and pulsing lights made her laugh. And he'd probably laugh at her if she suggested it.

While it might lead to an argument that would be delicious on camera, they'd have to actually be in public for that to generate maximum publicity. She couldn't think of anything that *would* work, though. Her lack of creativity lately was bleeding into the social arena as well, and it was bothersome. Almost as bothersome as the fact that she had a marketing presentation to give to her friends and business partners on Monday and it still didn't exist.

Formula-47 used nanotechnology to heal scars and reduce wrinkles. There were thousands of ways to market such a brilliant product. She should have two presentations by now.

That's what she had to focus on, not the two-word text message from Logan McLaughlin.

I'm in. Nothing else. No *let's meet for coffee and hash this out*. No *here are my conditions and expectations*. What? Was she supposed to do all the dirty work and organize everything? He had a stake in this, too.

By Thursday, she was ready to bite off the head of the next person who poked their toe into her office. When her phone beeped, she nearly shut it off. But then she saw Logan's name blinking at her. Eyes narrowed, she thumbed up the text message.

Charity gala tomorrow night. Guaranteed to have lots of cameras and press. Formal dress. Pick you up at 8.

Men. Logan had his share of nerve, assuming she could pull a formal ensemble together in less than thirty-six hours, not to mention she'd have to beg Franco for a last-minute appointment to get her hair done. Her regular nail girl was out of town, too. Trinity groaned and pushed back from her desk to go spend the rest of the afternoon shopping for the perfect dress to drive a man wild.

Logan McLaughlin totally deserved to spend the entire evening in the most painful state possible for springing this on her at the last minute. And if she secretly wanted to kiss him for getting her out from behind her desk and away from the reminders that her career might be circling the drain—she'd keep that to herself.

Miraculously, Franco had a cancellation, he personally found a replacement nail technician for her, and the most amazing dress fell into her lap. Logan might get a pass after all, but strictly because he'd stepped up when it counted.

When Logan knocked on the door of Trinity's penthouse loft in the Arts District, she was dressed and ready to go. Except for her lipstick. She swiped on a layer of Bohemian Rhapsody with a lip brush and dropped both into her clutch.

It was a ritual she'd always performed back when she'd dated more. Wait until he knocked and then apply lipstick, which left the guy on her doorstep for precisely the right amount of time. Enough that he'd start to wonder if maybe she wasn't dressed yet and was even at this moment throwing on clothes. Never hurt to dangle a visual in front of a man.

And then she would open the door to give him the real visual—her, dressed to the hilt in this smashing and sexy dress with cutout sides that displayed all her best features.

Except when she opened the door to Logan…in a tux…her tongue went numb and she dropped her clutch. Which he picked up for her.

Good God, did that man clean up well. The suit from the other day? Merely an appetizer to the main course of this gorgeous hunk of masculinity in a tuxedo that had clearly been custom-made for him.

Thank all that was holy that he didn't dress like that on a daily basis. The luxurious dark fabric spread across his shoulders, emphasizing the broad, dense build she shouldn't like as much as she did. Logan was too big. Too solid. Too...squeaky clean.

But the pièce de résistance was the single long-stemmed pink rose that he held out to her.

"Pink?" She took it and held it to her nose, trying not to be pleased but failing. A whole bouquet would have been overkill and completely unnecessary given that they weren't really dating.

One rose was classy. And well played.

"You wore a pink suit on the show," he said gruffly with a shrug and ran his now vacant fingers through his hair, sweeping it away from his face. "The association with that color and you is pretty much stuck in my head."

Her insides melted. She didn't know what to do with that or the best behavior vibe wafting from him. It was almost as if he'd lectured himself on the way over to remember he had a reputation for being a nice guy and maybe he should act like one.

She cleared her throat. "Thank you."

"Are you ready to go?"

Her brows rose. After three hours at the salon today, that was his comment? This sedate, boring version of Logan needed to vacate the premises, pronto, or they'd never heat it up enough for anyone to care about taking their picture.

"Don't I look ready to go?"

It would not kill him to compliment her dress. Her hair. Her punctuality. Something.

"You look like you should be spread across the floor of a Mexican restaurant," he said bluntly, with a once-over that totally contradicted his words. His gaze was more *I want to rip that dress off you* than *I want to eat tacos.*

Her hackles rose as she glanced down at her mosaic tile dress that nipped in so far at the waist it was almost two pieces. The large cutouts left her waist and hips bare, which meant when they danced, his palms would be on her bare skin. Something more along the lines of *thank you* would be highly appropriate here.

Was his vision impaired? She looked good. It wasn't arrogance. It was a fact, because she paid attention to details. If there was anything she knew how to market, it was herself.

"Well, don't hold back, honey. Tell me how you really feel about a dress that took me all day to find and set me back six grand."

"It's a little…risqué for a charity fund-raiser, don't you think?" His faint scowl told her he'd already decided the answer was yes.

"Considering Kendall Jenner wore the same dress with a different color scheme to the Met Gala, no," she countered and willed her temper back, because they hadn't even left yet. An argument now wouldn't benefit anyone, since there were no cameras around, never mind that she'd been trying to provoke him.

"I don't know who that is, but odds are good she'll never be dating me. You are. Maybe you could find a wrap?"

Hands on her bare hips, she contemplated her fake boyfriend, who was about to learn exactly how little that role entitled him to. "What's that supposed to mean? I'm not allowed to be myself because I'm dating the world's biggest Goody Two-shoes?"

His scowl grew some teeth. "Clearly we need to establish some guidelines to this…relationship. Partnership. Whatever it is. Ground rules are obviously a must."

Yeah, that was a day late and a dollar short. Honestly, she'd been a little surprised he'd agreed to this idea with no parameters.

She clapped enthusiastically. "Yay! I *love* rules."

Rules were going to go over about as well as the notion of a *wrap*. She was not putting a single thread on top of this Versace masterpiece, and he could eat his rule book. Though she was a little curious what rules he might throw down.

So she could break them all.

"Lose the sarcasm or this is going to be a very long night."

Her brows arched involuntarily. "That was always going to be true, and I'd rather lose the dress than the sarcasm."

"That can be arranged." The heat dialed up a notch as his gaze strayed to the straps around her neck that held the dress on her body.

"You wouldn't dare."

More's the pity. There was no way he'd actually strip her out of this dress simply to get his way.

Was there?

"Rule number one. Never dare me, Trinity," he said with so much wicked in his voice that she nearly pushed him on it, strictly to find out how good he was at undressing a woman in formal wear.

All at once, flashes of an ad campaign spilled into her head. A man sliding a dress off a woman and the woman stopping him before he reveals her scar. Cut to a shot of Formula-47 that would be called…

The rest blurred, sliding away before she could visualize the ending. But it was a start. And more than she'd had in a long time.

Holy hell. Where had that come from? Better yet,

could she get more of it if she told Logan to get lost so she could work?

Torn, she eyed him and swore. She'd agreed to do this fake relationship deal, and as she'd been telling herself all week, he had a stake, too. They had places to go and people to let photograph them. Lots of fake kissing to engage in—which she would deny to her grave she looked forward to.

She tapped her temple. "I dare say even I can remember that rule."

Seemed like a dare was pretty close to how she'd gotten him to kiss her the first time.

"Good. We can discuss the rest of the rules on the way. Grab your wrap so we can go."

"Counterproposal. You remember that this is a partnership and I don't answer to you," she shot back. "The whole point is to get eyes on us. This dress is guaranteed to be on a hundred fashion blogs by morning, and to be honest, your love life could use spicing up."

She'd done her homework on Logan McLaughlin, and the mice he normally dated barely registered a blip in the social media sphere. Photographs of him with a woman on his arm were rare in the first place, but the few she'd found—*please*. Either he liked invisible, unassuming women or his vision really *was* impaired.

He crossed his arms. "What's that supposed to mean?"

She almost grinned at his echo of her earlier comment, but only because things were starting to get interesting. Finally. "It means you're boring, darling. One of your players is dating a supermodel who posed for *Playboy*, and he gets more love in the press than anyone else on your team. Take a lesson."

"I'm aware." Logan's back teeth ground together. "I've asked him stop seeing her. It's distasteful."

"Oh, honey." She shook her head. That spine needed unstarching in the worst way, and she definitely had a lot of ideas on how to accomplish *that*. "Thank God you've hooked up with me. Now you listen. We're going to go to this charity deal, I'm not going to wear a wrap and we're going to sizzle. That's the only rule you need."

Logan regretted getting a limo the moment Trinity Forrester spilled into the interior. If he'd driven his own car, he could have occupied himself with the steering wheel. The lack of a place to put his hands hadn't been a factor on the way over. Now? There was entirely too much female skin right there within touching distance.

And God above, the will it took to stop himself from reaching out was monumental.

She smelled both divine and like the kind of sin that would put a man on his knees in a confessional before dawn. The paradox was driving him insane. And they hadn't even pulled away from the curb yet.

A butterfly tattoo flashed at her wrist. It had been covered before, and he was not happy about how much he liked it. He watched as she arranged her long skirt to let her sexy shoes peek out. The heels, of course, resembled ice picks, and only tiny straps held them to her feet, making him wonder how they actually stayed on.

Even her toes were sexy.

"Rules," he growled because he needed some. "Are—"

"Made to be broken?" she filled in sweetly.

The limo shuttled toward what promised to be a very long evening fraught with frustration and tension, most of it sexual, followed by a morning explaining to everyone he knew that he had not, in fact, lost his mind when he'd selected his companion for the evening.

"Rules are necessary so I—we—don't forget what we're doing here." Though he suspected she wasn't dealing with issues in that respect the same way he was. "Without rules, the world descends into chaos."

"Maybe your world does. Mine just gets more interesting."

"Case in point. The most important rule we need to establish is that behind closed doors, we're not a couple. Only in public. And it's not real."

The cockeyed gaze she shot him was further enhanced by her swirly makeup. Less Cleopatra today and more Picasso. It was very distracting.

"I kind of thought all that was a given."

"Well, that's why it's important to lay it out ahead of time. So there's no confusion." That way, there was no end-of-the-evening mix-up at the door where she invited him in for a drink, which was really code for sex, and he'd struggle to remember why he was supposed to say no.

Rules gave him that out.

And really, *this is all fake* was the only rule he needed. She apparently needed a few more, but he'd lost the battle over her outrageous dress and didn't expect he'd win any others—not tonight, anyway. He'd be a hell of lot more specific the next time they appeared in public together.

Rule number two—dress like a woman dating a billionaire who owned a wholesome sports team.

In all actuality, he'd never imagined such a dress existed. Her whole back was bare, dipping low enough to give a guy a tempting glimpse of her rounded bottom. The front wasn't much better, cinching in at the waist to reveal wide panels of her trim waist and abs, and rising over her breasts to cover her to her collarbone. Oddly, the lack of cleavage made his mouth water to unclasp the catch at the back of her neck and let the fabric spill to her hips to reveal the hard nipples tenting the fabric.

He could not get out of this vehicle fast enough.

The limo snaked toward the hotel where the charity ball was being held. When it was their turn to emerge, he got out first and held out a hand to her. He would not have been shocked if she'd refused, but this was it, their first appearance in public together since the kiss clip went viral, and they needed to make it work.

Her hand disappeared into his and he helped her from the limo, happy that she hadn't chosen this moment for their first public fight. Photographers lined the ropes on both sides of the entrance. Instead of beelining for the door like he normally did whenever someone with a camera was around, he paused and slipped an arm around Trinity. His date, for better or worse.

He nearly groaned as his fingertips hit the silky expanse of skin at her hip bone. She might as well be wearing a swimsuit for all the coverage the dress provided. It would take no effort at all to slide his hand inside the fabric and keep going, because there was no way she was wearing underwear. He had the strongest urge to verify.

"Smile," she hissed and snuggled into his embrace far too cozily.

Easy for her to say. She wasn't fighting an erection.

So far, the enormous effort associated with this plan far outweighed the benefit.

A million flashes proved him wrong. More people clamored at the rope than Logan would have ever credited, and every one of them had a lens aimed in his direction. Other couples walked into the building with zero fanfare. Completely ignored.

"Told you this dress would be the ticket," Trinity murmured out of the side of her mouth. "Trust me next time. Kiss me."

"What? Now?"

"What did I just say, Logan?" She smiled up at him, but the curve of her lips was strictly for the audience, because her gaze glittered with challenge. "Don't make me dare you."

He rolled his eyes and laid a chaste kiss on her lips that shouldn't have pumped up the erection in his pants as much as it did. But the score of flashes in his peripheral vision told him her instincts had been dead-on. So he didn't complain. Out loud.

He'd had enough of the spots dancing before his eyes and steered Trinity through the crowd and into the hall, refusing to think about how disappointing that brief kiss had been.

"What is this shindig again?" she asked, eyeing the decorations with enthusiasm.

"It's to benefit Roost, a foundation that helps families relocate and rebuild after a natural disaster. I'm on the board. I took my father's place."

His dad had established the foundation a year before his unexpected death, and Logan had gladly stepped in as the head of the board. It meant something to him to continue Duncan McLaughlin's legacy.

Of course the real heroes were the people doing the heavy lifting; Logan just funneled money into the coffers and ensured Roost's logo appeared regularly during baseball games. Occasionally, he showed up at a fancy deal like this one and gave a speech.

Her gaze cut to him and held far more appreciation than it should. "I've heard of Roost. I didn't know you were involved in it. It's a cause you're passionate about or is this just a family obligation?"

The offhand question dug at him, tripping more than a few wires inside. "Why can't it be both?"

She shrugged one bare shoulder. "I guess it can be. Just seems to me that if you're going to champion a cause, it should be your own. Not your father's."

"My father was my role model. I would do well to emulate him. So would a lot of people."

"Of course." But he didn't mistake her comment as agreement, and it did nothing to cool his suddenly boiling temper. "And you'd also do well to be yourself instead of a carbon copy of someone else. A philosophy you might guess I readily subscribe to."

A lecture on individuality from the woman with a tongue piercing was not on the agenda for the evening. Neither was a dissection of his desire to follow in his father's footsteps. "I'm happy with who I am, thanks. Roost is important to me. Have you seen what a house looks like after a tornado tears through it? It's my pleasure to drum up support for people who have lost everything."

"I'll write you a check later," she murmured as several people picked that moment to ask for an introduction to his date. "It's the least I can do."

"You're already doing the least you can," he commented under his breath and dived into the social minutiae required at such an event before she could come up with what would no doubt be a cutting rebuttal.

It was nice to win one occasionally.

Trinity chatted up the curious guests with ease, clearly in her element, while Logan thought seriously about leaving early. Wearing a tux ranked about last on his list of fun things to do, followed shortly by eating in a formal setting. As a member of the board, he had the dubious privilege of being seated at the head table, where all eyes stayed trained on him and his flashy date.

His uncomfortable awareness of her dimmed not at all as they worked their way through steak and asparagus that probably tasted great when it wasn't flavored by visions of whirling a woman into the shadows to see just how naked she was under that dress.

When the band struck up a slow jazz number, Trinity's hand snaked beneath the table to squeeze his thigh. He avoided jumping like a teenager, but just barely.

"What?" he muttered.

"Ask me to dance, ding-dong," she shot back in a whisper.

He checked his ninth or tenth eye roll of the evening and stood to offer her his hand. "Would you do me the honor, Ms. Forrester?"

She didn't bother to check her own eye roll as she let him help her to her feet. "Are you trying to sound ninety, or does it come automatically?"

"I never come automatically." He cursed. That had slipped out and probably told her far too much about his mental state.

"I'll keep that in mind." She sounded like she was trying not to laugh.

They walked out on the dance floor and his hands drifted into place at her waist as if he'd done it a thousand times. Which, theoretically, he had—if you counted all the times he'd done it in his mind since opening the door earlier that evening.

She felt so good that his fingers spread across her skin without any prompting on his part, but he couldn't help wanting more contact. The point was to give the appearance that they were into each other. He just wished it wasn't so easy to fake that part.

Unlike earlier, no crush of cameras clamored to capture their every move, but there were still plenty of eyes on them, which meant they had to make it look good. It helped that she moved in sync with him as they danced, a shocking turn of events. If anything, he'd have expected her to try to lead, to boss him around—anything other than the fluidity they fell into instantly, as if they'd danced before.

She peered up at him from under her lashes and smiled, which hit him with the approximate force of a fighter jet at Mach 5. Apparently she wasn't on board with the respectable distance he'd put between them, because she scooted closer, deliberately brushing his body with hers as she swayed.

It took far too long to unstick his tongue from the roof of his mouth. He was thirty-five years old, for crying out loud, and had certainly bedded a few hot women. Of course that had been a fair number of years ago, before he started looking for the future Mrs. McLaughlin.

"So," he said inanely. "Here we are."

One of the pitfalls of a fake relationship—they had to pretend they actually had things to talk about.

"Mmm, yes, we are here," she agreed easily.

Her hands meandered under his tux jacket to cup his butt, which she then fingered suggestively. Every drop of blood in his body drained into his groin, and his brain fuzzed.

"Um, what are you doing?" he choked out. "Are there cameras on us that I can't see?"

"Nope. I'm just naturally handsy. And curious." Her blue eyes glowed in the low ballroom light. "How can

I fake being hot and heavy with you if I don't actually know what your butt feels like when I grab it?"

He groaned as he envisioned the scenario under which she might be grabbing his butt—as she cried his name in her throaty voice, urging him on as he drove her to a blistering climax, for example. Or maybe as he pinned her to the wall and took her standing up. Or, his personal favorite, as she knelt before him and pleasured him with her hot mouth, sliding that tongue piercing across his flesh.

His vision grayed for a second, and he might have lost the feeling in his legs.

"Do I get the same courtesy?" he muttered, thoroughly impressed with himself that he wasn't laid out on the floor. "Because there's a lot of you I haven't grabbed yet, either."

They were so close, her laugh vibrated through his tight groin.

"What are you going to do if I say yes?"

"This." It was close enough to a dare that he locked gazes with her and slid two fingers under the fabric of her dress to caress one bare globe of her rounded bottom. No panties, as he'd guessed.

The temperature shot up as heat flushed through his body.

And then it was no longer a point to be proven, but an exploration of the woman he'd been angling to get his hands on all night.

God, she felt amazing, like warm silk. Heat flared in her expression, winnowing through his blood until he couldn't stop himself from pressing closer, desperately seeking more of her, questing for relief from the needy ache she'd induced.

"I don't recall actually saying yes," she said. Instantly he withdrew, a millisecond from spitting out an apology, when she grinned. "But I wasn't saying no, either."

"Make up your mind, woman," he growled.

"I'm not the one who laid down the ground rules. Wasn't there something about none of this being real?" She shimmied her hips in a practiced rhythm against his painful erection. "That feels pretty real to me. Are you sure *I'm* the one who can't make up her mind?"

She'd baited him on purpose. Probably had deliberately worn this dress with the easily accessible butt cheeks to drive him insane. This was exactly the reason he should have said no to this ridiculous fake relationship. Trinity Forrester was too bold, too exotic, too… *sensual* for a man who just wanted a nice girl to come home to at the end of a long day.

Nice girls didn't constantly make him think about getting naked.

"Why do you have to make everything about sex?" he grumbled. "Can't we just dance?"

And now he sounded exactly like what she'd accused him of: a Goody Two-shoes. A ninety-year-old. A stickler for rules.

That was not who he was. This woman had been manipulating him all night, and he was done with it. He'd agreed to this fake relationship but he hadn't agreed to let her run roughshod over him.

That stopped now.

"Me?" She had the audacity to feign surprise. "I've never so much as uttered the word *sex* one time."

"You don't have to. It wafts from your pores." Eyes narrowed, he spun her around until he could dance her off the marble floor and into the shadows at the back of the room.

She had reasons for why she was so overtly sexy, so in-your-face with her asymmetrical hair and tongue piercing, and none of them were because she was a free spirit who reveled in her individuality.

She was hiding something behind her shock value.

Let's just see how you handle a man who has your number, Ms. Forrester.

Before she could blink, he had her trapped against the wall, his body pressing hard against hers. Exactly where he wanted to be, every nerve primed to sink into her.

More than that…he wanted to expose her secrets in the same way she'd peeled back his need to be like his father.

"Cameras?" She peered around his shoulder in anticipation.

"No idea." He tipped up her chin, guiding her attention back where it belonged. "I'm just curious about whether kissing you feels as good as I remember."

Her expression heated as she zeroed in on him, ignoring the crowd. "Well, that doesn't sound like it's in the rules according to Logan."

"It's number three," he corrected silkily. "When a woman has been begging you for something all night, you give it to her."

And exactly like the first time he'd kissed her, he couldn't stop himself from caving to the blinding need to have her mouth under his. Their lips connected, and instantly, he parted hers to savagely seek her taste.

It exploded on his tongue. Back and forth, give and take, he kissed her with every ounce of pent-up longing and passion and frustration that he'd been battling since the moment she'd slid into his limo. Since before that. Since that first kiss.

He wanted to strip her raw and tunnel under her outrageous appeal in hopes of tempering it somehow.

The cool hardness of the steel rod through her tongue skated along his hot tongue, and yes, the contrast and the sheer uniqueness of the sensation was as affecting as he remembered. More so. Because there were no cameras on them this time and he didn't have to think about decorum if he didn't feel like it.

He didn't feel like it.

They'd be so hot together. He wouldn't have to think about anything but pleasure. She'd tell him what she wanted, take it, give it back tenfold, and there'd be nothing but miles of skin and Trinity's laugh.

Her hands were everywhere, in his hair and caressing his face, against his back.

He returned the favor, groaning deep in his chest as he slid both hands beneath the fabric of her dress to take as much of her bare bottom into his palms as would fit. Which wasn't much, because the stupid wall was in the way. He eased up his full-body press enough to go deeper, and that got a moan out of her that was like music to his ears.

"You're stopping," she murmured. "Don't stop."

He groaned. Again. Oh, yes, it would be so easy to wedge his hand between her legs and continue his exploration of the secrets under that dress. But they were in public, with other couples taking advantage of the shadows a mere few feet away.

He'd never been so tempted to throw caution to the wind.

"If I touch you like that, I want to be someplace where you don't have to be quiet," he advised her. His name tearing from her throat as she came over and over again would be perfect.

She smiled and nipped at his lips with hers, rolling her hips against his erection. "Trust me when I say I have a lot of practice letting a man pleasure me in places where noise isn't kosher."

He sucked in a breath. He so did not need to hear that. Too late. His mind started filling in the blanks, calculating how wild and insane an affair he and Trinity could actually indulge in and still stick to the rules—after all, they weren't behind closed doors.

His body nearly made the decision for him, straining toward her in eager anticipation.

No. He had more control than this. He could not let her drag him under her spell. No matter how slick and ready she must be. No matter how much he ached to find out if she was as turned on as he was. "You've never done that with me. I seriously doubt you could keep it together."

"Only one way to find out."

"That's not going to work this time." He shook his head. The only reason it wouldn't was because he seriously feared that if he gave in, she'd suck him so far down into her bad-girl fantasy that he wouldn't ever be able to cut himself free.

And he needed to be disentangled if he ever hoped to find something real.

Four

The sketches refused to come together.

Trinity threw down her pencil and let her head drop into her hands. A whole Saturday wasted on the premise of the ad campaign she'd glimpsed in her mind while with Logan last night. Wisps of it had floated through her consciousness while they'd been dancing. Then when he'd kissed her—it was like her entire body had woken up from a hundred-year sleep.

Glorious, wonderful inspiration flowed like lava. And then the man had flooded her, pushing out everything but him as he lit her up with his mouth. His hands had done a good job igniting sparks, too.

When he forgot to be a stick in the mud, Logan McLaughlin set her on fire.

Coaxing him out of his all-American shell had become somewhat of a favorite pastime. She hadn't gotten him there yet, not all the way, but he'd veered much farther toward the dark side than she'd have expected.

No more fantasies about teaching him everything she knew.

Back to work.

Instead of beating her head against the brick wall of her creativity, she checked a few of her social media accounts, where she'd reposted several of the better pictures from last night. A few shares. Nothing had gone viral like the video from the show. Of course, the majority of the photos circulating this morning were the posed ones in front of the limo where she'd practically had to order Logan to kiss her. The pictures were nice. Sweet. Not enough to generate a buzz in her stomach, so she held little hope they would generate much of a buzz with the public, either.

If only someone had captured Logan's hand down her dress as he kissed her within an iota of stripping her naked—*that* would have burned up the web. But alas, no one with a camera had been in shooting distance of those shadows, apparently. Shame. They'd have to do better next time, be more deliberate about their choice of locales.

Shadows.

What if… She picked up her pencil and sketched a quick drawing of two silhouettes engaged in a very hot kiss. Ad copy could go something like, *With Formula-47, you don't have to stay in the shadows. Because it fixes your scars.*

Eh. That wasn't exactly award-winning stuff, especially if she had to explain the concept. If only she could come up with a name, the rest would definitely fall into place. She had until Monday. And then the only things that would fall if she didn't have her act together were the faces of her friends and business partners, who were expecting a marketing presentation designed to sell the living daylights out of their signature product.

So, this was not helping. Maybe if she could generate a better showing for her brand-new fake relationship, some of the pressure would be off and her muse would get with the program.

Palming her phone, she sent Logan a text message asking if he was free tonight before the little voices could start laughing at her feeble attempts to make excuses for wanting to see him. Yeah, she'd had fun last night after figuring out that the key to everything was getting him hot and bothered. It wasn't a crime to admit she'd rather press those buttons than sit here failing at being brilliant for the rest of her Saturday.

The return message came back instantly.

It's the ninth inning, so I can jet in a couple of hours. What did you have in mind?

Crap. Should have thought that through a little better. What she had in mind and what was feasible to actually do in a crowd were two different things, despite what she'd told Logan last night about her public exploits. But it was only fair that she come up with an event since he'd done the work last night.

Something that didn't require hours to get ready would be great. And necessary, since it was already four o'clock. Something public, where she could goad him into a fight, preferably, because that seemed to have worked the first time to get so many shares.

Nada.

It wasn't like she never did social stuff. But for so long, she'd done them with her friends, met interesting men wherever they ended up, and then gone home with one if she was in the mood. Or not, as the case had been lately. And her friends had all gotten married, leaving her at loose ends and restless.

Married friends might be a saving grace right this minute.

There was nothing to do but ping Cass and ask if she and Gage were by some miracle in Dallas today instead of Austin and if they had plans. Maybe the CEO of Fyra might be up for a double date, and there would be the added benefit of having two more social powerhouses with her, since both Cass and Gage regularly made the society columns in both of the cities they frequented.

Cass texted her back almost immediately.

We have invitations to a party in Deep Ellum to benefit Children's Advocacy Center, but we're skipping due to all the smoke and loud music. Baby on board, as Gage likes to remind me. You want to go in our place?

Trinity did a victory dance. Looked like she'd be taking Logan to a club after all, and the timing was perfect. She texted him to pick her up at eight, then shut her laptop lid so she didn't have to stare at the blank screen any longer.

Humming, she took a shower, then did her makeup. Harper had just come up with a really great new eye shadow that she'd asked everyone to test. The deep emerald color matched Trinity's mood and had a touch of sparkle, perfect for a dark venue. She poured herself into a faux leather catsuit in black with a silver chain ring belt and donned six-inch platform heels that complemented the outfit but didn't totally scream *dominatrix*.

Logan's expression when she opened the door later said that he didn't quite get the distinction.

"No." He shook his head and shut his eyes for a beat. "I'm not going anywhere with you dressed like a cross between Catwoman and Lady Gaga."

That was such a ludicrous statement, she actually glanced down. "Are you kidding? Lady Gaga would laugh at how tame these shoes are. Also, we're not having this argument every time, are we?"

"Apparently." He crossed his arms over his Dallas Mustangs T-shirt, bunching up his biceps in the way that drove her mad. Because she still hadn't gotten her hands on them, not properly. "Until you get the memo that I'm a conservative, God-fearing baseball team owner who sells hot dogs, foam fingers and memories, not bondage equipment."

"Honey, you're about as conservative as a Ferrari." And twice as sexy. He was a little windblown, as if he'd driven from the stadium in Arlington with the windows open. "No one who kisses a woman like you do could ever be described as tame."

Windblown Logan was delicious. Almost as much as tuxedo-clad Logan. Maybe more. The tux had lent him an almost inaccessible air, too beautiful to mar, but today he had a ready-to-rumble look that said he'd throw down if she pushed. And she was in the mood to push.

"Tame and conservative are not the same thing," he said with a once-over that had enough bite that her lady parts perked up. "Kissing you directly benefits my goals. You wearing that outfit does not."

She crossed her arms to mimic him and let a slow smile spill over her face. "I'm not changing. We're going to a club in Deep Ellum. I guarantee you I will blend in. You won't."

"Good. Then we'll attract more attention if we don't blend." Without asking, he barged into her condo like a bull with the red cape in his sights, then whirled in the marble entryway. "Which direction is your bedroom?"

"Well, if I'd known that's all it took to get you there, I'd have worn this outfit the first day."

He scowled. "Stop being dense. You're wearing different clothes. I need to find your closet."

"Oh, that's a terrible reason to be in a woman's bedroom. Just curious, are you going to wrestle me out of this outfit?" Leaning on the open door frame, she contemplated him and pointed down the hall. "Because if the answer's yes, my bedroom is that way."

"Fantastic."

And then, without any warning, he swung her up into his arms as if she weighed no more than a child, slammed the door shut with his foot and carried her to her bedroom. Her pulse tripled as the hard planes of his torso cradled her body. God, he was as solid and strong as she'd always imagined, but he held her gently, as if he didn't want to break her. If she hadn't already been snuggled into his embrace, her weak knees might have put her on the floor.

Even though she knew he'd only done it to avoid the rest of the argument, the gesture was so…gallant. As many men as had crossed her threshold, not one had ever treated her like she was delicate, and honestly, she'd have shown every last one of them the door if they had.

There was something about Logan and his old-fashioned streak that hit her between the eyes, almost as if he refused to see her as a sex object, no matter how she regarded herself. It shouldn't be so affecting. But there it was.

He deposited her on the bed without a word and strode to her closet, throwing wide the doors without hesitation, as if he'd dressed many a woman in his day. And maybe he had.

Oh, hell. She kind of wanted to see what he'd pick out.

"Here." He came out of the closet with a pair of 7 for All Mankind jeans and a simple black T-shirt that she wore to spin class sometimes. "Put this on."

She couldn't help it. She laughed. "So we can be twins?"

He threw the clothes on the bed and hunted around in her drawers until he found a bra and panties, both black, which was an interesting attention to detail she appreciated, completely against her will. When was the last time a man paid *that* much attention to her?

Handing her the undergarments, he stared down at her on the bed. "No. So I can see the real you underneath all of your deflections."

The earnestness in his expression froze her lungs and dried up every scrap of amusement in this situation. "What do you mean, the real me? This is as real as I get."

Before she could move, breathe, blink, he knelt on the bed and grabbed one foot, slowly unbuckling her platform sandal. Transfixed, she watched, too curious where he was headed to stop him.

"In public, it's not real. Behind closed doors, we're not anything but two people who don't know each other. All bets are off. I want to see what you're hiding underneath all of this outlandishness."

Oh, God. He was serious. And so intent that it bobbled her pulse. But she was nothing if not voraciously attracted to new experiences. What was the worst thing that could happen? Her pulse thumped as he tossed the first shoe over his shoulder. His gorgeous hazel eyes did not have an ounce of hesitation in them.

"By all means, strip away." She granted him permission to continue with a wave of her hand as if it didn't matter, but that would be a lie.

This was far from the first time a man had undressed her. But the way he was doing it tripped a hundred sensors in her chest, warning her it wasn't going to be like any of those other times.

Despite the heavy awareness spreading across her skin, this wasn't about sex, and neither of them was confused about that. It was about something else. A quest for knowledge.

She'd always considered herself an open book, but as he dropped the other shoe to her hardwood floor, she suddenly wondered if he'd sense all the dark and personal corners of herself that she'd never shared with anyone.

The brokenness inside wasn't something she liked to think about.

And that made her want to slam the book shut.

But it was too late. He peeled the catsuit from her shoulders and dragged it to her waist, his gaze locked on to hers, never straying to the skin he was revealing. Somehow, that made the act of him undressing her *more* sensuous.

She'd expected him to look, to ogle her naked body, because come on. He *was* a man, as red-blooded as any she'd ever met, and he had pulled out a bra and panties. He knew she didn't have anything on under this outfit.

Carefully, he lifted her hips and kept going, unwrapping her so slowly that her throat burned. When she twisted to release the fabric from under her legs, his fingertips grazed the brilliant green ivy tattoo twining around her thigh. She could feel the question in his touch, and her muscles quivered.

"It leads to the garden of Eden," she murmured as he laid her bodysuit aside. "Or so the story goes."

His gaze cut to her eyes.

"What's the real story?" he asked quietly. Unobtrusively. Sincerely, as if he really did want to know who she was.

"Ivy is hearty. It climbs. The vine grows little feet and will cling to almost any surface until it's taller than the structure it's climbing on. That resonates with me."

"You're tenacious." He nodded and slid the panties over her legs and trailed his thumb across the tattoo as he settled them into place. "That's a good quality."

She shrugged, mystified why he'd picked that word from the concept she'd thrown out. She'd always thought of it as survival and then domination of her surroundings, because it was that or be trampled underfoot. Ivy was one of those plants that when you stumbled over ruins, it would still be thriving. Maybe even overtaking the entire structure.

The butterfly tattoo on her wrist had meaning to her as well. Everything she'd done to decorate her body had significance. She wasn't sure how much she liked that he'd immediately dug that out of her.

His thumb continued stroking her thigh, and she got very aware of his hands on her very fast. "Your thumb is a little low. The garden is underneath those panties you just put on me."

"Are you asking me to touch you?" His voice was rough with a need that thrilled her. "Because that is very against the rules."

"Make some new ones," she said and let the challenge roll through the space between them, of which there was way too much for her taste. Maybe this hadn't been about sex at the start, but it could be now. It *should* be. "I'm just going to ignore them all anyway. I'm very good at being bad."

To demonstrate, she slid her fingertips up his leg to brush his groin, but just as she was about to curl her palm around his shaft, he grabbed her hand, removing it forcibly.

"Why do you do that?" he said point-blank, holding her hand in his as far away from his body as he could.

"Do what?" She stared at him, desperately trying to figure out where she'd miscalculated. He wanted her, and there was no way he could lie about it when she'd felt the evidence herself. "Refuse to pull punches when I want something? I'm not going to apologize. I like sex."

"No, you don't. You like control, and seduction is how you get it." He stared right back. "It amuses you to lead a man around, and sex keeps him occupied so he doesn't dig too far down into places he's not welcome."

Shock made her hand go limp. "I don't do that."

She did. She so did.

How the hell had he figured that out when they hadn't even slept together yet?

"You do. You flirt and wear outrageous clothes and advertise your availability purely as a distraction. What are you afraid I'm going to find out?"

That she longed to be the kind of woman a man wanted to stay with. Since she wasn't, she might as well get something out of a man's company. Orgasms worked for her.

She tossed her hair. "I'm not the one who's afraid, McLaughlin. It bothers you that you're so attracted to me. That's why you want me in boring clothes, so you can keep pretending you don't have a secret desire to do all sorts of wicked things to me. Things you know I'd like. You're throwing all of this in my face because you're the one who needs a distraction. Stop being such a Goody Two-shoes and take what you want."

"What I want is for you to put these clothes on so we can go." The catch in his voice said he wasn't as unaffected as he'd like her to believe. "Good sex stems from intimacy. Connection. I like to have that with someone I'm sleeping with."

I want to see the real you.

He'd meant it. That hadn't been a ploy to get her out of an outfit he'd hated.

And all at once, she wanted to give it to him. To have this thing between them be real. She could confess all her secrets, tell him how he made her feel feminine for the first time in a long time. He wouldn't care that she couldn't have babies; he'd like her for her.

They'd have something between them besides sex.

That's when her fantasy dried up and blew away. What did she know about how to be in a real relationship? Nothing, obviously, or she'd have figured out how to keep Neil around once she'd told him she'd conceived.

Dutifully, she let Logan hook her bra into place and raised her arms so he could pull the T-shirt over her head, suddenly grateful for the cover. She felt oddly exposed, as if the sheer act of informing her that he was stripping away her shields along with her outfit could actually accomplish it.

And she had enough appreciation for the psychology behind his assessment to be a little freaked that he'd come up with such a tactic. Enough that she let him pull her from the bed so he could slide her jeans over her hips and then button them, fully concealing her. It marked the first time in her life that a man had dressed her, only for her to wind up more naked than when she'd worn nothing.

The appreciation shining in Logan's eyes as he laced his fingers with hers put a different kind of heat low in her belly. This barely-make-a-blip outfit had more effect than the in-your-face sexy one. For Logan, at least. What was she supposed to *do* with him?

"You're a beautiful woman, Trinity." He stated it like a fact, but that didn't decrease the potency in the slightest. "Dressed like this, you make so much more of an impact, because it allows you to be the star instead of the outfit."

Her knees did go weak at that, but she locked them. Now was not the time to get mushy over Logan McLaughlin. No time was good for that. This was all fake and designed to go his way so he could control his image. Nothing more.

She had to remember the most important rule— none of this was real. That was the reason he hadn't undressed her and used it as an excuse to cop a feel or ogle her. He wasn't attracted to her other than at a base level, and only then because it was involuntary physiology, not the connection he was looking for.

Good. She didn't want that. Not with Logan, not with any man.

Except maybe she did, and she did not like that he'd uncovered a longing she'd had no idea was there. A longing she had no business indulging in, because she didn't work like other women, couldn't. Her body wasn't made for pregnancy, and her ability to trust the opposite gender didn't exist. She had to stop this nonsense cold.

"Maybe I like my clothes to be the star," she muttered, and to her mortification, tears pricked at her eyelids. What in the hell was this man doing to her?

A better question was, why was she letting him?

"Wearing this outfit will get us the top spot on people's social media feeds, I guarantee it," he said mildly. "Do me one last favor and wear the shoes, though. I like it when you're tall enough for me to put my arm around you."

Oh, really?

The tears coupled with the unexpected exposure and longings that shouldn't even be a factor put her in a dangerous mood. "I call BS. You like these shoes because you have secret bad-girl fantasies."

He rolled his eyes. "It's not a stretch to say I like sexy shoes on a woman. I readily admit to that."

That set her back. The man was honest to a fault, and it kept throwing her off. He was supposed to lie to her and act like an ass and pull immature ghosting routines where he pretended his phone was off when she tried to reach him.

Maybe he'd already lied to her. Like when he said he wanted intimacy instead of sex. Or was he actually lying to himself about what he wanted?

"If I wear the shoes," she murmured throatily, "do I get a reward?"

Suspicion clouded his expression. "Like what? A gold star?"

She shrugged. "Maybe you take me to the bathroom in the club and see how far your hand goes down these jeans. Or didn't you notice how tiny these panties are on me?"

"I noticed," he said shortly and ran a hand through his hair, a habit she'd started to clue in meant he felt uncomfortable. "Trust me, I'm not that much of a good guy."

News to her. "Tell me. Would it be so bad to let your bad boy out to play occasionally?"

His eyes narrowed. "Yes, it would."

When he didn't elaborate, her curiosity went through

the roof. So he wasn't denying that he had a wild streak. Interesting. Because if he had denied it, she'd have called him on that, too. No man who put his hands down a woman's dress in a crowded ballroom with scarcely a glance around could claim he'd never done anything like that before.

Seemed like Logan might be hiding behind his public persona, too. What would he be like if she stripped him of his conservative armor?

Suddenly, she was ready to get him out in public, where she could flirt and seduce and provoke him into putting his hands on her again without fear. Because behind closed doors, it wasn't real. She had to get out of here before she forgot they weren't a couple with an interest in getting to know each other beneath the surface.

By ten o'clock, Logan had a pounding headache that beat against his temples in perfect time to the garbage being pumped out of the speakers at the Deep Ellum club Trinity had dragged him to.

The Mustangs had lost today—again—and what he should really be doing was combing through his roster—again—to see where he could make improvements.

As a whole, the team's manager had point on the fine details, but he had to work with the talent Logan gave him. It was the general manager's job to get the right guys onto the field for the best price. Bang for the buck was key when it came to the financials of a ball team. Managing money should come easily considering his DNA, but it didn't. He had to work at it.

So instead of crunching numbers and looking at possible trade angles, Logan leaned against the bar nursing a light beer that wasn't fit for unclogging a drain. The view was nice, though. Trinity perched on a bar stool, clutching a highball, one jeans-clad leg entwined with his. She'd done that a while back in a seriously sexy *back off, ladies* move that had raised his eyebrows, but he kind of loved it.

They couldn't exactly talk due to the music, yet the contact created a sense of intimacy he'd never have expected. As a result, he'd been sporting a semi in his pants since the moment her leg had snaked possessively around his.

All right, the fact that she was wearing jeans and a T-shirt that he'd personally put on her body might have a little more to do with the hard-on. When he'd said he wanted to see the real her, he hadn't expected to like it so much, or to discover a burning desire to uncover more. He'd barely scratched the surface of what lay beneath Trinity's outrageous exterior. And that thirst for knowledge was at least 50 percent of the reason he was still here.

The bump in ticket sales was the other fifty. Myra couldn't control her glee earlier when she'd phoned him in the dugout to say that today's game had hit an all-time high for attendance. Which unfortunately wasn't saying much, but it was saying *something*.

There was definitely room to get some more press, though.

And he needed to do it before his skull split in two.

A photographer had been circulating near the front of the club, and he bided his time until he saw her headed toward the bar. From the corner of his eye, he tracked her progress until she was close enough to guarantee she wouldn't miss it if he tossed her a great shot.

Logan plucked the highball from Trinity's grasp. Before she could squawk, he swiveled her stool and cupped her face in both hands, bringing it up to his. Their lips connected.

It should have been a token kiss, just show. But this was Trinity, and she didn't hesitate to open her mouth. That steel piercing slid hard across his tongue, sensitizing him all the way to the bottoms of his feet. Her arms raced down his back. She flattened her palms against it and shoved, grinding his erection straight into her center, hard enough to put stars across his vision.

God, yes, more of that. Aching, fiery need exploded between them, and he wrapped a hand around her thigh dangerously close to the ivy tattoo under her jeans, hauling her leg higher on his hip. The angle opened her wider and the stool was just the right height to make everything feel unbelievably good.

Deepening the kiss shouldn't have been so effortless, but she was as into it as he was, her moans vibrating her chest against his, or maybe that was the thump of the bass jarring them both. Whatever it was, this was the hottest kiss he'd ever participated in.

The music wasn't loud enough to cover the hoots of the surrounding partygoers, though, and somehow it filtered through his head that he'd more than accomplished his goal of laying a photo-worthy kiss on his date. And publicity was the only reason to be doing it. The only logical reason, anyway, and the only one he'd admit to.

With far more reluctance than he'd like, he ended the kiss and pulled away, but Trinity was having none of that. She threaded her fingers through his hair, pressed against his neck and nuzzled his nose with hers, brushing their lips together, and suddenly they were kissing again.

But this time, it was a slow slide into an intense web of awareness. Everything faded and time stopped as he tasted heaven. The floodgates of his body opened, welcoming her in. This was connection, the kind he'd said he wanted. It was so much more than a kiss, and he craved it like he craved blood to his heart.

This was what it was like to kiss the woman behind the curtain. No barriers. He'd been looking for the essence of Trinity and he'd found it. More importantly, she'd given it to him. It spread through him, warm, thick, sweet, and it was so right that it became a part of him instantly, as if she had always been there.

One of her hot hands slipped under the hem of his shirt, scrabbling at his waist as if she'd slide off the stool if she didn't hold on. He totally understood that. Because he was careening down a slippery slope as well, hitting a hundred miles an hour with no brakes.

And that's what finally snapped him out of it.

When he'd told her he wanted intimacy, he'd expected her to balk. It was supposed to put another barrier between them, a reminder that he wanted a home and hearth kind of woman, not one who threatened to incinerate every bone in his body.

This time, when he pulled back, she let him go, her arms falling into her lap. She blinked, reorienting herself, apparently as befuddled as he was by what had just happened.

"Did she get the shot?" Trinity murmured, and instantly it was business as usual.

"She better have."

If not, he was done with this farce. There was no way he could keep this up. Because it was starting to feel way too real even when they weren't behind closed doors.

When Logan's phone rang at 8:00 a.m., *Mom* was the last name he expected to see flashing on the screen.

He groaned and put a pillow over his head, but it still felt like each chime of the ringtone cut straight through his temples. He knocked the phone onto the bed without looking and dragged it under the pillow. "Don't you have church?"

"Hello to you, too." His mother was way too chipper for a Sunday morning. "I'm about to leave, yes. You should come with me."

"I have a game today," he reminded her, which she should know, since she had box seats and came to most home games. When he was free, he didn't mind taking his mom to the church she'd attended with his dad for over thirty years. He hated that she had to go by herself now.

"Judging by the pictures your grandmother forwarded me, you'd do better to come with me to church," his mother said and he could hear her raised eyebrows in her tone. "Who is this woman you were kissing like you wanted to swallow her whole?"

"Trinity Forrester." He could not have this conversation at 8:00 a.m. on a Sunday. Or any time on any day, for that matter. How did he live in a world where Grandma got her mitts on photos posted to the internet and tattled to his mother about them? "And it was just a kiss."

It was so not just a kiss, and odds were the photographer had captured the scene at the club last night at the height of the frenzy. Logan hadn't seen the pictures yet, but they must have been really good if they warranted an early-morning call regarding the subject of his eternal soul.

"Would it be too much to ask if I could meet her? Since you're seriously involved and everything?"

Logan groaned. "Mom, I'm not marrying her. We're just…dating."

"That's not what the caption says."

He sat up, knocking the pillow to the floor. "What? What does it say?"

"'Billionaire owner of the Dallas Mustangs celebrates as Fyra Cosmetics executive says yes to his proposal.'" She cleared her throat. "That's verbatim. I'm reading it straight off my screen."

Since he didn't need any more invitations to church, he bit back an inventive curse. "It's…complicated, Mom."

He couldn't flat-out deny it, not until he knew if Trinity had planted the story on purpose. She better not have. He'd already told her his views on a fake engagement. His temper set off at a slow boil.

"Oh. So are you engaged or not?"

He couldn't lie to his mom, either. They'd always been close, but since his dad had died, Logan made sure that his mom wanted for nothing. They'd made the agonizing decision together to sell McLaughlin Investments, the online stock trading company his dad had founded, and then split the money in half. It had bonded them in a way nothing else could have. "I'll call you later and tell you. How about that?"

"As long as the answer is yes, sure."

Of course that was what she'd say. She'd been bemoaning the lack of a daughter-in-law for going on ten years now and recently had started in on the lack of grandchildren. *You're not getting any younger*, she liked to remind him, *and I'm certainly not*.

He had a ticking clock in his head, too, and didn't need any help feeling like the life full of family and kids that he saw when he closed his eyes did not even slightly resemble the one he lived every day. The line of eligible women wrapped the block twice, but he couldn't seem to find the *right* future Ms. McLaughlin. Certainly he would not increase his chances by parading a fake one around.

A shower did not improve his mood, and neither did the images that had been flashing across his mind since the undressing of last night. Trinity's body was the stuff of legends, and he was not the nice guy she'd painted him as.

Oddly, thinking about that second kiss put more wood in his shed than visualizing her perfect breasts as he peeled off that outfit made of sofa cushion material. So horrible. But once it was gone? So beautiful.

The woman. The kiss. The way she'd made herself vulnerable to him, both on that bed as he'd stripped away all of the outer trappings that hid Trinity from the world and on that bar stool as he explored what he'd found. So amazing.

He palmed himself and took care of the worst of the aching need, but he suspected he wouldn't ever fully absolve it until he gave in to the inevitable.

Which wasn't happening.

When he got out of the shower, he hunted up something to eat in the enormous kitchen that had come with the house he'd bought in Prosper because it was close to the Mustangs training facility and the school district was one of the best in north Texas.

Yeah, it had occurred to him that the woman he eventually married might like to pick out her own house, but he'd fallen in love with the property the moment his Realtor showed it to him. Twenty rolling acres spread out around the main house with plenty of room for kids and dogs, and a stable sat up on a hill overlooking a lake that he'd stocked with fish. Now all he needed was the wife.

Apparently he'd been granted step one in that process without his consent, and since he really couldn't put it off any longer, Logan snatched his laptop from the built-in desk near the fireplace in the great room and booted it up as he mainlined coffee.

The shot spilled onto his screen, and yeah, it was hot. He was standing between Trinity's legs, back to the camera and his hand on her thigh. The photographer had captured the kiss perfectly to show Trinity's face and expression—rapturous.

Logan's entire body cued up at the memory. This wasn't a picture of two people faking it for the camera. They wanted each other more than they wanted to breathe, and it was all there in full color for the world to see.

That's what his mom should be worried about, not whether the caption had any validity, although it did say exactly what she'd said it did.

Trinity Forrester was not the woman of his dreams. Fantasies? Sure. It would be impossible not to think about finishing that kiss with all her clothes on the floor. But the idea of her being his fake fiancée did not sit well. At all. He needed to call her, but it was barely nine o'clock on a Sunday and despite all of the evidence burning up his laptop screen, he did have a small sense of decorum left.

His phone beeped with a text message from none other.

Looked like she wasn't a late sleeper, either.

Did you see? It's all over my social media. I need a ring.

That pushed far more buttons than he should have allowed, and his temper flared. A fake relationship was one thing, because frankly, it wasn't all that fake. They *were* dating, and no one had asked how serious it was, so there had been no reason to lie. Until today.

He called her. Some things couldn't be properly conveyed via text message.

"Isn't it great?" she gushed by way of answer. Clearly she'd been sitting on her phone waiting on a return text and was perfectly fine with a conversation instead. "My publicist already called me. She's thrilled with the response. One of her trackers says the picture with the proposal caption has been shared twenty-five thousand times."

The phone nearly slipped from his suddenly nerveless fingers.

"Twenty-five thousand? Really?"

God, the nightmare just kept going, didn't it? How was it possible that people cared so much about something as unimportant to their daily lives as two people they'd never met getting engaged? And it was a lie, besides.

"That's just the one with your hand on my thigh. The other one is better, but it's not getting as much traction, probably because it's not as splashy."

The other one? Wedging his phone against his ear, he did another search and so many results scrolled onto his screen, he could hardly fathom it. There. He clicked.

The photographer had gotten a one-in-a-million shot in that moment after Logan had pulled away, in between the first and second kisses, just as Trinity had started to reel him back in. They weren't kissing, not yet, but the raw desire on her face was unmistakable. This picture was worth a thousand words, perfectly encapsulating what he'd felt as he'd been sucked into her—as if flesh and bone had dissolved, leaving only their essence behind.

She'd felt it, too. And he hated sharing what should have been a private moment with the world.

He hated a lot of this.

"I'm not buying you a ring," he muttered. "Are you the one who planted that caption?"

"No, I was just as surprised as you were. It might have been my publicist, but she won't admit it."

"We have to set the record straight. That's nonnegotiable. I don't mind letting a bunch of strangers think we're dating, but it's not fair to the people in my life to let them think there might be a wedding in our future when there's not."

"Why do we have to say anything?" She waved off all of his concern with that one airy statement. "No one is asking for an interview. Let it ride. See how your numbers are Monday morning and then let's strategize some more."

Easy for her to say. If the Mustangs won today, he'd most definitely be in front of a dozen sportscasters, and he'd bet good money they'd ask him about his love life.

They didn't win.

But by noon on Monday, he had evidence in his hand that people were buying tickets regardless, in record numbers. Logan McLaughlin had become the poster boy for the Dallas Mustangs ball club, and Myra had very specific ideas for how to capitalize on it.

Logan bit his tongue and picked up the phone to call Trinity.

Five

There was literally nothing about baseball that had matched Trinity's expectations. Case in point: when Logan had called her to ask if she'd go on a road trip with him, she'd actually thought he meant a *road trip*. Like the kind every single person on the planet except Logan would interpret as two people in a car driving somewhere.

Not what he'd meant.

Fortunately, jetting off to San Francisco for a few days to watch the Mustangs take on Oakland fit her need to not be at work on Monday. She might even call herself pathetically grateful to have a valid excuse for why she couldn't be at Fyra giving the nonexistent Formula-47 presentation.

Also, Logan had failed to mention that the Mustangs had a private plane for away games, which made the trip even more fun. The entire fuselage had been fitted with first-class-size seats, which made her feel even tinier in a cabin full of large men, but she reveled in the luxury.

Shortly after takeoff, the flight crew began circulating with drinks and food. Logan casually took Trinity's hand, lacing their fingers together. Strictly for show. She knew that. But it put a little tingle in her stomach that she secretly didn't hate.

She was looking forward to a lot more *tingle* in her future. After all, this trip was the perfect opportunity to take their relationship to the next level, both on camera and off.

"Tell me again," she murmured with a nod at the middle-aged man Logan had introduced her to earlier as the Mustangs' manager. "You're the general manager and that guy is the manager with no other title in front of it?"

"Right. It's a weird baseball thing. I never think twice about it." Logan's thumb brushed over her knuckle as he spoke and she wondered if he even realized he was doing it. "Gordon is the coach and I'm the CEO."

Prior to today, Logan had been almost deliberately affectionate, as if he was only paying attention to her because their on-camera relationship required it. She was trying not to ascribe any meaning to his seemingly subconscious touch other than the obvious—he was technically at work and probably focused on that.

Besides, they weren't a real couple. There didn't have to be meaning to anything he did. In public, everything was fake. She didn't have to dissect his moods or worry if he was thinking about ditching her. None of that mattered, which was what made it great.

"CEO, huh? So everyone reports to you and you could fire them all?"

He nodded with a shrug.

That was a job she was glad Cass had signed up for at Fyra. Trinity would hate having so many people looking to her for answers.

She scooched down in her seat. Wasn't that still the case with the marketing campaign for Formula-47? Skipping town on the wave of positive publicity didn't absolve the fact that a lot of people depended on her to hit a home run on this one.

And Logan had apparently invaded her consciousness to the point where she was making baseball analogies.

She'd noticed that around Logan, her muse was inspired. She'd gotten a double dose of inspiration from that scorching-hot round of kissing Saturday night, but the dozens of half-finished sketches hadn't moved her much closer to her goal. Something much more…*encompassing* than mere kissing might be the ticket, and she had a four-day trip ahead of her to prove her theory.

The next time she got naked with Logan, there would be a whole lot more happening than a conversation, and no one would be putting on clothes for quite a while. But she didn't want to clue him in that she had a stake in taking this very public flirtation behind closed doors.

When they got to the hotel, a slew of photographers waited outside the sliding glass doors. The limo Logan had chartered slid to a stop near the valet stand, but he didn't get out right away.

"By the way, I tipped off the local press that we were coming to this series. Together," he said. "As a couple. I hope that was okay."

"Brilliant." She'd wondered if this was the typical welcome a baseball team received in a host city. But it was the general manager and his girlfriend-slash-fiancée that they'd come to see. Nice. "Maybe we should think about hiring someone to follow us around with a camera. I like the organic reach of having unbiased third parties pick up the story, but it couldn't hurt to goose things a little."

"Got it covered. My publicist does, anyway," he amended as Trinity lifted her brows in question. "She's sending someone to all three games to take photos of us in my suite."

"We have a suite?" Like with a bed? Suddenly the prospect of sitting through three baseball games got a little more interesting. "You should have mentioned that way before now. Maybe we can take an adult nap during the middle part when nothing happens."

She waggled her brows to be sure he picked up on the double entendre.

His chuckle warmed her enormously. "It's not like a hotel suite. It's a skybox with seats for people to watch the action on the field, but with air-conditioning and a bar. I also invited several acquaintances to come hang out with us. It'll be a party."

Oh. That still sounded better than being outside in the sun while watching guys in uniforms hit a ball. "I shall be attentive and adoring in front of your friends. And the photographer."

Just that morning, a new article had made the rounds with damaging allegations about Fyra's animal testing practices. Cass had already involved their lawyer to see if they could sue. But anything Trinity could do to negate that bunch of BS would only help.

He climbed from the limo and helped her out, slipping an arm around her waist to guide her inside. The porter began pulling luggage from the limo's trunk as people surged forward, cameras poised to begin snapping money shots of the couple they'd come to photograph.

"Nice shoes," he murmured in her ear as flashes went off around them.

Yeah, she'd worn her six-inch Prada heels even though her ankles got puffy when she flew. The straps were cutting into her flesh and she'd lost feeling in her toes at least three hours ago. But she liked it when he could put his arm around her, too.

"You're welcome."

He grinned, and she promptly forgot about her ankles. Maybe she could talk him into an adult nap right this minute. Just to take the edge off. Her insides had never quite cooled after that second kiss Saturday night, and she'd be quite happy to pick up where they'd left off.

But then she distinctly heard him tell the hotel clerk *two rooms*. "What?"

He glanced at her. "One sec. I'm checking in."

"I realize that." She smiled at the clerk. "Excuse us for a moment, please."

The charter bus the rest of the team had ridden in from the airport picked that moment to unload. A wave of testosterone flowed through the doors, raising the noise level to a dull roar as the athletes, coaches and staff members sorted themselves out.

Dragging Logan to an uncrowded corner of the lobby was no small feat given both her precarious balance and his resemblance to an immovable mountain. But he came willingly, which she appreciated. She raised her brows. "Are you insane? We can't have separate rooms."

"We not only can, we are." He crossed his arms. "As soon as I get the keys, that is."

Aghast, she stared at him, but he looked perfectly serious. "After you went to the trouble to hire photographers, what are the odds they'll snap a picture of us going into separate rooms? Like a hundred and ten percent."

He scowled. "So? We can be a chaste couple waiting for marriage, can't we?"

His scowl deepened the harder she laughed. When she finally got herself under control, she gingerly dabbed at her eyelashes without fear thanks to Harper's waterproof, smudge-proof, morning after–proof mascara, all of which Trinity had personally tested.

"Did you actually look at the pictures from Saturday night?" She had. A lot. And twice she'd had to finish the job he'd started herself. Her vibrator hadn't ever gotten so much action. "They had ten times the reach that the ones from Friday did. The posed red carpet thing? Not for us. The spontaneous, hotter-than-hell, can't-wait-to-screw-each-other vibe is what our fans like. What they want to see."

His expression didn't change, and her panic level started an uphill climb. She needed him. Needed to get hot and heavy away from the camera. Inspiration was in short supply, and he was hogging it all.

"No. It's not happening. I've already made huge concessions—"

"Like what?" Hands on her hips, she forced her voice back down into a lower register before someone overheard them. She didn't mind if the photographers captured a public fight, but she did not want them to splash the cause of it across the web. "I'm the one constantly changing my clothes and—"

"One time you changed, and only because I forced you—"

"You so did not force me. I let you change my clothes because it suited me. Make no mistake, you don't control me."

"I don't want to, Trinity!" He apparently had no concept of volume, and several heads swiveled in their direction.

"Shh." She jerked her head at the press, who had

definitely clued in that something was afoot and started snapping away. Hopefully they'd get some good shots. "Act like you're mad all you want, but we can't afford any prying ears."

"I'm not acting," he growled. "I've already had phone calls about our impending engagement, despite your certainty that no one was going to ask about it. I don't like being put in that position. Nor do I want to be in the position of defending my personal choices regarding sleeping arrangements."

Gee whiz. His old-fashioned streak went a whole lot deeper than she'd credited. What a fun new challenge she'd stumbled onto here. Gaze narrowed, she swept him with a once-over designed to put a few thousand degrees of heat under his skin. "You must not be aware of what I have planned, then, if you think this is about sleeping."

Instantly, wariness and a fair amount of caution snapped across his expression. Who was throwing up shields now, hmm?

"Separate rooms," he said firmly.

"Fine."

She threw up her hands, but only to make it look like she still hated the idea, when actually, she'd realized it worked in her favor. It was a much juicier story if they had separate rooms but, oh, look, someone just caught them macking down in the hall outside one of them. And then they could both duck inside to take the super-hot kiss to its natural conclusion.

It was also in her best interests to ensure it was his room…so she could accidentally on purpose let someone photograph her sneaking away from it at dawn.

"Separate rooms. But you have to take me to dinner," she insisted. "Otherwise, we'll miss a golden opportunity to get more lens time."

He nodded with a smug smile. Probably because he thought he'd won. She let him think that. By the end of the night, he'd realize they'd both won.

One thing she could say for Logan, he did not cheap out when it came to putting up his fake girlfriend-slash-fiancée in a hotel.

Trinity took a long soak in the garden tub and used every ounce of the bubble bath the hotel had provided from their signature spa, strictly for market research purposes.

One hot-and-heavy sheet session with Logan could do the trick to get her muse back in the game full-time. But she was fully prepared to go all night with him if need be. Three or four orgasms fit into her schedule just fine, especially when Logan was the one delivering them. The man got her hotter than concrete in August.

In deference to her agenda, she selected a very simple white shift dress strewn with tiny colored flowers that covered her almost to the neck. It looked spectacular on her even though it didn't advertise any skin. To make up for the conservative dress, she put a pink stripe down the side of her hair and wore lace-up heels that crisscrossed her ankles a bajillion times. It would take both an enterprising and patient man to get these shoes off, and she shivered in anticipation of the foreplay that could be involved.

Logan knocked on her door.

She answered. His gaze dropped to her dress and lingered, hot appreciation blooming on his face. Score one for Trinity.

How had she missed that he liked her *that* much better in conventional clothes? He'd been so turned on by the simple jeans and T-shirt, but she'd mistakenly believed that had been a result of him being the one to put them on her.

"I expected to have to redress you," he threw out casually, but she did not miss the undercurrent of disappointment. He not only liked her in conservative clothes, he liked picking them out. Road trips made for interesting fonts of information, that was for sure.

"I was feeling generous."

"Noted. I will return the favor by escorting you to a nice dinner."

Where she would be charming and pretend that dinner was the only photo op of the night.

As predicted, a few photographers were still hanging around in the lobby, and she and Logan dutifully stopped before continuing on to the restaurant, allowing pictures. It didn't matter that the photos were staged, because they would all pale in comparison to the ones later on tonight, anyway. These chaste pictures got them nowhere.

Dinner was surprisingly normal. And nice. Logan exhibited incredible patience as Trinity peppered him with baseball questions that he must have found tedious. But she liked listening to him talk about his passion, and baseball was clearly it. He talked with his hands, smiled, laughed. If she didn't know better, she'd think they were actually dating.

No. Slipping into a fantasy about this whole thing being real was the surest path to problems.

"Walk me to my room?" she asked casually after noting several photographers had drifted away. Only the most tenacious had hung on, which meant they would likely be the most interested in being thrown a bone.

"Sure." Logan laced his fingers with hers in what had become a very common move for him. She liked it, but that was a deep, dark secret she'd never spill.

Was this what normal couples did, how they acted with each other? Was that why so many people did the relationship deal despite the surety of things going south? If nothing else, participating in a fake relationship gave her an inkling why Cass, Alex and Harper had all jumped on the marriage bandwagon.

But none of her friends were broken. Obviously. Just because real relationships had happened for them didn't mean it would for Trinity. That's why this one was so great—it would end before anyone got attached.

Of course, they hadn't exactly established an expiration date, but he could announce one any second. Letting go of Logan suddenly felt like the very last thing she'd be okay with, and her throat tightened along with her hand.

He squeezed hers back and oh, God, she didn't want to let him go. Not tonight.

They stepped out of the elevator on her floor without any reporters following them, and she didn't care. None of this was about the press or sales. He was a man and she was a woman and she needed him. For a lot of things, some she didn't even want to articulate to herself, let alone to him.

Logan must have sensed her distress, because he lifted her hand to his lips and kissed two knuckles as they arrived at her door. "What's wrong? You're shaking."

"Nothing." *Blow it off.* Not letting a man see her weaknesses was so ingrained, she did it automatically. "Just thinking about our missed opportunity to get photographed kissing downstairs."

"We have the next three days. We'll have plenty of opportunities."

She couldn't let him leave. Desperately, she shook her head and smiled, easily falling into seduce-and-conquer mode. Because that's what she knew how to do. "Maybe we should practice."

He laughed. "Kissing? You saw the pictures from Saturday. I don't think lack of practice is our problem."

"No, it's not," she murmured. "Our problem is that we always stop."

A glint popped into his gaze that she couldn't read. But he wasn't walking away. "We stop because we're in public and our agreement doesn't extend to making X-rated films."

But not because he *wanted* to stop. She pounced on that small distinction and held up her card key, then deliberately dragged it down his torso until she hit his belt. "So don't stop."

If he didn't, it would be her one chance to pretend Logan could be hers for real. Just for one night.

The little white dress Trinity wore had been killing him since he'd first glimpsed her in it. All Logan could think about during dinner was putting his hands under it to see if she had on virginal white underwear or had gone full-bore bad girl with a racy thong, maybe in red.

Either one would work.

The mystery could be solved very easily. All he had to do was sweep her into his arms, open the door and lay her out on the hotel bed.

He didn't. There were rules in place. For a reason.

"Are you inviting me into your room?" His voice had dropped, going raw with need that he couldn't control if he tried. So he wasn't trying. "Because that would be a no-no. We're only a couple in public. A fake couple."

"Oh, right. We're still worried about your rule book." She didn't sound worried. She sounded like she was about to rip all of his rules to shreds. And maybe some of his sanity, too. "If it would make you feel better, we could leave the door open."

A technicality. It had potential. If they left the door open, they'd theoretically still be a couple. It was only behind closed doors that he'd established any sort of parameters.

"That doesn't make it real," he cautioned, and he was pretty sure she realized he was talking to himself more than her.

Kissing in public was one thing, but to take it behind closed doors meant he had to admit his fierce attraction to Trinity went far deeper than it should. She wasn't the right woman for him.

Her laugh ripped through his groin, hardening his shaft to the point of pain.

"For the love of all that's holy, Logan. Please tell me what about the sizzling-hot thing between us isn't real?"

She had a point, one he wished he didn't like so much. Real was relative.

They had a real attraction. A real interest in getting each other naked. The only fake part was how it had started. And how it would end. He'd always defined a real relationship as one with potential to be permanent, but again, perspective.

"What are you saying, that we'd become a real couple?" he asked.

What did that even mean? How would they manage the logistics of that?

"Sweetie, you're thinking about all of this way too hard." She took his hand and flipped it over, exposing his palm, where she laid her room key as some kind of offering. Or challenge. "We don't need rules or definitions. That's how things get all messed up. All we need is to know that once we step through that door, we're both going to have a lot of orgasms. Together."

Something akin to relief rushed through his body along with a very strong lick of lust that put every nerve on high alert. She was doing her best to make this all about sex. Which was working. What did it matter whether she was a woman he could marry or not? That wasn't on the table, for either of them. Why was he even struggling with this?

She closed his fingers around her room key. "This is your show, Logan. If you want to play this as a publicity angle, I'm all for it. Think about how much sizzle photographs of us will have if we're actually burning up the sheets. It's a no-brainer."

The key to everything was literally in his hand. She'd given him the choice—wisely—because then he couldn't say he hadn't made it. "You're just going to keep throwing out my rules until I give in, aren't you?"

Wickedness laced her smile. "I'm pretty sure I already have. Oh, wait. I forgot rule number one. Logan McLaughlin, I dare you to take what you want. Let me fulfill every last fantasy you've ever had but were too busy being nice to indulge in."

That was the sexiest thing a woman had ever said to him.

"Every one?" he murmured. She didn't move, but thick, dense awareness rolled between them like fog with teeth, weighting his words. "I'm afraid even you couldn't keep up with my vivid imagination. It's been in high gear pretty much since the moment you told me you had a tongue piercing."

"Try me."

The chemistry that had been building since day one exploded inside him, and he pressed her up against the door before he could think. Not thinking worked for him. She'd given him permission to feel and he planned to.

Mouth on hers, he angled her head in a fiery kiss that flowed through him, hot, molten. When she added her tongue, he sucked it in greedily. Sensation cleaved across his flesh as she worked that steel bar.

He had so many fantasies about that thing. Where to start?

Her lush little body didn't fit against his the way he wanted, so he wedged a hand under her thigh and boosted her higher against the door until his raging erection slid into the valley between her thighs.

She moaned in a register that drove him insane. When she felt pleasure, she let him know. That was powerful, and it burst open something inside him. He wanted more of that, more of her under his mouth, more of her crying out his name.

But they were still in the hall. Because he hadn't yet committed.

It was time to take this behind closed doors.

Scrabbling with the plastic in his hand, he somehow got it into the slot without letting go of her. The door swung open, and just so there was no opportunity for either of them to throw down another roadblock, he picked her up to carry her across the threshold. It was symbolic, maybe more for him than her, but her feminine sigh unfolded something inside him as he kicked the door shut.

When he laid her out on the bed, he meant to immediately dive back into the kiss he'd had to cut short with the room entrance logistics. But he paused for a half second to drink her in, because she was a stunning sight, lounging there on the bedspread wearing that simple white dress. She'd put it on for no other reason than because she wanted to please him.

She had. She did. Constantly, even when they were crossing swords. A lot of times, he didn't even care if he won the battle because the act of fighting it turned him on. It should bother him. How messed up was that? But everything about her turned him on, and he was done resisting it.

But before he could get started on the million or so fantasies he'd lined up in his mind, she rolled to her knees and reached for his belt buckle, drawing him closer as she peered up through her lashes. "I can't wait to taste you."

His shaft grew impossibly harder, and it took a supreme amount of will to gather his faculties enough to still her hands. She'd already gotten his belt unbuckled and had started to pull it from its mooring.

"No," he said hoarsely. "That's not what I want."

Obviously his meaning did not compute, because she cocked a brow and broke free of his hold to yank the belt completely off. "In case I'm not being clear, I'm going down on you. Right now."

"I wasn't confused."

His eyelids shuttered closed as she trailed her fingers across his erection. Her touch through his clothes felt like liquid fire, and he nearly came at the thought of her mouth on his flesh. The real thing would probably be the death of him, but he wasn't going to find out. Not at this moment, anyway.

What she wanted was to stay in control. She wasn't going to get her wish.

The sound of his zipper sliding open put a little more urgency in that thought. Encircling her wrists, he drew her quick fingers away from his body. "Stop, Trinity. As good as I'm sure that would be, that's not what I fantasize about."

Bewilderment marred her face. "Really? Not ever?"

He groaned. "Of course I've thought about it. I'm not the Goody Two-shoes you seem to think I am. But neither am I a selfish ass who only thinks about how great it would be to have a woman go down on me."

"You'd be in a small minority of one," she muttered. "I have to ask. What in the world do you fantasize about then?"

Now they were talking. He eased her backward on the bed, still holding her wrists, until they hit the bedspread. Nuzzling her neck, he held her hands captive as he lightly sucked on her skin, diabolically pleased with the gasp that burst from her throat.

"I fantasize about being the man you moan for," he murmured against her skin. "The one who makes you come so many times, you don't remember what it's like to be with anyone else. I'm guessing you've had a lot of sex in your life, Trinity. But you've never been with me before, and I guarantee you this will be nothing like any of those times."

"So it's a competition thing?"

That was so not it. But neither did he know how to be someone other than who he was. He liked to feel something inside when he made love to a woman. A connection. His gut told him the surest way to get that with Trinity was to not let her do things the way she always did.

"Is it so difficult to believe that I want to give you a unique experience?"

"When it comes down to a choice between me pleasuring you or the other way around, yeah." The disbelief in her voice sliced through him, and it scored a place inside he wouldn't have said she could reach.

As many times as she'd surely gotten naked with a

man, had she never had *one* who cared about her pleasure above his own?

That was not okay.

He lifted his head and released her wrists at the same time in favor of threading her inky hair through his fingers. The thumb he brushed across her cheek put a note of tenderness in the moment that he hadn't intended... but there it was. "So then I have to ask. What do *you* fantasize about?"

Something akin to shock zipped across her expression, but she covered it almost immediately. "Making a man come with my mouth."

He grinned. "How many times have you said that? You must practice in the mirror, because it was impressive how you spit it out without having to think about it. Now give me the real answer. Otherwise, I'm going to have to work my way through all the things I can think of until I figure it out for myself."

"Maybe that's what I want," she said flippantly. "Maybe that's what I was after all along."

Yeah, he didn't think so. The wild uncertainty in her gaze told a different story, one that he should be ashamed he liked so much. But Trinity unsettled and off-kilter might be the sexiest she'd been yet. That was a state he could get into a whole hell of lot more.

He wanted her naked and writhing under him as he gave her orgasm after orgasm until she was so spent, she forgot all about her need for control.

And she was going to like it.

Six

Trinity swallowed as Logan's big palms engulfed her face. The kiss he laid on her lips had far too much sweetness in it. Like he wanted this thing between them to be real as much as she did.

I want to see the real you.

The request—demand—he'd made when he'd changed her clothes suddenly took on new meaning. Maybe she'd let him see her for reasons she hadn't fully admitted to herself. Her chest quivered with some nameless, unfathomable emotions. Which was not supposed to be the deal.

She'd given him permission to make this about nothing more than sex. Tried to stick to that herself. She'd practically had his zipper down and her hands on his rock-hard shaft, which she wanted to see with her own two eyes but hadn't yet, because he'd shifted gears so hard in the other direction, she still didn't know what had happened.

He'd *stopped* her from giving him the first of many climaxes.

What was he trying to do to her?

"I've been wondering," he murmured, "about what you have on under that dress."

"I've been wondering how long it would take you to find out," she shot back. Except the sassy note she'd tried to slip into her tone hadn't come out like she'd wanted.

Instead, it had sounded wistful.

With a wicked smile that shouldn't have tripped so many alarms in her head, he put his hands on her knees to situate her the way he seemed to want: shoes on the ground, bottom nearly to the edge of the bed, thighs open wide. He knelt between her legs and slid both palms along her skin, his rough hands thrilling her as he gathered the fabric in a slow reveal that hitched her lungs.

The ivy tattoo appeared. He settled his mouth on the first green leaf and dragged his tongue across it. Gasping, she bowed off the bed and levered herself up on her elbows, because she didn't want to miss anything.

The sight of his beautiful mouth on her thigh did it for her like nothing else.

"More where that came from," he murmured.

He licked her tattoo clear up to her panties, shoving back her dress and fingering the fabric of her white thong. "I'm going to take this off."

"You don't have to check in with me," she informed him breathlessly. Now that he'd so thoroughly turned the tables, she couldn't get air into her lungs. She ached for him to touch her intimately, and she wanted it now. "Really, I'm game for whatever you have in mind."

He glanced up, his expression hooded and implacable. "It would be best if you'd clue in right up front that I do things my own way. Therefore, I will be telling you what I'm doing to you as I do it. For example, I'm about to put my tongue between your legs."

The promise raked heat through her core. Logan McLaughlin had a dirty mouth, and she was a huge fan of it.

Hooking his fingers at the waistband of her thong, he slid it off and tossed it over his shoulder. His gaze went hot as he looked his fill at her uncovered sex. No one had ever done anything like that before. Sure, she'd had men go down on her, but usually in the dark, and most of the time it had a mechanical, scripted vibe as if there was some unwritten rule that she had to get off before her partner got his turn. In short, not very romantic.

This…was.

Logan had already eliminated his pleasure from this equation, and it was as unsettling as it was exciting. It was easy to take what she wanted from a man after he'd done the same to her, but she had no idea how to accept pleasure freely given.

"Trinity," he murmured, and her name floated across her skin like a prayer. "You're so gorgeously made. I want to taste all of you at once. I hardly know where to start."

She fought the urge to say something outrageous, to deflect, to ease her discomfort. She didn't know how to deal with a man who wasn't letting her run the show. He took away her dilemma by easing his thumbs up her thighs until he hit her slick center, where he went on an exploring mission that instantly lit her up.

Eventually, he replaced his thumbs with his lips.

Her core flooded with heat, and she gasped as he draped one of her knees over his shoulder, moving closer to her, increasing the pressure, the hot, wet sensation that had her crying out as she soared toward the ceiling. His tongue—it felt like it was everywhere at once, thanks to the sheer power of suggestion.

His big, solid hands held her in place as her hips bucked against his mouth. He welcomed it, going deeper, harder, faster until her skin incinerated under his onslaught and she came with his name on her lips.

"Again," he murmured, his lips grazing her core as he spoke. "Don't hold back. I want to watch you."

He fingered her pulsing channel, catching the faint echoes of her orgasm and whipping her into a frenzy instantly. Her back lifted from the bed as he shot sparks through her entire body, shoving her over the cliff a second time. She crashed into the release with something akin to shock, letting it play out in a way she never had before. In a way she'd never been able to before.

Bleary eyed, she stared up at him as he covered her, dipping his head to take her mouth, sharing the earthy taste of herself on his tongue. It was as arousing as it was intimate.

Good sex stems from intimacy. It wasn't just a throwaway comment he'd made. The man meant what he said. Always. Instead of enticing the all-American boy to take a walk on the wild side, he'd yanked her firmly over to his side. But she had no time to reflect on the irony of that as he shifted her to her stomach so he could unzip her dress.

This time, he offered no explanation as he stripped her of her dress and bra. When she was naked, he laid her back on the pillow and picked up one foot. He took one look at the tangled mess of strings and grinned. Wickedly.

"Is this some kind of Mensa test?" He yanked on one

firmly tangled string. "Let's see if the good ole Texas boy is smart enough to figure out how to get this off."

"Maybe." She shrugged and matched his smile. "Maybe it's an opportunity to prove how badly you want it."

"Sweetheart, you underestimate me." With that, he dropped her shoe to the bed. "I can do all sorts of things to you without taking them off, which I don't mind one bit, and you're the one who has to wear them during, so…we'll have a discussion later about our individual intellects."

With that, he rolled from the bed and did the most provocative striptease she'd ever seen in her life. First he slipped all his shirt's buttons from their moorings and inch by inch revealed the torso she'd felt plenty of times but was only now getting her first glimpse of.

There might have been drooling.

Then he took off his shirt, first from one broad shoulder, then the other, and the final product dried up her mouth to the point where drooling was definitely not in her future, along with not breathing. The man was magnificent, hard, sinewy, clearly not an executive who spent a lot of time behind a desk. Or wearing a shirt. He had a tan line where the sleeves of his many and varied T-shirts hit his biceps, but he must do something outside with his chest bared because it was deliciously sun kissed, highlighting what blew past a six-pack into uncharted territory.

She'd have to count the indentions across his abs. With her tongue.

The prospect unleashed a shiver. He undid his pants and let them drop to the floor along with whatever underwear he might have had on, and then she was really glad she was already lying down, because holy hell.

Powerful thighs. Thick erection. Too much to take in. No words.

But she didn't need any as he retrieved a handful of condoms from his pants pocket, which she scarcely had time to register. Though they'd circle back to the fact that he'd had condoms *in his pocket* the entire time.

And then there was no more thinking as he gathered her up and settled her into the grooves of his body. The hard, brutal planes of his physique had no give, and she thrilled at the feel of it against her bare skin.

He tipped up her head with both hands and she fell into the kiss, instantly drowning in Logan. Their legs entwined and his muscular thigh came up between hers, seeking her sweet spot…and finding it, rubbing hard at her still-sensitive bits until gray blurred her vision and a gasp tore from her throat.

Her skin heated so quickly she feared she might burn to ash. His hot hands spanned her waist, rolling her to her back. Taking one nipple in his talented mouth, he nipped and sucked until her back arched, and she had enough brain cells to realize he was doing exactly as he'd promised—pleasuring her with no thought to himself. He'd already made her come twice and seemed in no rush to stop.

What do you fantasize about?

She'd done precious little of that in her life. Her creativity was usually drained by the end of the day, and by the time she got naked with a man, it was never about what she wanted.

Why was it never about what she wanted?

Logan's teeth hit a spot on her nipple that barreled through her like a freight train, and she cried out.

"I love it when you do that," he murmured. "It's like an aphrodisiac."

Since aphrodisiac should be his middle name, she liked it, too. "Maybe you should see what switching to the other side gets you."

He chuckled and did exactly that, dragging his tongue across the valley between her breasts as he went, and then sucked her other nipple into his hot mouth. But he coupled that with a very well-placed finger between her legs, and the dual sensations spun her off into oblivion again. Breathless, she clenched her way through another spectacular orgasm that encompassed her whole body.

Logan had a condom rolled on and was poised at her entrance, pushing inside before her vision cleared. Mewling sounds tore from her throat as the pressure built, and it was so good, so unbelievable on the heels of a release. He grabbed one stiletto and tugged her knee nearly to her shoulder as he widened her.

"Relax," he murmured. "I'm…big."

Yeah, she'd noted that for herself. "You say that like I should be disappointed. That's usually on the pro side of a girl's checklist."

Oh, yes, he *was* big. Her whole body went liquid as the exquisite feel of his length slid along her sensitized flesh.

But not too big. Perfect. Especially after he'd primed her to the point where she was so swollen and wet that he slid in easily. And she didn't miss that he'd done so. Even in this, he was thinking about her pleasure instead of taking his own.

When he'd buried himself inside completely, he sucked in a breath and froze, bliss stealing across his features. "You feel so amazing."

How was he forming coherent sentences? Her own body had wheeled off into the stratosphere, greedily sucking in all the new sensations as he began to move, circling his hips as he thrust. She couldn't have stopped the moans pouring from her throat at gunpoint and she didn't want to. He murmured his encouragement with well-placed phrases as they came together again and again.

The best was when he wrapped her leg around his waist and let go of her stiletto in favor of cupping her jaw. But he didn't kiss her, just watched her as he plunged deep inside, his eyes dark and focused. Fingers tangled in his hair, she couldn't look away, even when his face tightened and turned tender with release. It was so powerful to witness such a strong man showing his vulnerability that she nearly came apart inside.

When was the last time she'd done it missionary style? It was her least favorite position—or at least it had been until Logan.

He made it exquisite, an experience. Not just sex, but pleasure combined with connection, both beautiful and precious.

This was what she fantasized about. A man who would be the same in bed or out, day in and day out. Still there in the morning. Strong, capable. Honest. One who cared about her over his own selfish needs.

She fantasized about being loved.

And she'd spent the last few years of her life systematically ensuring she'd never have to think about the fact that she didn't have that, wasn't capable of having that.

Which meant she had to shove that particular fantasy back into the deep. Where it belonged.

The pictures from outside Trinity's door the night before shot their fake relationship into the stratosphere.

Apparently some of the photographers from the lobby had followed them after all.

Logan downed the first of what would likely be many cups of coffee that morning as he ate breakfast in the small dining room of the hotel restaurant and reread the email from Myra crowing about his brilliant strategy to be photographed kissing Trinity outside her hotel room.

If you could call it that. Strategy hadn't been forefront in his mind. And it was hard to label it something as innocuous as a kiss.

The scene was almost pornographic, raw and sensual, and the photographer had timed it perfectly to show Trinity's card key clutched in his fingers as he searched blindly for the slot without even lifting his mouth from hers. The urgency burned visibly between them.

He almost couldn't look at the picture. It was too much truth, too intimate. Had Trinity known a photographer had followed them upstairs? Was that the only reason she'd given him the green light?

Last night had been real—to him, anyway. As real as the ache in his elbow from the vigorous activity, which had caused his old injury to flare up. And it didn't sit well that something so personal had been captured and then turned into a marketing gimmick by his and Trinity's respective publicists.

But that's what they'd been doing all along. Why was this picture different? He didn't like the answer. Or the kick to his stomach as he glanced up to see Trinity breeze into the restaurant and take a seat at his table without so much as a hello.

God, she was gorgeous. Even with an inch-wide green stripe running down the nonshaved side of her hair. He was almost accustomed to the heavy hand she used to apply her cosmetics, and honestly, it was part of the overt style that bled from her pores. She wore a flowy, hair-stripe-matching grass-green dress that covered her to her calves and tied up around her neck. She looked so sizzling hot that he had his suit jacket unbuttoned before he realized he'd been about to take it off so he could cover her up with it.

Moron. She'd shredded his brain cells last night.

It was a very respectable dress. It was what was under the dress that got him, and he didn't just mean the body. Trinity was fierce on the outside, but when he'd gotten her behind closed doors, she'd melted into his arms, becoming so sweet and impassioned he could hardly fathom it.

That had been a huge surprise. And all he wanted to do this morning was pull her into his lap and stick his nose into that juncture of her neck and shoulder, where it most smelled like her. Then he'd start peeling back her outrageous shell again.

"Lara called me already," Trinity said as she smiled at the waitress and ordered coffee. "My publicist. She's thrilled with the traffic on our website. I have a couple of calls in to Alex to get some prelim sales numbers now that it's close enough to the end of the month to have the data."

"Good morning to you, too," he said and almost didn't choke on it.

Trinity shot him a look. "Get up on the wrong side of the bed? Or maybe in the wrong bed entirely? I told you to stay. You were the one who insisted on propriety and left."

Because he'd had to. Sleeping in the same bed with her put a stamp of permanence on this association that he couldn't afford. Not as far as the outside world was concerned; it was already too late for that. But in his mind. They were a real couple now, for better or worse, and he wasn't sorry they'd taken things to the next level. But it was *temporarily* real.

He couldn't forget that. Sleeping with her, wrapped up in each other all night long, would be a mistake.

Instead of letting the unsettled restlessness in his chest take over his mood, he lifted her hand from the table and kissed her palm. "My publicist is happy with the results as well. Act like you're enjoying yourself. There's a slew of photographers across the way."

She peered in the direction of his subtle head jerk from the corner of her eye to where a crowd of people lined the lobby, visible over the low wall separating the restaurant from the rest of the ground floor. "They're here early. And I don't have to act like I'm having fun with you. I just do."

Really? He eyed her. "You're in Oakland, California, at a hotel eating crappy breakfast food, and I'm about to make you watch a baseball game that you don't want to sit through. You should have higher standards."

Her smile heated him so fast, his vision grayed. "It's what will happen after the game that's keeping my spirits up."

And now he was thinking about that, too. He'd been trying not to, because they hadn't really established any morning-after rules, like how frequently they'd take their relationship behind closed doors. Given that they'd be doing deliberate on-camera work today as well, maybe she'd want a break. What did he know about what went on in her head?

"The endless interviews and postgame strategy sessions?" he commented. "Yeah, that'll be a blast for you."

She'd agreed to do the whole nine yards' worth of

press junkets in hopes of getting some extra exposure, which had seemed necessary at the time but now felt excessive given that they were already burning up the internet with their presex activities in the hall.

"You're so sweet to worry about me." Her hand was still in his, and she thumbed his knuckle almost affectionately. "But I can amuse myself. All I have to do is think about how much it'll be killing you to stand next to me, knowing that I'm completely naked under this dress."

Hot coffee scalded his throat as he choked on it.

Clearly nowhere nearly as concerned as she should be—since his inability to breathe or swallow was her fault—she arched a brow. "Are you okay?"

"What do you think?" he growled. "Are you really commando? Like, one hundred percent?"

She nodded with a sly smile. "And I plan to sit really close to you during the game. Maybe there will be a table that might cover a wandering hand or two?"

That dress took on a whole new definition of shock value—and now he definitely wanted to cover her up. With his naked body.

Going commando under a simple dress should definitely be a morning-after rule. He just couldn't decide if the rule should state *never* or *always*.

Trinity chatted some more about strategy and photo ops while drinking her coffee and refusing to eat anything, a female tendency he could never understand. The team had already left for the stadium so they could get started on their pregame rituals. Ballplayers were a superstitious lot, and you couldn't pry their customs from their cold, dead fingers. They always ate at the ballpark, mostly so Gordon could watch the players like a hawk, but also because hotel food sucked.

Normally, he'd be with them, angsting alongside the coaches. But instead of doing his job, Logan was still at the hotel, listening to his fake girlfriend–slash–real lover talk about how great it was that this partnership was paying off.

"Fyra was featured in a cosmetic review on *Allure's* website," she gushed. "And it was so positive that our northeast distribution warehouse is out of stock of Bahama Sunset eye shadow and the mascara they mentioned. They panned us last time, claiming the products they tried were overpriced. Like anyone cares about value when it comes to whether your mascara clumps or not."

"Uh-huh." Her lips moved constantly and he couldn't help but think about how quiet she got when it counted. When talking wasn't necessary because they were communicating perfectly with their bodies.

He wasn't done with his fantasies, that was for sure. And for the first time in his life, he resented the fact that he couldn't just watch a baseball game with a gorgeous woman and then take her back to his room for some postgame activities. Maybe he could cut things shorter than normal. He was already making concessions by not being on the field at this moment.

"We'll leave in about an hour," he told her as they left the restaurant after breakfast.

"Oh. Isn't the game at one o'clock?"

He hid a smile. "Yeah, but the team usually gets there about six hours early. I'm cutting you a break since it's your first time."

She hit the lobby an hour later, exactly on time. The day was perfect for baseball—cloudy with a slight breeze off the bay, which put the temperature near sixty degrees. Logan loved this area, especially in the summer, when it routinely reached 110 in their home stadium in Texas. Trinity shivered as they stepped outside the glass doors to the valet stand.

Without hesitation, he stripped off his jacket and draped it around her shoulders. Gratefully, she smiled and slipped her arms into the sleeves. He didn't feel guilty at all about getting extra clothes on her and bit his tongue instead of asking if she owned a sweater.

He was pretty sure he already knew the answer to that.

Somehow he resisted putting his hands on her during the limo ride to the field. The stadium sat overlooking the bay with a great view of the Oakland bridge. Across the bay, San Francisco gleamed in the low light of the morning, and he was extraordinarily glad they didn't have to venture to that side of the bridge. The traffic in the Bay Area rivaled Dallas, and he was not a fan of sitting in the car for hours.

Of course, he'd never done it with Trinity. That might make a long commute worth it.

The stadium was less grand than some others, but he got a rush walking through the gates regardless. The smell of popcorn lingered in the air, something almost all stadiums had in common, even the open-air ones. He'd never lost the sense of being on sacred ground, and no matter what time it was, he could hear the thunk of the ball against his glove, the shush as it sailed through the air, the roar of the crowd in his head. God, he could still feel the energy even though it had been nine years since the last time he'd pitched here.

Some days it felt like his life had ended when his career had.

Trinity slipped her hand into his, squeezing it. More strategy? If she'd noticed he'd slipped into a funk, she didn't say anything, but the timing couldn't be a coincidence. She'd somehow tuned in to him and he didn't hate it, no matter how weird it felt to be here with a woman, especially one wearing his suit jacket. Weird, but nice.

Trinity oohed and ahhed over the skybox he'd borrowed from a friend. He tried to see it through the eyes of someone who'd never been in one before, but he'd grown up in the box his dad owned, often hanging out for hours on random Saturdays during the season.

It was odd to be above the field when his team was on it. The players were warming up, and he automatically assessed each one.

Trinity's unique feminine scent hit him a moment before the woman did. She joined him at the glass overlooking the field. "Are you okay? You seem distant."

He shrugged, mystified how she could do that when he hadn't clued in on her moods to the same degree. "I'm an in-the-trenches guy. It's very unusual for me to watch my team play from this vantage point."

"Why are you here, then?"

It was a valid question. No one else was here yet. The party wouldn't start for a couple of hours, closer to game time. And there certainly weren't any photographers around. "I don't know."

He literally had no idea how to integrate a woman—fake, real or otherwise—into the rest of his life. Sure, he'd dated a few women here and there since buying the Mustangs. But they'd never been serious enough relationships to bring the lady to a game.

Which of course begged the question—how serious was this one?

There might have been a hundred other things he

could have taken his fake girlfriend to besides an away game, where they'd be stuck together for three more days until they went home late Thursday night. Yet he'd pounced on Myra's suggestion. Why, because he'd wanted to see how Trinity fit in here?

Trinity cocked her head, contemplating him. "If you're normally down on the field, the only conclusion I can draw is that you're here for me."

He made the mistake of meeting her ice-blue eyes, which had gained a great deal of warmth as she watched him.

"I am." No point in lying about it. "I didn't want you to be alone. This is a big stadium, and you don't know anything about baseball."

Okay, that part might not have been the whole truth. But he wasn't sure what was.

She laughed. "I'm a big girl, Logan. I can find things to do no matter where I am. But since you've made such an excellent point, tell me about baseball."

Eyeing the green dress and sandals she wore, he crossed his arms. "Really? Like all of it?"

"Sure." She uncrossed his arms for him without his permission and guided him to the long leather couch on the front row of the seating in the box. "We have time, right?"

He settled onto the cushion next to her, but only because he'd just realized the benefits of having this suite to themselves with no danger of her undergarments going missing.

The protective one-way film on the glass suddenly seemed like genius on the part of the stadium planners. No one could see in. No one could enter the suite without the lock code, and all the people who were privy to it wouldn't arrive for quite some time.

He had a temporary pass to have real sex with his fake girlfriend. That was the only thing he should—could—focus on right now. It was all they had between them that was real. All he could allow to be real.

Things had just gotten a hell of a lot more interesting.

Seven

"We have a couple of hours," Logan told her and picked up Trinity's hand to raise it to his lips, nibbling on her fingertips because he wanted to and he could. "What do you want to know about baseball?"

"I want to know everything."

Her voice had dropped into that register that somehow plugged straight into his groin, lighting it up. She pulled her hand from his grasp deliberately, with a little tsk. Without taking her eyes off him, she hiked up her skirt to flash him a very quick peek at her naked sex and levered one gorgeous leg over his lap, settling herself astride him.

Oh, God, yes.

Her heat ravaged his instant erection, burning him thoroughly even through his clothes. She leaned forward, rolling her hips to increase the contact between their bodies, and nuzzled his ear as she murmured, "Tell me what baseball means to you."

His pulse went into a free fall.

"Baseball is like breathing," he said hoarsely as her fingers went to work on his buttons.

He should stop her for...some reason. Because she was taking control. That was a bad thing. But he couldn't find any fault in the way she worked her hips against his length, and he groaned as she laved at his exposed collarbone.

"Breathing?" she prompted, tonguing her way up his throat.

He liked her out of control, when he was the one calling the shots. But his head tipped back easily as she cupped his jaw to move him into a position she liked better, and he was pretty sure he wasn't going to stop her. "I don't have to remind myself how much I enjoy the way my lungs function. They just do. I step on the mound and my body automatically cues up into the right stance to throw."

"What else?" She opened his shirt, her clever hands sliding down his torso to explore every inch of it, and her touch enflamed him. His thoughts fragmented as he fell into a sensuous haze, and words just spilled out from somewhere inside.

"My mind turns the ball over and over, examining it, hearing the way it sounds in the air. In my peripheral vision, I'm checking out first base to see if the guy has a little too much of a leadoff. The sun is usually high in the sky and I have to adjust my cap. But that guy at bat? He's not getting a piece of my arm."

"Logan, that's beautiful," she murmured and cupped his face with her hot hands, laying a kiss on his lips that he felt deep inside. When she pulled back, her eyes glowed with something he couldn't name, an appreciation, maybe, for what he'd shared without really meaning to. "You're a pitcher."

It wasn't a question, but he nodded as his throat worked, and he couldn't swallow all at once. None of that should have come so automatically, and she'd clued in that it was significant. Somehow. He'd never told her that he'd played professionally. That it still killed him on a regular basis that he wasn't down on the field at this moment warming up.

Sometimes being in the dugout with the team let him pretend for a few moments that he would actually don a uniform. Up here in a box? No way to maintain that illusion.

So here he was perpetuating another one. With Trinity.

When had he become so dependent on fantasy?

And how had she figured that out about him?

Before he could gather his scattered wits, she kissed him again, but this time, it had far more intent. Her mouth slanted against his, growing more heated and deliberate. Her tongue wound against his, seeking more, going deeper, and he helplessly fell into her, because he didn't care if it was supposed to be fake.

He wanted this woman as bare to him as he'd just been to her.

The tangle of their bodies pressed intimately together and her hips circled harder, faster against him. He reacted instantly, his insides turning molten until he couldn't feel his bones any longer. *Closer.* He needed her, ached to be inside her, and put his hands on her waist to hold her in place as he ground into her core, his shaft so hard between them it was a wonder he didn't bruise her tender flesh.

"Logan," she murmured. "Let me pleasure you."

And then she easily broke his hold, dropping to the ground between his legs. Her lithe hands went to work on his belt buckle, and before he could think of a reason to stop her, she yanked down his zipper, burrowing into his clothes to hit bare flesh.

He sucked in a breath as she peered up at him and simultaneously cupped him in her hot hands, running his tip along the line of her lips. He jerked involuntarily as sensation rocketed up his length.

The raw mood she'd uncovered twined with the physical reaction, making everything feel ten times more powerful.

"You're so beautiful," she crooned. "I'm going to take care of you. Let me show you how good this tongue piercing can make you feel."

So much blood rushed south he didn't understand how his heart could still be beating, but his pulse thundered in his ears, so things must still be in working order.

And then the entire world slid sideways as she dragged her tongue up his length. The bite of the steel coupled with her hot, rough lick nearly separated his bones from his skin. Then she sucked him fully into her mouth and he was lost to the dual sensations of cold and heat.

The emotional vortex inside him heightened everything.

Higher and higher she spun him. It was so good that his hips bucked automatically, shoving him deeper into her mouth, but she took him, *all of him*, and it felt unbelievable. So amazing that he couldn't hold back, couldn't stop the flood of Trinity through his blood, and his thighs tensed with the effort it took to simply keep breathing.

The release pounded through his entire body, ripping

a cry from his throat that was one hundred percent primal, and it was easily the hardest he'd ever come in his life. She finished him off expertly and he fell back on the couch, nerveless and so spent he couldn't feel his toes.

But the sated serenity that stole over him was so very right.

The sight of her on her knees before him, with her lips wrapped around him, had burned into his mind indelibly. She tucked him away and disappeared for a moment, then came back to settle into his side on the couch, lifting his arm so she could snuggle against his chest with his arm around her.

It was so nice, his eyes closed automatically as he soaked in the feel of her warm body bleeding through his. "You know I won't ever think about pitching again without thinking of your tongue piercing, right?"

She laughed, her fingers toying with one of the buttons hanging from his shirt. "I wanted to give you a unique experience. Since you did that for me. Last night."

The information she'd just shared filtered through his poor, beleaguered brain. "You mean I was successful?"

Of course, their conversation had been extremely limited last night because their mouths had been on each other, not talking.

Her smile was a little misty. "Let's just say I have a lot of selfish men in my past and I'm not sorry they're in my rearview mirror. Plus, I'm looking forward to how you're going to repay me for that."

"Yeah?" he growled. "Lucky for you I've got hours and hours to come up with something spectacular."

Unfortunately, it would have to wait, because what he had in mind would not work in their current environment, given that people might start arriving at any time. And that he'd stupidly left all the condoms back at the hotel. But honestly, he'd never have considered a baseball stadium ripe ground for a sexual encounter.

He would not make that mistake twice.

Once he had all his clothes in order, Trinity stood with him at the glass and listened intently as he explained the mechanics of the game—at her request. She asked intelligent questions and genuinely sought to understand the rules, of which there were a lot.

"No wonder you're such a fan of rules." She rolled her eyes good-naturedly. "My eyes glazed over ten minutes ago."

No, they hadn't. She'd absorbed every word, even when he'd gotten entirely too impassioned in his defense of the concept of a designated hitter, which he should hate as a pitcher. Former pitcher.

But all at once, he didn't feel like he had to make the distinction. He was still a pitcher even though he didn't do it professionally any longer. He didn't have to pretend it wasn't a part of him. Trinity hadn't labeled him as a former pitcher or asked if he used to pitch. She'd just understood that baseball wasn't a job, it was his essence.

And then gave him the most amazing sexual experience he could imagine.

How in the hell was he supposed to go back to a one-color, lackluster, *boring* woman after that?

Short answer—he had to. Trinity was temporary. He couldn't be constantly distracted from his life by a sex-on-a-stick marketing executive. Especially not one who'd just demonstrated a remarkable ability to entice him down a rabbit hole of fantasy, which was apparently an Achilles' heel he'd just discovered. They should start talking about exit strategies, stage a public fight. Surely their fake affair had done all the good it was going to do.

But the universe wasn't finished knocking his plans around.

The Mustangs won. And Trinity instantly became a good-luck charm. What was he going to do now, drag her to every game from now until the end of the season?

It was not cool how great that suddenly sounded.

Logan had not been kidding about the interminable rounds of interviews that happened after the game. Trinity lost count of the number of times she heard him repeat the same phrases to yet another reporter.

"Johnson can absolutely repeat that three ninety tomorrow," Logan said easily, which was always followed by, "O'Hare is still on the DL, but we're calling up a reliever from Round Rock who will knock your socks off."

Three ninety—that might have been a reference to the mysterious stat called a batting average that Logan had mentioned earlier. But she wouldn't put money on it at this point. DL meant nothing to her.

It was like a secret code that only the kids in the know could crack, and by the time dinner rolled around, she was jonesing for a glass of wine. Spending an hour on her stuffed-to-the-gills email inbox wouldn't be out of line, either. Her face hurt from smiling as she stood by Logan's side, but his arm never left her waist, and the photos would be brilliant, especially since she'd worn this green dress that would pop on camera.

Several of the reporters asked about her, and Logan eagerly introduced her without a label, but the adoring look he gave her told the story vividly and none of the eagle-eyed cameramen missed that shot.

"You're a much better actor than I would have given you credit for," she murmured as they held hands and dashed for the limo after Logan had finally deemed them both done. "Even I almost believed we were headed for the altar soon."

She'd meant it as a joke, but it twisted at her heart painfully because it was frighteningly easy to pretend the adoring looks weren't faked.

He laughed and kissed her cheek playfully. "Wasn't an act. I'm very fond of you right now."

"Um…really?" She glanced at him askance.

"Did you not see the scoreboard at the end?" He picked up her hand and kissed her fingers, a habit she could get very used to. "Mustangs put one up in the win column. Thanks to you."

"Me?" Had she blown his brains out earlier? She wasn't bad in the pleasure department, but no one had ever actually lost their mind afterward. "Pretty sure I never picked up a bat the whole game."

"You didn't have to. You're good luck. Obviously."

The stress he put on the word *obviously* was like a verbal eye roll, except she still didn't get it. "What, like I'm your Blarney stone now?"

That piqued his interest, and he swept her with a once-over. "Yep, which means I have to kiss you in order to get my dose of luck."

"Now that has possibilities." She let him pull her into his lap to get started on that, which effectively dropped the subject. Fine by her.

By the time the limo reached the hotel, they were both breathless and she'd nearly hit a high C twice as he fingered her under her dress, dipping his talented fingers into the pool between her legs again and again.

"Have dinner with me," he murmured as they hustled through the lobby, ignoring the coaches and players she vaguely recognized. Some of them called out to Logan, but his gaze was trained on her. Deliciously so.

"Think there will be more photographers here later?"

She glanced around, but the lobby was bare of the press. For once. Had they finally gotten tired of the story? Her spine stiffened and a cold chill crept along each vertebra. If there wasn't a story, what did that mean for this fake relationship?

"Trinity." He waited until she glanced at him to continue. "I'm asking you to eat with me. Not because it's good for my ticket sales or to get people to buy more mascara. Because you have to eat, and why not do it with me?"

That was too much like a date. Which was a ridiculous thing to be wary of. They'd been on plenty of dates already. Seen each other naked and put their mouths on each other in places that would get them arrested if they'd done it in public.

All at once, she realized—it *wasn't* like a date. She'd been conveniently standing there when he'd decided he was hungry, that was all. He wasn't asking her to spend time with him because he liked her. What if he had? Would that make a difference? It didn't matter. He wasn't supposed to like her. She didn't like *him*. This wasn't real.

Maybe she'd blown her own brains out earlier. Furious with herself for turning into a waffling, idiotic crybaby, she shook her head, totally unable to fathom why she couldn't get rid of the crawly feeling on the back of her neck.

"I need to catch up on work after spending all day at a baseball game."

"Okay." He nodded like it was no big deal, and why

wouldn't he? It wasn't a big deal. Convenient dining companion was unavailable. So what?

But then he pulled her into his arms by the elevator and gave her a scorching-hot kiss that curled her toes. His tongue talked to hers in a timeless mating ritual that her body responded to in ways no man had ever evoked. He'd literally just made her come in the limo before they'd arrived, and already she was hot for him again, wishing she'd given him a different answer when he'd asked her to dinner.

That's why it was so much better that she'd said no. She didn't need a man to entertain her, and she'd already gotten a couple of orgasms out of the deal. What more did she want?

They weren't dating. This wasn't real. The more she had to remind herself of that, the farther away from Logan she needed to stay.

When she got back to her room, her face still stinging from his stubble, she sat down at the desk to boot up her laptop. The long list of bolded unread emails flashed onto the screen and she nearly cried. Choosing emails over Logan McLaughlin. She was certifiable.

But the job of the chief marketing officer did not stop simply because the woman with the title spent the day watching a bunch of guys in tight pants whack some balls around. The only reason she'd met Logan was because she'd been doing her job, and she needed to keep focusing on that.

An email from Alex with the title Preliminary Sales Numbers jumped out from the screen. She clicked on it.

And blinked. The first line of Alex's email had fourteen exclamation points. For a numbers girl, that was so out of character. Trinity's eye immediately scrolled to the bottom line of the profit/loss statement.

"Holy crap."

It was three hours later in Washington, where Alex lived, but this was too important to wait until tomorrow. Trinity thumbed up Alex on her phone and hit Call.

"Seriously?" she said when Alex answered. "A seven percent increase in sales this month?"

"Would I lie to you?" Alex's indignation spat over the network. "No. I would not, especially not about something as sacred as my balance sheet. You are a star, my dear. Whatever you're doing, don't stop. You've almost singlehandedly halted this smear campaign in its tracks."

Trinity sank down in her seat and shut her eyes. Figured. This had been personal for so long and she'd put her all into reversing the tide. Did this mean she and Logan had to keep going no matter what?

And how long could she actually keep it up without dissolving into a puddle of feminine confusion? Didn't matter. She couldn't quit now.

She plied Alex with a few platitudes, asked after Phillip and the twins her friend was carrying, avoided the topic of Logan like a champ and hung up, determined to make some headway on the campaign for Formula-47 now that everything in her life was on track.

The design program she pulled up sat there mocking her, and her mind drifted to who else? Logan. The way his hair always fell into his face and he shoved it back—she loved touching his hair, threading it through her fingers. Which of course reminded her of his big, solid body over hers...

Funny how that was the strongest image she had of him. But Logan was a closet romantic, and she sighed a little over how he expressed it. Like the single long-stemmed rose he'd given her on their first date, which she might have pressed into a book simply because no one had ever given her a rose that matched the outfit she'd been wearing the day they'd met.

The rose popped out in her mind. And twirled loose some other images. In a flash, the entire Formula-47 campaign unrolled with a million and five different bursts of inspiration.

Her fingers flew to the keyboard and when she next looked up, two hours had passed and she had a crick in her neck.

Bloom. The product was going to be called Bloom.

What better image to sell people on the idea of a cream that regenerated skin cells? *Fyra's Bloom promises to make your skin do exactly that. You'll bloom; your youthful self will bloom; your skin will bloom.* The concept had so many applications, she still had new ad copy and packaging ideas zipping through her mind despite having just devoted two hours to dumping the contents of her brain onto the screen.

It was so perfect, even she was impressed, and once she had the name, the whole thing exploded into exactly the multimillion-dollar marketing push it needed to be—and she had Logan to thank for it.

Before she could think of the ten million reasons it was a horrible plan, she ordered a bottle of the most expensive champagne on the hotel's room service menu. Then she changed into the most seductive black bra and thong she owned, threw on a little black dress that showcased her legs and went to find the only person she had any interest in celebrating with.

When she knocked on his door, he answered with his shirt unbuttoned and hanging loose over his gorgeous chest, as if he'd shrugged it on. His blank expression melted into one of easy appreciation as he swept her with a look that burned her nerve endings.

"Wasn't expecting you. I like the wardrobe change. As long as we're not going out."

She held up the champagne bottle, choosing to ignore his comment about her wardrobe. "I might be convinced to share this with the owner of today's winning baseball team."

"No more work tonight?" He still hadn't moved from the door, blocking the entrance as if to say he had every intention of determining her intent before he let her in. But the sizzling look in his eyes told her he'd clued in pretty fast to why she was here, and it wasn't to ask him to dinner.

"None. I had a breakthrough on a sticky problem and Alex told me we have a seven percent increase in sales this month. I thought you might be up for a celebration."

He stepped back and held the door wide, allowing her to brush past him, but she didn't get far. Snagging her arm, he took the champagne bottle and set it down on the dresser near the door, then whirled her into his arms for a kiss that rivaled the one by the elevator earlier.

Her body went up in flames. Hungrily, she kissed him back as he stripped away every ounce of doubt about what they were doing here with nothing more than his hot mouth on hers.

She moaned and he backed her up against the door, his hard body pinning hers. The contact sang through her and she didn't even mind that they hadn't gotten to the champagne yet. It would keep. And it had been an excuse to seek him out anyway.

She wanted *him*. Against all reason.

Her fingers found the edges of his shirt, and in a flash, she yanked it off to let it drift to the floor, letting her palms delight in the feel of his back, which never ceased to thrill her to the marrow.

"You're barefoot," he growled. "You're too short now."

She laughed as he circled his erection against her stomach, which was so very far north of where they both wanted it. But she could be flexible. "I don't have to be wearing shoes for this."

He groaned as she spun him and pressed him against the door so she could mouth her way down his beautiful abs. That part was like an extra-special treat, perfect for her tongue. The steel bar dipped in and out of the crevices, exploring, tasting. Dipping below the waistband of his pants. But when she reached for the zipper, he stopped her with his hand to her chin, tipping it up.

"Trinity."

All at once, her feet left the floor as he picked her up and carried her to the bed, throwing her down on it. He rolled onto it next to her and immediately picked up that kiss, but now that they were horizontal, it took on new urgency. Their legs tangled together and his fingers tugged on the zipper of her dress, yanking it down until he could peel the fabric from her shoulders, which he followed with his mouth, kissing down the curve of her back as he revealed her skin inch by inch.

When he got the fabric to her waist, he sucked in a breath as he took in her lacy black shelf bra. "That's the most gorgeous sight I've seen all day."

"Better even than the scoreboard?" she teased.

He glanced up at her from under his lashes. "Sure you wanna go there?"

"I, um… It was just a joke."

"That was no joke." He laid her back against the pillow and kissed the valley between her breasts, hooking the straps of her bra with both thumbs to drag them down her arms. "The Mustangs play one hundred and sixty-two games a year. Every win counts, but it's just another day at the office. You can't dwell on one win. We have another game tomorrow with a blank scoreboard."

Transfixed, she watched as he threaded the straps of her bra through his fingers, winding them up until his hands were bound to her arms.

"You, on the other hand," he continued. "Are exquisite. Every time I see you, there's something new to explore. And I was expecting you to be naked under that dress. Because you were earlier. It was a surprise to find this bra. I like that."

Her throat froze as he bent his head to trace the top swell of one breast with his tongue and then dipped behind the wall of lace to curl the tip around her covered nipple. The visual of him licking her underneath her bra put a shower of sparks at her core.

He was telling her that she was indeed the most gorgeous thing to him and he valued her above his team's winning score. What was she supposed to do with that?

All at once, he yanked on the straps, revealing her breasts to his ravenous gaze, and with his fingers still tangled against her arms, it effectively trapped her. Mercilessly, his hot mouth descended on her, licking her, sucking at her sensitive flesh. Moaning his name, she writhed under the sensuous onslaught.

She was supposed to let herself go, obviously.

The little cries she gasped out increased his urgency. He liked it when she made noise, and she liked the result of it. In a matter of moments, he had her clothes on the floor and her naked body decked out on the bed for his blistering perusal. She squirmed a little as his gaze traveled over her and his arousal bulged in his pants, clearly advertising how much he liked what he saw. But he didn't undress, suit up and plunge in. Instead, he rolled her to her stomach and knelt over her, the whisper of his bare torso skating up her back.

The first exploratory touch of his lips on her spine tightened her whole body. He lifted her hair away and licked at her neck, traveling in lazy, delicious circles as if in no hurry to quench the flames he'd ignited under his lips. He kissed the small of her back and kept going across her buttocks, down one leg until he reached her foot, where he sucked at the arch.

The pressure lit her up as he explored an erogenous zone she hadn't been aware she possessed. Gasping as he added his tongue to the party, she nearly came up off the bed.

Apparently he was going for some kind of record in how many new experiences he could find to give her. She did not have a problem with that.

Fabric rustled, and she turned her head to see him finally shedding his clothes. Since that was her favorite show, she watched with unabashed glee. His body was so beautiful. Powerful, sinewy, solid—she could perfectly imagine him in another age as a model for an Italian sculptor.

"Just getting comfortable," he told her with raised eyebrows, but still he didn't seem to be in a hurry to get to the main course.

No arguments on that front, either.

He knelt back in place and licked his way up her leg, lingering around her knee as if he had all the time in the world and was not in fact driving her insane with the combination of his mouth and whiskers on skin that rarely saw more action than a razor blade in the shower. Under the blitzkrieg of Logan's brand of seduction, however, her core exploded with unfulfilled promise, aching to have that same treatment.

He gave it to her. Slowly, he worked his way north until he hit the crease between her legs, and before she had time to wonder about the logistics involved when she was still facedown, he demonstrated by tonguing her from top to bottom, teasing the flesh of her rear with his fingertips at the same time. White lightning forked through her, and automatically, her hips rolled, seeking more, grinding her nub against the mattress so hard, pinwheels of sharp desire exploded everywhere at once.

His fingers worked magic in tandem with his tongue, and she came so fast she scarcely had time to register it was happening before it ripped her apart inside.

Midquake, Logan covered her with his big, solid body, lifted up her thigh and slid home in one fluid, exquisite shot that had them both groaning. His mouth latched on to her neck as he levered out and pushed back in slowly. It was so amazing that she shut her eyes, sinking into the mattress as he sank into her.

It was a long, slow slide into perfection, and she reveled in it, savored each sharp intake of his breath. The feel of him was like nothing she'd ever experienced, lush and tight. He pushed her closer and closer to the edge, one tiny step at a time, and she'd be fine if this lasted for an eternity.

But his urgency increased, driving hers until she couldn't stand it. Pleas fell from her lips as she met him with backward hip thrusts, desperate for more of him, aching for him to fill her faster, harder, deeper. His fingers slid down between the mattress and her stomach to find her center, doubling her pleasure until she came so hard that she had to bite back the scream he'd ripped from her throat.

His teeth bit into her shoulder as he groaned through his own climax, and his undulations set off another round of ripples in her core until she couldn't feel where she ended and he began.

Collapsing to the mattress, he pulled her tight against him, raining weak little kisses on her shoulder where he'd nipped her, apparently in apology, but she didn't care because her body was in a state of bliss.

But then he stiffened and swore. The string of curses was far more explicit than anything she'd ever heard from him, so she half rolled to check in with him when the gush of wetness against her thigh clued her in on the source of his consternation.

"The condom broke," he said tersely. "Extra strength, my ass."

She bit back a curse of her own. But she managed to choke out, "I'm on the pill. It should be fine."

He didn't look relieved. "I appreciate the pass, but it's not fine. I shouldn't have tried that position. I can't even say I'm sorry, because it can't possibly cover how crappy I feel right now."

"It's not your fault," she insisted. "It was an accident."

Just like the first time she'd gotten pregnant. But she hadn't been on the pill then. In all the years since then, she'd never had so much as a scare. It *would* be fine.

His tentative smile went leagues toward quelling her panic, as did the way he held her like he never intended to let go.

"You're very forgiving," he murmured, his voice gruff with an emotion she wasn't sure she understood. "And don't take this the wrong way, but as accidents go, that was an amazing way to have one."

She nodded against his chest because, yeah. The condom had broken for a reason—the sex had been earth-shattering.

Before she was fully ready to lose his body heat, he

rolled from the bed to dispose of the condom remains, then snagged the bottle of champagne, tore off the foil seal and expertly pried it open. "Shall we drink to how real this relationship just got?"

Her pulse jumped into her throat. "What are you talking about?"

Scouting around near the mini fridge, Logan came up with two flutes and poured the champagne. "If you get pregnant, I'll want to be involved. One hundred percent. Can't get more real than the reality of failed birth control."

She took the flute from his outstretched hand and downed it in one gulp, then held it out for more.

"Nothing has failed." And wouldn't. She could not handle another miscarriage, another guy who was fine with sex but not the responsibility that came with it. Sure, men got in line for orgasms, but midnight feedings? Forget it.

Except that wasn't Logan. He'd just said so.

He glanced at her and tossed back his own champagne. "Would a positive pregnancy test be so bad? I mean, let's play it out. I'd be the baby's father, no matter what. We'd have to be coparents, which is a relationship in and of itself. Why not make it official and just coparent as a couple?"

Her heart ached as the sentiment pinged around inside her, seeking a place to land. She wished all at once that he'd meant he wanted to be with her because he'd developed feelings for her. Because he couldn't stand the thought of being apart. But of course he was just talking about the reality of the consequences, not happily-ever-after tied up with a bow.

Fine. She didn't want that. Or at least she was going to convince herself she didn't. Really soon.

Besides, her confusion didn't matter, because there wasn't going to be a pregnancy. Secretly, she'd always assumed that the horrific nature of her miscarriage had rendered her infertile, but she'd never had it officially checked out.

"I can't possibly tell you how much I appreciate that," she said slowly, keeping the rest of her swirl of thoughts under wraps.

His expression warmed. "I've always dreamed of having a family."

"But we don't have any idea if that's what's going to happen," she countered firmly. "Nor will we for some time. Can't we just put it away for now?"

"Sure." He dinged his newly full champagne glass to hers. "For now."

With all of this academic talk about babies and families and a future with Logan in it, a yearning she'd never allowed to gain traction reared its head, settling into a place in her heart. She was pretty sure it wasn't going away any time soon.

Regardless, she was not the right woman to fulfill his dreams, which meant she *should* find a way to stay far away from Logan McLaughlin.

Except she didn't want to.

Eight

Trinity left to go back to her room, but Logan couldn't sleep. The whole day had been wild, and the conversation they'd just had put the crazy sauce on the sundae.

He couldn't stop thinking about the definition of real and how easily he could envision trying to create something that sounded a lot like that with Trinity.

This whole situation had unraveled alarmingly fast.

He'd always thought he'd get married first, then he and his wife would eagerly get on with baby making. They'd take their first pregnancy test together and she'd throw herself into his arms when it turned positive. Happiness would ensue.

Obviously the broken condom had presented another possibility that he might have to get used to—being with Trinity long-term as coparents and maybe more.

Was that what he wanted? Was that what *she* wanted? They hadn't really finished the conversation, not to his satisfaction, but he'd been willing to shelve it for the time being, since there was little reason to discuss it at this point.

Except for the fact that he *liked* the idea of having something real more than he should.

His chest hurt as he reminded himself that he and Trinity weren't at all suited for anything that smacked of real, no matter how he defined it. He'd known from the beginning that they weren't right for each other. Nothing had changed.

And yet everything had changed.

By unspoken agreement, they continued the rest of the trip as planned. Trinity came to the games, his guys played baseball and reporters took pictures afterward of the general manager and his girlfriend. Every time Logan felt like pulling her into his arms to lay a kiss on her that would communicate how much he still wanted her, she came willingly, and he liked her in his bed better than he should as well.

The heat between them sizzled for the camera and sizzled behind closed doors. It was like they couldn't quit each other now that the boundaries had evaporated.

The Mustangs won both games. Naturally. Because of Trinity, he was convinced. His team was convinced, too, and treated her like royalty, sending her flowers and chocolate, cards with funny cartoons. The Mustangs' shortstop, the one who was dating the supermodel against Logan's wishes, convinced his girlfriend to call Trinity about doing ad work for Fyra Cosmetics as a token of goodwill.

When Logan asked her about it, Trinity grinned and told him she had a meeting with the model's manager next week. All in all, it felt like a great match, she said. At night, she worked on a campaign for a new product that she chattered about endlessly during her midnight treks to his hotel room. He loved listening to her talk about the things that mattered to her.

On the plane ride home to Dallas, Trinity sat next to him and they held hands like they had on the way to the West Coast. Somehow it was different. As if the broken condom had created an unspoken agreement that they were testing out how things might go if they did slap a "real" label on their relationship.

If anyone had asked him how he'd like the concept of Trinity Forrester as a permanent lover, he'd have said there was no way it would work. But the last few days proved that was a lie.

What was he supposed to do about that? Unless she got pregnant, there was no call to have any sort of discussion about labels.

Maybe he didn't have to do anything. Maybe he could just let it ride, see how things played out. No one had breathed a word about stopping what they were doing.

Before he could think of a reason not to, he reached out and brushed her jaw with a thumb. Intimately. She didn't miss it and raised her brows at him.

"I wanted to touch you," he murmured. "Sue me."

She laughed. "You don't have to apologize for touching me. I like it. So no lawyers needed."

"Then you should know I plan to keep doing it once we're home," he advised her.

"Oh? I'll be curious how that's going to work when we both have jobs."

"Yeah. We'll have to adjust. Give some things up, maybe." When she made a noise in her throat, he did a double take. "What, you can't make our relationship a priority? We're still trying to generate publicity. Right?"

"Lest you forget, I'm an executive running a multi-million-dollar cosmetics company." She spiked her tone with enough irony to get her point across. "I told you I was working on a new product campaign. I have a strict deadline. Some of us don't get to take trips to the Bay Area and stay in fancy hotels for our work. And when we accompany those of you who do, we have to burn the midnight oil to make up for it."

"I want to spend time with you."

That had not been what he'd meant to say. But now that it was out there…he couldn't help but be curious what she'd do with it.

She scowled as the plane flew through a thick bunch of clouds, temporarily throwing the cabin into shadow. "My career is more important than breezing by your bed to pick up a couple of orgasms."

That wasn't all they had between them, and she knew that wasn't what he'd meant. Her refusal to admit things had shifted between them rankled more than he'd like, but he couldn't force her to be honest. He could only be smart enough to outwit her.

And she hadn't pulled her hand from his, a telling point that he had no problem exploiting.

"Your career is definitely more important than orgasms," he agreed smoothly. "But they shouldn't be exclusive of one another. After all, you found a way to seamlessly integrate one with my job. Let me do the same for you."

"I do like the way you think." There was still a note of caution in her voice. "What do you have in mind?"

"You know the guys need you, right? You're their Blarney stone." He pulled her hand to his mouth for what should have been a quick kiss to her fingertips, but he liked the taste of them so much, he kept them there and talked around them. "Come to the home games with me. I'll pick you up. It's on the way."

"That's not putting my career first, Logan. What happens to your luck if I say no?" Her fingertips curled against his lips in a deliberate caress that immediately made him sorry they were on a plane with a hundred other people.

"You can't. They need you." He was pretty sure she heard the unspoken *I need you* in that as well, but he didn't care. "I'll make it worth your while. Look what I've already done for your career. Seven percent increase in sales isn't anything to sneeze at. I'll figure out a way to blend work and orgasms to your satisfaction. Trust me."

"Okay." She snuggled down in the seat. "It's good for us to keep being seen together anyway."

"Absolutely," he agreed and didn't bother to hide his smile. He'd definitely won that round, and if she wanted to pretend like they were still seeing each other for publicity reasons, he could live with that.

Ticket sales were at an all-time high after a three-game winning streak and the extra boost from the publicity surrounding the road trip he'd taken with Trinity. When he got back to his office at the ballpark, he dived headfirst into his job, which he'd sorely neglected lately. Trinity wasn't the only one with deadlines. Some crucial trade agreements had finally landed on his desk—also thanks to the positive publicity his team had recently seen—and he worked through those without pausing to think about her laugh more than about a dozen times. A personal best.

Trinity came to the games and the Mustangs didn't lose. Their winning streak stretched to five games. Then eight. They were on fire, a flame eclipsed only by the one between Logan and Trinity as they burned up the sheets after games. Sometimes she brought her laptop and worked while the team tore the competition to shreds. Sometimes she put it away and cheered alongside him, occasionally coming up with relevant comments about the action on the field, which showed that she was learning baseball whether she'd meant to or not.

With his fake girlfriend by his side, Logan hadn't watched a game from the dugout since the Mustangs played Oakland. It was a huge shift in his managerial style, one that his coaches hadn't failed to comment on. He let them think it was because Trinity had caught him by the neck and wouldn't let go. Secretly, he was convinced it was part of the good luck that she'd brought them. It was simple math. If he went down to the field, they'd lose. So he stuck to his box and sometimes used the seventh-inning stretch to make sure Trinity felt like she was getting her share of orgasms out of the deal.

The subject of the broken condom hadn't come up, and he trusted she'd tell him if there was something to report. Everyone was getting what they wanted.

A call from the commissioner's office burst Logan's bubble. Cal Johnson, his star player, was the subject of a doping investigation and would likely be suspended pending a long string of meetings that Logan had just been cordially invited to attend. The devastation this news would create could not be overstated. He'd go to the meetings and then see what was what.

Without pausing to question the decision, he drove from his office to Trinity's condo, parked and texted her.

I'm outside. Can I come up?

Her response was immediate.

Of course.

When she opened the door, he forgot everything he'd been about to say, even though he'd seen her yesterday.

She looked so good, gorgeous in a pair of jeans and a T-shirt, which signified she'd had no plans to go anywhere this evening. Of course she had on her facial armor, but her eye makeup was more subtle than normal. But even if she had done her Cleopatra thing, it was part of her whole package, one that he could secretly admit he liked on her. She was bold, outrageous, and he couldn't get enough of her.

"What's up?" she asked, and it was obvious from her expectant expression that she'd assumed the reason for his visit had something to do with their publicity campaign.

"I wanted to see you."

Suddenly, he felt foolish showing up unannounced when in reality, he didn't know what was up. He'd done more wicked things with this woman than with any other woman of his acquaintance, but that didn't give him any better ability to understand how to communicate with her. What was he supposed to do, come right out and admit that he'd been dealt a devastating blow and she was the only one he wanted to be with right now? Because that felt way too real for what they were doing here.

Something shifted in her expression. "Then come in."

He must be more transparent than he thought. He'd never just dropped by like this. Their association started and ended with being seen together for publicity purposes, which he was using as an excuse to continue having sex without committing to anything else.

This was crossing a line. An irreversible line.

He came in.

"I brought you something." Before he changed his

mind, he fished the jewelry box from his coat pocket. "To say thank you."

"For what?" She eyed the long flat box like he'd pulled out a tarantula. "There aren't any reporters here to capture this moment for all posterity. Sure you don't want to wait and give that to me later?"

"No," he growled. "I don't want to wait. This is personal and I don't want it on camera. I…"

Have no idea what I'm doing here.

Instead of floundering around like a moron, he snapped the lid open and showed her the eight-carat diamond necklace he'd painstakingly picked out at the jeweler earlier that day. Before he'd gotten the call from the commissioner's office, finding something to commemorate the Mustangs' eight-game winning streak— a club record—had been his top priority.

"What the hell, Logan." Fire flashed from her gaze, which was not the reaction he'd been looking for. "You can't give me something like that. It's gorgeous."

He couldn't help the laugh that bubbled out. "You have a funny way of showing your appreciation."

Cautiously, as if afraid it might bite her, she held out one finger and touched the teardrop stone. "It's pink. Like the flower you gave me."

Yeah, because the instant he'd seen it, he'd thought of her and how it would look against her beautiful skin. "Does that mean you like it?"

"It's too much for a thank-you." But she nodded. "I like it."

"Shut up and let me put it on you then."

She held up her hair and presented her back without further argument, thank God. He drew the fine chain around her neck to clasp it, then took advantage of the absence of hair to kiss her exposed flesh. She didn't move away. One second against her skin became two, and that was the extent of his self-control.

He mouthed his way to her ear and yanked her backward into his embrace so he could thoroughly ravage her. She melted into his arms and he walked her toward her bedroom, a path he knew from the handful of times they'd ended up naked after games.

But this was the first time they weren't high on the public displays of affection they'd indulged in. The first time he had no excuse to be here other than the obvious—he couldn't stay away.

When he hit the edge of the bed, he lifted his mouth from her neck long enough to strip her and himself, then rolled her to the coverlet. He reached for the condoms she kept in her bedside drawer and then pleased them both by sucking at every one of her erogenous zones until she was wet and swollen enough to take him fully. And she did, with a little gasp that thrilled him.

That pink diamond sparkled in the low light from the neon outside her floor-to-ceiling view of downtown Dallas. He'd never given a woman jewelry before, and the sight of the chain around her neck when she had nothing else on her body except him put a glow in his chest that felt a hell of lot like something that shouldn't be there. As he sank into Trinity again and again, building the fire until they were both moaning with it, the significance of what was happening here overwhelmed him.

This relationship was as real as it got. And he liked that.

He refused to take time to sort that out as she bowed up, thrusting her breasts high. This, he understood, and he took one of those rosy nipples between his teeth, rolling it almost savagely as he thrust faster, spiraling his hips the way he knew drove her insane, silently powering her to a climax that would trigger his. Because they knew each other's bodies, how to please, how to gratify. Physically, they were a perfect match, but not in any other way.

So why was he so wrapped up in her?

They exploded together, and he bit his lip to keep the wash of emotions inside, where they belonged. Afterward, he spooned her into his body the way they both liked it, and she curled into his embrace.

"What's the real reason you came over tonight?" she murmured.

His eyes shuttered automatically. Would she ever *not* be so good at reading him? He couldn't do that with her. It wasn't fair. But that didn't give him any better ability to lie to her, either.

"Johnson is probably going to be suspended. I'm..." What was he? Disappointed? Frustrated? Furious? "Not sure what's going to happen to the team as a result."

"That's crappy." She squeezed his arm with her soft hand. "What did he do?"

"Performance-enhancing drugs, or so they say. They're against the rules. I'm cooperating with the investigation, but I have to go to New York for some meetings."

With neither of them at the away games, the Mustangs' winning streak would most likely come to an end. A brutal but inescapable truth.

"Do you want me to come with you?" she asked, and the note of genuine concern in her voice unfolded all the emotion inside that he'd been trying to keep under wraps.

Silently, he kissed her shoulder, worried something inappropriate—like *yes*—would slip out if he tried to speak. The fact that she'd offered meant more to him than he could say.

Because she deserved an answer, he finally choked out, "No need."

She rolled in his arms and glanced at him, her eyes warm and huge. "This is really bothering you, isn't it?"

He shook his head. Why he'd denied it, when it was obvious she'd already figured that out, was a mystery to him. "I don't know. Yeah. Maybe. I feel like I should have known or something."

Of course doping went on. It was no different today than when he'd been pitching. Everyone knew who was doing it and who wasn't. Logan had never touched the stuff. Fortunately, he'd been good enough that he'd never been pressured like some of the guys.

Maybe Johnson had felt some of that pressure. Had Logan inadvertently been one of those pressure points?

"You didn't do this, darling. It's not on you."

"I'm the boss," he said simply. "And I feel like I failed at keeping my team strong. My dad ran a billion-dollar company for years and years, and he never let anything like this happen to him."

"You're not your dad, Logan. And this is a totally different industry with different rules and strategies. You have to lead like you." She fanned her fingers across his cheek, lightly caressing as she spoke the gospel according to Trinity. "You can't compare yourself to someone who's gone, either. You don't know what might have happened if he'd lived. Maybe someone in his organization would have been brought up on insider trading. Would that have been his fault for hiring someone who made bad choices?"

No. Of course not.

"You're not allowed to make me feel better with logic," he grumbled.

But her point was not lost on him, and some of the

weight lifted. Exactly what he'd hoped would happen when he'd gotten into his car to come over here. Somehow, she made life…brighter.

She laughed and kissed him sweetly. "What if I make you feel better a whole other way?"

Her legs tangled with his, and her wandering hands left no doubt how she intended to make good on that. Since he was pretty sure she could deliver, he let her.

But the whole time he was pondering some huge questions of his own—like, if he wasn't his dad and it was okay to do things his own way, did that mean he could admit he didn't want a nice, unassuming woman? And that maybe the reason he'd never met the right woman had to do with the fact that he hadn't met Trinity yet?

But the most important question of all was, what would she say if he told her that despite all of his objections to the contrary, he was falling for her?

Logan left to go to New York, and Trinity spent a lot of time pretending she didn't miss him.

Funny how she'd never watched sports in her life, would have claimed under oath she hated the concept of grown men throwing balls around in some macho contest. But for God knew what reason, she couldn't go to sleep at night unless a baseball game was on in the background.

The Mustangs' winning streak ended as Logan had predicted that night before he'd gone to the meetings. But they won the next one even though she wasn't at the game to provide good luck, which was such a silly concept. Of course she'd never say that to Logan's face, since he took his superstition so seriously.

He texted her occasionally with updates, but there

was nothing in the messages that indicated his state of mind or whether he was thinking about her like she thought about him. Days stretched into a week, but neither of them approached the subject about when he was coming home or if they'd pick up where they left off when he did.

The Formula-47 marketing presentation had been rescheduled a couple of times due to everyone's crazy travel schedules, but finally, Cass threw a dart at a day and told everyone they better attend or else.

That morning, Trinity had a nearly impossible time dragging herself out of bed. Despite having subscribed to her cable channel's baseball package—which she would deny if anyone called her on it—there hadn't been one game on the night before, and sleep had come fitfully.

While she was busy not sleeping, her mind kept turning over whether Logan was using this trip to New York as a break—from her. Fyra's numbers were up. Logan's ticket sales had gone through the roof. There was little reason to continue seeing each other. But she didn't want to be done. Selfishly, she'd used their publicity campaign to pretend their relationship was real, and she'd liked it far more than she'd expected, especially given that it had been a very long time since she'd spent time with a man outside of bed.

As she dressed in a teal-green suit and did her makeup, she tried on the idea of casually mentioning to Logan that maybe they could still see each other occasionally, if their schedules permitted. Which sounded crappy in her head and probably wouldn't be improved by saying out loud. The problem was that she didn't know how to tell him that she wanted something more, something real, when she had no clue how to do either one.

When she got to the boardroom, Cass was already there, keying in the virtual meeting details on her laptop. Alex and Harper popped up on the split screen TV.

Harper blinked. "Holy crap. What is that around your neck, Trin?"

Fingering the pink diamond that she couldn't bear to take off, Trinity frowned and opened her mouth to say it was a loaner, and to her absolute mortification, she burst into tears instead.

Cass shoved her chair back and rounded the table to pull Trinity into an embrace, a trick and a half since her expanding belly got in the way. But Cass pulled it off with her typical togetherness, murmuring soothing words until the waterworks subsided somewhat.

"I'm sorry," Trinity sputtered. "I don't know what that was about."

Alex and Harper made noises and talked at the same time until Cass shushed them.

"I think I speak for everyone," Cass said with a smirk, "when I say we've all been there. Let me guess. Things with Logan aren't so fake after all."

"That obvious?" Trinity thought about putting her head down on the boardroom table, right on top of the printed materials she'd brought for the campaign. "I don't know what's real and what's fake and why I'm upset about it or what to do about it. I can't sleep and I'm exhausted all the time."

Cass cocked her head. "Have you talked to him about what you're feeling?"

"I can't," she wailed. "He's in New York at meetings about a very big problem for his team and I just want him to come home and sleep with me, like really sleep. I want to wake up with him in the morning and have coffee and just be together. We've never done that. I don't do that with anyone. I don't know why I want that now. It's ridiculous to feel so clingy and out of sorts and—"

"Trinity." Alex's voice rang out from the TV. "Breathe. That sounds like hormones talking. Maybe after your cycle, you'll feel better."

"I'm not on my period," Trinity snapped. Like Alex knew anything about that. She'd only been pregnant for forever. "I'm not even due to start until—"

The first. What was today? Trinity glanced at her phone. The sixth. *Oh, my God.* It was the *sixth.* And she was always so regular.

Panic slammed through her chest as she did the math. It had been almost three weeks since the broken condom incident. With all the baseball games and juggling the Bloom campaign and missing Logan, she'd totally lost track of the calendar.

"I'm sensing we're having a revelation in the works," Harper said cheerfully. "Should we reconvene another day while you go take a pregnancy test?"

A pregnancy test.

The phrase made literally no sense, as if Harper had spoken Swahili. Trinity hadn't taken a pregnancy test in eight years. Because she'd never had the slightest doubt about what the result would be.

"I have a couple of extras in my desk," Cass offered. "From when Gage and I were trying. If you want to know now."

Numbly, Trinity nodded at the woman who had been her best friend since eleventh grade. The distance that had grown between them due to their very different life circumstances vanished. There was no one else she'd want holding her hand as she verified whether her problems with Logan were exponentially greater than she'd supposed.

After an eternity that was really more like ten minutes later, she had her answer.

Amazing how she could actually see the plus sign though all the blurry tears. *Pregnant.* With Logan McLaughlin's baby.

"Should I say congratulations or I'm sorry?" Cass asked quietly.

Trinity didn't answer, just tossed the positive test onto the counter and sank to the ground to put her head on her bent knees. Her whole body shook with a cocktail of nerves and wonder and disbelief and hope. But she had to squash that. Now.

There was no way she'd carry to term. Her body didn't work like that. The little miracle inside would be snatched from her before it had a chance to form, and she'd have to deal with it. Again.

Oh, God. A new round of horror tore through her. What was she going to tell Logan? She'd promised she'd let him know if this happened, but that had been back when she'd been ridiculously certain her birth control would stick. Obviously her pills had failed her and her secret belief that she couldn't get pregnant again was false.

"I don't understand how this happened," she sniffled out brokenly to Cass through the sobs still racking her chest. "What am I going to do?"

"Do you want the baby?" Cass asked, cutting to the chase in her usual style. And of course that was the most important question, and Trinity knew the answer instantly.

"Of course. But that's not in the cards—"

"Stop. You don't know that. You're going to get the best prenatal care possible," Cass countered. "And then we're going to stage sticky-baby sit-ins, ply you with peanut butter, whatever it takes to make this work for you this time. Your womb has had eight years to develop, to mature."

The words filtered through the crushing pain in Trinity's chest but did nothing to absolve it. She couldn't do this, couldn't bear the idea of eventually—soon—having absolute confirmation that she was indeed as broken as she'd always assumed.

But what if Cass was right? What if the baby actually stuck? What if this was the start of the most amazing chapter in her life? For today, right now, she was pregnant with Logan's baby.

Fledgling emotions that she'd never allowed herself to embrace welled up and over with the realization that she had a piece of him inside her, that the universe had conspired to make their relationship real in the most wonderful way possible.

She could admit that when he talked about having a family, she wanted that, too.

And then she realized. She couldn't tell him.

Instead of fearing that he'd take off, the opposite would be true. He'd want to be there every step, to go to the doctor's appointments, pick out a crib. That's who he was, and he'd be devastated if—when—she miscarried. And then she'd have to deal with it alone, because what else would bind them together? He'd be done with her at that point, forever.

She could not take the double loss.

They had nothing between them except a successful publicity campaign and a mass of cells that would never become anything but another heartbreak.

Nine

New York had been brutal. Johnson's forty-five-game suspension destroyed the Mustangs' morale, precisely as Logan had expected when he'd received the verdict.

He'd appealed, naturally, which meant extending his stay longer than he would have liked, but the appeal would take a while to work itself out. Plus, it was strictly a formality; the inquest had Johnson dead to rights, including video of him frequenting the clinic that sold the PEDs.

The whole thing was disheartening.

Once a day, he'd reached for the phone to call Trinity and beg her to fly to New York, just so he could see her. So he could touch her. Hear her laugh, lose himself in her sweet body at the end of a long day of meetings that ripped his team apart. He wanted to be with her, to let her make the horrible reality better.

He wanted more.

But he never dialed. It wasn't fair to start that discussion over the phone. So he held off until he got back to Dallas. While waiting for his luggage to appear from the bowels of the airport, he texted her.

At the airport. Can I come by Fyra to see you?

God, that was bold. Trinity had a job. *He* had a job. Jumping off a plane and driving straight to her wasn't smart. But it was the only thing he wanted to do.

She didn't text him back right away. Probably in a meeting. He went home, which was what he should have done anyway. The house smelled stale and musty from disuse, even though he'd only been gone for a few weeks. The emptiness crawled onto his last nerve, and he hated it. Why had he bought such a monstrosity of a house when he had no one to share it with?

What was today? Thursday? Maybe he'd see if Trinity would ditch work tomorrow and spend a three-day weekend at his place. He'd never brought a woman home, and he could picture Trinity draped across his bed with frightening ease. She'd like his giant marble garden tub, too, he had a feeling. Or rather, she'd like what he did to her while she was in it, which was practically the same thing.

They could order takeout, or maybe he'd cook steaks on the massive grill in the outdoor kitchen that overlooked the pool. Afterward, he'd strip her down to her bare skin, pick her up and lower her into the hot tub at the north end of the pool, cleverly tied into the design via an outcropping of natural river rock.

He checked his phone, but she hadn't texted him back yet. His plane had landed four hours ago. Maybe she hadn't seen the message. He called her this time.

No answer. Fine. She was busy. He'd been gone for a while, and they hadn't really talked much since he'd left Dallas.

Thursday stretched into Friday, and he made the long trek from Prosper to his office in Arlington. The team was in Pittsburgh playing a three-game series and getting their asses handed to them. Myra had some very depressing numbers regarding the decline in ticket sales, which of course had taken a hit with the double whammy of losing the Mustangs' marquee slugger and the lack of new, steamier pictures from the club's favorite poster boy.

But oddly, the most unsettling thing in Logan's world right now was the distinct absence of Trinity Forrester. He missed her keenly, had for weeks, and he could not seem to focus on anything but the three, maybe four, unanswered text messages he'd sent since landing yesterday.

He'd made a mistake not calling her while he'd been in New York, that much was clear. He had to fix it. But if she wasn't responding to his messages or the voice mail he'd left, it was entirely possible she'd lost her phone. It happened.

By Friday night, he couldn't stand it any longer and drove to her condo. Stupid. He couldn't get into the building unless she buzzed him in, but she didn't respond. He could see her Porsche in her designated spot in the parking garage from here.

His temper flared. She was here but not interested in seeing him? That was not cool.

The gods of security smiled on him when a well-dressed couple came out of the building and glanced at the flowers in his hand as he skulked about outside.

"Is she not answering? You must be early, then," the

elderly woman surmised with a misty smile, apparently drawing her own conclusions about the situation. "That's so nice to see."

"Yes, ma'am," he replied, because there was really no other answer.

"Come on, then." She winked and held the door open. Once he was inside…he had no idea if Trinity would even answer the door.

One way to find out. He took the elevator to the fifteenth floor and banged on the door in case she had music on. She answered almost immediately, clearly frazzled, her hair mussed and her ratty sweatshirt a marked contrast to her normal style.

And she wasn't wearing any makeup. She'd literally never been more beautiful. He could not tear his gaze from her.

All the color drained from her bare face. "Logan."

Not expecting him, obviously.

"Surprise." He held out the flowers. His pulse hammered in his throat, and he wanted to sweep her into his arms so badly his hands were shaking.

She eyed the bouquet, her expression frozen. Why wasn't she taking the flowers?

"You, um…didn't respond to any of my messages."

Which judging by the ice chips currently jetting from her eyes, she already knew. "I've been busy. You shouldn't have come by."

The long process of dealing with the PED inquest and fatigue and sheer confusion swirled together to step on Logan's temper. "I wanted to see you. Can I at least ask why the reverse isn't true?"

Warily, she shrugged, but not before he noted her expression. She wasn't as unaffected as she'd like him to think. It settled his temper a touch.

"It was a good time to break things off. I really thought you were on the same page with your lack of communication over the last few weeks."

That speared him right through the chest. She had been avoiding him. On purpose.

"My fault," he agreed smoothly, mystified why there was this distance between them. It felt like she was trying to push him out.

"Let me make it up to you," he said with a smile. "And I don't mean in bed. Unless that's what you want."

Her eyelids shuttered, hiding her thoughts from him. But then, he'd never been able to read her, and the frustration of it almost snapped the stems of the blooms in his hand before he realized the pain in his palm came from the thorns digging into his flesh.

"I'll pass, thanks."

Something was very wrong. Fatigue pulled at her eyes, and all at once, he clued in that her death grip on the door frame wasn't designed to keep him out—she was holding herself up. Alarmed, he made his own guess about why she wasn't wearing makeup. *Idiot.* When her face had drained of color, he'd assumed she'd been unhappy to see him, but in reality, she was sick.

"Is it the flu or something more serious?" he asked.

"It's…nothing," she lied when it was so clearly something. And then she weaved as her knees buckled.

Tossing the flowers, he scooped her up in his arms and shut the door with his foot, refusing to recall the last time he'd done this—when they'd ended up naked together. He couldn't even enjoy the fact that he was touching her again after an eternity apart.

She felt so insubstantial in his arms, weakly protesting as he strode to her bedroom and laid her out on the bed, then wedged in next to her to stroke her hair.

"What is it? Can I get you something? Water or—"

"No, I'm fine," she whispered but her eyes closed and her head pushed into his palm like a cat seeking affection. He was more than happy to give it to her. It pleased him to have his hands on her, even in this small way.

The longer he stroked, the more she relaxed and the less his chest hurt. If she was sick, it explained why she hadn't immediately jumped on his text messages. Probably she'd had one of those silly moments where she'd railed against having him come over and see her without makeup, like he cared about that.

Didn't she know she was beautiful to him regardless?

All at once, she moaned, and it wasn't the good kind. Helplessly, he watched as she turned over, curling in on herself. That was not going to work. But what should he do?

Leaving her on the bed, eyes still squeezed tight, he ventured into her bathroom to see if she had some kind of prescription or over-the-counter medication. And maybe if he found something, it could clue him in to what the hell was wrong with her.

There was nothing on the counter except a small mirrored tray covered with tiny, expensive-looking bottles of perfume. The drawers on the right side of the espresso wood–and–marble vanity held her cosmetics in an array of holders and shelves and various hidey-holes that made his skin crawl, so he shut them and pulled open the cabinet on the left.

Hair spray and various other female things lined the bottom. Including a small white plastic wand with a blue tip. It was face up and he could easily read the words Pregnant and Not Pregnant, next to a plus sign and a negative sign. The big circle prominently featured a blue plus sign.

Logan's brain went fuzzy as his knees gave out and he plopped onto the bathroom floor, half on the short-pile bath mat, half on the white marble tile.

Trinity was *pregnant*. That's what was wrong with her.

"I didn't want you to find out this way." Her low voice floated to him from the doorway.

He glanced up to see her standing there, leaning on the door frame as if it was the only thing keeping her from joining him on the floor.

"What way did you plan for me to find out?" It came out a little harsher than he'd intended, but she'd promised to tell him if this happened, and after ignoring all his messages—

The first tendril of blackness snaked through his stomach as he stared at her flushed face. The lack of welcome. The way she could barely look at him. The cold silence on her end of the line once he'd returned from New York.

"You weren't going to tell me, were you?" How he got that sentence out around the baseball in his throat was nothing short of miraculous.

After the longest pause in history, she shook her head. "But not because I didn't want to. Because—" Something choked off her words and she bent nearly double, scrubbing at her face with the heel of her hand.

He had no trouble filling in that blank. Because it wasn't his baby.

Dark, ugly jealousy flooded his chest as he stared at her. While he'd been falling for her and trying to reconcile all of these strange, wondrous emotions, she'd been seeing other people. Why wouldn't she? They hadn't established any exclusivity. He'd just assumed...

And look where that had gotten him. He followed

the rules and she broke them. She'd never had any interest in having a family, not the way he did. They were always going to be opposites and pregnancy was an irreversible showstopper.

Thank God he hadn't told her he wanted more like he'd half considered while in New York, or this gutting would definitely be worse. Though he had a hard time seeing how when it felt like his stomach was on fire.

How was it possible that he'd been trying to figure out how to take the next step with her while she'd been backing away as fast as she could?

The longer Logan sat on her bathroom floor by the open cabinet, the more Trinity genuinely thought she might throw up right then and there.

Morning sickness had picked a hell of a time to whack her. She'd called in sick to work, a first, but Cass had totally understood despite the fact that she'd never once done it herself.

Trinity was too miserable to care that she was not the champion pregnant woman among Fyra's executives. Now Logan had forced her to deal with him, too.

When she'd opened the door, the first thing that had slammed through her body was relief. *Thank God.* He was here and she didn't have to do this by herself. All she'd wanted to do was fall into his arms, to babble endless words about how much she'd missed him, how beautiful and strong and solid he was. How she knew he was going to make everything better.

Good thing she hadn't. As soon as she realized he was in the bathroom going through her cabinets, she'd hurled herself out of bed to stop him. But it was too late. And judging by the look on his face, this pregnancy conversation was not going to end well.

He was furious.

"You didn't want to tell me?" he ground out through clenched teeth. "You didn't think I had a right to know?"

She'd never heard his voice sound so tightly controlled, so much like he was holding himself in. It frightened her a little. Hadn't he said he wanted kids and had every intention of being in the baby's life? Or had she completely misremembered that?

"I…"

Have no defense.

Really, she didn't. It was only due to her own cowardice that she hadn't told him right away, and as a result, she'd ended up alone over the last couple of days anyway. Nausea turned her stomach over and threatened to expel the chicken noodle soup she'd eaten earlier to settle it.

"I can't do this now," she whispered and sank to the hardwood floor outside her bathroom. She'd thought… well, it didn't matter that she'd thought maybe there was a chance things might magically work out.

"Or ever?" he countered. "You didn't want to tell me because you realized our publicity campaign would be over, right?"

Stricken, she stared at him. He thought she'd kept this quiet because she was worried about *publicity*? "That makes no sense, Logan. Why would our opportunities for publicity end just because I'm pregnant?"

As if that was the most important thing to hash out. He hadn't asked how she was dealing with it, how far along she was. Whether she'd gone to the doctor. None of the things she'd expected. His reaction was almost… cold.

A shiver worked down her spine. This situation was unraveling fast. Potential for miscarriage aside, now that he knew, she'd honestly expected more of a positive reaction.

"Oh, you're right," he said silkily in a dark tone that did not sound like that of a man happy to find out he was going to be father. "Why not continue faking our relationship no matter what? Should be easy. We've been doing it this long, pretending we like each other for the camera. What's an unexpected pregnancy between *friends*?"

There was nothing friendly about his sarcasm, and his point cut through her. He'd been faking it this whole time. While she'd been fighting her feelings and trying not to fall for him, he hadn't been engaged in a similar battle. She'd created a fantasy in her head because he'd given her a few intense looks during sex.

Nothing about their relationship was real. Hadn't she learned that lesson by now? She should have. The pain radiating through her chest was exactly what she deserved for daring to pretend they'd been building something neither of them could walk away from.

"My mistake," she said, proud of how substantial her voice sounded when in reality, her insides felt hollowed out. Fitting that she could fake even this. "I misspoke. It seems as if it might be best if we ended our public relationship. The sooner the better, so we have time to work on a recovery plan."

"And our private one, too." Then he twisted the knife in farther before she had a chance to fully process that. "That's why you didn't tell me, I'm guessing. You knew it would be the end of us and opted to keep the devastation to a minimum."

Miserably, she nodded and shut her eyes against the blackness spreading across Logan's face. At the end of the day, that was the gist of it. She hadn't told him out of pure selfishness. She'd eventually miscarry anyway and there'd be nothing holding them together. But even that had been imaginary, because there was nothing holding them together now, either, apparently.

Why not let him leave now instead of then? It was a simple matter of timing.

Obviously he didn't want her or the baby. Or maybe he didn't want the baby strictly because it was hers. Hadn't he always said she wasn't his type? They were ill suited for each other. That was why he'd always asked her to dress differently, after all.

"I can't do this now, either," he growled. "Congratulations. You've successfully provoked my temper. I have to get out of here."

She scuttled out of the doorway so he could stride from the bathroom. Without a backward glance, he stormed from her condo and took the majority of her heart with him.

The only piece left was tucked in next to the fetus still growing in her womb. For now. She lived in fear of the day she'd wake up in her own blood and know that she was once again alone.

Trinity forced herself to lie in the bed she'd made, continuing to go to work and do her job, but it was far more rote than she would like to admit. Her body hurt all the time and her creativity fled along with her ability to feel anything other than miserable. Thankfully, she'd gotten far enough along in the Bloom campaign that her creative team could run with it.

Logan didn't call. She kept her phone in her hand constantly and cursed every time it buzzed and there wasn't a message from him.

Funny how when he'd been trying to reach her after

returning from New York, each contact point had sliced through her and she'd prayed he'd stop, that he'd leave her alone to figure out how to manage this huge, terrible secret between them.

Now that he had actually broken off all communication, each moment of silence cut even deeper. He really wanted nothing to do with her or the baby. Nor would he be a strong hand to hold when she miscarried. He wasn't the man she'd thought he was, and that was perhaps the worst realization of all.

Late one afternoon, Trinity roused herself out of her stupor to help Harper and Alex throw a baby shower for Cass. It was good for her to stop stewing over things she couldn't change, and it was definitely better to quit dwelling on what had not yet happened, which she had zero control over. Plus, Cass was her best friend, no matter how distant they'd been lately.

Maybe it was time to change that.

Harper flew in from Zurich for the occasion and coupled the trip with some on-site meetings with her lab staff. Alex's twin girls weren't technically due for another six weeks, but her doctor in Washington was convinced she'd deliver any day now, so she participated remotely. As soon as she had her babies, Fyra's CFO would take six months maternity leave.

Once, Trinity would have labeled that ludicrous and pretended a woman's career should trump everything else. When really, it was solely Trinity who had grabbed on to her job with both hands in lieu of seeking what her friends seemed to fall into so easily—a supportive relationship with a husband who loved his wife and couldn't wait to be a father.

Now she could readily admit she was so jealous she couldn't stand it.

As the four pregnant executives gathered in one of the conference rooms at the company they'd built from the ground up, Trinity had enough energy to hug Harper, whom she hadn't seen in person in quite some time. Never would Trinity have thought they'd all have pregnancy in common a few weeks ago. Fyra's chief science officer had finally developed a belly, which she patted when Trinity commented on it.

"Dante calls him Amoeba. I tried to get him to quit, but he thinks it's hilarious." Harper rolled her eyes at her absent husband, whom she'd left behind in Zurich, but only because he was filming his television show about the science of attraction. Otherwise, he'd have been following his wife around like an overprotective caveman, wearing a goofy, adoring expression that communicated how very much he loved Harper and their baby.

Obviously Trinity could use some pointers on how to find a man like that—she should have been watching Dr. Gates's show all along. Then it wouldn't have been such a shock to find out Logan hadn't been falling for her all along like she'd been for him.

Tears pricked at her eyelids and she let them fall. Didn't matter how hard she tried to hold it all in, everything came gushing out anyway. Why fight it?

"Oh, honey." Harper rubbed a sympathetic hand along Trinity's forearm. "It gets better."

Cass settled into the chair on Trinity's other side and drew her into a hug, bopping the balloons tied to nearly every surface of the room. "You still haven't talked to Logan?"

Trinity shook her head against Cass's shoulder without fear, because Harper's combo foundation and powder was bulletproof against smearing. Maybe that could be the genesis of a new ad campaign. But her thoughts refused to jell, like everything else in her life. Her creativity had left the moment Logan walked out of her condo. Which was of course appropriate, because he'd become her muse along with her reason to breathe, the father of her baby and the sole thing that occupied her thoughts 24-7. Ironic, much?

"You have to talk to him," Alex called from the TV screen. "He has legal obligations to you and the baby regardless of whether he likes it or not. Child support, if nothing else. Phillip is texting you the name of a lawyer right now who will get you everything you deserve."

What did she deserve? Half of Logan's fortune? Season tickets to the Mustangs' home games? To be alone because she'd spent her adult life pretending she didn't want the fantasy she'd created with him?

Cass nodded as Trinity sat back in her chair. "Also, things are not always how they seem. I thought Gage and I were destined not to work. And we tried it twice. I never would have predicted that he'd storm into my office with an engagement ring in his pocket."

That was different. Everyone had known that Gage had it bad for Fyra's CEO.

"Phillip kidnapped me on the way home from the hospital, after that time I passed out, so he could talk me out of divorcing him," Alex threw in. "Men can be very unpredictable when they decide they want something."

Harper laughed. "Dante flew from Zurich to Los Angeles, then to Dallas almost back-to-back to tell me he'd screwed up when he left. I've been in love with the man for ten years. I would have taken a phone call. But it was nice to feel like I was his number-one priority."

"You all deserve the happiness you've found," Trinity sniffed. "But you married men who wanted to have children—"

The gales of laughter interrupted her as all three women wiped tears of mirth from their eyes.

"I cannot even begin to tell you how wrong that is," Cass said when she'd gained a small measure of control. "Becoming a father to a one-year-old was probably the hardest thing Gage ever did. He looks like a pro now, but trust me when I say it took a lot of soul-searching on his part to get where he is today."

Harper laced her fingers with Trinity's and smiled. "You do remember that Dante is not the biological father of my baby, right? It took me forever to convince him to go to the doctor with me as my *friend*, let alone for him to decide he wanted to be the baby's father. It nearly broke us apart, but we figured it out. If it's meant to be, you and Logan will, too."

"And if it's not," Alex countered, "you're a strong, independent woman. We'll be there for you as you raise your baby."

"If the pregnancy sticks," Trinity reminded everyone. Because that was the biggest hurdle. It didn't matter what she *wanted*. It mattered what her body decided to do with the baby, which she had no control over. That was probably messing her up the most.

But the love in her friends' words filtered through all the misery anyway, and Trinity smiled for the first time in a long time. "Thanks. You guys mean the world to me, and I appreciate your support. You would have been well within your rights to tell me to stick my self-righteousness where the sun don't shine when I got pregnant."

Harper grinned. "I thought about it. You were pretty smug when you swore you'd never get knocked up. I should get a medal for not blabbing that fifty percent of all pregnancies are unplanned."

"Statistically speaking," Cass said drily, "I think the four of us proved that in spades."

"Yet we still manage to run a multimillion-dollar company." Trinity smiled because that was still amazing. "Even though we apparently suck at launching a secret revolutionary product."

"Hey." Cass scowled. "Your marketing proposal for Bloom is brilliant. We're launching the formula on schedule despite numerous setbacks with first the leak to the industry about our unannounced product, then the legalities of the FDA approval process nightmare. We navigated the tainted samples and triumphed over the public smear campaign. Each of us according to our strengths. That's how we started this business and that's how we'll keep on doing it."

Flinging her red hair over her shoulder, Harper leaned forward with her pit-bull face on. "I wasn't going to mention it since this is supposed to be a party, but since we're on the subject, when I met with my staff earlier, I had an idea for how to catch our culprit. I'm pretty sure I know who it is. But I need everyone's help to close the deal."

"Like a sting operation?" Alex's raised eyebrows reflected in her tone loud and clear. "We're executives, not Charlie's Angels."

"But our lawyer already advised us we couldn't go to the police because we didn't have enough evidence," Trinity argued. Honestly, the whole thing sounded like exactly what she needed to get her mind off everything else. Alex didn't have to ruin all the fun with her logic and reason. "At least hear what Harper has to say."

They bent their heads together and talked through

Harper's thoughts, which Cass insisted was more productive and beneficial than opening gifts containing clothes the baby couldn't even wear until it was born.

Finally, they had a solid plan for how to deal with the hits their company had taken over the last year as they dared branch into a new product line. They were still four strong and would prevail.

Right after they made their plan, Cass, Harper and Trinity devoured the finger sandwiches and cakes Melinda, Fyra's receptionist, had ordered for the party. They were all eating for two, after all.

Ten

Logan groaned and put a pillow over his head as his phone rang at the god-awful hour of…9:45 a.m.

How was it already almost ten? Did he have a game today? Was someone calling to see where he was? His brain would not connect any dots.

Juggling the phone into his hand, he launched out of bed. His big toe collided with the heavy wood nightstand, and when his foot jerked back automatically, his ankle crashed into the bed frame.

The curse he bit out wasn't fit for a dive bar, let alone the caller on the other end of the phone.

"Logan Duncan McLaughlin." His mother's voice had that no-nonsense thing down pat. "I will personally come over there and wash your mouth out with soap if that's how you're going to talk to me."

"Mom, please. I'm really not in the mood."

His head hurt from the copious amounts of alcohol he'd poured down his throat last night after the Mustangs lost their third game in a row. And now he had matching aches on the other end of his body. Rubbing his throbbing toe, he sank back onto the bed and fought the wave of agony inside that was far worse than the physical discomforts.

No amount of alcohol could fix how miserable he was without Trinity.

"Well, I'm sorry, but I don't enjoy learning things about my son's life from the internet." Her tone softened a tad. "I saw an unconfirmed rumor that you and your maybe fiancée broke up. Is it true? Because if it's not over, I still want to meet her."

Wasn't that the million-dollar question? It *should* be over. But he couldn't stop thinking about her, missing her, wanting her.

He flung himself backward to stare at the ceiling in his master bedroom that was far too masculine for his tastes, but the decorator he'd hired had insisted that he'd like the heavy, depressing jewel tones and dark wood. Honestly, he suspected the only thing that would fix it was a woman with a penchant for bold fabrics and colors, who wasn't afraid of slinging her particular brand of style around.

One woman in particular.

He sighed. "The thing with Trinity never really started in the first place. The whole relationship was staged to generate positive publicity for our respective companies."

He braced for censure, shock, something. Who knew what? What he'd just confessed was no doubt blasphemy of the highest order to someone who'd had a great relationship with a man for nearly forty years.

"Oh, please." His mother gave a very unladylike snort. "It might have started out that way, but anyone can take one look at those photographs and see that you care for her."

"Well, *she* doesn't fall in that category, unfortunately." And Trinity was the most important one in that equation. If he wasn't so wrecked, he'd have the energy to get really pissed about it all over again. But all he could muster up was a dose of profound sadness.

"I think you're too close to the situation. She's got it as badly for you as the reverse is true. So why don't you tell me what's really going on?"

He almost smiled at that, but only because his mom sounded like Trinity, reading his mind and his moods with ease. "How do you know anything is going on? We had a fake relationship and now it's over. What more could there be?"

Everything. And nothing. Because he'd been naive enough to think what they'd had was special. Real. Instead, it was all an illusion, and he'd walked right into it without even realizing it was vanishing around him until it was gone.

"Please. I was married to your father, wasn't I? The day I can't understand a man with McLaughlin DNA is the day I gladly go to meet my maker. Spill. Or I'm coming over there."

Which was not an idle threat. She'd do it, too, and drag the whole story out of him while cooking him something full of fat and calories and love.

Suddenly that sounded so nice, his throat went tight. "I'd be okay with that."

"Oh, sweetie. Is it that bad?"

"She's pregnant." Why had he blurted that out? It was too early for this kind of ambush.

"What? Give me that girl's phone number right now!" His mother's outrage nearly burned up Logan's phone, his fingers and his ear. "I cannot believe that woman would try to use you to extort money—"

"Mom, she didn't try to get money out of me."

"She…tried to pass the baby off as yours?" Obviously that was the more delicate issue in her mind.

"No, she didn't do that, either."

"So. Let me get this straight. You had a fake relationship with her but you had an agreement to not see other people?" When he muttered *no*, she blurted, "I'm drawing a blank here, then. It's like you gave up within sight of the finish line. What did she do that was so horrible that you can't tell her how you feel?"

"The baby is not mine!"

"So? What does that matter?"

The phrases echoed through his head, condemning him, because suddenly, he didn't know the answer. It felt like there should be some kind of rule that said you didn't stay with a woman who'd gotten pregnant by another man. But Trinity had never conformed to the rules, and she'd certainly proven her ability to get him to break them often enough as well.

"I—"

"Have a temper and let it ruin your relationship?" she guessed easily. But his mom wasn't done icing that cake. "Do you love her?"

"Of course I do." He blinked. "I mean…I don't know. Yeah. I thought I was moving in that direction, but it all fell apart."

"Honey, you basically just told me that a pregnant woman had a billionaire on the hook and chose to be honest with you about what was going on. Sounds like a keeper to me. Get off your butt and go get what you want."

Was his mother *daring* him to be with Trinity anyway? "It's not that simple."

"Then move on," she advised. "Put this chapter behind you. There's this really nice girl I want to introduce you to. She just joined my church. That's why I called, actually—"

"Thanks, Mom, but no."

He stood up as conviction roared through his chest. He didn't want a nice woman. He wanted a shocking one who didn't put up with his crap and dared him to take what he wanted. A woman like his mom.

Maybe he was more like his father than he'd credited.

For the first time since he'd left Trinity's condo, his world made sense. He was in love with Trinity and he'd screwed up by walking out on her. Period. Everything else was just incidental.

Now he had to convince her that while they were busy faking it, reality had crept up and changed everything.

The sting operation—such as it was—had been a huge success. Fyra's four executives had delivered Harper's lab manager into the hands of the police, along with her venom-filled confession recorded digitally on Trinity's phone.

It was so great to have finally taken control of *something*.

"That woman deserves to burn," Harper spat as the detective the Dallas police department had sent finally left. "Imagine the nerve. Assuming she deserved any credit for Formula-47. That was my baby. I gave up my life for two years to develop it. All she did was take notes. *Dante* did more than she did when he created the new FDA samples after *she* ruined the first ones."

The woman had been so angry about the perceived lack of credit that she'd confessed to causing all of their problems in hopes of ruining Harper for the snub. In reality, the lab manager had little to do with the creation of Bloom. Psychological screening was definitely in order.

"It's over now," Cass said soothingly and glanced at Trinity's phone, which was still on the table in front of her after she'd played the recording for the detective. "We should go celebrate."

Trinity sank into a swivel chair in the conference room where they'd met with the police, clutching her weak stomach. "That doesn't look like the face of a CEO who just plugged the leak in her company."

"I, um…think you should see this." Cass held out Trinity's phone to show her a text message. From Logan. "I didn't mean to read it, but it popped up with the preview."

"It's okay."

Numb, she tapped up the whole message. She probably wouldn't have read it now—or ever—if Cass and Harper hadn't been sitting there staring at her. But she had to talk to him sometime. Avoidance wasn't a good coping mechanism.

The text jumped off the screen.

We need to stage a public breakup. I left a ticket to today's game at will call. Come by before the seventh inning and we'll get it on camera.

It was a good idea. Brilliant, in fact. Maybe they could still generate some publicity with another fight. Except her stomach heaved so much that she genuinely feared she might throw up.

So this was it then. Logan was really lost to her. In

keeping with the painful theme of their relationship, it didn't seem real.

"Want me to drive you?" Cass asked quietly.

Disoriented, Trinity nodded. Cass didn't try to talk to her on the way to the stadium, a blessing because she didn't know what she'd say. At will call, Cass insisted on buying her own ticket, even though Trinity tried to pay for it as a thank-you for driving her. She couldn't have done this alone. For a woman who claimed to value independence, she'd grown remarkably unable to stand on her own two feet lately.

Per the additional instructions Logan had texted her en route, Trinity found the security guard expecting her, and he led both women through a warren of hallways and out onto the field where Logan was supposed to meet her. They hung back, well out of the way of the cameramen and other personnel.

The game was in progress. Top of the seventh, so she'd made it before the stretch as instructed. The Mustangs were up to bat, two men on base and two outs. She eyed the lineup. The next batter couldn't afford a sacrifice fly because the runner on second wasn't fast enough to tag up—God, what was she doing? Where did all that stuff even come from?

Well, no mystery there. Logan had infused her with his passion so easily because she'd loved hearing him talk about baseball.

LA's left-handed pitcher took out the right-handed batter in three easy strikes and the inning was over. The players streamed from the field, and a woman in a US Air Force dress uniform sang "God Bless America." Trinity had seen this routine several times now, but never from the field. The perspective was dizzying.

As the last notes faded, a figure shadowed the stadium lights, and Trinity glanced up.

Logan. Big, beautiful and such a hit to her already strung-out nerves. How dare he stand there with that killer smile, looking so amazing that her knees actually buckled before she could catch herself? Apparently her body hadn't gotten the memo that she didn't go for men who bailed when the going got tough.

"You rang?" she called out sarcastically and crossed her arms before he noticed her hands were shaking. "Looks like even I couldn't save Walker's RBI, so your plan to get your good-luck charm on the field failed. LA's reliever is hot."

He shrugged good-naturedly. "Win some, lose some."

"Close your mouth, Trinity," Cass muttered from behind her. "There's a camera on you. And it's streaming your conversation to the big screen."

Somehow Trinity hinged her jaw back into place, but not because of the camera. The whole point of her being here was to put this madness behind her once and for all, and she had to actually talk in order to get this argument started.

No matter how much it hurt.

"Win some, lose some?" she repeated incredulously. "Who are you and what have you done with Logan McLaughlin?"

Because the guy she'd known would never say that. Maybe that was part of the point. She hadn't ever really known him.

His brow arched. "I told you, the scoreboard is not the most beautiful thing in my world. You are."

Something was off here. They were supposed to be staging a public breakup, not rehashing stupid things they'd said to each other. Hands jammed down on her hips, she scowled. "You hate my clothes."

"I do like you better naked," he agreed readily. "But I don't hate your clothes. I just like the ones I pick out above the ones you pick out. But we can compromise."

"Compromise?" Now she felt like a parrot. "Can you even spell that? You're dictatorial, inflexible and frankly, I have no idea how you walk around under the weight of all the rules you've got slung over your shoulder."

Now they'd get into the knock-down, drag-out part of the agenda. He hated it when she made fun of the stick up his butt.

But instead, he nodded. "That does sound like me. That's why I need a woman like you in my life to shake things up and point out when I'm being too narrow-minded. I lost the best thing that ever happened to me when I walked away. So this is your public apology. I'm sorry."

The stadium lights swirled into a big blob as her vision tunneled and the roar of the crowd's approval swelled up and over the sudden pounding of her pulse. This wasn't an argument. He'd lured her here under false pretenses so he could *apologize*?

"What are you doing?" she whispered. "We're supposed to be breaking up."

"But that's not what I want." Logan inched forward on the grass, capturing her hand in his and bringing it to his lips like he'd done so many times. "Forgive me. I didn't handle our last discussion well and I'm asking you for another chance. Publicly. I'm also giving you the opportunity to humiliate me, because I deserve that far more than I deserve you."

Her throat clogged with unshed tears that shouldn't

be there. None of this could be real. "Why will this time be any different?"

Which was not at all what she should have said.

There was an angle here that she wasn't getting.

That's when he smiled and the tenderness in his expression washed over her. "Because this time, I'm admitting right up front that I'm in love with you."

Blood rushed from her head so fast that she nearly passed out. When she wobbled, Logan's expression shifted instantly to concern and he waved the camera off, scooping her up in his arms.

This time, she wholeheartedly agreed with his tactics, because holy hell. "Did you just tell me that you're in love with me?"

"It's okay," he murmured as he carried her through the warren of halls. They passed people getting ready for the eighth inning now that the team owner's theatrics were over, but no one stopped them and finally he found a private, unlocked room. "I'm not totally used to it yet, either."

He settled her into a chair and knelt by her feet, caressing her face with questing fingers, likely to verify whether she was about to face-plant on the floor. His heat faded from her body far too fast. All she could do was drink in his precious face, hair falling into it and all. God, she'd missed him, missed the feel of him under her fingers, missed the rush of him through her blood.

"Why would you say something like that?" she burst out. Now that they were alone, all her emotional consternation over the last few days squished her chest. Which wasn't going to work. She needed to be calm and rational instead of a hairbreadth from flinging herself back into his arms, where she felt safe and beautiful and loved. "None of what we had was real."

"Because I'm trying to make it crystal clear that what we had before might have been fake, but what I want to have going forward isn't." Quietly, he surveyed her. "We're starting off with no misunderstandings. The way I feel about you *is* real. I should have told you before now."

"But I don't understand." Her voice gained a little strength as some of what he was saying filtered through the ache in her heart. "You didn't want anything to do with me or the baby. What changed?"

He didn't so much as blink. "I realized that I was being shortsighted by letting something like a past relationship stand in our way. I can accept a baby that isn't mine. As long as you come along with it."

The ground slid away at an alarming rate. Words. Buzzing in her ears. No context.

"What past relationship?" And then *isn't mine* registered. "Are you accusing me of having *slept* with someone else while we were dating?"

Before she could stop herself, she slugged him on the arm. Her knuckles glanced away and started smarting like she'd hit a brick wall. Which wasn't far off.

"It's okay," he said soothingly. "We didn't have an exclusive agreement. I was being a Neanderthal about it."

"The baby is yours, idiot," she ground out through clenched teeth as his face went ghost white. "*Men.* Oh, my God. Really? When would I have had time, Logan? Of *all* things. I went to four million baseball games with you. I went to *Oakland.* What do I have to do to prove that I was invested in us? If you've made me miserable for the last few days because you didn't bother to ask me one of the most basic questions—"

Air whooshed from her lungs as he snatched her into

his arms, holding her so tightly she couldn't breathe. But she could still hear him repeating *sorry* over and over.

Squeaking, she shoved at his rock-hard pecs until he eased up a bit. "Seriously? You thought the baby wasn't yours?"

Oh, God. All of this started making a wonderful, terrible sort of sense.

"I…made my own assumptions about why you didn't tell me right away," he confessed miserably. "I'm so sorry. I should have clarified before storming out. It's really mine? I'm going to be a father?"

As she nodded, the clearest sense of wonder stole over his features and his smile spread through her veins, warming her. "Really. No question."

He wanted the baby. Raw, gorgeous emotion beamed from deep inside him so clearly that those unshed tears inside her welled up and over, falling down her cheeks unchecked. This was what it *should* look like when you told a man you were having his child. Beautiful. Bonding. Amazing.

His smile turned a little misty. "You're right. I'm an idiot. And you can feel free to call me one for the rest of your life."

"Are you going to be around that long?" she murmured, her eyes widening as he pulled a square box from his pocket and unhinged the lid. "What are you doing?"

Exactly what she'd dreamed of, obviously. Giving her the one thing he'd never given anyone else, because he thought she deserved the unique experience reserved for the future Mrs. McLaughlin.

"Proposing," he verified as her stomach twisted. "But not on camera. Because this is for me and you only."

The ring sparkled in the light, shooting pink flares into her eyes and nearly blinding her to all the huge problems with what he was about to do. Everything came to a head in one horrific shot. She swallowed and shook her head. "No, you can't."

He eyed her. "Why not?"

I might say yes.

He deserved better than a defective bride. Her frozen hands wouldn't move, wouldn't stanch the flow of pain. "You didn't ask why I kept such a big secret. I have a history of miscarriages. This baby might not ever be born. Then where will we be?"

His eyelids shuttered for a moment, and when he opened them, the compassion there nearly crushed her anew.

"Let's start over." His voice broke as he held out his hand, which she didn't hesitate to take, letting his big palm cover hers. "My name is Logan McLaughlin and I own a baseball team that I bought because I thought it was going to fill a void in my life that throwing out my elbow had created. I was wrong. *You* fill the void. I love you. Whether you can carry a baby to term or not."

Finally, she'd stripped him of his conservative armor and gotten to the real man underneath. Her heart filled so full of him that she could hardly speak. But she had to as she pumped his hand slightly for good measure. "My name is Trinity Forrester and I married my job as a marketing executive because I thought I was too broken to ever have what I really wanted. *You*," she clarified as he raised a brow in question. "I want you. For real. Forever."

And he'd uncovered the woman behind the outrageousness. Probably he'd done that the first day. Because he was exactly her type, a strong, solid man who stuck around no matter what.

Whether she lost this baby or it decided to grace them with its presence after all, Logan would be there by her side, holding her hand. Loving her. He was her every fantasy come to life, and she was holding on tight. Not because she feared he'd vanish. But because she never wanted to let him go.

Epilogue

Four local TV stations, two TMZ correspondents and a liaison from *Entertainment Weekly* covered the wedding of the year between Trinity Forrester and Logan McLaughlin. The mother of the groom told anyone who would listen that she was going to be a grandmother.

Bloom launched the very next day, but Trinity and Logan were busy cheering the Mustangs as they won their seventh straight game. They planned to take a honeymoon somewhere exotic and expensive after the season was over and before Trinity got too big. At twelve weeks, Dr. Dean had proclaimed Trinity's pregnancy mostly out of the woods. There was still a chance she'd miscarry, but the odds went down significantly enough that Trinity stopped walking around on pins and needles.

Her condo in Dallas sold in one day and she moved to Logan's Prosper estate, which she'd fallen in love with the moment she'd laid eyes on it. Slowly, her style permeated the property until it became theirs. They bought two dogs, a male and a female, and named them Nolan and Estée.

Best of all, Logan had an extra closet built off the master bedroom for Trinity's clothes and shoes and almost never complained about what she wore from it—as long as she let him take it off her at the end of the day. Win-win in her book.

The positive publicity from the apology heard round the world, which went viral nearly instantaneously, guaranteed the launch of Bloom would go well, and it did. Its success far exceeded the expectations of Fyra Cosmetics' C suite, and Alex celebrated by giving birth to healthy twin girls. Phillip, the proud father, sent his private plane to Dallas to collect her friends, and Cass and Trinity in turn collected their husbands to travel with them. Harper flew into Washington, DC, from Zurich with Dante, and the six of them gathered at the hospital to meet the babies.

Logan's big hand never let go of Trinity's as they stood at the end of the bed. Her face hurt from smiling. The babies were so precious, and Phillip's and Alex's expressions as they each held one were priceless. *Awestruck* barely covered it.

"That's going to be us soon," Logan murmured in her ear.

"We don't know for sure," she whispered back, because this was Alex's day, not hers, and negative talk had no place here. "I'll be okay either way."

And she would be. Logan had told her several times that if the worst happened, they'd look into adoption. Or wait and try again. Or buy a horse. All of the above. Whatever she wanted. That fit perfectly with her plans, because she wanted it all—a family with a man who loved her by her side.

As she glanced around the hospital room at the three women with whom she'd built a cosmetics empire, their husbands, children, babies to come…it didn't matter what happened with her own pregnancy. She had it all already.

* * * * *

LET'S TALK

Romance

For exclusive extracts, competitions
and special offers, find us online:

- facebook.com/millsandboon
- @MillsandBoon
- @MillsandBoonUK

Get in touch on 01413 063232

MILLS & BOON

THE HEART OF ROMANCE

A ROMANCE FOR EVERY KIND OF READER

MODERN

Prepare to be swept off your feet by sophisticated, sexy and seductive heroes, in some of the world's most glamourous and romantic locations, where power and passion collide.
8 stories per month.

HISTORICAL

Escape with historical heroes from time gone by. Whether your passion is for wicked Regency Rakes, muscled Vikings or rugged Highlanders, awaken the romance of the past.
6 stories per month.

MEDICAL

Set your pulse racing with dedicated, delectable doctors in the high-pressure world of medicine, where emotions run high and passion, comfort and love are the best medicine.
6 stories per month.

True Love

Celebrate true love with tender stories of heartfelt romance, from the rush of falling in love to the joy a new baby can bring, and a focus on the emotional heart of a relationship.
8 stories per month.

Desire

Indulge in secrets and scandal, intense drama and plenty of sizzling hot action with powerful and passionate heroes who have it all: wealth, status, good looks…everything but the right woman.
6 stories per month.

HEROES

Experience all the excitement of a gripping thriller, with an intense romance at its heart. Resourceful, true-to-life women and strong, fearless men face danger and desire - a killer combination!
8 stories per month.

DARE

Sensual love stories featuring smart, sassy heroines you'd want as a best friend, and compelling intense heroes who are worthy of them.
4 stories per month.

To see which titles are coming soon, please visit

millsandboon.co.uk/nextmonth

JOIN US ON SOCIAL MEDIA!

Stay up to date with our latest releases, author
news and gossip, special offers and discounts, and
all the behind-the-scenes action
from Mills & Boon...

 millsandboon

 millsandboonuk

 millsandboon

It might just be true love...

MILLS & BOON
MEDICAL
Pulse-Racing Passion

Set your pulse racing with dedicated, delectable doctors in the high-pressure world of medicine, where emotions run high and passion, comfort and love are the best medicine.

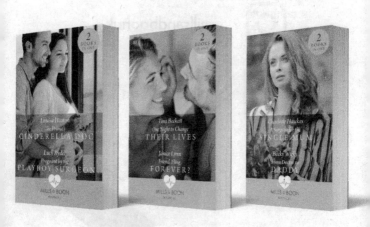